Dear Readers:

Aaron McCarver has long been a favorite author of mine since his earlier works with Gilbert Morris. It's been my absolute pleasure to get to know him better and hear his heart for writing, history, and God. Aaron is an amazing storyteller with a rare talent for weaving in the subtle nuances of history while giving the reader a gentle spiritual message. I'm so blessed to call him friend.

Diane Ashley is a new friend who has impressed me over the last few years with her love of history and God. Her gentle spirit and loving heart spills out on the pages she creates, and I find her to be one of those up-and-coming authors to watch.

Now as Diane and Aaron combine their talents, I'm reminded of stories by Eugenia Price and Nancy Cato. Stories of life on the river hold me spellbound, and Diane and Aaron have captured the heart of riverboat epics while giving the reader a strong feeling of Southern grace and beauty. I found it nearly impossible to put this book down as I found myself caught up in the story of Lily and the obstacles she faced in the pre-Civil War South.

I have a special fondness for Southern literature and if the same is true for you, I think you're going to find Lily, book one of the Song of the River series, to be a pleasurable gem. So find your favorite comfy chair and settle in for a fascinating story of romance, intrigue, and forgiveness. You won't be sorry!

—Tracie Peterson, award-winning,
bestselling author of over ninety-five books,
including the Striking a Match series and *House of Secrets*

*Our mission is to publish and distribute inspirational products offering exceptional
value and biblical encouragement to the masses.*

DIANE T. ASHLEY *and*
AARON McCARVER

Lily

SONG OF THE RIVER

Book No. One

BARBOUR
PUBLISHING

Dedication

Aaron: I dedicate this book to my best friend, William D. Devore, Jr. It is hard to put into words how much you mean to me. The closest of friends for over twenty years, God has used you in so many ways in my life. I have learned so many things from you: how to be more patient, how to not allow life to stress me out, and how to be a true friend, to only name a few. Like David and Jonathan, God has knit us together as true brothers. You are indeed a special gift from God to me, one that I will always treasure. "As iron sharpens iron. . ."

Diane: For Deborah and the "Walleen" sisters: Good memories with great friends. Thanks for your supportive words, caring hearts, and wise advice. The true measure of our friendship is that it remains strong even when our pathways diverge. All three of you are precious to me, and I treasure the times when we are together. May God continue to bless you as you have blessed me.

Acknowledgments

We, of all people, know what a collaborative effort a book truly is. We would like to thank the many people who helped us with our newest endeavor:

Our agent, Steve Laube, who tirelessly works on our behalf and muddles through legalese and other languages foreign to us.

Our editors, Becky Germany and Becky Fish, and the wonderful team at Barbour. May God bless our work beyond what we can possibly imagine to bring about His will.

And a special thank-you to Dr. Don Hubele and his Bibliography and Research class of Spring 2011 for your invaluable research assistance: Naomi Ahern, Amanda Barber, Christopher Bonner, Kirsten Callahan, Salina Cervantes, Alexander Crowson, Samantha Edwards, Ebony Epps, Kathleen Hennessy, Erin Hoover, Evan Jones, Allison Kalehoff, Krista Kliewer, Bonnie McCoy, Angela Morgan, Mary Morris, Aubry Myers, Chelsea Randle, Karisa Rowlands, Mark Samsel, Megan Timbs, Isaiah Tolo, Deanna Vanderver, Phillip Williams.

Chapter One

Natchez, Mississippi
Spring 1859

Lily Anderson watched the passing scenery from the comfort of her uncle's carriage. Stately mansions with manicured grounds gave way to the smaller, sturdy homes of local merchants as they traveled toward the Mississippi River. They passed a busy mercantile and several shops before the carriage took a sharp leftward downturn toward the raucous, bustling dock that lay far beneath the genteel residences of Natchez's wealthy plantation owners and merchants.

Natchez Under-the-Hill. She sniffed the air appreciatively as she disembarked, picking up the scents of fresh coffee, burning wood, and fish. How she loved the river. She barely noticed the disreputable, rickety inns and saloons that sprouted like weeds on either side of the winding road called Silver Street.

Roustabouts slumbered in the scant shade of ramshackle buildings while a pair of glassy-eyed Indians staggered down the street, each clutching a brown bottle close to his chest. Lily's eyes widened at their blatant drunkenness, but their presence did not deter her eagerness to absorb every detail of her surroundings as she followed Aunt Dahlia.

Voices shouted in an exciting mix of languages. . .English, French, German, and even lilting Norwegian dialects. The latter brought disturbing memories, but Lily pushed them away, determined to enjoy her outing on the river.

As she and her aunt picked their way past bales of cotton and barrels of tobacco, her gaze absorbed the myriad boats lining the banks. Rugged keelboats and waterlogged rafts butted up against lofty steamboats, each awaiting cargo or passengers to be transported downriver to the port of New Orleans.

"Don't dawdle, Lily." Aunt Dahlia's annoyed tone drew her forward.

Lily would have liked more time to soak in the energy and color of the busy landing area. If she had her way, she would spend every afternoon down here. Sometimes she dreamed she would even have her own riverboat, *Water Lily*, and ply the crowded waters of the wide river. If not for the accident that took her parents, she would not have to dream. She would already live on the river.

A snap of her aunt's fingers brought Lily back to the present. "Come along, girl. Quit gawking like a simpleton." Aunt Dahlia shook her head. "One would think you had not grown up in Natchez."

Lily glanced toward her aunt, comparing her to the memory of her mother, the sweet and gentle woman whom God had called home far too quickly. Her aunt could never match the beauty and spirit that flowed from Mama. Aunt Dahlia was more...commanding. At a height of five foot eight, she towered over the other ladies and most of the gentlemen in Natchez society. Mama had been much shorter and more genteel. Even though her mother had died nearly a decade ago, if Lily closed her eyes, she could see Mama's shiny blond hair and laughing blue eyes. Aunt Dahlia, however, had inherited her father's coloring, her hair and eyes as brown as the river flowing along the nearby bank. When she was vexed, her upper lip thinned out and nearly disappeared. It was hard to imagine that Mama, so happy and carefree, was Aunt Dahlia's sister or that the two women had shared a common upbringing.

"I'm coming, Aunt Dahlia."

"I've never seen you move so slowly, girl. What's the matter with you?" Her aunt sniffed and reached for the handkerchief in her reticule. "One would think you don't appreciate your good fortune in being able to attend the Champneys' party. The invitation indicated we should arrive prior to three or risk being left at the dock."

Sunlight beamed down on them, warming Lily's shoulders. "It cannot be—"

A young boy barreled into Lily, nearly knocking her over. "Oof." Sharp pain distracted her as her teeth stabbed her tongue. A sudden tug separated her reticule from her forearm, and the child raced off, triumphantly escaping with her belongings clutched to his dirty chest.

Forgetting that she was not chasing one of her sisters in the gardens at home, Lily grabbed her skirts and dashed after him. "Stop, thief!"

Heads turned, but no one seemed to absorb the meaning of her words, or perhaps no one wanted to help.

Lily couldn't let him get away with her reticule. It held too many valuables, like the handkerchief her sister had embroidered for her last year. Was the distance between them narrowing? It seemed so. She pushed her legs to their limit. He would have to stop running at the bank. There was nowhere for him to go.

But she underestimated her quarry. He glanced back, and she caught a glimpse of his wide green eyes. She bunched her skirt with one hand and reached out with the other, nearly catching hold of his skinny arm.

The boy avoided her grasp by inches and sprinted up the muddy bank. He hesitated a bare instant before leaping across a narrow stretch of stagnant water to land like a cat on the deck of a barge laden with wooden casks.

Lily stood panting, her gaze clashing with the young thief's. "Come back here with my bag!" Forming the words made her tongue sting, but she ignored the pain.

An impish grin split the boy's freckled face. "Come take it from me." He made a face before turning away.

Frustration boiled through her. Lily measured the distance to the boat. She would have to leap across nearly two feet of water. She would never make it.

The boy walked to the front end of the barge and jumped from it to a side-wheeler, one of the steamboats whose giant paddle wheel was mounted along its center instead of its back end.

She paralleled his progress on the bank, hoping to find a way to reach him. Squinting against the sunlight, she thought she could see a gangplank ahead that had been extended to the bank. Perhaps she could catch up with him there and wrest her property from his thieving hands.

A steamboat whistle blew its mournful tones, and a nearby paddle wheel began to thrash the water. The sound must have distracted the boy as he jumped once more because he misjudged the distance. Lily watched in horror as his feet teetered on the edge of the steamboat deck he was trying to reach. Then he fell backward into the river and disappeared.

"Help!" She croaked the word, her throat dry from her exertions. Lily took a deep breath and tried again. "Help—man—overboard!" Her shout was louder and garnered more attention from the nearby deckhands.

The many boats vying for space near the bank made the water appear paved with decks. Lily pointed a shaking hand to the place where the towheaded boy had disappeared. Time stretched endlessly as she waited to see if he would resurface. Had he drowned?

Her heart faltered. She should not have chased him. A prayer of supplication slipped from her lips as guilt pressed down on her.

"What's going on out here?" A tall, dark-haired man strode onto the deck of the steamboat where the child had fallen. His eyes, as blue as a summer sky, sharpened as he glared at her. "Are you responsible for all the noise?"

She gulped in air and nodded. "Child. . .overboard. . .chasing." The steamboat rocked gently in the water, and she gasped. If they started the huge paddle at the back of the boat, the child might be dragged into it and killed.

His gaze left hers and swept the water. A gurgle alerted him, and he ran to the edge of his steamboat, dropping to one knee in a fluid movement and reaching into the water. When his hand lifted up, she could see the child's wet blond hair and waxen face. The stranger heaved mightily and lifted the boy onto the deck.

A roustabout appeared from the darkened recesses of the steamship. He looked over to her before swinging a narrow plank toward the bank.

Lily ran across as soon as it touched the ground.

"You ought to keep a closer eye on your child." The tall man knelt over the boy, but his gaze speared her.

She could feel her cheeks warming under his intense stare. How rude. Did he really think she was old enough to be the boy's mother? Her mouth opened and closed, reminding her once again of her aching tongue.

The boy coughed and pushed himself to a sitting position, relieving her concern that he had drowned.

The stranger slapped him on the back. "You're going to be okay, son."

The boy nodded and coughed again.

"Don't you have anything to say for yourself?" A lock of coal-black hair fell across the rescuer's forehead, making her want to reach out and push it back. Shocked at the errant thought, she dragged her mind back to the subject at hand.

"I'm. . .he's not—"

"He's not dead, no thanks to you." The man stood up and pushed back the lock of hair with an impatient hand. His eyes were hard and cold.

Before Lily could order her thoughts, the discharge of a gun made her jump.

The stranger took two steps forward, placing his body between her and the dock. "Get back." He pulled his own weapon free of his holster, holding it easily.

Lily's heart thumped in time with the paddle wheel on the boat next to them. She sidled up closer to the tall stranger and peeked around his shoulder. "What's going on?"

The man did not answer. All she could see was a knot of men standing on the dock. One of them was pointing back the way she had come, and Lily suddenly thought of Aunt Dahlia. Had she been hurt? Robbed? Had the cutpurse who had gotten her own reticule been a distraction to separate the two of them?

Unseen hands shoved rudely against the small of her back, unbalancing Lily. She tried to stop her headlong sprawl, but it was no use. She fell hard against the stranger, and he tumbled toward the deck, too. Squeezing her eyes shut, Lily waited for what seemed an eternity for the impact.

Crash. The deck wasn't as hard as she had thought it would be. She opened one eye and looked into his startled blue gaze. The stranger's body had cushioned her fall. Somehow he had landed on his backside, so now she was lying on top of him, her nose squashed up against the brass buttons of his brocade vest. "Oh!"

"Are you hurt?" His hands grabbed her shoulders.

"No." The sound was so soft she couldn't hear it herself. She'd never had so much trouble with her voice. Lily swallowed. "I'm fine." Much better. She pushed against his chest but somehow felt bereft when his hands let go of her. It must be relief she was feeling at being freed. It couldn't be disappointment. . . .

"This is what I get for being a Good Samaritan." The irony in his voice stung like a wasp.

Lily slid off him and sat up, one hand checking to see if her hat, a small white cap edged with the same blue lace as her dress, had been knocked awry. It was still firmly affixed. Probably due to Tamar's careful work of securing it this morning.

The stranger stood up, holstered his gun, and brushed dirt from his clothing, taking an inordinate amount of time. He reached out a hand to help her stand.

She would have liked to refuse it, but she didn't want any of the strangers on the dock to witness her efforts to stand on her own, so she grimaced and put her hand in his.

He pulled her up with ease, nearly jerking her arm out of its socket. "Don't expect me to continue rescuing your rambunctious son, madam." Again with that thick irony.

How dare he? She was not some wayward female. She was the victim. "He's not my son!" There, she'd finally gotten the words out.

"Well, whoever he is, he's not staying around to thank his rescuer."

Lily swung around to see the thief disappearing around a bend in the road. "He took my reticule."

"I see. Well, I doubt your reticule survived the dunking in the river. I suppose now you expect me to chase after him, but you'll have to look elsewhere for a knight-errant." He turned on his heel and stomped toward the interior of the steamboat.

Lily looked after him for a moment before collecting herself. She wondered about the gunshot that had distracted her and the stranger but shrugged. No telling in this part of town. It could have been an argument over words, goods, or even a loose woman.

She made her way to the bank and plodded tiredly back to her aunt. Lily sighed, steeling herself for the lecture she was sure awaited her arrival. At least Aunt Dahlia seemed unharmed, if not happy.

Chapter Two

"Where have you been?" Snapping brown eyes inspected Lily's appearance. Aunt Dahlia's exaggerated sigh reminded her of the woman's penchant for blowing every incident out of proportion. "Do you have to act the hoyden?"

"He took my reticule." Lily dropped her gaze to her feet, unable to bear her aunt's look of censure. She wished she were anywhere but standing in front of her angry chaperone. She was a grown woman. Hadn't she been mistaken for the mother of the young boy who had stolen her purse? Not that she wasn't a bit miffed at being connected to the raggedy youngster. But she was old enough to avoid being treated like a child no older than nine-year-old Jasmine, her youngest sister.

"This is a lawless, wild area. Even in the daylight it's not safe for women to travel unaccompanied." Aunt Dahlia raised her ruffled parasol and opened it with a click. "Let's get to the boat. Hopefully there will be adequate protection amongst our own kind."

Lily didn't argue, but she didn't much feel like the guests at the party were "her own kind." She felt more kinship with the stevedores and sailors walking up and down Silver Street. They loved the river as much as she did, and she envied them their ability to make their living on the river. With all its hazards, the Mississippi called to her like Homer's mythological sirens.

"You look as flushed as a washerwoman, Lily Catherine Anderson.

I declare I don't know what to do with you." Aunt Dahlia shook her head and looked to the cloudless sky. "Your uncle and I have tried to raise you three girls to take your rightful place in society."

"Yes, ma'am, I'm sorry." Long experience had taught Lily it was the best answer to give. Silently she listened as her aunt bemoaned all the trials she had endured because of Lily and her sisters.

She followed a step behind her aunt to the boarding platform of the *Hattie Belle*, grateful because arriving at the party would end her aunt's harangue.

A line of finely dressed matrons were attended by their equally well-dressed spouses. A group of young ladies about Lily's age were standing in a tight circle, whispering behind their fans and watching the antics of the young men vying for their attention.

Why had she asked permission to attend this soiree? Although the invitation sent by the newly arrived Champney family had intrigued her, she should have known it would be a disaster. Maybe she could salvage a tiny bit of the expectation that had led to her attendance.

She and the other guests were to enjoy a leisurely float down the river to the Champney plantation, where they would disembark and enjoy a light luncheon on the grounds overlooking the river. Then they would return to the steamboat and chug back up to Natchez Under-the-Hill. She supposed it would have been easier and less expensive to go to the Champney mansion by coach, but she was glad their hosts had decided to transport their guests by boat, where there would be dancing—a different kind of ballroom to be sure.

A warm breeze teased at the ladies' skirts and the men's hats as the Champneys' guests waited to cross the gangplank and board the beribboned steamboat. There were three levels on the boat, with the bottom floor almost completely taken up by two forty-foot-long cylinders. Lily knew these were the boilers that would push the long pistons back and forth. The movement of the pistons turned the paddle wheel at the back, which propelled the boat through the water.

Her father had always known by its sound if a boiler was building up too much pressure and might explode. He'd said it was the first thing a sailor should learn about his boat. She could remember spending hours listening to the *hiss* and *whoosh* of his boat's engine. Being on board this afternoon brought back feelings she thought were long buried—memories of grief and betrayal caused by the death of her mother and her father's subsequent desertion of his three daughters.

She shook off the dismal thoughts and concentrated on the present. Her interested gaze took in the graceful curves of a wide staircase that led to the second floor, probably the level on which they would dance. The third-level hurricane deck was open to the sky, limited only by the pilothouse and a pair of tall, black smokestacks that would soon belch smoke, ash, and red-hot cinders.

Mr. Dashiell Champney, a tall, handsome man with dark hair shot through with white, stood next to a much shorter and rounder woman who must be his wife, Gabrielle. Lily waited behind her aunt while she exchanged greetings with their hosts. Then her aunt introduced her. Hoping her skirts showed no tears or dirt from her recent adventure, Lily curtsied deeply. She comforted herself with the thought that Aunt Dahlia's keen eyes would have spotted any problem. Her exacting aunt would not have hesitated to point out any shortcomings.

"What a charming young woman." Mr. Champney bowed over her hand. "You look more like your mother than your father."

Her shocked gaze met his. "You knew my parents?"

Mr. Champney frowned and glanced toward her aunt.

Aunt Dahlia tittered. "Oh, you misunderstand, Monsieur Champney. Phillip and I are not Lily's parents. Her mother, my sister, died some years ago, and Lily and her two sisters were left with my parents." She laughed as though her words were humorous. "Of course we consider the girls as dear to us as our own children."

Lily clenched her jaw to keep it from falling open. What an exaggeration. Aunt Dahlia and Uncle Phillip tolerated her and her sisters because they had no choice.

Aunt Dahlia put a hand on her shoulder, and Lily schooled her features into a polite expression. "Monsieur Champney is doing some business with your uncle, dearest. I suppose he was talking about his concern for your future." She turned back to their host. "I'm certain that's how the misunderstanding occurred."

"Our English is a little. . ." Mrs. Champney glanced toward her husband.

He patted her hand. "Shhh, Gabrielle, we will learn."

Lily's soft heart was touched. She put aside her shock and reached out toward their embarrassed hostess. "My papa also struggled with accents."

"You are sweet, *enfant*." Mrs. Champney smiled at her. "Such a kind heart you have. Go on inside and enjoy yourself."

"Thank you." Lily could feel her face flush. Expectation made her stomach clench. When her grandparents had introduced her to local society two years ago, it had been the same—terrifying and exhilarating all at once as she entered any ballroom.

Mr. Champney passed a white handkerchief across his forehead before turning to greet the next guest.

Lily moved down the line behind her aunt and came face-to-face with the Champneys' son, the young man who, according to rumor, was the real reason for today's party. He was said to be a bachelor on the lookout for a compliant wife. Her heart sped as she wondered which lady he would find interesting.

He bowed and kissed the air above her hand. "It is a pleasure to meet you."

"Thank you, Monsieur Champney."

His smile was wide and inviting, transforming his face from pleasant to handsome. Two dimples bracketed his mouth, and his dark eyebrows rose in the center. "My father is Monsieur Champney. You must call me Jean Luc."

For once Lily's face didn't flame. But a dozen butterflies seemed to have awoken in her stomach.

"And I hope you will save a dance for me."

Was he teasing her? She searched but could find no hint of mischief in his expression. "I. . .I would be gl—"

"Come along, Lily. You must not monopolize our host." Aunt Dahlia's voice seemed to come from a distance.

Jean Luc's impudent grin drew an answering smile from her. He squeezed her hand briefly. "I will find you later."

"I—" Her voice came out in a squeak, betraying her once again. Lily pulled back and took a deep breath to steady her nerves. "Thank you, monsieur." That was better. She sounded more confident, less terrified. "I look forward to having you partner me."

Then her aunt whisked her away. Lily didn't know whether to be relieved or disappointed. Was Jean Luc Champney flirting with her? What an odd feeling. And one she could easily grow accustomed to.

As she followed her aunt to the second level of the steamboat, Lily realized how glad she was that she had worn her new dress, a tailored suit with a fitted top and wide flounced skirt. Jaunty blue ribbon outlined each flounce and fluttered with every step she took. The sleeves were soft and generous, with blue-edged cuffs. A line of pearl buttons decorated the bodice from the edge of her beribboned collar to the wide blue grosgrain ribbon at her waist. The outfit was perfect for this party. Even though she would never be as beautiful as her middle sister, Camellia, Lily's fashionable attire and Jean Luc's obvious admiration made her feel pretty.

She held her skirt aloft with one hand so she wouldn't trip while her other hand traced a bronze handrail rubbed to a rich sheen. A welcome breeze brushed by as she reached the main landing.

The stateroom was a large, open area with floor-to-ceiling windows that provided light and a view of the Natchez bluffs. At one end, a full orchestra awaited the arrival of the guests while a wide, arched doorway dominated the other end, its leaded-glass doors thrown open to coax river breezes into the room.

The boat whistle sounded. Several guests hurried outside to watch the ropes loosened and the gangplank lifted away from the wharf. Some young ladies covered their ears because of the clanging boilers and hissing stacks. The boat shuddered as the long pistons began to move back and forth, slowly at first but with increasing speed and thrust.

Lily rushed outside to see the stern-wheeler begin churning the brown river water. The busy dock receded quickly as the *Hattie Belle* slipped into the strong current. Someone joined her at the rail, and Lily turned to see Jean Luc standing next to her. Unable to contain her exhilaration, she smiled widely. "Isn't it glorious?"

"Yes." But his gaze was fastened on her.

Unable to think of anything to say, she gazed at the green banks slipping past. Silence fell between them, almost like they were in their own private bubble that none of the other guests could inhabit. Her shoulders tensed with each second that ticked by.

Jean Luc moved a tiny bit closer. "Is this your first time on a steamboat?"

The romance of the moment fled. Lily shook her head. "My. . .my parents had a steamboat." She swallowed hard. "My mother d–died in an accident."

"How terrible for you." He put a hand on the one she had rested on the guardrail. "I didn't know."

Lily appreciated the kindly tone, but she pulled her hand from underneath his. "It was a long time ago. I was only a child."

The orchestra began playing a lively tune, and Lily pushed away from the rail.

"Wait, Miss Anderson. I didn't mean to pry." He offered his arm to her. "Please forgive me."

She hesitated before resting her hand on the crook of his elbow. "It's not your fault. Being here has brought old memories to the surface."

"Do you want me to have the captain turn the boat around?" His features were drawn in a frown of concern. "We can reschedule the picnic for another day."

Lily was touched by the offer but shook her head. "I wouldn't dream of depriving your guests for such a selfish reason." She pasted a wobbly smile on her face. "I'm just being overly sensitive."

"Good afternoon, Monsieur Champney." Grace Johnson, the beautiful, tawny-haired daughter of one of Natchez's wealthiest tobacco merchants, floated toward them, her movements as elegant as a swan's on a moonlit lake. She opened a fan and fluttered it in front of eyes as blue as chicory blossoms. "What an exceptional idea your family has conceived to host a floating gala. I predict they will become all the rage."

A hard look from Grace made Lily realize she should not monopolize their host's attention. She wanted to protest that he had followed her, not the other way around. Yet she felt guilty, so she started to remove her hand from his arm. She was stalled when he placed his hand over hers and applied a slight pressure.

"Thank you, Miss Johnson." Jean Luc's dimples appeared as he smiled. "Please excuse us. Miss Anderson has just agreed to let me partner her on the dance floor."

Lily's heart tripped. Dance? She couldn't dance with him. They would be the focus of everyone's attention. She would trip over her dress or step on his feet. . .or somehow make a fool of herself. Her mind screamed warnings even as he led her into the ballroom. She barely heard Grace's huff of irritation over the cacophony in her head.

Then they were in the center of the room. Jean Luc placed one arm around her waist, leading her into a waltz. She concentrated on following his lead for the first few bars but relaxed when she realized she was not going to make a fool of herself. The lessons she had complained about were paying off. She was thankful Grandmother had been so insistent.

"I'm glad you and your aunt were able to come this afternoon. Especially since I now know about your aversion to the river."

"Oh no, Monsieur Champney, I am not averse to the river." She could feel his fingers tighten around her waist. "On the contrary, I love the river. It is so alive! So full of intriguing characters and beautiful scenery. I deeply regret that my mother lost her life while boating, but I fault my father's lack of foresight rather than the river itself."

His midnight-dark gaze speared her. Lily could feel her heart flutter at the intense scrutiny. A blush heated her cheeks.

"Mademoiselle, you are an intriguing young woman. As fascinating as the ladies of Paris."

"You have been to Paris?" Lily jumped at the chance to change the subject. "Please tell me all about it."

He swept her into a complicated series of turns. She could feel the material of her gown swirling out and hoped the movement was not so energetic that her ankles were exposed.

"Paris is a very sophisticated city. There are endless things to do—balls every night, the opera house, the zoo, and of course Versailles."

"You have been to the Palace of Versailles?"

"Oh yes. It is *magnifique*, though the emperor, Napoleon III, does not reside there, of course. It is too much the symbol of Bourbon imperialism, and Napoleon and his wife are populists."

Lily nodded and tried to think of some dazzling remark. Like why a populist had become emperor. Hadn't he been elected president of France? She was not sure enough of the facts to question him. "I suppose they would avoid it."

"But a pretty girl like you does not want to hear about dreary politics." Chagrin deepened his voice. His mouth turned up on one corner. "I should be telling you how lovely your dress is and how your eyes sparkle. How light you are on your feet and how much I want to spend the rest of the evening at your side."

A blush heated her cheeks. Did he really think she was pretty? "N–not at all. I find your descriptions fascinating. You have seen so much more of the world than most of the men from Natchez. And you understand so much more than they."

Their dance came to an end before he responded, and Lily wondered if her compliments had been too gushing. Perhaps he had interpreted her enthusiasm as an attempt to flatter him, but she had been sincere in her sentiments.

He returned her to her aunt, who was visiting with some of her cronies in a corner of the room. Jean Luc bowed to them and chatted for a moment before excusing himself.

Aunt Dahlia drew Lily away. "Where did you disappear to, Lily? I was about to introduce you to a special friend of your uncle's, but I could not find you anywhere."

"I went outside to watch as the captain steered the ship away from the docks."

Her aunt shook her head and sighed. "I should have known. One would think you had no thought for your future. Are you content to always be a burden to your poor grandparents?"

"I danced with the Champneys' son," Lily defended herself. She had imagined her aunt would be pleased. Why was she so disgruntled?

"I'm sure he was just being polite. The Champneys have exquisite refinement, and surely their son has been schooled to spread his attention equally among his guests." She nodded to the other side of the room where Jean Luc stood talking to a group of young ladies.

Lily noticed Grace Johnson among their number. Her heart dropped like a heavy stone to her toes. How had she let herself be swept away by Jean Luc's easy charm? Plainly, her aunt was right. He was nothing more than a kindly host doing his duty. She dropped her gaze to the floor.

"I declare, I don't know why I keep trying to instruct you. It seems you will never learn the basic rules governing our little corner of society." Aunt Dahlia opened her fan and fluttered it.

Lily could feel the fan moving air against her warm cheeks. How could she have so easily forgotten herself? She was not beautiful or artistic or even witty. Her talent lay in her practicality, her ability to watch out over others and steer them from trouble. A girl like her would never be able to secure the interest of someone as debonair, charming, and cultured as Jean Luc Champney, the heir apparent to his father's vast shipping interests.

The first indication Lily had of trouble floated toward her in a cloud of strong cologne. She opened her own fan and used it to disperse the overpowering smell.

Aunt Dahlia's overly bright tones were the second indication. "Oh, good. Mr. Marvin has returned. I know you're going to be delighted by his interest."

Lily glanced at the man who approached. Her heart sank. He was old! As old as Uncle Phillip and Aunt Dahlia. Surely this was not the man her aunt wished her to meet. Casting one last, longing glance toward the lively group of young women surrounding Jean Luc, she sighed and waited for her aunt's introduction.

Mr. Marvin asked Lily to dance, and Aunt Dahlia practically shoved her at him. But Mr. Marvin did not seem to notice. They exchanged the usual pleasantries as they moved about the room in time to the musicians.

When the music ended, he returned her to Aunt Dahlia with aplomb. From that point on, she was handed from one partner to another, some more skillful with their steps than others. Even though she had not attended many balls, she knew most of the guests, as they were from local families.

She was dancing with Louis Roget when a disturbance at the ballroom door drew their attention. "What do you suppose is happening?"

His hazel eyes narrowed. "It looks like a message is being delivered by someone's slave." Roget halted as the orchestra's notes died away.

Lily recognized the black man who was making his way toward Aunt Dahlia. It was Amos, Grandfather's personal slave. Her heart began to hammer. She pushed her way past the couples still standing on the dance floor and reached her aunt just as Amos straightened, his message apparently delivered.

She glanced at her aunt, surprised to see that the color had washed from her face. "What is it?"

"We have to go. Something has happened to Father, and Mother wants us to come immediately."

Lily helped her aunt stand and followed her out of the room, all thoughts of the river, her dance partners, and the attractive Jean Luc Champney fading like mist under the concern blazing through her.

Chapter Three

Jean Luc Champney yawned and glanced toward his papa, who was writing a letter to *Grandmère*. What could he find to write about this boring town? How did his parents expect him to find a proper wife in this backwater?

They had invited everyone from the area to the party a few weeks earlier, and he hadn't found a single girl worth remembering. Well, maybe one or two. The tall blond had been interesting until she laughed. He couldn't remember a more horrible sound. What was her name? Grace somebody-or-other. And then there had been the quiet girl who he thought might be interesting to pursue. Her eyes had sparkled with interest and intelligence when he'd talked about his travels. She'd even been able to ask questions to show her interest. But then she'd left the party early.

He lifted his crystal snifter to his mouth and took a long drink, savoring the thick liquid before letting it slide down his throat. Realizing he had emptied his glass, Jean Luc pushed himself up from the leather chair and sauntered to his father's desk. He unstoppered the leaded decanter and splashed a generous amount of the liqueur into his heavy goblet.

"You'd better slow down, Son." His father looked up from his correspondence. "It's not gentlemanly to drink yourself into a stupor."

Jean Luc put down the decanter with a thump. "What else is there to entertain a gentleman in this mud hole?"

A sigh answered him. "Natchez is a bustling port city."

"What does that matter when you won't let me take part in your business?" Jean Luc could feel the old resentment building in his chest. What kind of father didn't trust his own son? The situation made Jean Luc furious. How was he supposed to learn the shipping business if his father refused to include him?

"Your mama and I have been discussing that very thing." The older man put down his fountain pen and folded the stationery with deliberate movements.

Silence built in the room. Was his father serious? Or leading him on? Jean Luc wanted to say something, but he didn't want to jeopardize his chances, so he returned to his chair and sipped from his snifter.

His father unlocked one of the drawers in his desk and pulled out several sheets of parchment. "We think it's time to give you some responsibility, so I'm deeding one-half interest in the *Hattie Belle* to you."

Shock made Jean Luc gulp down too much of the alcohol. He put the glass down on a table at his elbow and coughed. And coughed.

"Are you okay, Jean Luc?" His father rose from his seat.

Jean Luc nodded, but his thoughts darted back and forth like startled minnows. He could not believe it. His father did trust him. The *Hattie Belle* might not be the newest or grandest in his father's fleet, and he was receiving only partial interest, but she did move a great deal of cargo up and down the river. Once he got his coughing under control, Jean Luc stood and held out a hand. "Thank you, Papa."

His father shook his hand, clapped him on the back, and handed him the parchment. "This makes it official. In a year or so if everything goes well, I will turn over the controlling interest, and the *Hattie Belle* will belong to you. Be sure to keep your deed in a safe place."

His mother entered the room, and Jean Luc greeted her with an enthusiastic hug.

"It's good to see you happy, Son." She kissed his cheek. "Dare I hope it's because you have found a young lady who meets with your approbation?"

Papa cleared his throat. "I gave him the deed."

"*Eh, bien.*" Mama nodded. "We love you, Jean Luc, and we want you to be happy." She crossed the room and settled in the padded armchair next to Papa's desk. "A large part of that happiness will stem from your settling down with a local young woman and starting a family."

Jean Luc wasn't sure his mother's idea of future happiness mirrored his own, but this evening he would be amenable. "I met a few likely candidates at the party."

"I should think so." His father's right eyebrow rose. "We only invited the best families."

His mother nodded her agreement. "What about the young Anderson girl? She seemed like a sweet young woman."

"I did dance with her, but then she and her chaperone were called away."

"A pity." Mama patted a pocket in her skirt. "I received a note of apology from her aunt. It seems the girl's grandfather had a seizure."

"I'm sorry to hear that." The words came easily, although Jean Luc had no real feelings on the matter.

Papa trimmed the nib of his quill with a small knife. "Perhaps you should pay a visit to the young lady."

"I will consider doing that tomorrow." Jean Luc would have promised his parents anything. He would even have agreed to propose to the girl. Not that they would suggest such a thing. Even they wouldn't expect him to marry someone he'd only shared one dance with.

After the conversation turned to more general topics, Jean Luc excused himself and retired to his bedroom, his deed clutched in one hand. He looked around for a safe place and finally settled on the ornate box his parents had given him years earlier. He smoothed the pages and perused the document one last time before placing it in the box, which he locked with a key he wore around his neck. That should keep it safe.

His personal slave, Meshach, slipped into the room. "Do you need help with yo' boots, Master?"

He shook his head. "I'm too excited to retire. Do you know anything about the *Lucky Lucy*?"

Meshach shook his head and looked down.

"I've heard she boasts an honest game of an evening."

When no answer was forthcoming, Jean Luc sighed. "No, I don't guess you would know about that. Tell them to saddle my stallion. I will come out to the stable to get him." Feeling expansive, he waved a hand at the slave. "After that, take the rest of the evening off. I'll undress myself when I return."

"Yes, sir." The door closed behind Meshach with a quiet click.

Why hadn't he asked his papa for a gun while he was in such a giving mood? Jean Luc sighed and picked up the long knife he'd bought off a trader earlier this week, sliding it into the top of his boot. He hoped he wouldn't need a weapon, but Natchez Under-the-Hill had an unsavory reputation. Not that he was worried. He was young and strong, and his father had made sure he was accomplished with swords and had received training in pugilism.

Slipping quietly downstairs, he avoided his parents, who still sat in the parlor. They wouldn't understand his restlessness. He crept to the stables, mounted his horse, and galloped toward the distant yellow lantern glow at the river's edge.

It didn't take him long to find the *Lucky Lucy*. She was a smaller, older boat, but she seemed to be drawing quite a crowd.

His eyes widened when he entered the main cabin. He'd imagined it would look like the gambling salons he'd visited in Paris, but the layout was much simpler. Half a dozen straight-backed chairs surrounded a large round table covered with a piece of oilcloth. Most of the guests were filling plates from a pair of long, narrow tables laden with steaming dishes of food, while others stood in small groups talking and enjoying liquid refreshment. It looked like he had stumbled into his mother's drawing room rather than a gambling establishment.

"Welcome." A tall man with dark hair and blue eyes walked over to him. "We've plenty of food and drink." His eyes narrowed as he looked at Jean Luc closely. "But you look to me like a man who wants to match wits at a card table."

Jean Luc hadn't realized how tense he was until his shoulders relaxed. He smiled and extended his right hand. "Jean Luc Champney."

"Well, Mr. Champney, I'm Blake Matthews." The man had a firm handshake. "If you're looking for an honest game, you've come to the right place."

Another man joined them, a rueful smile on his face. "That's right. No cheating allowed." He turned his pockets inside out. "That will not guarantee you a win, but you stand a better chance here than at any other place under the hill." All three of them laughed.

Jean Luc was so glad he'd decided not to stay home. This Matthews fellow was quite likable. For a moment, he envied Blake's lifestyle. How exciting to sleep all day and entertain all night. From the looks of the lavish spread, the man had plenty of money to spend in making his guests comfortable. The fancy pastries, fresh vegetables, and huge platters of roasted meat reminded Jean Luc of the party his family had hosted to introduce him to the local planters. "What type of game do you offer, Mr. Matthews?"

"Poker." The other man's smile warmed. "Would you care to join us?"

"I'd be delighted." He jangled the coins in his pocket. "But I don't know if I brought enough money with me."

"I understand." Mr. Matthews waved a hand toward the buffet tables. "It was a pleasure to meet you. Please help yourself to food and libation. And don't forget where we're moored if you decide to come back another day."

Jean Luc was impressed when the man didn't try to coerce him into playing. He was not a cardsharp looking for easy prey. A servant offered him a glass of champagne. Jean Luc accepted and stood sipping the bubbly liquid as he watched several cardplayers take seats at the round table.

Mr. Matthews sat on the far side, allowing him to have his back to the wall. Many a gambler had met an untimely end from a bullet in the back. At least Mr. Matthews's position meant he stood a better chance of not being caught off guard.

Jean Luc watched the card game progress. Finally deciding he could gamble as well as most of the men playing and better than others, Jean Luc sidled up to the table. "Is it too late for me to join?"

Mr. Matthews looked up and nodded toward an empty seat. "Not at all." He introduced Jean Luc to the other players. "Sit down, and I'll deal you in."

Chapter Four

Blake Matthews reached for a boot and tugged it on. As he pushed his left foot into the other boot, his eyes lit on his soiled clothing piled in a corner. He would have to make the trek up to Natchez today to drop them off at the washerwoman's shop. He didn't trust the women in Natchez Under-the-Hill to do a proper job, and he had learned early on that appearance and personality were as important as his skill with cards. His subsequent addiction to cleanliness had paid off nicely, drawing in fastidious, rich customers who were ready to wager large sums at his table.

A pleasant feeling brought a smile to his lips. Thanks to a particularly generous client last night, he was no longer a nameless gambler eking out a living between port cities. He supposed he ought to feel a little guilty for fleecing the young man of his property.

But he wasn't in the business of raising youngsters. All of them had an equal chance at winning or losing. The only edge he held was an ability to read his opponents from their gestures and expressions—and that he remained sober when most of the men were at least half-lit. But he neither dragged them onto the *Lucky Lucy* nor poured liquor down their throats. And he ran an honest game.

Still, he shuddered to think about the scene that had likely occurred in the Champney household when Jean Luc had confessed his loss to his parents. Blake shrugged. He'd probably done the young man a favor—he wouldn't soon forget the dangers of drinking and gambling.

Blake drew on his brocade vest and thought about how his life was about to change. He was a businessman now. He was the owner of a boat. A picture of his father flashed in his mind. The old man couldn't accuse him of being a ne'er-do-well anymore. How he would enjoy informing the stodgy puritan of his success. Perhaps one day he would chug his steamboat upriver and make a visit.

A sigh escaped. Probably not. Even if he did, Blake had the feeling reality wouldn't be as fulfilling as his imagination. Besides, he had left that life long ago. There would be no going back for him. Not that he wanted to. No, he and his father would never see eye to eye. It was better for them to be as separated by distance as they were by belief.

Blake shook his head as he sauntered across his stateroom to the bureau that held all his belongings. His holster and gun were draped across the top. He checked the gun carefully. Natchez Under-the-Hill was far too rowdy a town for him to wander about unarmed.

Satisfied the weapon would fire if needed, he laid it down and picked up his leather gun belt, securing it around his waist and letting the holster dangle against his upper thigh. He tied the strips of rawhide around his leg and dropped his gun into the holster. He hoped he wouldn't have to use it. He'd never yet shot a man, but there was always the first time. The danger surrounding his occupation was part of its attraction.

He opened the top drawer and pulled out two blades—a genuine Bowie knife, made famous right here in Natchez, and his sword cane, his weapon of last resort. He slid the knife into the inside top of his left boot, where he could reach it quickly. He leaned the cane against the wall and shook out his frock coat before putting it on.

A deck of cards slid into a pocket. A new purchase, they had proven to be worthy of the money he'd spent. He dumped his soiled clothing into a gunnysack and tossed it over one shoulder, grabbed his cane, and made for the door. Blake glanced in the mirror at the smile curving his lips. It was going to be a wonderful day.

Summer was quickly approaching. Warm air slapped him in the face like a wet facecloth when he stepped outside. Amazing. It was hardly past the middle of May. Blake hoped his neckcloth would stand up to the humidity.

"Good afternoon, Mr. Blake. We sure had a good crowd last night."

Blake turned back to the corridor where the boat's cook/steward stood. Jensen Moreau was not a handsome man, but his thick shoulders and brawny arms had brought him a fair share of respectful glances from those who visited the *Lucky Lucy*. An inch or two shorter than Blake, Jensen had swarthy skin and dark features that hinted at mixed ancestry. He also sported a thick scar over his left eye. Apparently whatever had caused the scar had severed a muscle, making him appear to squint all the time.

"It's good to see you, Jensen." Blake held out his right hand. "Yes, we did have a crowd. I don't doubt it's your food that draws them in for a visit."

The shorter man's smile was as wide as the river. "Mr. Blake, you're a real jokester. Everyone knows they come here to play an honest game or two of cards. So many would cheat and steal to take their money. Word's gotten out you run a straight game. That's why we fills up the boat every night."

"Even if that's true, your wonderful meals keep their bellies full." Blake smiled at the ruddy color filling Jensen's cheeks. "Which puts me in mind of a matter I wanted to discuss."

Jensen straightened his shoulders and brushed off his apron. "Yes, sir?"

A chuckle rumbled through Blake. "I'm not going to shoot you, man. I want to offer you a job."

"A job?" A frown brought Jensen's left brow down. "What kind of job?"

"Were you paying attention to the game last night? Especially a certain young man who had more money than sense?" Blake glanced to see if Jensen remembered.

He looked confused, so Blake continued. "This young man holds the title to some rather valuable property. Or I should say he used to hold the title. It has come into my own hand."

"Wow! You're a landowner?" Jensen's right eyebrow crept up, making Blake think of a caterpillar.

"Not a landowner. Something much more suited to folks like you and me." Blake tossed a smile at Jensen. "You're looking at the proud owner of the *Hattie Belle*."

"You don't say." Jensen's smile lit up his face. "That's amazing. And it happened last night? I didn't realize what high stakes you was playing."

"Yes, and I'm on my way to pick up the papers in a little while. I don't know exactly when I'll take possession, but I'd love to have you come on board with me. If you agree to work for a percentage of the table, you'd be my very first crew member."

"I'd be honored, sir. You'd be a good man to work for."

Blake slapped him on the back. "I'll get with you once I know more details. It's always been my dream to have a floating palace for gambling. Then if the locals get puritanical on us, we can shove off and go where we're more welcome."

"Exactly right. And we can always look at moving some cargo, too. A big ol' steamboat like the *Hattie Belle* has plenty of decks to accommodate a few barrels of whiskey or bales of cotton."

"We'll see." Blake wasn't sure he wanted to be a trader. He did much better when he was seated at a card table. But a wise man always kept his options open. "I'd better get out of here before my appointment gets the idea I'm not interested in claiming my winnings." He stepped back into the warm afternoon sun and crossed the deck of the *Lucky Lucy*. He would talk to the captain later, once he found out exactly when he'd be leaving.

The gunnysack thumped against his back with each step. No matter that Blake shifted its weight from shoulder to shoulder, by the time he reached the top of the bluff, he was ready to toss the irritating bundle into a ravine. Eventually he reached the shanty where the washerwoman lived and worked.

He dropped off his clothing and dickered with the old woman, whose back was bowed from years of bending over hot tubs and scrub boards. Normally she would have delivered the clean clothes in a few days, but since Blake wasn't sure where he'd be living, he told her he'd come back to collect them in three days. By the time he left, both of them were satisfied with their arrangement.

The trip down the hill was easier and cooler. He could see a boat chugging its way upstream, loaded with immigrants. It was a common sight. Dozens of families crowded onto steamboats. The lucky ones could afford to rent rooms in the interior of the boats while the poorer immigrants had to eat, live, and sleep on the upper decks, exposed to all weather conditions.

As he made his way back to the river, the boat docked, and her passengers flowed onto the muddy banks like ants from an overturned mound. Some of them headed uphill while others stayed in the lower town, probably wanting to remain closer to their boat. He hoped they would stay away from the trapdoor saloons, a row of buildings clinging to the river south of the docks. They were perched on tall stilts to avoid damage from frequent floods, but they housed the most dangerous inhabitants of Natchez Under-the-Hill: hardened criminals who were on the lookout for easy prey. Unwary travelers were sometimes clubbed to death inside the saloons and stripped of their valuables. Then the hapless bodies were tossed through trapdoors into the river below. Most of them ended up caught in the eddies of a wide curve just south of the city, aptly named Dead Man's Bend.

Blake nodded to several men who had gambled at his table the past few weeks. Natchez had been good to him, giving him enough money for food and shelter. Now it had also given him his dream.

His musings were brought short by a shout from a nearby brothel. The front door flung open, and two men stumbled onto the wooden sidewalk. Judging from the angry words being exchanged, the argument had begun when the two conceived a desire for the same woman.

One of the men, a short, broad-shouldered Cajun who sported a red rooster's feather in his black slouch hat, backed into Blake and nearly fell. "Watchit!" His snarl was as threatening as a mad dog's. "Whaddaya doin' here?"

Part of Blake's mind registered the smell of alcohol on the short man's breath even as his hand clamped down on his sword cane. Should he back away from the combatants? Or would that be perceived as cowardice and end with his receiving a bullet between his shoulder blades? Should he try to be a calming voice in the quarrel between the two men? Or would they then join forces and attack him?

The irony of the situation did not escape him. He was finally beginning to see his dream come true. Would he die this afternoon, the accidental victim of chance?

"Excuse me, gentlemen. I was wondering if either of you knows the way to the Silver Nickel? I'm meeting a client there in a few minutes." He hoped his bogus question would take the attention off him. As far as he knew, there was no such place in Natchez.

The taller combatant dropped his fists and scowled. "What? Silver Nickel? I ain't never heard of it. How 'bout you, Pierre?"

Pierre's shoulders lowered slightly. He looked from one man to the other and scratched at his head, almost dislodging his hat. "Never heared of it neither."

"Oh well, thank you, gentlemen." Blake took a step past them, watching for any sudden movements toward a gun or knife. "I guess I'll continue my search."

The two men resumed their argument. Blake reached a corner, breathing a sigh of relief when he knew he was out of their line of sight. They were too drunk and belligerent to come looking for him. All he had to do was make sure he didn't bump into them again. Even though his current route would take a few extra minutes, the safety it brought was worth it.

He arrived at the saloon and stopped a minute to check for an ambush. When a big prize was at stake, it was prudent to be extra careful. Seeing nothing suspicious, he stepped inside and looked around for Jean Luc Champney. Several patrons perched at the bar, but he didn't see any sign of the man he was supposed to meet. Deciding it was too early to be concerned, he sat at an empty table and ordered a cup of coffee from a frowsy-headed waitress.

She put one hand on her hip. "Don't ya want anything stronger?"

Blake used his most winning smile. "No, thanks. Coffee will be fine. Tell me, have you seen a young gentleman in here this afternoon?"

"Well of course, honey. I seen lots of men in here. That's why they call it a saloon."

"I'm looking for one in particular. A little shorter than me. Good looking with expensive clothes."

She wrinkled her nose. "No. But give it a few minutes. I'm sure he'll be right in." She flounced off, her long skirt dragging across the dirty floor.

The saloon grew more crowded as time wore on, but still Blake saw no sign of Jean Luc. If he didn't show up soon, Blake was going to have to go in search of him. At least he knew the young man's last name. It shouldn't be too hard to discover his whereabouts.

The next time the waitress came to check on him, Blake showed her a gold coin. "I need some information."

Her eyes watched the coin as she nodded. "I'll be glad to help ya."

"I need to know where the Champney family lives."

She wrinkled her nose before answering him. "I don't rightly know, but I can ask my boss."

He nodded, but when she reached a hand out to take the coin, Blake shook his head. "Information first."

She huffed and walked away. He watched as she talked to the bartender. He nodded and pointed toward the roof. Then more gestures as he apparently described the exact location of the Champney home.

Blake had the coin ready when she came back. "Well?"

She repeated the instructions, although she didn't use as many gestures as the bartender had.

Blake asked a couple of questions to make sure he understood before handing her the money.

She placed it in a tiny pocket in her skirt. "Thanks."

Blake stood up. "Have a good evening."

Her pout was supposed to be attractive, but Blake was unmoved. She was more pitiful than voluptuous. He wished he could tell her to go home and find a husband.

Instead he picked up his hat and settled it on his head. He had more important things to see to. . .like claiming his boat and the new future that awaited him.

Chapter Five

When he met his mother's concerned gaze, Jean Luc realized he should have gone out instead of taking a meal with his parents.

"You've hardly touched your dinner, enfant. Are you ill?"

He shook his head. "I'm fine."

"But it's not like you—"

Papa interrupted. "Leave the boy alone, Gabrielle. He doesn't have to stuff himself at every meal."

Jean Luc shared a sympathetic gaze with his papa.

Mama pushed her chair back. "I will leave you gentlemen alone, then. Will you join me in the parlor later?"

"We won't be long." Papa's voice lost some of its irritation.

A slave moved to open the door, and Mama sailed through. "We'll need a tray in the front parlor." The slave nodded and left to do her bidding.

Papa tossed his napkin on the table. "I was surprised you didn't come to the office today."

Grasping his goblet, Jean Luc drained the wine in one gulp. "I was busy."

Silence filled the room. He could almost feel his father's piercing gaze burn straight through him, but he refused to look up. Papa would see the truth. Another thought made his heart stutter. Did Papa already know? Against his will, Jean Luc's gaze rose and smashed into his father's.

Feeling like a youngster, Jean Luc gulped. He tried to marshal his thoughts, but his mind wouldn't function properly. He opened his mouth to confess when a knock on the door interrupted them.

"I wonder who that can be?" Papa rose from his chair and opened the door.

"Good evening. You must be Mr. Champney."

It could not be. Jean Luc started at the sound of the voice that had dogged him through every waking minute today. He coughed in an attempt to ease the dryness in his throat.

"I'm afraid you have me at a disadvantage, Monsieur. . ."

"Matthews. Blake Matthews."

Papa waited, a look of mild curiosity on his face.

"I need to speak with your son, sir."

Papa's gaze raked Jean Luc before turning back to Matthews. "Come in. You've arrived too late to join us for dinner, but perhaps you would care for a glass of brandy." He moved back to the table.

Matthews followed. "I don't believe so, sir. I don't wish to disturb you. I was only coming by to make sure Jean Luc was not ill. He missed our appointment today."

Papa raised an eyebrow. "With all this concern over his health, I'm beginning to wonder if I should send for a doctor."

"Before you do, sir, could I have a few moments alone with your son?"

"Whatever you have to say to Jean Luc can be said while I'm here."

Jean Luc pushed back his chair, indignation and horror fighting inside him. Had he stumbled into a nightmare? Surely Blake Matthews hadn't dared to come here to demand payment. But he could not ignore the evidence. "Shouldn't you be on your boat?"

A tight smile appeared on the man's face. "I would be, but I cannot gain access."

"I'm sorry to hear that." Jean Luc tried for an imperious stare. All he needed to do was imitate his father's expression. "But I don't understand what I have to do with that unfortunate circumstance."

"I'm not talking about the *Lucky Lucy*." His eyes glittered like shards of glass. "I'm referring to the boat I won from you last evening, the *Hattie Belle*."

"What?" Jean Luc's father looked from Matthews to his son. "What is he talking about, Jean Luc?"

"I'm sure I haven't the slightest idea." Jean Luc dropped back into his dining chair. "Mr. Matthews must have me confused with someone else."

The genial host he vaguely remembered from the night before had disappeared. In his place stood an angry volcano. Mr. Matthews took two long strides toward the table, his hand reaching for something in the inside pocket of his coat. Was he going to shoot him here in his family's home?

The gambler pulled out a sheet of paper and held it in front of Jean Luc. "Are you going to deny this IOU?"

Jean Luc opened his mouth, but no sound came out.

His father stalked over and grabbed the piece of paper. "What is this?" His eyes perused the short statement. "It says that you have sworn to turn over the deed to the *Hattie Belle* in lieu of the debt you owe Mr. Matthews." He balled up the paper and tossed it on the table.

All three men watched as it bounced off the edge of Jean Luc's dinner plate and rolled toward a pair of lit candles in the center of the table.

"That paper has your son's signature on it. And I have half a dozen witnesses who will verify he signed without any duress. He was certain he held the winning hand, but alas, the cards were against him."

"You were against me, you mean." Jean Luc could hear the note of panic in his voice. He cleared his throat and looked at his father. Papa's face had aged ten years in ten minutes. A stabbing pain of remorse shot through him. But it was too late for remorse. He would bluff his way through this. Surely his father would believe his word over that of some stranger. "I don't owe this man anything."

"Did you go to his gambling hall last night?"

"Yes, but—"

His father pointed a finger toward the note. "Did someone else sign that or force you to?"

Reluctantly, Jean Luc shook his head.

More color drained from his father's face. "Go upstairs and get the deed."

"But Papa, the game was fixed."

A sound from Mr. Matthews indicated he was ready to defend himself. Jean Luc's father turned toward him. "I apologize for my son. He has no excuse for his words or his behavior."

"You don't have to apologize for him. Jean Luc is a grown man."

"Apparently he's more immature than I had hoped." Papa turned back to him. "Get—the—deed. Now!"

The last word propelled Jean Luc from his chair. He practically ran from the room, his humiliation complete. How could he have been so stupid? How could he have gambled away the first thing his father had entrusted to him? How would he ever make up for his colossal error?

The questions chased him upstairs and circled in his mind as he unlocked the box. Hot tears blurred the words on the deed. He wiped them away with an angry hand before they could fall on the paper. He would be a man about this.

Jean Luc considered several scenarios. Could he claim the deed had disappeared or been stolen? No one would believe such a coincidence. Besides, since Blake had the IOU, he could force Jean Luc to have an attorney draft a new deed.

He had to give the deed over to the nefarious gambler tonight, but he would find a way to get it back. He had been cheated. None of the provincials in this backwater town could have defeated him honestly. He had played in some of the best gaming halls in France, and he'd never had such ill luck.

He had hoped to have a few days to find out how he'd been cheated, but that was not to be. He had to temporarily admit defeat. But one day he would prove his suspicions and wrest his property back from Blake Matthews. He would do whatever was necessary, no matter how difficult. He would once again bask in the glory of his father's approval. On the day he succeeded, he would make Mr. Matthews pay for his humiliation. On that day, he would put his boot on Mr. Matthew's neck and make him scream for mercy. On that day, everything would be right again.

Halting steps brought him back to the dining room. It was galling to have to look up at the man as he handed him the deed. Before his father could prompt him, Jean Luc bowed. "I hope you will forgive me for what I said earlier. I was overset."

The other man's shoulders relaxed a tiny bit. "It is hard to admit one's mistakes."

"Yes." He watched as Matthews took his leave, studying each movement the man made. He needed every advantage if he was going to defeat his adversary.

Chapter Six

Birds chirped in the warm air, undisturbed by grief or other human concerns. Lily wanted to shoo them away. Perhaps if they weren't singing, she could summon tears like those that washed the cheeks of her grandmother and her sister Camellia.

But her heart had turned to stone. It was as though her emotions had left when Grandfather's soul departed his mortal remains. She moved through the days like a shadow, drifting from room to room as she considered what life had become without him.

His strength had seemed indomitable. But in the end, he had succumbed to death as any other man. In the end, he had left her alone to fend for herself in much the same way her father had all those years ago. Of course, her father had chosen to leave her; Grandfather had remained until his health failed.

Lily picked at the heavy black material of her wide skirt as Camellia placed a bouquet of fresh flowers on Grandfather's grave. She was worried about her sister. Camellia had always been Grandfather's favorite, his perfect little lady.

Golden ringlets moved with Camellia as she traced the marble headstone with a gloved hand. "I miss him so much."

"As do we all, Camellia." Grandmother's voice was choked with tears but still managed to convey warmth. "It is hard to say good-bye to our loved ones, but it is given to man to die."

"Grandfather would be pleased with the flowers." Lily forced her lips to curve upward as she met Camellia's blue gaze. The smile became more natural as she considered how beautiful her fair sister looked in her mourning clothes. Not that Camellia ever looked less than lovely.

"Do you think so?" Camellia's hopeful words wrung her heart.

"I think Grandfather is flying around heaven with his new wings." Jasmine flapped her arms and ran around a nearby tree, her black dress making her look more like a crow than an angel.

Laughter threatened to bubble up as Lily thought they probably looked like a flock of crows in their black dresses.

"Jasmine, get back here." Aunt Dahlia clapped her hands. She turned to Lily, a frown on her face. "I don't know where she gets her manners. Can you not do anything to control her?"

Lily felt the stab of her relative's disapproving gaze. "Jasmine, please come here."

With a whooshing sound, the young girl complied, letting her arms drop to her sides.

"You must learn to act like a lady." Aunt Dahlia clipped her words as though her tongue were a pair of scissors. "You should try to emulate your sister Camellia."

Lily wanted to contradict her. One prissy girl was enough for any family. She loved Camellia, but she had none of Jasmine's playful exuberance. Lily put a protective arm around her youngest sister and squeezed.

Jasmine looked up at her, her violet-hued eyes wide. "I'm sorry."

"I know you are, Jasmine, but you need to think before you act."

"I won't do it again." The young girl's lower lip trembled. Tears threatened.

Lily wanted to comfort her, but she could feel her aunt watching them so she sighed and nodded.

"Tamar, come take the girls back to the house." Aunt Dahlia beckoned to the middle-aged black woman standing a little apart from them. "We need to talk a bit before we rejoin Phillip for afternoon tea."

Lily supposed she should be flattered to be included as an adult, but she had an idea she was not going to enjoy the talk her aunt had in mind.

Her bonnet ribbon fluttered in a light breeze, tickling her cheek. Lily caught it between her fingers and pleated it with restless fingers.

"Quit fidgeting, child." Aunt Dahlia's frown deepened. "It's no wonder Jasmine is so restive."

Grandmother closed her eyes. "That's enough, Dahlia."

Aunt Dahlia's mouth dropped open. She was not used to anyone challenging her opinions. She unfurled her fan, whipping up a breeze to cool her reddened cheeks. "I suppose I should not be surprised, Mother. You never have exercised enough control over your granddaughters. If you are not careful, Lily will become a spinster and rely on you to provide for her the rest of her life."

Grandmother stepped closer to Lily and took her hand. "You're being ridiculous, Dahlia. Lily is barely eighteen years old. She has plenty of time to choose a husband."

"That might be true if we were speaking of Camellia. But Lily is no raving beauty."

If she had not been so numb, Lily supposed the cruel words would have hurt.

"Lily has a great deal to offer any man lucky enough to win her affection." Grandmother's defense had the same effect as Aunt Dahlia's attack.

"Win her affection?" Aunt Dahlia blew out a harsh breath. "It's not as though the whole town is lined up at my niece's door. As far as I know, she doesn't have a single suitor."

Lily wasn't surprised at her aunt's remarks. It was true. No perspective beaus were knocking down her door. And why should they? Although she expected to inherit a respectable dowry from her grandfather, the bulk of his money and his entire estate would go to Aunt Dahlia and Uncle Phillip.

And Lily had never been under any misapprehension about her looks. She was too short to be considered fashionable, and her waist was several inches thicker than her middle sister's. Instead of Camellia's changeable blue gaze or Jasmine's exotic violet irises, she boasted dull brown eyes that refused to sparkle no matter the number of candles in a room. Her hair was lifeless, too. No long, fat ringlets for her. Instead, Lily had to be satisfied with a sensible bun at the base of her neck.

Aunt Dahlia snapped her fan shut. "Luckily for you and Lily, Phillip and I have not been sitting idly by. I believe we have found a suitable candidate who is interested in courting Lily. He met her at the Champneys' party, and even though we had to leave unexpectedly, he has assured Phillip he finds my niece acceptable."

Clarity struck Lily with the suddenness of a lightning bolt. Her stomach clenched. The man from the party. The old man. She could stomach her aunt's unflattering assessment of her chances to find a husband, but she refused to consider linking herself to a man who was at least twice her age.

Grandmother drew her shoulders back. "You ought to be ashamed of yourself, Dahlia Leigh. We are still grieving. All but you. You and your husband are both too busy trying to take over the estate."

"That's not it—"

"Stop right there, Dahlia." Grandmother pointed her fan at Lily's aunt. "I have listened to you, and now you will pay me the same courtesy." When Aunt Dahlia said nothing, she continued. "Have you forgotten that you told me the Champneys' son danced with Lily? She lacks none of the social graces, and while she may not be a raving beauty, she has many admirable qualities."

Lily was thankful for her grandmother's defense, but part of her wished she were as beautiful as either of her sisters. Why did she have to be the one with admirable qualities? As young as Camellia was, men were already drawn to her whenever she was in public. Ashamed of the envy trying to take root in her heart, Lily tamped down her thoughts and concentrated on her relatives.

"Even if you were right, Dahlia, which I do not for one moment believe, Lily will always have a place of honor in my home."

"Surely you'll not reject this man before you meet him." Expecting an explosion of rage from her volatile aunt, Lily was surprised at the reasonable tone of her words.

A sigh came from Grandmother. "I suppose you may invite him to visit my home, but that is all."

"Of course, Mother." Aunt Dahlia kissed Grandmother on the cheek and turned to retrace her steps back to the porch, her strides long and purposeful.

"That must be the attorney arriving." Grandmother's voice drew Lily's attention to a carriage that had arrived at the front steps just ahead of Aunt Dahlia. "I suppose we should go in and hear what he has to tell us about your grandfather's will."

After a few steps, however, she turned back to Lily. "I don't want you to worry about your aunt's plans. She has no say in the running of the household. I promise you she will not force you into a loveless marriage."

Lily nodded, but a new worry took root as she watched her grandmother's unsteady steps across the front lawn. She might always be welcome in Grandmother's home, but one day Grandmother would join Grandfather in heaven. While she prayed that day would be far in the future, what would happen to her then? Would her aunt and uncle be as loving toward her? Would they allow her to live with them, or would they expect her to find another home?

And what about her little sisters? What if they had not yet found men they wished to marry? Would they have to accept the first offers that came their way?

She would not—could not—allow that to happen. Her sisters had to be protected. . .no matter what.

Chapter Seven

$\mathscr{B}$lake looked up at the fancy sign boasting a picture of a stern-wheeler with the words CHAMPNEY SHIPPING emblazoned below it. It hung on the facade of an equally fancy building and seemed to fit with the self-assured owner he had met so recently. A much more shrewd businessman than the son, Jean Luc. But he was ready for this meeting, ready to describe his plans to his new business partner.

Funny how things turned out. When he had finally received the deed, he had been disappointed to learn that it represented only half ownership of the *Hattie Belle*—49 percent to be precise. He wondered if it galled Monsieur Champney to be in business with a gambler as much as it galled him to find he was not the sole owner.

After some time angrily pacing the contours of his room, Blake had realized the situation could be salvaged. Partial ownership was better than nothing. From that thought came an idea to present a plan to Mr. Champney. The man would be a fool to turn down easy profits. With his knowledge of the gaming world, all his partner had to do was sit back and reap the profits.

Blake twisted the polished brass knob sharply, entering the main room of Champney Shipping with a firm step. His gaze rested on a narrow-shouldered clerk sitting behind a polished oak counter. "Good morning."

The man looked up and adjusted his spectacles. "May I help you, sir?"

"I'm here to see Mr. Champney."

The man frowned and glanced over his shoulder toward the door that must lead to the owner's office. "Do you have an appointment, Mr. . . ?"

"Yes." Blake tapped the rolled papers into his open palm. "He's expecting me to come by with this proposal."

"If you'll wait here a moment." The clerk slid off his stool and knocked on the door to Mr. Champney's office. After a moment, he opened it a few inches and spoke to someone inside. When he turned back to Blake, his face held a warmer expression. "You may come in, sir."

Blake stepped around the end of the counter and entered the room, his heart beating hard. Was it excitement or dread? Probably both.

A thick carpet cushioned his footsteps, its rich burgundy and navy colors a pleasing contrast to the oak-paneled walls of Mr. Champney's office, walls that were interspersed with tall mahogany bookshelves. This was luxury. His gaze wandered over the books and ledgers stored inside the office before finally resting on Mr. Champney's desk. Ornately carved and larger than a formal dining table, the desk was situated between two floor-to-ceiling windows that commanded a spectacular view of the river below.

"I didn't understand your note exactly, Mr. Matthews, but I have a little time to listen to your proposal." Mr. Champney's cultured voice focused his thoughts.

He could be impressed by the man's property later. For now he needed to impress Mr. Champney with his plans for the *Hattie Belle*. Blake cleared his throat. "I'm sorry if I was cryptic." He moved forward and placed his roll of papers on one polished corner of the desk. "I have some ideas I think will interest you."

"Captain Steenberg mentioned you had visited the *Hattie Belle* several times this week."

"I don't plan to be a silent partner." Blake unrolled his plans with a flourish. "I know you are much more familiar with the shipping business than I, but I have some knowledge of other areas you may be lacking. I am hoping to combine our strengths and make the *Hattie Belle* more profitable than you ever dreamed."

"You have my complete attention." Mr. Champney leaned forward. "What do you have in mind?"

"Most of your expenses with the *Hattie Belle* come from moving her up and down the river with heavy loads of goods?"

"Yes, but that's what shipping is all about."

"What if you didn't have to move her at all? What if you could make just as much money from her here in Natchez, maybe even more?"

A frown creased the older man's brow. "I don't understand."

"For the past six months, I've been running a profitable business from the main deck of the *Lucky Lucy*. My proposal is to create a luxurious, floating casino that would rival the gambling houses of Europe. We could reserve a couple of staterooms for those who come a distance to play at our tables, but the rest of the boat would be dedicated to games of chance." His words came faster. "I have always run fair games, so our reputation would spread like wildfire. Everyone would be welcome—planters, farmers, traders, anyone who has a little money to spend on entertainment. We'd fill every floor of that boat with people who want a chance to leave with more than they had."

"You certainly seem passionate about this." Mr. Champney sat back.

Blake wanted to press the point, but he had learned early in his career not to push someone too hard. Allowing a man to make up his own mind generally yielded the same result without any hard feelings. So he waited.

"I find your proposal interesting if unusual, Mr. Matthews." Mr. Champney steepled his hands. "But I don't know if I want to be associated with the dubious world of gambling."

"That's where I come in. I run a clean ship as I mentioned before. You can check with anyone who has gambled on the *Lucky Lucy* since I came to town at the beginning of the year. Except for one or two who may be sore about losing at my table, you will find nothing but good reports. I have sent a host of men away winners."

"Then how do you make a profit?"

Blake leaned forward. "There's a saying in my world, sir. Gambling money always makes its way back home. And when you own the house where it lives, you cannot help but profit."

Silence slipped into the room as Blake waited, his confidence building with each second that passed. He was good at reading what a man was thinking. It was one of the reasons he was successful in his chosen profession. He was sure Mr. Champney wanted to throw in with him.

Champney nodded. "What will it take to put your plan into action?"

Trying to keep his jaw from dropping, Blake flipped through his paperwork. He might need to work on his divining skills more. Although he had seen the other man's desire to partner in his venture, he hadn't expected his wholehearted support. But he might as well take advantage of it. With Champney's financial backing, he could make the *Hattie Belle* even more spectacular. She would be a showplace! "I can have you a list by the end of the day."

Mr. Champney rose from his desk and held out his right hand. "Ask my clerk for a list of businesses in town with whom we trade. He'll make sure they extend you credit." His eyes narrowed, and his grip on Blake's hand tightened. "But if I have any suspicion you are not being honest with me, our deal will be off."

"You won't be disappointed."

"I had better not be. I am not a good man to cross, Mr. Matthews. Although it would pain me, I would rather sink that boat than let you take me for a ride." He released Blake's hand.

"I understand, sir." Blake wanted to stretch his hand but refused to show any weakness. He slowly rolled up his papers and tapped them into a neat cylinder. Let Mr. Champney threaten all he wanted. Soon his new business partner would learn to trust him. Soon the money would begin rolling in. This was going to be a profitable venture for both of them. He was certain of it.

Chapter Eight

"Aren't you excited to meet your suitor?" Camellia stood at the window, keeping watch for their dinner guest.

Lily rolled her eyes and turned slightly, forgetting for a moment the curling iron Tamar was applying to her hair. "I am not."

"Hold still, Miss Lily, or you'll get burned."

Lily obediently turned back toward the mirror and made a face at her reflection. "It might be worth it if it kept me upstairs during dinner."

Camellia came to stand beside the dressing table. "I wish I could go in your place. I'd adore having a handsome man gazing at me and telling me how beautiful I am."

"Oh, Camellia, you have no idea what you're talking about."

Her sister put her nose in the air. "I know Aunt Dahlia said you'll have to marry Mr. Marvin, or you'll be a burden to her forever."

"Now you be quiet, Miss Camellia. You shouldn't be repeating gossip, especially hurtful things like that." Tamar's fingers twisted the curling rod, pulling it from Lily's hair. "I'm sure you misunderstood your aunt. She only wants the best for all her nieces."

Lily shook her head now that it was free of the hot iron. "I think she's more worried about her comfort than our futures."

"I think it's romantic." Camellia sighed. "Do you think he'll propose tonight?"

"I hope not." Lily shuddered. The tight coils Tamar had so painstakingly fashioned began to sag and droop. She felt like doing the same.

Tamar tsked and reached for the iron once more.

"Just pull it back like always. No sense in torturing either of us any longer. I still have to put on my hoops and that dress."

Camellia reached for one of the hairpins on Lily's dresser. "Don't you want to get married?"

"Of course I do, but marriage is a serious decision, an oath that cannot be broken. When you marry someone, you should be certain he is the right one according to the dictates of the Lord."

Tamar put the finishing touches on Lily's hairstyle and moved across the room to retrieve the hoops that would be fastened over her chemise. "You should listen to your sister, Miss Camellia. She's very levelheaded. She'll never let herself be carried away by a gentleman's looks."

Lily wondered if she was as levelheaded as Tamar thought. Her mind went back to the party on the Champneys' steamboat. Dancing with Jean Luc Champney had been much more thrilling than her dance with Mr. Marvin. She closed her eyes to conjure up memories of that night, surprised when Jean Luc's dark gaze was supplanted by eyes as azure as a summer sky. Now why had she thought of the stranger who had accosted her before the party? He might have been handsome, but he had also been rude, judgmental, and uncouth.

Her unruly thoughts were interrupted as the door to Lily's bedroom burst open and a dark-haired windstorm swept in. "Jasmine." She stood up and held her arms out in welcome, unwilling to chastise her youngest sister for her lack of decorum. Jasmine was such a happy young lady, taking joy in every moment. As the oldest sister, Lily had a duty to make sure both of her sisters behaved, but she couldn't bring herself to dampen Jasmine's pleasure. She was only nine years old, after all.

Jasmine threw her arms around Lily. "I love you, Sissy."

Who could resist such warmth? Lily placed a kiss on Jasmine's forehead. "I love you, too."

Camellia crossed her arms. "Aunt Dahlia said you need to stop calling her sissy. It makes you sound like a baby."

Jasmine stuck out her lower lip. "It does not."

"Tell her, Lily."

Lily shook her head. "As long as it's just us, I don't see the harm."

"You always take her side." Camellia plopped down at Lily's dressing table. "I think you love Jasmine more than me."

"Don't you be saying such things about your sister." Tamar shook out the folds of Lily's skirt as she spoke. "You should be ashamed of yourself. Miss Lily loves both of you more than anything else in this wide world."

Lily held up her arms so Tamar could lift the skirt over her head. "It's all right, Tamar. I know she doesn't mean it. Camellia is disappointed because she has to stay up here and entertain Mr. Marvin's children."

"What do you suppose his children are like?" Jasmine had a dreamy look in her eyes. She was probably hoping to meet children her own age.

Lily often worried that Jasmine had no one to play with. Her youngest sister had been a toddler when Lily lowered her skirts and put up her hair, and Camellia had not been far behind.

With only three years between them, she and Camellia had shared both their lessons and their dolls. They'd had plenty of skirmishes over the years, but they had also spent hours together pretending and exploring.

Jasmine had been too young to romp with them. Camellia was six years older than their youngest sister and could have played with her, but she was too fastidious. Sometimes Lily thought Camellia was growing up faster than she was.

Her heart turned over as she watched them perusing her hairpins. She might get outdone with one or the other at times, but Lily's sisters were so precious to her. Sometimes she felt as protective as a mother would be. No one else could love them more than she did.

"Here's your fan." Tamar's words snapped Lily out of her pensiveness.

Jasmine turned from the dressing table, her mouth forming a perfect O. "You look beautiful, Si—Lily."

"Thank you." Lily took a deep breath. "I suppose it's time for me to go face the music."

"There's going to be dancing, too?" Camellia's voice was full of envy.

A nervous giggle bubbled up and escaped Lily's throat. "It's just a saying. Think about it. Have you seen any musicians coming to the house?" She pointed to the black material of Camellia's dress. "You know dancing wouldn't be proper while we're in mourning."

Camellia hunched a shoulder, but Lily ignored her ill temper. She hugged both of her sisters tightly. "I wish you could come downstairs with me."

Jasmine threw her arms around Lily's neck and hugged her with enthusiasm. After a brief hesitation, Camellia returned her hug, too. Lily's heart throbbed. She wished the moment of total accord could last forever, but the sound of a carriage announced the arrival of Mr. Marvin's children. Lily straightened and headed for the door, a smile pasted to her lips and a prayer in her heart.

"You need to move away from that window, young lady. What if your guests saw you spying on them?" Tamar tried hard to hold on to her frown. She understood Miss Jasmine's curiosity, but if Miss Dahlia caught one of her nieces staring out the window, she would scold Tamar. "Come over and sit beside Camellia."

Jasmine turned, a pronounced pout evident. "But I won't be able to see Mr. Marvin's sons."

"They'll be up here with us soon enough. In the meantime, you should work on your sampler."

"I don't want to."

"Young ladies must learn how to make neat stitches, or you'll never get married." Camellia's voice was a perfect imitation of her aunt Dahlia's.

Tamar shook her head. "Miss Jasmine is much too young to be thinking on such things."

"Aunt Dahlia says one is never too young to be a lady."

"I'm sure she's right, Miss Camellia, but that doesn't mean your little sister should be worrying about marrying." But that day would come. Miss Lily was likely to be wed before the year was out, and no one could doubt Miss Camellia would be snapped up before she was eighteen.

It seemed like only yesterday when the three girls had come to live with their grandpa and grandma. So sad they'd been to lose their ma in that terrible storm. Tamar's heart had been torn by their tears, even though she'd never rightly known her own ma. That was to be expected for a slave. But not for the privileged white children of a wealthy family. Then they'd lost their pa, too. She'd heard the others slaves say Master Isaiah had made him promise to stay away. Such a sad thing—

Her thoughts were interrupted when the door to the nursery burst open, and two young men stepped inside. One sported a thatch of straight red hair while the other had a head of dark, curly hair. But their relationship was obvious in their facial features and stocky, square bodies.

The older one sketched a bow and advanced to the sofa where Camellia and Jasmine sat. "I'm Adolphus Marvin Jr., and this is my little brother, Samuel. It's a pleasure to meet you." A smile of assurance turned up the corners of his mouth.

A handful that one would be. Tamar shook her head and picked up Miss Jasmine's porcelain doll, placing it carefully on a shelf. He was the type who would catch a girl in the shadows and steal a kiss or even more, if possible. She might be a slave, but she could recognize trouble when it walked into the room.

The younger boy wore an expression of admiration as he watched Adolphus Jr. talking to the two girls. It seemed Samuel was likely to follow in his older brother's footsteps.

Tamar continued to move around the room, straightening the books and toys that had not been put away as she listened to the children getting acquainted. They talked about whether they would become related and how odd it would be if the two girls were to become their aunts. A smile touched her lips at the idea.

"I brought my marbles." The younger Marvin boy held out a hand to show off four shiny orbs. "Do you want to play?"

"Of course they don't want to play, Samuel." The older boy rolled his eyes. "They're girls. They can't sit on the ground to play."

"I can." Jasmine put down her sampler and slid from the sofa to the wooden floor. "See?"

Tamar stepped toward her. "Now, Miss Jasmine, you're going to get your dress all dirty."

Adolphus Jr. sneered. "Leave her alone, slave. It's not up to you to tell your betters how to act."

Tamar stepped back as though she'd been slapped. She might be a slave, but as the maid to the beloved granddaughters of the Blackstone home, she had earned a place of respect. Miss Dahlia might scold her for some perceived infraction, but no one ordered her around like one of the field hands.

Both Marvin boys laughed. Camellia giggled, but Jasmine stood up.

"You don't talk that way to Tamar. She's my friend."

Camellia's face went slack with surprise. She glanced from her little sister to the two boys, who were laughing. "Stop laughing."

Samuel made a rude noise. "You can't tell me what to do."

Tamar knew it was her duty to maintain order in the nursery, but she *was* only a slave. She didn't need to make any enemies, especially if these boys were going to visit often. She had heard below stairs how much Miss Dahlia and her husband wanted Lily to marry Mr. Marvin. They might not react well if she defied the man's children and the boys complained.

All four children were glaring at each other. Jasmine made a fist and shook it at them. "You're dreadful, mean boys."

"I can do whatever I want." The younger Marvin boy took a step toward Jasmine, but the dark-haired girl stood her ground.

"Leave my sister alone." Camellia put a hand on his arm.

Tamar gathered her courage. "The good Lord must be shaking His head at you boys. What are you going to do? Have a fistfight with girls?" She hoped her words would ease the tension in the room.

The redhead looked at her, his gaze inscrutable. Then his shoulders relaxed. He cuffed his brother on the shoulder. "Put your marbles away. We'll find something else to play with."

Tamar's heart sank at his calculating expression. What was he planning to do? The younger one, whose dark curls had made her think he might have a sweet temperament, birthed a smile of pure evil.

"Maybe over here." Adolphus went for the shelf of dolls, pushing them onto the floor. When the shelf was empty, he looked around for another target.

His brother mimicked him, attacking the books on the other side of the room. Soon they were in a heap on the floor.

"Stop that!" Camellia ran after Adolphus, swatting the boy around the head and neck. He shrugged off her blows and kept up his destructive actions.

Jasmine took a step toward them, but Samuel grabbed her arms in his chubby hands. "What do you think you're going to do?"

"Let me go!" Jasmine struggled to get free. "Let go."

Another crash sounded as Adolphus jerked a drawer loose and emptied its contents on the floor.

Tamar's instinct took over. She stepped forward to pull Jasmine free of the younger guest's grasp. Jasmine must have decided to take matters into her own hands. She kicked the boy holding her. He howled and bent over Jasmine, his mouth locking onto her arm. Jasmine screamed and began crying, falling to the ground when Samuel released her.

"Let me see your arm." Tamar cuffed the boy before scooping Miss Jasmine into her arms. She didn't care if she got in trouble. No one was going to hurt one of her girls.

Startled by Jasmine's cries, Adolphus had stopped strewing the girls' belongings and watched, his eyes traveling from Tamar to Samuel to Jasmine. "Quit being such a baby."

Camellia picked up a parasol from one of the heaps on the floor and used it to attack him. "You're a boorish oaf." She landed several blows on his head before he wrested her weapon out of her hands. Undaunted, she pointed at him. "I hope my sister never marries your pa. Get out of my house."

Tamar was proud of her. Camellia was finally showing her true mettle. She watched as the two boys slunk away. "What should we do now?" She stroked Jasmine's shoulder and whispered comforting phrases in the little girl's ear. But Jasmine would not be comforted.

"Do you want me to go get Aunt Dahlia and Uncle Phillip?" Camellia fell onto the sofa as though exhausted.

Tamar shuddered at the thought of breaking up the dinner party downstairs. "No, I don't think that's a good idea. Maybe I can draw Lily away without too much commotion. She always knows how to calm Jasmine, and she can make certain the others know exactly what happened."

Camellia nodded. "Come here, Jasmine. Let Tamar go downstairs and get your sissy."

Tamar left the two of them leaning against each other on the sofa and went in search of Lily. This night could not end fast enough.

Chapter Nine

*A*nd that's the way I found him almost two hours later."

Everyone seated at the dinner table laughed at the humorous story Mr. Marvin told about his oldest son, Joshua. Lily had to admit he was a gifted storyteller who had kept them enthralled with tales of his travels and his sons. He had a self-deprecating air, as though he was grateful for whatever attention he received.

Lily realized she liked Mr. Marvin. If only he weren't so old.

"Adolphus, I don't know when I've laughed so much." Grandmother took a sip of water before returning her goblet to the table. "When Dahlia told me she wanted you to come over for dinner, I had my doubts. But after what we've been through recently, genuine laughter is a welcome diversion."

"Thank you." Mr. Marvin captured Grandmother's hand in his own. "I was so sorry to hear of your loss. If I've helped in even a small way, I will consider the evening a momentous success."

Was that a blush on Grandmother's cheeks? Lily's heart pounded when Grandmother looked toward Aunt Dahlia and nodded. Was she trying to signal her approval of Mr. Marvin as a suitor for Lily? What a frightening turn of events. No matter that Mr. Marvin seemed to be a nice man. She had no interest whatsoever in marrying him. Ever.

Grandmother pulled her hand from Mr. Marvin's. "That's very kind of you, Adolphus. We must have you over again soon."

Uncle Phillip nodded his agreement. "I concur, Adolphus. You should consider yourself a member of the family." Lily's heart sank further as she glimpsed the determination on her uncle's features. She had always thought of him as a weak man, controlled by Aunt Dahlia's whims, but recently she had seen him in a different light. He was the man of the family now that Grandfather was dead, and he seemed eager to embrace the role. That would not have bothered her except that his primary objective seemed to be arranging a marriage between her and Mr. Marvin.

Mr. Marvin glanced at Lily. "I would like that very much."

"Shall we retire in the parlor while the men gather in the study?" Satisfaction had settled on Aunt Dahlia's face.

Lily slid her chair out quickly, ready to escape the dining room. How had this happened? Grandmother was supposed to be on her side. It was bad enough she had to worry about Aunt Dahlia and Uncle Phillip trying to hurry her off into a loveless marriage. Now Mr. Marvin had managed to turn her only ally against her.

"Are you enjoying your evening, Lily?" Grandmother sat down on the black horsehair sofa and patted the place next to her. "I found Mr. Marvin engaging, didn't you?"

"She ought to fix his interest." Aunt Dahlia took a seat in the red brocade chair on the opposite side of the sofa table and reached for her sewing bag. "You could do a lot worse than marry him, you know."

Feeling besieged, Lily tried to come up with an answer that would satisfy them. A knock at the door followed by Tamar's familiar face seemed like a reprieve. "What's wrong?"

Tamar stepped inside the room. "It's Miss Jasmine. She's crying for you."

Lily stood.

"Where do you think you're going?" Her aunt's voice halted her escape.

"I'm going to see about my sister, of course."

"I don't think that's a good idea." Aunt Dahlia stabbed at the sampler with her needle. "I doubt there's anything terribly wrong with her, but if there is, Tamar or another of the girls can see to her."

"Let her go, Dahlia." Grandmother smiled. "Don't you remember what it was like to look to your older sister?"

Aunt Dahlia sighed. "Well, be quick about it, Lily. We don't want

Mr. Marvin thinking you are trying to avoid him."

Lily made her escape and hurried up to the nursery. The normally tidy room had been turned upside down. Toys lay scattered about, and several pieces of furniture were upturned. "Did an army invade while I was eating?"

"Near enough." Tamar righted a chair. "It's those imps whose father is courting you. I don't know what he's taught them, but it wasn't company manners. They fair terrorized your sisters before Camellia told them to leave."

Lily could hear faint sobbing coming from the bedroom attached to the nursery and hurried inside to find Camellia sitting next to her younger sister's bed. Jasmine lay facedown across the bed, her pillow muffling her sobs.

Lily sat on the edge of the bed and ran a hand through Jasmine's thick hair. "What happened?"

Jasmine sat up and threw herself into Lily's arms.

"Master Samuel Marvin bit her." Camellia took Jasmine's hand in her own and held it so Lily could see the circle of teeth marks.

"How barbaric." She rocked back and forth, whispering words of love and sympathy.

Jasmine's tears slowly abated, and she hiccuped.

Lily put her hand under Jasmine's chin and tilted her face upward. Dark eyes ringed by darker lashes stared at her. "I'm sorry, Jasmine. Do you think we should bandage it?"

Jasmine's eyes grew larger. She nodded.

"Tamar, go see if Alice has any bandages in the housekeeping supplies." Tamar turned to do her bidding. "And check with Mary about the strawberry-rhubarb tarts she fixed for tea yesterday. If she has any left, bring them back with you. I know how much better I feel when I eat one of her fruit tarts."

Camellia hovered around them, alternately patting Jasmine's shoulder and fussing with the bows on her own dress. "Those boys ought to be whipped. They were nasty to Tamar, and they rushed around the nursery, pulling all our things onto the floor."

"I don't like the way they acted." Lily got up and dipped a cloth in the washbasin next to Jasmine's bed. She handed it to Jasmine before turning her attention to Camellia. "But perhaps they have some excuse since they have no mother to care for them."

"We have no mother," Camellia declared. "But do you see us tearing up our rooms or terrorizing little children?"

Was this a foretaste of what her life would be if she allowed her family to coerce her into marrying Mr. Marvin? Lily wondered. Her resolve hardened. She would not bend, no matter the cost. But for now, she needed to calm her sisters. "We are blessed to have Grandmother and Aunt Dahlia to teach us how to behave."

"Lily, I know why they're so bad." Jasmine's voice was dreamy, like she was about to fall asleep.

"Why is that, little one?"

"Cuz they're made of 'snips and snails and puppy dogs' tails.'"

Laughter bubbled up. "That's right." Lily hugged her sister close. She glanced up at Camellia and saw her lower lip protruding. She no longer looked like she was on the cusp of becoming a woman—she looked like a little girl who needed comforting. "Come over here, Camellia. You're too old for cuddling, but I think Jasmine would appreciate an extra hug, and I know I would."

For once Camellia forgot her dignity. She crowded onto Jasmine's bed.

Silence filled the room, and contentment spread through Lily as she put an arm around her middle sister. She wanted to save this tender moment for future remembrances. It had been far too long since the three of them had sat together with their arms wrapped around each other. Although Lily was sorry for the trouble that had arisen, she would much rather be up here than downstairs with the adults.

Tamar bustled in with a tray laden with treats and bandages. "Those boys are in the kitchen running around like a couple of heathens."

"I hope they're not causing Mary too much trouble."

"She has plenty of help down there. More than your sisters and I had when they attacked the nursery." Tamar set her tray down on a piecrust table and handed the roll of bandaging to Lily.

Jasmine lay back against her pillows while Lily and Camellia cleaned the wound and wrapped it in soft cotton.

"Can I have a tart?" Jasmine's eyelids looked heavy, as though she would fall asleep at any moment.

"Of course, dearest." Lily nodded to Tamar, who took a plate from the tray and put a tart on it. "If you can stay awake long enough, that is."

Camellia rolled up the bandaging while Jasmine took a few bites from one of the treats.

"Thank you, Sissy." Jasmine handed the plate to Lily before settling back against her pillows once more.

Lily pulled her coverlet up to Jasmine's chin, relieved to see the returning color in her cheeks. Putting a finger to her lips, she signaled Tamar and Camellia toward the nursery. They spent the next half hour discussing the day, ending with the earlier disaster.

Camellia wiped her mouth after finishing one of the delicious tarts and folded her hands in her lap. "I couldn't believe it when that boy bit Jasmine." She looked toward Lily, tears welling up in her blue eyes. "I was trying to get the other one to stop tearing up our things, but I should have been protecting Jasmine."

"It wasn't your fault, dearest. You did what you could. And you had Jasmine mostly calmed down before I got here. I'm sure that's why she fell asleep so quickly."

Looking pleased, Camellia stood up. "I suppose I shall go to bed, too. Is your dinner party over?"

Horror overcame Lily. "I forgot. As soon as I help you straighten up in here, Tamar, I'll go back down and see if Mr. Marvin is still here. I hope he is. I have some hard words for him about his children."

"You go on down, Miss Lily." Tamar returned their dishes to her tray. "I can clean up this mess in no time."

Camellia added her voice to Tamar's. "I can help her, Lily."

"Are you sure?"

Both of them nodded, so Lily shook out her skirts. Checking to make sure there was no rhubarb on her skirt, she left them working and went downstairs.

On her way to the parlor, Lily noticed the door to Grandpa's study was open. Certain the men had joined the women in the parlor by now, she stopped to pull it closed. But with her hand on the doorknob, she heard a voice. Someone was inside! Who could it be? The terrible Marvin boys? She leaned closer to make sure before going in to confront them.

"I tell you steamboats are what you should be investing in." She recognized Uncle Phillip's voice and realized the men were still discussing business. "They are the easiest, fastest, safest way to transport people and goods. If you've never seen the inside of a steamship, you should do yourself the favor of taking a trip, say to New Orleans or Memphis. You will be amazed at the luxury to be had. The quarters are comfortable, the food is as good as our cook prepares, and the scenery is astounding."

Knowing she should turn away, Lily couldn't. Would Mr. Marvin be interested in purchasing a steamboat and raising a family on the river? She might change her mind about the man if she could be assured of living on the Mississippi River.

"I don't know, Phillip. I'm not a man to take risks."

"I tell you there is no risk, no risk at all. Everyone connected to a riverboat makes money—from the shipwright to the crew, not to mention the planters, farmers, and shipping tycoons who rely on the river to deliver their goods."

Lily closed her eyes as she imagined the scene in the study. Her uncle would be sitting in Grandfather's leather chair, a cigar in one hand and a glass of brandy in the other. Mr. Marvin would be sitting on the other side of the desk, leaning forward with eagerness to learn more of her uncle's ideas.

"I'm not saying I'm ready to take the plunge, but if I was, how would I proceed?"

Lily leaned closer.

"I normally wouldn't tell anyone this, but since you are so close to becoming a member of the family, you should go to Dashiell Champney." Her uncle's voice was quiet, confidential, like he was sharing a deep secret. "He owns several boats and would likely have one or more for sale. It's better than having money in the bank. I don't know how your finances are, Adolphus, but it never hurts to have a goose to lay a few golden eggs, eh?"

"I don't know if you should be so hasty to consider me a part of your family." Mr. Marvin coughed. "Your niece is less than receptive to my overtures. She seems more concerned about her sisters than finding a husband."

"You let me worry about that. As long as you would like to have her as your bride, all you have to do is propose." Uncle Phillip chuckled. "I'll make certain Lily says yes."

Mr. Marvin's laughter joined her uncle's, creating a revolting noise. Uncle Phillip was supposed to be her protector, not someone willing to pawn her off on the first man who approached. Or had Uncle Phillip approached Mr. Marvin? Either way, she would not stand for it.

All thought of rejoining the dinner party evaporated. She could not abide the idea of being polite to either Uncle Phillip or Mr. Marvin. Lily picked up her skirts and fled to her bedroom. Shutting the door with a firm click, she flung herself across her bed. Hot tears flooded her down pillow as she fell victim to despair.

What would she do? What could she do? She was only a girl, a girl who had inherited nothing more than an adequate dowry. The same amount of money each of her sisters had inherited. If there was some way to put all their money together, she might be able to come up with a solution. What she needed was a way to take care of all three of them.

Inspiration struck. Mr. Champney was Jean Luc's father. He had seemed interested in her when they danced. He could use his influence with his father to allow her to purchase one of his steamships. All she had to do was convince Grandmother to let her have her dowry now. It might be sufficient to buy a boat, but if it wasn't, perhaps Mr. Champney would sell her the boat if she promised him a large percentage of the riches she would earn transporting goods along the river.

Lily sat up in bed, her tears drying as she considered the idea. She would take Camellia and Jasmine with her. They could make a home for themselves on the river. It would be unconventional, but it would also be free of the restrictions they faced here. No one would be able to tell them what to do or whom to marry.

The more she thought about her idea, the more excited Lily got. When Tamar entered to help her get ready for bed, she could hardly contain her emotions.

Tamar combed out her long hair and braided it. "It seems someone has stars in her eyes. Are they stars of romance?"

Lily rolled her eyes. "I don't know what you're talking about." Her plans were far too vague to share with Tamar. Perhaps in the days to come, but tonight she would keep the information secret. "I didn't speak to him after I left you and Camellia. The idea of being polite to him after seeing what his child did to Jasmine was too much to bear. I hope he understands I'm not at all interested in him."

Tamar cocked an eyebrow. "Maybe the child needs a mother to teach him how to act."

"Maybe so, but I don't plan to take on that job, and I pity the woman who does."

"I thought your aunt and uncle were in favor of a match." Tamar pulled back the covers and waited for Lily to climb into bed.

"They may be, but Grandmother assured me I do not have to marry anyone I don't wish to."

Lily thought she would be too excited to sleep, but her eyelids grew heavy as soon as Tamar blew out the last lamp. Schemes and dreams blended, and she barely had the energy to bid Tamar good night before sleep claimed her.

Chapter Ten

Blake wiped his forehead with a grimy sleeve. "I'm not used to this kind of work anymore."

Jensen grunted. "I thought you never worked with your hands."

A laugh burned his throat. "There was a time all I knew was physical labor. Every bite of food I put in my mouth came from hard work."

"I never heard you talk about your past." Jensen gave a final tug to the drapes he'd spent the past hour hanging. "You were a farmer's son?"

How he wished the days of his youth were so easily described. Blake shook his head. "Ma taught us how to plant a garden, or we'd have perished from starvation."

He leaned over the wood he'd been sawing and started work again. His mind, however, had been primed like a pump. Memories flooded through—cold nights, empty stomachs, his baby sister crying for milk. No longer able to bear her pitiful sobs, he'd stolen out of the house after dark, climbed a fence to get into Farmer Weems's pasture, and squeezed nearly a quart of fresh milk from one of his cows. Of course his father caught him feeding Ada and had rained down the punishment prescribed in the Bible for spoiled children.

Blake had taken the whipping without a sound, focusing his attention on the way Ada had looked when her hunger was satisfied. Afterward, his father had tried to comfort him. Blake still remembered the hatred and shame he'd felt. Not because of what he'd done, but because his father insisted on relying on God to feed his family. What kind of God demanded starvation and poverty? Not the kind of God he wanted to worship. Blake hadn't darkened the door of a church since he'd left home. And he was much happier for it.

"You sure can make that saw sing." Jensen's shout interrupted his thoughts.

Blake pushed down once more, surprised when his saw met little resistance. He'd nearly sawed the plank in two without realizing it. With another quick pull and thrust, he finished. Standing up, he rubbed his back and grinned at Jensen. "It's funny you say that."

"Why?" Jensen's unscarred eyebrow rose. "You was working harder than a lumberjack trying to meet his boss's tally."

"Back home, some people use saws like this to make music." He held the tool to his chest and pretended to drag a bow across its back. "They can make a saw sing with a voice as clear as an angel."

Jensen's face was a mixture of curiosity and doubt. "Are you trying to humbug me? I know I don't have much learning, but I'm not a daft old coot."

"Not at all. When you can't afford to buy fancy violins or pianos, you look around for alternate ways to entertain during a long winter's night."

"Well, if that don't beat the Dutch." Jensen scratched his head. "I heard of blowing into a bottle, and I've seen men beating out a rhythm on an upturned washbasin, but I've never seen nobody making music with a saw."

The floor shifted under Blake's feet. "I wonder who that could be. Maybe the captain has decided to return." He set his saw down and strode outside. "Lars, is that you?" Only silence answered his call.

From his vantage point on the second floor of his boat, Blake had a wide view of the dock and the first-floor decks. As far as he could see, no one had come aboard. He looked out toward the river, wondering if they'd been jostled by a passing boat, but saw no sign of recent activity. He shrugged. Maybe a gator had nudged them.

He looked around at the curtain of trees separating them from civilization. As soon as he'd taken possession of his boat, Blake had decided to move it away from the bustling dock at Natchez Under-the-Hill. He would need to make major renovations to *Hattie Belle* to meet his needs, and he wanted peace and quiet while he worked. Shaking his head, he walked back inside.

"Who was it?"

"No one as far as I could see."

Jensen's face whitened. "There's spirits living in some of these backwaters."

Blake would have laughed, but he could see his friend was serious. "I imagine it was more likely an alligator. You'll find a lot more wildlife than ghosts out here. Besides, it's not even noon. No self-respecting ghost would be out in broad daylight."

"Go ahead and make fun of me, but I've seen things on this river that would make you stop and think." Jensen nodded in emphasis. "Many a unsuspecting traveler's been attacked on the Natchez Trace, robbed and killed and left without a proper burial. What's to stop them from rising up and wandering around out there in the woods?"

"Death would do it, I'd think." Blake stacked the planks he'd sawed and grabbed another.

Jensen shook his head. "One of these days you're gonna see something that'll make you stop and scratch your head."

"Maybe so, but until then I prefer to put my faith in the natural world." Blake sent Jensen downstairs to fix some lunch and got back to work on his final project. As soon as he had his bar finished, the gaming room would be complete. Then he'd move back to Natchez and open up the most amazing gambling hall this part of the world had seen. He hoped it would become so famous they'd hear about it upriver, all the way up in Hannibal. A tight smile twisted his lips as he imagined the reaction of one man in particular—the Reverend William Matthews.

Chapter Eleven

I don't know if this is a good idea, Lily." Grandmother pulled out a stack of golden coins, each valued at fifty dollars, from the safe Grandfather had installed in his study years earlier.

"The money will be safe in the bank and earn interest." For the past half hour, Lily had been trying to convince her grandmother to let her deposit her dowry at Britton's Bank.

"And what if the bank has to close its doors before you are ready to collect your dowry?"

Lily understood her grandparent's distrust. In the past, banks had closed, and people's banknotes had become nothing more than worthless paper. She remembered hearing of two such disasters from Grandfather.

If she had been planning on depositing her dowry with Mr. Britton, she might have had second thoughts, too. But she intended to spend the money as soon as she could. On a steamship. Telling her grandmother her real plans, however, would result in a bigger argument if not an outright refusal.

Wishing she could be honest with her grandmother, Lily sighed. "Things are different now, Grandmother. My money will be safe."

"It is your money, even though your grandfather intended it for your dowry." Grandmother closed and secured the safe. "I only hope nothing happens to it before you wed. Once you are safely married, your husband will be the one to decide how to keep it safe."

"Yes, ma'am."

"Speaking of husbands, what did you think of Mr. Marvin?" Grandmother opened the top drawer of Grandfather's desk and pulled out a leather pouch.

Lily shrugged. The last thing she wanted to discuss was Adolphus Marvin. He'd become a veritable nuisance in the last few days, sending notes or dropping by to pay a call. It had taken all her ingenuity to avoid him, and she had the feeling her efforts would soon be curtailed by her uncle. "He seems to have many virtues."

Grandmother nodded. "But?"

Another shrug. "I don't know, Grandmother. I've always dreamed of meeting a special man." She chose her words with care. "The Bible says God made Eve from one of Adam's ribs—that He designed her as Adam's mate, a woman he would love above all others."

"And that's what you hope to find?" Grandmother sighed. "That's your youth speaking. Once you have met a few more eligible bachelors, you will realize any one of a number of men can love you and care for you."

"Yes, ma'am." Lily folded her lips together. Even if her grandmother was right about there being more than one man she could love, there had to be someone much better suited to her who would allow her to follow her dreams. She would wait for him to find her. . .even if it took the rest of her life.

Grandmother scraped the money into the leather bag and handed it to Lily. "Is Dahlia going with you to town?"

"No, ma'am." Lily's attention was on the heavy pouch. Her future—and her sisters' futures—were represented in its contents.

"I hope you are not planning to go alone." Grandmother pointed a finger. "It's not safe for a young girl to gad about alone, especially with all that money."

"Tamar will be going with me." Lily leaned over to kiss her grandmother's cheek. "Thank you so much."

"I don't know what your uncle is going to say."

"He won't say anything if you don't tell him." Lily adopted the most innocent expression she could manage. "It's not like I'm stealing something that belongs to him, after all."

"I suppose you're right."

As she left the room, Lily felt a pang of guilt. Grandmother had always been accommodating. But since Grandfather's death, she had become as easily swayed as a rudderless boat in a hurricane.

Hardening her heart, Lily told herself it was necessary to use her grandmother's kindness to achieve her goals. Aunt Dahlia and Uncle Phillip were influencing Grandmother with their ideas—ideas that would ensure a bleak, loveless future for Lily. She had a different future in mind. One that would include hard work and sacrifice, but that would come with many rewards such as pride, wealth, and freedom.

Lily took a moment to dream about one day landing at Natchez Under-the-Hill, happy and successful. She would smile patronizingly at her uncle when he looked with envy on her beautiful boat. Everyone would heap praise on her for her daring. Her sisters would be happy with their exciting lives on the river. Her breath caught as she imagined a man standing beside her. Her husband—tall, handsome, and kind—a man who made women swoon, a modern-day David with a heart for the Lord.

Yes, once she bought a steamship and moved her sisters aboard, no one would be able to force her to do anything she didn't want to do. Until then, she had to keep her plans hidden. She had no doubt Uncle Phillip would put a stop to them if he found out.

A shiver of dismay whispered down her spine. What would God think of her deceit? But she wasn't deceiving anyone. Lily was going to tell them the truth. . .later. The Bible didn't say it was wrong to choose one's timing. She truly believed buying the steamboat was God's will for her and her sisters, to give them freedom from society's dictates. She would have to tell her grandmother as soon as she could.

Feeling better, Lily asked one of the footmen to call for the carriage and hurried upstairs to get her bonnet and gloves. Her sisters were in the classroom, working hard on their lessons. She peeked in but didn't want to break their concentration, so she put a finger to her lips and shook her head at the tutor.

Grandfather had been insistent all three of them learn to read and write, as well as have a strong grounding in literature and history. He had always told her to study the past or be prepared to repeat its mistakes. Once they moved onto their steamship, she would never be able to afford to pay the fussy little man who was currently teaching her siblings, so Lily would have to teach them what they needed to know.

Tying a large bow under her chin and pulling on her gloves, Lily checked her appearance in the reflection of her bedroom window. She needed to present a professional image and impress Mr. Champney.

Lucretia Mott would be her model. The Quaker woman had been so outspoken in her views about women's rights, the abolition of slavery, and other important issues. She could be as strong as that lady. These were modern times, after all, even if things changed more slowly in the South. Lily would not be hindered by others' views of a woman's proper duties. She would bring change to Natchez and the other ports along the river. Perhaps one day people would read about her crusades in the newspaper. Perhaps other young women would strive to be like Lily Anderson—strong, fearless riverboat captain.

She could almost hear the mournful sound of her steamship's whistle as they rounded the bend and sailed majestically into Natchez. The cannons announcing their arrival would boom like thunder. All the people of the town would stand along the bluffs and wave at her. It would be wonderful. All she had to do was persevere, and one day her dreams would come true.

Lily's thoughts occupied her all the way to town. She could tell Tamar was curious, but she didn't want to reveal her plans just yet. Plenty of time would be available once she had bought her boat. By then it would be too late for anyone to interfere.

She directed the coachman through the streets until they reached the large building of Champney Shipping.

"What business could you possibly have here, Miss Lily?"

"Nothing much." Lily waited until the coachman let down the step before disembarking. "Only the future of my family."

She stepped to the door and twisted the doorknob, taking a deep breath. The clerk's shocked expression did nothing to bolster her courage, but Lily knew she could not allow herself to retreat. She lifted her chin and marched forward. "I would like to see Monsieur Champney."

The man gulped, apparently as frightened as she felt. He nodded and stood. "Who should I say is calling?"

Divulging her name might jeopardize her plans if word got out of this office. "I'm a friend of the family."

His Adam's apple worked once more before he opened a large oak door and disappeared behind it. When he reappeared a few moments later, Monsieur Champney was with him.

The older man's dark eyes twinkled with recognition as he swept his arm in a welcoming gesture. "Bonjour, mademoiselle. Please come into my office."

Lily entered the sumptuous room and perched on the edge of a large chair.

"How may I be of assistance?" The shipping magnate settled into his even larger chair on the far side of his gigantic desk, a polite expression on his face.

She couldn't think of any way to ease into the subject. "Do you have any steamboats available for purchase?"

"I, uh. . ." Monsieur Champney cleared his throat. "The short answer is yes, but—"

"Excellent. Then all we need to concern ourselves with is the asking price." Lily wondered where her newfound courage sprang from. Fear of failure? She squeezed her hands together and prayed for guidance. She had to succeed. If she didn't, she and her sisters would be separated forever. She wouldn't be able to care for them, guide them, or watch them grow into the self-assured young women she dreamed they would become.

Her host studied her, his dark eyes reminding her of his handsome son. What would Jean Luc think if he knew she was doing business with his father? Would he admire her pluckiness or decry her boldness? And why did she care? She would soon be captain of a steamboat, plying the muddy waters of the great Mississippi River. She might never see him again.

"I have an idea." Monsieur Champney's words grabbed her wandering attention. "You are familiar with the *Hattie Belle*, no?"

"Yes, sir." Excitement zipped through her. The *Hattie Belle* was a beautiful boat. And huge. Far larger than she had hoped to be able to purchase. If only she could afford it, she and her sisters would be certain to succeed. "But I don't know if I have enough—"

He waved away her words with one hand. "I have been thinking for some time that I should sell her, but I didn't want to let that beautiful boat be ruined by the wrong owner." He smiled broadly. "I can see what a determined young woman you are, the perfect owner for *Hattie*. There is, however, one small consideration."

Lily nodded. "I have my money with me." She could hardly contain herself. Never before had God been so quick to answer her prayer. She thanked Him mentally and made a promise to spend time on her knees that evening in gratitude and praise. But for now she needed to close this deal.

His eyebrows rose. "You do not want to take a tour of the boat before making your purchase?"

"No, sir. I've been on board, remember? My aunt and I attended your party."

"Of course you did." Monsieur Champney looked through the various stacks of paper on his desk before pulling out a leather-bound portfolio. He focused his attention on the papers he held. "Here we are. I thought I had the proper paperwork on my desk. I'll need your signature here so the transfer will be properly recorded."

She barely heard his explanation, nodding as he talked about deeds and rights and filing. She signed where he indicated and handed over the money she had received from Grandmother, her mind occupied with thoughts of the river.

Her dream was coming true. She could see herself standing in the pilothouse, looking for the next port to load or unload her lucrative cargo. Her sisters would be at her side, watching the water for hidden dangers. It would be a glorious way to spend their days. Of course, the *Hattie Belle* was large enough to take on passengers as well as freight, an unexpected development for their first boat.

Wouldn't her parents have been proud to see their children following in their footsteps? Her eyes burned with unexpected tears. Sadness for Mother's death battled against the anger she felt at their father's abandonment.

Determined to turn her thoughts from the past, Lily concentrated on the idea of sifting through the backgrounds of prospective passengers before selling them berths. It would be awful to expose her little sisters to the riffraff. She would only accept the most unexceptionable people—parents with children of their own or aristocratic couples. Perhaps President Buchanan would one day petition them for passage.

"And I believe we have completed all the necessary paperwork." Monsieur Champney held out a hand. "Congratulations, you are now the proud owner of the *Hattie Belle.*"

Lily's emotions nearly overwhelmed her as they shook hands to seal their arrangement. She had really done it! Her future and her sisters' futures were secure. They would make their fortunes on the river. She could hardly wait to break the good news to them.

❧

Foreboding made Tamar's heart thud as the carriage made its way back to the plantation. What had happened to the quiet girl she had cared for all these years? Lily had bloomed into a determined young woman who would not blindly follow the wishes of her elders. Yet had there really been a change? Or was Lily's decision a natural outcome of her love for her sisters?

While Tamar envied her charge the freedom she had to control her own future, she also was unsettled by Lily's ability to enter into a man's business and make a shocking, unheard-of purchase. "Tell me again exactly what you've done."

Color rode high in Lily's cheeks. "I've bought a boat—a beautiful, glorious boat called the *Hattie Belle*. It's going to be our home. I'm going to give Camellia and Jasmine a taste of life on the river. What better place for them to learn about life as they become young ladies?"

Tamar shuddered. She could think of several places.

"And we want you to come live with us, Tamar. I'm going to ask Grandmother to let you come. Won't it be wonderful?"

"I don't know." The words came out slowly. Tamar's mind went back to the first time she'd ever seen Lily—a tall, thin, towheaded child with skin as brown as a nut. A heartbroken little girl who had lost her mother and was about to lose her father. A girl determined to protect her baby sisters. That had been eight. . .no, nine years ago. In the intervening years, things had changed—Lily's skin was white and her hair had grown darker. But she was still as fiercely protective of her sisters. "Won't it be dangerous to live on a boat?"

Lily's eyebrows drew together. "I suppose you are referring to the accident that took Mother's life." Sadness invaded the carriage, an echo of the grief that had once been a part of Lily's daily life.

Tamar summoned a shaky smile. "I'm sorry, Lily dear. I didn't mean to dredge up old memories. All I meant is we're always hearing about boats catching on fire or getting sunk or attacked by pirates. Living in your family's home seems a safer choice."

It took Lily a moment to respond. Tamar wished she could find the words to bring Lily some comfort.

"I don't care." Lily's raised chin was an indication of her strong will. "It might have been safer at one time, but since Grandfather died, things have changed. I'm afraid that Aunt Dahlia and Uncle Phillip will convince Grandmother to make me marry Adolphus Marvin. She's already half-certain it would be the right thing to do."

"Your grandmother loves you, Lily. She wouldn't force you to do anything you don't want to do."

"You're probably right, but I cannot take the chance." Lily sighed. "I have to grab this opportunity. Uncle Phillip says it's a sure way to make a fortune. Besides"—a smile lit her face—"I have river water in my veins. Father always said so."

Tamar wanted to argue with Lily, but she didn't know what else to say. "I'm sure everything is going to be all right." Where had those words come from? It seemed highly unlikely that anything would be all right if Lily stuck to her plan. The list of things that could go wrong was longer than Tamar's arm.

As the carriage turned into the drive leading to Les Fleurs plantation, peace spread over her like a familiar quilt. It was the Lord. He was whispering that He was in control. It was the same voice that had brought her comfort throughout her life. The voice that had strengthened her when she needed it, reassured her whenever she took the time to listen.

Tamar smiled. "Everything is going to be all right." This time when she said the words, she knew they were the truth.

Chapter Twelve

Jean Luc strolled down the boardwalk, swinging his walking cane. Even though his world had crumbled...again...he would not wear his problems on his sleeve. The *Hattie Belle* was lost to him for now, but he would recover. He must recover.

Last night he had taken a few dollars and returned to the *Lucky Lucy*, only to find his nemesis had left the day before. He sat down and played a few hands of poker, retaining enough sense to get up and leave the table when he doubled his stake. If only he'd had that much sense a week ago.

The money jangling in his pocket was evidence that he was too good a gambler to stay behind forever. Too bad his father didn't see it his way. Every gambler knew all he had to do was to keep gambling. Eventually everything would flow his way.

A carriage pulled away as he turned the corner of Canal Street. A common occurrence at Champney Shipping. His father dealt with most of the prominent businessmen in town.

Jean Luc raised his cane in greeting as the carriage drew even with him, but his hand froze in mid-salute when his gaze discovered a large pair of sparkling brown eyes. A lady! She didn't seem familiar to him, although he found something arresting about her expression. Something that teased at his mind.

She couldn't be one of the young women he'd met at the round of social gatherings, could she? There were so many beautiful Southern belles. Blonds, brunettes, redheads. He'd met every marriageable daughter in town and most of the ones from the outlying communities. A shame they all blended together into a single image—empty, vacant, subservient. He wished he could find one who had some spirit.

Her cheeks colored, but the young lady did not look away from him. A slight smile turned up the corners of her mouth, again striking some chord in his mind. Jean Luc could not place her, so he looked to see if he recognized those she traveled with.

A female slave sat beside her, a middle-aged woman with a stern look on her honey-colored face. No brother, father, or other male accompanied them. That fact alone piqued his interest.

Was the mystery woman a young widow? No, she looked far too innocent for that role. Maybe she had dropped off some family member at his father's office and would pick him up when she finished shopping. Deciding this must be the case, Jean Luc bowed as her carriage picked up speed and passed him.

It would be interesting to meet her relative and find out more about her. So far, all the young women paraded in front of him had left him yawning at the least, horrified at the worst. He wished his parents were not so anxious for him to find a bride. At least not here. If they would allow him to travel to New Orleans, he had no doubt he could find an acceptable candidate, but sophistication could not be found at the back of beyond.

A derisive smile curled his lips. The newspapers proclaimed the Mississippi River the gateway to the West, the muddy divide between civilization and wilderness. To his mind, Natchez should be on the far side of the river. The whole state of Mississippi, as far as that went, should be moved to the wilderness. It seemed to be composed of nothing but impenetrable forest and provincial settlers.

With a sigh, he opened the front door and strode past the clerk, entering his father's sanctum after a brief knock with the silver head of his cane.

His father reached for his pocket watch and grunted. "It's about time you arrived, Son."

Jean Luc yawned and flopped into one of the chairs opposite his father. "Mama didn't mention a time when she told me you wanted to see me."

His father's lips folded into a straight line. He leaned back in his chair, causing the wood to creak ominously. Jean Luc refused to be intimidated by his father's tactics. He'd already heard plenty about his stupidity at the gaming tables. But Papa would soon find out who knew more about that.

He lifted his cane and studied the snarling panther's face. He felt a kinship with the predator. Jean Luc might have to lie in wait until the time was right, but one day he would pounce. On that day, everyone who had ever bested him would be sorry.

"I've managed to take care of the problem we have with the *Hattie Belle.*"

Jean Luc glanced up at his father. "What do you mean?" A vision of Blake Matthews floating lifelessly in the eddies of the river came to mind.

"I had an interesting interview with a young lady you may remember, Miss Lily Anderson, whose grandfather, Isaiah Blackstone, recently died."

Jean Luc cocked his head to one side. A collage of images took form in his mind—a distraught young lady at the launch of the *Hattie Belle,* that same young lady eyeing him with admiration as he twirled her about on the dance floor of his boat, a concerned girl who left behind an air of mystery, and the young woman he had just seen in the carriage. Lily Anderson.

"It seems Miss Anderson will not inherit her grandfather's estate, at least not yet. But she did receive a generous settlement, a dowry of sorts."

"How generous?"

His father cocked an eyebrow. "Not enough to support your habits."

Jean Luc sat back, a flash of anger passing through him. He was tired of being gigged about how he spent his leisure time. Why could his father not forgive and move forward? Deciding that to ignore the pointed comments was the best response, Jean Luc composed his features into a mask of nonchalance and waited.

"It is, however, enough for her to purchase my portion of the *Hattie Belle.*"

The cane clattered to the floor. "You sold controlling interest to a girl?"

"That's right. Imagine the surprise Blake Matthews will receive when he discovers I am no longer his partner." A bark of laughter came from Papa. "I almost wish I could be there."

Jean Luc's mind whirled. Lily Anderson had managed to possess the thing he wanted most to get his hands on. Why hadn't his father offered it to him? Or had he? It suddenly occurred to Jean Luc that selling to Miss Anderson might be his father's way of offering the boat to him. An attempt to kill two birds with one stone. Ownership of the *Hattie Belle* was a prize for which Jean Luc might pursue a marriage in earnest.

He picked up his cane and stood.

"Where are you going?" Papa's voice was dark with emotion. "I'm not through talking to you, Jean Luc."

"I have a lady to meet." He threw the answer over his shoulder as he headed out the door. He had absolute confidence in his skill with the ladies. Miss Anderson would be like putty in his hands. He would woo her and win her affection. Then he would force Blake Matthews to sell his interest in the *Hattie Belle*.

Even if it meant playing into his father's hands, Jean Luc had to take advantage of this situation. Papa might have won this skirmish, but Jean Luc was determined to win the war.

Chapter Thirteen

Someone's driving up to the house." Jasmine struggled against Camellia to retain her place at the window.

"Move, Jasmine. I can't see who it is."

Lily held her breath, waiting to hear her sisters' pronouncement. She prayed it would not be Mr. Marvin. She had no desire to spend half an hour in the parlor ignoring her aunt's pointed looks and thinly veiled suggestions. "Serve Mr. Marvin his tea, Lily. Show Mr. Marvin what an excellent needlewoman you are. Walk Mr. Marvin to the door, Lily." The incessant directions came each time he visited. Could her aunt make her plans any more obvious? It was humiliating enough to think her relatives wanted to throw her at the first man who came courting. But they could wait until the period of mourning for Grandfather was over, or at least until a few months had passed.

"I don't recognize the carriage, but the driver is quite distinguished." Camellia glanced over one shoulder toward Lily. "Do you think it's another suitor?"

With a shrug, Lily traced the monogrammed initial in her handkerchief. Camellia had been kind enough to sew one to replace the handkerchief lost to the cutpurse in Natchez Under-the-Hill. "I doubt it. More likely a business acquaintance of Uncle Phillip's."

Camellia made a face and wandered away from the window. "I wish someone would come visit me."

"Are you going to marry Mr. Marvin?" Jasmine stood next to Lily's chair. Her lower lip trembled slightly.

Lily gave her youngest sister a reassuring hug. "No." She considered telling her sisters about their steamboat, but she had decided to wait until she could show them the *Hattie Belle*. She hadn't yet found a way to tell Grandmother, either. "I don't plan to marry anyone right now. Especially if it means leaving you here with Aunt Dahlia and Uncle Phillip." She reached out, taking one of each sister's hands. "I have a different idea for my future and yours."

A knock at the door preceded Tamar's entrance. "You are wanted in the parlor, Miss Lily."

Her fearful glance met Camellia's. Was it Mr. Marvin after all?

Camellia shook her head, her golden ringlets brushing her cheeks. "It's not Mr. Marvin. His coach is not nearly as fine."

"I wonder who it can be." Lily released her sisters' hands and stood.

Tamar frowned. "You have a spot on your collar." She hurried over to Lily's bureau. After a moment of searching, she pulled a length of black-dyed cotton from the top drawer with a satisfied sound. "Here's a fresh one. Let's get that one off."

Lily removed the offending collar. "I don't know why you must make a fuss."

"You are my responsibility, Miss Lily. I'd never let you appear to guests looking less than your best." Tamar smiled as she tweaked a lock of hair into place. "Your grandmother would have a fit if you showed up in her parlor looking like a ragamuffin."

Knowing it was useless to protest, Lily allowed Tamar to fluff the ribbon around her waist and fuss with her skirt. Finally Tamar stepped back and nodded. "Go on down, now, before your grandmother sends someone to find you."

A giggle threatened to escape. Lily swallowed it as her gaze once more met Camellia's. "I'll be back before long and tell you all about it."

Camellia shrugged as if she did not care, but Lily knew better. Both girls would be antsy until she returned.

Lily descended the stairs, her heart tripping as she considered who might be awaiting her arrival. Although they had received many visitors since Grandfather's death, most of them had been older. Perhaps this was another visitor of the same ilk. But why the summons to the parlor?

She stood outside the door and took a deep breath. Pinning a smile on her shaky lips, Lily pushed open the door and stepped inside. The man who rose from the couch made her mouth drop open. It was Mr. Champney, Jean Luc Champney, the son of the man she'd bought the *Hattie Belle* from. Had he come to tell her family of her purchase? Or perhaps he was coming to tell her the sale was invalid.

"Good morning, Miss Anderson." He bowed over her hand.

She sank into a curtsy, acting on instinct as her mind considered half a dozen reasons their guest might be here. "It's a pleasure to see you, Mr. Champney."

His smile was as attractive as she remembered from the afternoon they had danced on the upper deck of the boat she now owned. "I am honored you remember me."

Lily took a seat on the sofa and nodded toward her grandmother.

He sat down on the sofa, too, but on the far end as was proper. "The weather is so nice today. I hoped you might be interested in a leisurely drive this morning."

This was better than she'd imagined. He was interested in getting to know her better. Perhaps he was considering a courtship. Lily's cheeks warmed at the idea of being alone with him. She glanced at her grandmother for permission and received an encouraging nod. "I would greatly enjoy that, Mr. Champney." Perhaps he would be amenable to taking her to the river so she could tour the *Hattie Belle*. Her boat. The words thrilled her. Did he know she had purchased the boat?

Grandmother sent Tamar for Lily's cape before giving Mr. Champney strict instructions on their outing. She was to be returned home by the time lunch was served. He was to keep his carriage on the main roads, and they were to take Tamar with them for propriety's sake.

Once she and Tamar were ready, Mr. Champney helped Lily into the front seat of his fancy cabriolet. His footman assisted Tamar into the backseat located on the outside of the fancy carriage. As Mr. Champney climbed into the front seat and settled himself beside her, Lily hid a grin. Tamar was muttering under her breath about the dangers of traveling. Something about breakneck speed and her desire to use her own God-given limbs.

Mr. Champney raised his riding whip to encourage the pair of horses, and they set off. "Do you have any place in particular you would like to go?"

How nice of him to consider her wishes. Lily couldn't help comparing the man beside her to the one her aunt and uncle were trying to foist on her. If they had chosen Mr. Champney, she would not have been forced to find her dire solution. Of course, she would also not be about to realize her dream of living on a riverboat like her mother. "I'd love to go to the waterfront."

He nodded. "I suppose you want to visit your boat."

Lily could feel her cheeks heating. "Please don't mention it to my family."

"They don't know you purchased the *Hattie Belle*?"

Lily shook her head. "I don't want them to stop me. As soon as I make sure everything is ready, I plan to move my sisters and myself aboard. We're going to live on the *Hattie Belle*."

His hands jerked on the reins, and his horses swerved. For a moment he had to concentrate on the horses, but as soon as he had them under control, he turned to stare at Lily. "You can't live on a riverboat."

Lily stared at him. Wasn't his family involved in shipping? "Why not? My parents did. My father was the captain of his own boat, and he and my mother often took trips together before th–the accident."

"That's precisely why you should abandon this idea. It's far too dangerous for a lady."

A wagon trundled toward them, its bed empty. Lily wondered what it had carried to the river. Cotton? Sugarcane? Corn? Or maybe some handmade goods? Whatever the cargo, it had likely been loaded onto a steamship destined for sale in some distant city. Her heartbeat accelerated. Maybe it was even now sitting on the *Hattie Belle*, waiting for her arrival before sailing off.

"You can't say anything to change my mind." Lily looked away. "I'm going to make a home for myself and my sisters. A place where we can make our own choices and live our lives the way we wish."

Silence fell between them as they entered Natchez. The traffic was heavy, and Mr. Champney had to pay attention to their route. She could feel his disapproval like a wall between them, but it only made her more determined. No obstacle would stop her. Living on the *Hattie Belle* was a dream come true.

"Very well, I'll take you to your boat." His voice held a note of something she could not name. Amusement or resignation? "I only hope you won't be too disappointed."

He guided the carriage through town but did not take the road to Natchez Under-the-Hill.

"Where are we going?" Lily could not keep the suspicion out of her voice.

"To see your boat."

"But I thought—"

"Miss Anderson, I have only your best interests at heart. I hope you will one day learn to trust me."

His tone made her feel guilty. Abashed, she watched the road silently. Soon they came to a bend, and she caught sight of the brown water of the Mississippi River. She caught her breath as a pair of white smokestacks appeared. She turned to Mr. Champney and had to fight the impulse to hug him.

His dark gaze seemed to read her mind. His smile widened, giving it a wolfish quality she had not noticed before. Before she could react, a banging sound turned her attention back to the *Hattie Belle*. "What is that?"

"I would imagine that is Blake Matthews." He brought the carriage to a standstill and waited for his footman to come to the horses' heads. "My father said he was making some alterations to the boat."

"Is he the captain?"

"Not exactly."

Lily was beginning to lose her patience with Mr. Champney. What kind of game did he think this was? "Is he one of the crew?"

"I suppose you could say that." Mr. Champney climbed down and came around to help her disembark, his hand outstretched.

Lily put her hand in his and leaned forward, trusting him to balance her weight until her feet could touch the ground. To her shock she found herself caught in his embrace. "What are you doing? Put me down!" She pushed at his chest to no avail.

"Hold still, Miss Anderson. The ground here is quite muddy." With several long-legged strides he reached the boat and stepped aboard before setting her gently on her feet.

Not sure if she should be angry or thankful, Lily straightened her bonnet and stepped back. "You might have warned me." His teasing look brought a smile as Lily realized how silly her complaint was. "Thank you." She glanced back toward his carriage.

"Shall we begin our tour?"

"Tamar is still in the carriage awaiting help."

The teasing look disappeared from his coal-black eyes. "You want me to assist a slave? She can make her own way to the boat."

The disdain on his face brought her up short. Tamar was more than a slave. She had mothered Lily and her two sisters from the time they first came to live with their grandparents. She had wiped away their grief-stricken tears and bandaged their scrapes. "Tamar may be a slave, but she's part of my family. She is also my chaperone, and I refuse to take one more step until she is standing beside me."

His lips tightened, and he gave her the briefest of bows before returning to the carriage. He carried Tamar as though he held an armful of firewood. His attitude might not be uncommon in this part of the world, but he should have some consideration for Lily's feelings.

"Who's out there?" The gruff voice sounded vaguely familiar to her.

"It's Jean Luc Champney. I've brought the new owner of the *Hattie Belle*."

She liked the sound of that. The new owner. Before she could fully savor the introduction, her thoughts were cut short.

The man responded with a crude epithet.

Who did he think he was to speak so before checking to see if a lady was present? Lily's ears burned. "Please mind your tongue. I am not accustomed. . ." Her words trailed off as he stepped onto the deck above them. The man who had accused her of being the mother of a thief. The man who had already given her the rough side of his tongue, although he had refrained from curses that day. The man whose strong arms had encircled her and held her protectively close when it had seemed someone might be shooting at them. Hot blood flushed her neck and cheeks as she remembered the feel of his muscular chest cushioning her fall.

"And I'm not used to idlers who interrupt my work with foolishness." He stared down at them.

Lily's gaze made note of his leather shoes before traveling up the length of his dark trousers. They might have been black, but she couldn't tell because of the liberal coating of dirt or dust. His shirt, which she supposed had once been white, was now a dingy yellow from the same dusty substance. Her gaze halted for a brief instant on the open collar of his shirt, as it allowed more of his chest to show than she was accustomed to seeing. Raising her eyes to meet his gaze, Lily was mesmerized by the blue fire in them, a fire that set free a host of butterflies in her stomach. She gulped in some air to quiet the tickling sensation and reached for Mr. Champney's arm, her fingers gripping with the strength of an eagle's talons. "I don't know what work you could possibly have on *my* boat."

His jaw dropped. He disappeared inside, and she heard his heavy footsteps descending stairs before he reappeared, his broad shoulders filling the main entrance. "What on earth are you talking about?"

Mr. Champney coughed, and she thought she saw him hide a smile.

Letting go of her escort's arm, Lily opened the strings of her reticule to pull forth her deed to the *Hattie Belle*, glad a last-minute impulse had made her bring it along. "I recently purchased this boat, and you are to vacate it immediately." She waved the vellum sheet toward him for emphasis.

He grabbed the deed and unfolded it.

Lily didn't see why he should be so interested in reading about her purchase, but she supposed it wouldn't hurt for him to see the proof in black and white.

"What kind of trickery is this?" The man ignored her and directed his question to Mr. Champney. "Or have you been gambling again?"

Her breath caught as Mr. Champney's face turned bright red. Was he about to demand satisfaction for the insolent words?

The butterflies in her stomach turned into a hardened lump. "I don't know what you're talking about, sir."

"He's no 'sir.' His name is Blake Matthews." Mr. Champney's voice had an edge she had not heard before. "He's nothing but a gambler—a man who relies on Lady Luck to make his living."

The anger she had sensed in Mr. Matthews dissipated suddenly. He folded the deed and handed it to Lily. "Yes, I'm a gambler, and I depend on my wits to survive. I like to think of my lifestyle as being free of the strictures of modern society." His gaze speared the man beside her. "It's better than being the wastrel son of a conniving businessman."

Mr. Champney's brows lowered once more. "Be very careful who you slander."

"What slander? Your father decided to bail out of our business deal by selling his interest to a naive young girl who ought to be home, batting her eyes for an adoring husband."

The air seemed to thicken. How dare this man—a gambler—patronize her! She drew herself up to her full height of five foot three.

"I don't know what you're doing here, Mr. Blake Matthews, but I suppose it is an arrangement you had with Mr. Champney when he was the owner of the *Hattie Belle*. Since that is no longer the case, I would greatly appreciate it if you would gather your belongings and remove yourself from the boat."

"And if I don't?" The look in his blue eyes reminded her of a stalking cat—predatory, dangerous.

Lily lifted her chin. "Then I will call on the sheriff to remove you."

"That will be hard to do, my dear." His lips curled into a triumphant smile. "You see, barely a week ago the upstanding young man next to you lost to me in a card game. And he gave me his deed to the *Hattie Belle* as payment."

"But I own—"

"If you read your paper carefully, you'll find you own a portion of the boat we're standing on."

Lily unfolded the deed once more and saw the language he meant. "Controlling interest?" She skipped the legal wording that made no sense to her and found that she owned exactly 51 percent of the *Hattie Belle*. Her mind spun. She didn't own the boat outright? After all the money she had spent, she had to share her boat with someone else? Tears sprang to her eyes as her dreams collapsed.

She had been duped. Tricked by Jean Luc's father. The sunlight dimmed, and the sounds of the river seemed far away. What was she going to do? What could she do? Beg her uncle for help straightening out this mess? Unthinkable. She would have to make the best of it. Hadn't she planned to face down any obstacles to her plans? She would not give up at the first challenge.

Her mind raced. She could still make this work. Surely a few trips delivering cargo would give her enough money to buy the rest of the boat. She nodded and lifted her gaze to meet the blue eyes of the man standing in front of her. Her partner. Her temporary partner. "As soon as I have sufficient money, I will buy you out."

His eyebrows rose. "You're going to buy me out? I don't think so. I have my own plans for the *Hattie Belle*."

"And that will be fine as long as they meet with my approval."

"Your approval? You're only a girl."

That might be so, but Lily had been raised on a thriving plantation, and she had seen her grandfather handle myriad problems through the years. She drew on that experience for her reply. "Nevertheless, I am the one in charge."

Mr. Champney coughed. Was he amused? She didn't have time to be affronted, so Lily ignored him, concentrating instead on Mr. Matthews. "I would like a tour of our boat."

His face looked as if chiseled from a block of stone. She could read disapproval in every line of his body.

Part of Lily wanted to run back to Les Fleurs plantation. But that was her old life. Her new life was in front of her, if only she could summon the courage to embrace it. She would do this, for herself and for her sisters.

Mr. Matthews apparently recognized her determination. He bowed and swept his hand toward the inside of the boat. "Right this way."

Chapter Fourteen

Blake watched the little spitfire as he took her through the boat—their boat. Grudging admiration filled him for her spirit, but she needed to learn this was no place for a lady.

Maybe explaining the physical labor involved would convince her to be a silent partner. Instead of being bought out, he could likely put together enough money in a month or less after opening his casino to pay her off and forget she existed.

"We have constructed several tables for poker, and I am looking for a roulette wheel to purchase." His chest expanded as he detailed his plans. The *Hattie Belle* was going to be gorgeous when he finished. "I'll hang ruby-red curtains on the windows to keep the customers from realizing what time of day it is. That way we can run the games constantly. This boat will earn more money in a week than it could earn from six months of running cargo up and down the river."

"Delivering cargo will not strip wealth from people." Her disapproving tone matched the look on her face.

What had he expected? She was no doubt too puritanical to immediately agree. But if he could make her see the profits at stake, surely she would change her mind. "We'll have food and libations available at all times. I already have an excellent chef who will take care of the meals."

Jensen stepped from the doorway of one of the staterooms, and

Blake heard a soft sound from the spitfire. He expected to see an expression of horror on her face, but instead sympathy filled her large brown eyes. Her gaze met his, and he was instantly wrapped in her warmth. "This is Jensen Moreau, my steward and chef and handyman rolled into one."

Jensen seemed to be lost in a trance. He was looking at someone behind Blake, a silly expression on his weathered face. If Blake wasn't mistaken, adoration filled every inch of Jensen's face.

Blake turned to see what had caused such a response. Miss Anderson's chaperone? Curiosity kept his attention centered on the woman. She had to be a few years older than Jensen, and if he judged correctly, a necessary ability of a gambler, she was devoted to her mistress and would have no time for a romance.

"Good morning, Mr. Moreau." Miss Anderson stepped forward and curtsied.

Jensen came out of his trance, but the gentle smile that looked so odd on his face remained. He bowed, exhibiting more grace than Blake would have thought possible. "Welcome aboard the *Hattie Belle*."

"You may not realize it, Jensen, but you are welcoming your new employer." He shot a tight smile at Jensen's shocked face. At least he had managed to refocus the man's attention to important matters. "Miss Anderson has purchased interest—"

"Controlling interest."

Her interruption made him grind his teeth. He consciously loosened his jaw before continuing. "*Controlling* interest in the *Hattie Belle*, and intends for us to get the boat in shape to run cargo."

"I don't rightly understand." The man looked from Blake to the spitfire, but his gaze moved back to the slave and settled there. It appeared Jensen had been struck by Cupid's arrow.

Jean Luc made a disgusted sound. "Can we get this over with? I promised I would have Miss Anderson home in time for luncheon." He pulled a watch from his waistcoat. "We need to leave before much longer if I am to keep my word."

She tilted her chin upward in a gesture of defiance, showing she intended to stay as long as she pleased.

If Blake didn't want the lot of them here all day, he needed to come up with a distraction. "I do have a problem you could help me with, Miss Anderson."

Her chin came down a notch. Her brown eyes gleamed with triumph. "What is that, Mr. Matthews?"

"Jensen here needs to concentrate on getting the kitchens ready, but I cannot do all the carpentry by myself, much less the cleaning." He nodded to the scattered bits of wood and sawdust where he'd been working. "Perhaps you could hire some help."

She nodded, and her bright smile moved her face from the realm of pleasing to attractive. "Do you have a captain?"

Blake gathered his wandering thoughts. "I don't think we'll need a captain since the boat won't be leaving the bank."

"I see." She ran a finger across her chin. Miss Lily Anderson's frown was rather cute.

Blake steeled his heart. He couldn't afford to let her puppyish eagerness get under his skin. He would give her tasks to keep her busy until he could put together enough money to buy the boat outright. Then he would send her home where she belonged.

"You've given me much to think about, Mr. Matthews."

He bowed to the three of them and swept his hand outward. "This way to the stairs."

Jensen came up beside Blake as he watched Jean Luc help the women pick their way around muddy patches on the way back to the carriage.

"That's one mighty pretty girl."

Blake frowned. Was Jensen talking about Miss Anderson? He followed his friend's gaze to where the slave, Tamar, was climbing to her seat.

"I thought she turned your head, but I have to warn you, I doubt she'll leave her little chick. She'll probably want to stay with Miss Anderson until she marries, and perhaps even after."

Jensen sighed. "She'd never look at the likes of me."

"Don't be ridiculous, man. You're a fine fellow with a steady job and a good heart. Any woman would be lucky to be the object of your affection." Blake hid his doubts from the other man. Jensen would probably forget all about his attraction after a few days. As much as Jensen prized his freedom, Blake could not see the man settling into matrimony. But if his friend decided he did want to win Tamar's heart, Blake would do everything in his power to help him realize his dream.

Jean Luc whipped up his horses on the ride back to Lily's home. He needed to figure a way to turn the obvious enmity between Lily and Blake to his advantage.

Sliding a glance to the young woman perched beside him, Jean Luc wondered what had happened to her determination to use the *Hattie Belle* for ferrying cargo. She had seemed so certain of her plans. Had she been overwhelmed by the enormity of the work to be done? Or had she simply knuckled under the pressure applied by Blake?

Of course she was only a woman. Truth to tell, he was a bit relieved Lily wouldn't be joining the world of business. Women had no place in that sphere. He might not have put it as crudely as the gambler had, but ladies should concentrate on their families and households.

He stole another glance at Lily. What was she thinking? He couldn't tell from her expression, but it must be engrossing as she had not said a word for the last mile. "Is everything okay?"

She started as if awakened. Her brown eyes were full of apology as she turned to him. "I'm afraid I was caught up in my plans. Thank you so much for taking me to the *Hattie Belle*. I don't know when I could have gotten there on my own."

"It is my pleasure. When Papa told me what Blake intended to do with the boat, I thought you would want to know about it."

"Yes. And you knew right where it was docked. I doubt I could have found it on my own."

He basked in her approving words. At least she admired him. He could grow accustomed to her smile and the glow in her large brown eyes. It was a welcome relief after the vitriol he'd recently gotten from his parents. "I could not believe Matthews wanted you to hire help. I doubt you'll want to ask your uncle for assistance since you said you wanted to keep him from learning about your purchase, so I'd be glad to take on the task of interviewing some of the local workmen and sending them to the boat."

"Thank you, Mr. Champney. It is sweet of you to offer, but I won't be hiring anyone."

Jean Luc frowned. "Do you plan to leave Matthews and his servant to do the work?"

"Not at all." She beamed. "I plan to do the work myself."

Her words blasted him like a winter gale. "You plan what?" He was shocked to the core of his being. She must be teasing him. One glance at the determined set of her chin, however, told him she was serious. "But your reputation—"

"Oh, I will have plenty of chaperones." The look she shot him was full of mischief. "I'm going to take Tamar and my two sisters. We can do the cleaning and arranging in the kitchen and leave the men to work on the upper decks."

Jean Luc's shoulders shook with laughter.

"I don't see what you find so amusing, sir." The mischief was gone from her expression, replaced by cool disdain. "I assure you we are quite capable."

He sobered immediately. "You misunderstand, Miss Anderson. I wasn't laughing at the idea of you and your sisters working." He swallowed his laughter and slowed the horses some so he could concentrate on explaining himself. "I was just thinking of Matthews' expression when you tell him you are moving aboard."

A giggle answered him. "It won't be what he's expecting, but Mr. Matthews is going to find I am not some biddable female who will allow him to ruin the *Hattie Belle*. She is going to be my home whether he likes it or not."

It was an unconventional solution, to say the least. Jean Luc doubted even his father, the quintessential opportunist, could have foreseen this turn of events. But the more he considered her idea, the better he liked it.

All he had to do was lead her on. Lily was already showing signs of being bowled over by his knowledge and abilities. With a little work, he had no doubt he could make her fall in love with him. He might even marry her.

As her husband, he would control the day-to-day operations of the *Hattie Belle*. If Matthews could offer him enough incentive, he might let the man continue turning the boat into a casino.

Even if he didn't marry Lily, he could make sure she depended on him. Then when she tired of her foolishness, she would come to him for help. He would offer to take over. No matter which way he went, Jean Luc would end up controlling the *Hattie Belle* without having to spend a dime. And his father would have to admit he'd been wrong.

They were nearly back at the Blackstone plantation before another idea came to him. "You're going to need a captain."

She nodded. "I can put an advertisement in the *Courier* or *Free Trader*. There are probably many good captains in Natchez. I'll simply choose amongst them."

"You might find that more difficult than you think." Not wanting to offend her, Jean Luc chose his words carefully. "Although I don't agree with them, some men will be reluctant to work for a woman."

Her face puckered in a frown. "They would care more about that than about earning a good salary?"

"I'm afraid so." He let the horses slow to a walk. "But since my family owned the *Hattie Belle* until a few days ago, I know the man who captained her for us. I could talk to him privately and assure him of your ability."

"You would do that for me?" A slow smile appeared on her face. "I'd be very much in your debt."

"Think nothing of it." He leaned toward her, happy when she did not move away as she had earlier. "I want to be of service in any way."

Her cheeks suffused with blood. "Thank you, Mr. Champney."

"I have only one request." He felt her body tense, so he rushed on. "I'd like for you to call me Jean Luc."

"Is that all?" She relaxed and looked down at her hands. "I would be most happy to grant your request, Jean Luc."

He smiled as he turned the horses into the drive. He'd make sure Lars Steenberg reported to him daily on the activities aboard the *Hattie Belle*. And all he had to do to romance the girl sitting next to him was be patient and attentive. Miss Lily Anderson would soon give him everything he wanted.

Chapter Fifteen

It's a good match." Aunt Dahlia added her voice to her husband's. "You ought to be thankful your uncle has arranged your future for you."

"Maybe I want to plan my own future." Lily glanced at her grandmother, whose hands twisted in her lap as she listened to the argument. Grandmother understood her reluctance to marry a man she did not love. They had spoken of it on more than one occasion. But it seemed Grandmother was not going to support her now.

Uncle Phillip pushed away from the mantel and took up a position behind his wife's chair. "And what type of future do you think you can arrange for yourself, young lady?"

"I suppose she could be a governess." Aunt Dahlia sniffed. "Mother and Father have certainly paid enough to educate her over the years."

Lily shuddered. The idea of being cooped up with someone else's children held about as much appeal as marrying Mr. Marvin. "I want freedom. Freedom for myself and for my sisters."

Uncle Phillip's frown darkened.

She wished he would not be so angry, but she would not bow to his wishes. Lily was determined to stand up for herself. She closed her eyes and prayed for the words to convince her relatives her way was best.

"And exactly how do you propose to get that freedom?"

Her heart thudded in anticipation of the response her answer was going to bring. "I have purchased a steamboat."

"You've what?" Her aunt's screech made Lily wince.

Grandmother gasped, and Uncle Phillip's jaw dropped.

Lily had the sudden urge to tell him to be careful or he was likely to swallow a few flies. She stifled a giggle. Nothing about this discussion was funny. She had to keep her head...for her sake as well as Camellia's and Jasmine's. She had to be strong. "I took the money my sisters and I inherited from Grandfather and bought the *Hattie Belle*. Mr. Champney sold it to me on Monday, and I went to see it this morning. It is in need of some repairs, but I expect to be able to load cargo on it within the month and take it on the river."

"Preposterous." Her uncle sputtered the single word. "You're a girl. What do you know about running a boat? At best you'll end up losing every dime you've invested. At worst you'll end up as dead as your mother."

Lily could not believe the callous words. Tears stung her eyes. She wanted to lash out, to turn her back on her family. They obviously didn't love her.

"That's enough." Grandmother stood, ignoring her needlework that fell to the floor. "I will not have you casting aspersions on either my daughter or my granddaughter."

"But—"

"Not another word, Phillip. Lily has made her decision. She has already purchased a boat, and though I might have wished she had consulted me before taking such a drastic step, what's done is done."

"Surely you cannot support her in this madness," Aunt Dahlia challenged Grandmother.

"Lily is eighteen, and no longer a child. She should have the right to spend her inheritance in whatever way she sees fit." Grandmother sat next to Lily on the sofa and put an arm around her shoulders. "I love you, darling. I don't want to see you miserable."

"Thank you, Grandmother."

Uncle Phillip snorted. "Both of you have lost your minds. Lily's reputation will be in tatters if you allow her to go off on a riverboat."

"It may be unconventional," Grandmother said, "but the Blackstone family has never bowed to convention. Lily will be following in the footsteps of many of her forebears—men and women who risked everything to follow their dreams."

He turned his attention to Lily. "I don't know what bee has gotten into your bonnet, young lady, but I wash my hands of you. Don't think you can come back here and beg me to introduce you to any of my acquaintances."

"I'll keep that in mind." Relief flooded Lily. Did Uncle Phillip think his words were threatening? On the contrary, she ought to thank him for his promise.

"You ought to be ashamed of yourself, Lily." Aunt Dahlia shook her head. "Do you know how much effort your uncle has put into this match? And now he's going to have to tell Adolphus you are not interested in his suit."

Uncle Phillip put a hand on his wife's shoulder. "Can't you see that your words are falling on deaf ears? Your niece is determined to bite the hand that feeds her."

"That's enough," Grandmother interjected. "If you cannot keep a civil tongue in your head, Phillip, you can leave."

He closed his mouth with an audible snap, but the look he threw Lily promised more repercussions.

She lifted her chin and glared back at him. She refused to be intimidated. And thanks to Grandmother's championship, she didn't have to worry about her aunt and uncle's disapproval.

"How soon do you plan to leave, dear?" Grandmother's voice broke the staring match.

Lily turned her attention to her grandparent. "Tomorrow morning."

Sadness crept into her grandmother's violet eyes, eyes that reminded Lily of her youngest sister. "So soon?"

"There's so much to be done." Lily hesitated, hating to ask her grandmother for a favor at this time, but she couldn't see any way around it. "May we take Tamar with us?"

Aunt Dahlia's mouth dropped open. But Grandmother stopped her words with a raised hand. "Of course. I'll feel much better knowing you have her to watch out for you and your sisters."

Relief and anticipation filled Lily. She hugged her grandmother before standing. "I promise to take good care of Camellia and Jasmine."

"I'll hold you to that." Grandmother smiled through tears. "And I expect all of you to visit as often as you can."

"We will." Lily left the parlor, her mind already consumed with the things she needed to gather for all of them. She could hardly wait to tell Tamar and her sisters about the changes coming to all of them.

Chapter Sixteen

"Will we be back in time for my piano lesson on Tuesday?" Camellia's pout had not lightened all morning as Lily and Tamar rushed about to get everything ready for their departure.

"I'm not sure how long it will be before we can return for a visit." Lily knew Camellia was going to have a difficult time adjusting to life on the river. She loved the comforts that went along with being the pampered grandchild of a wealthy planter.

"Is there a piano on the boat?"

Lily closed the trunk she had just finished packing and sat on the lid. She tilted her head at her forlorn sister as she tried to remember whether the boat had the desired instrument. "They had one during the ball I attended several months ago, but I didn't see any sign of one yesterday." She patted her sister's knee. "Everything is going to be all right, Camellia. I'm only trying to do what I think is best for all of us."

When Camellia didn't respond, Lily directed, "We'd better finish packing. The morning is slipping away quickly."

A little before noon, the three sisters and Tamar finally climbed into the carriage. The family's largest wagon—usually reserved for carrying baled cotton to market—followed them, its bed piled high with clothing, trunks, and household items.

"Whooo." Jasmine leaned against the side of the carriage, looking out the window at the passing scenery. Jasmine would embrace this adventure, and Lily would have to keep a close eye on her.

Camellia's frustration boiled over as Jasmine continued making strange noises. "What are you doing?"

"Making the sound of a riverboat." Unperturbed, Jasmine turned from the window and smiled at Lily. "Have you heard the *Hattie Belle*'s whistle?"

Lily ignored Camellia's disgusted sigh. "Yes, it's quite distinctive. You'll love it."

"Could be none of us will hear it for a while." Tamar joined the conversation. "From the look of things yesterday, a great deal of work remains to be done before your boat will be ready to leave."

Tamar's observation had merit, but Lily hoped to be done with the cleaning and repairs in a couple of days. She made a mental note to ask the captain about securing profitable cargo to load. Excitement zipped through her. She could hardly wait until they pushed the *Hattie Belle* away from the bank and headed out on their first adventure.

"I see it! I see it!" Jasmine bounced up and down. "There it is!"

Tamar put a quieting hand on the little girl's arm. "Yes, it is, but you must not hop about like a grasshopper. Once we are on the water, you are liable to fall overboard."

An awful vision of Jasmine flailing about as the river swept her away formed in Lily's mind. Had she made a terrible mistake to bring her sisters? But she could not stand the idea of leaving them behind. She would simply have to be vigilant.

The carriage came to a halt, and Lily gathered her skirts. "Be careful where you step. The ground is very damp. I don't want either of you to fall into a mud hole."

Camellia shuddered and closed her eyes. "Perfect." Sarcasm dripped from the two syllables.

"I'll be careful, Lily." Jasmine mimicked Lily's motions as they waited for the coachman to let down the steps and open the door.

Lily stepped from the carriage, relieved to see the sun had dried the ground some since her earlier visit. "Tamar, will you direct the loading of our things while I introduce the girls to Mr. Matthews and Mr. Moreau?"

Lily picked her way across the fern-strewn bank and stepped onto the boat before turning to help her sisters. Her unseen partner must be still abed. No doubt that was why he had not accomplished much work.

Well, he would soon learn better habits. "Mr. Matthews, I have returned with my best labor force."

Nothing answered her but the loud song of a bird along the riverbank. Finally the stomp of boots on the staircase heralded his approach, and she took a deep breath. She fully expected a battle with Mr. Matthews when he learned of her plans.

"What on earth are you doing back here?" His voice reached them before he did. When his large frame appeared, Camellia gasped. Jasmine made no sound, but her hand tightened around Lily's fingers. "And what are you doing with a gaggle of children? You were supposed to bring me workmen."

"You will find that my sisters and I are hard workers. We've spent many hours putting up vegetables and fruits. We can clean better than most men. And we won't charge an exorbitant fee for our services." Lily was proud of her calm voice. The sentences tripped off her tongue just as she had practiced as she lay in bed last night. No hint of trepidation betrayed her true feelings.

Blake Matthews quirked an eyebrow and stared at all three girls, his blue gaze finally coming to rest on her face. "I suppose Jensen and I can do the heavy work if we leave the cleaning and organizing to you ladies."

Lily's pent-up breath whooshed out. Where was the battle royal she had expected?

"Let me show you to the kitchen." He moved out onto the deck. Lily and her sisters fell back a step to let him pass, but he froze, his attention caught by something on the bank. "What is that—that stuff they are bringing aboard?"

Turning her head, Lily saw the men from home approaching, their arms full of burdens. "Those are our belongings."

His gaze swiveled back to her, and his face paled. "Your belongings? You and your sisters are going to live aboard the boat with Jensen and me?"

Lily nodded.

"You don't mind being exposed to gambling and drinking?" His voice was incredulous.

"Of course I would, but no gambling or drinking will occur aboard the *Hattie Belle*."

He raked a hand through his dark hair. Several locks fell across his forehead, giving him a mysterious, slightly dangerous appearance.

Lily could feel her heartbeat accelerate. Blake Matthews was very handsome and probably used to getting his way with women as a result. Well, he would find she was impervious to his charms. That was one thing for which she could thank her worthless father—she would never fall in love with any man. Never again would she put herself in the position of being abandoned. Even Grandfather had failed her when he died—

A tug on her hand interrupted her thoughts. Camellia pulled free of her grasp and executed a graceful curtsy, her blond hair gleaming in the midday sun. "Please excuse my sister's lack of manners, sir. I am Camellia Anderson, and this is my little sister, Jasmine."

The brooding air lifted from Mr. Matthews's face, replaced by a look of bewilderment.

Camellia rose and stretched out a white-gloved hand for him to place a salutatory kiss. "I'm sorry, but I didn't catch your name."

Lily sighed. Trust Camellia to attempt a flirtation with the man. She was not nearly as concerned with guarding her heart. But then she didn't know about their father's true perfidy. She and Jasmine had been told that he had died. Their grandparents had decided that would be the best way to handle the situation. Only Lily knew the truth—Papa had not loved them enough to stay with them. "His name is Mr. Matthews, Camellia, and as soon as he shows us the way to the kitchens, you and Jasmine will don your aprons and begin working."

"Right this way." He walked stiffly down the right side of the riverboat.

Lily followed his lead. "Be careful," she instructed Camellia and Jasmine. "The wood looks damp where it's in the shade." She was relieved when their guide opened a door in the approximate center of the boat.

"This way, ladies." He bowed, irritation obvious in the stiff movement of his arm. "I trust you won't be overwhelmed."

The dark room felt like a cave. Lily waited for her eyes to adjust to the gloom. "Aren't there any windows?"

Mr. Matthews sighed and walked outside.

"Where did he go?" Although she couldn't see, Lily recognized Jasmine's fearless voice.

A clunking sound came from outside, and sunlight blasted into the room. Mr. Matthews must have removed a shutter.

Something skittered into the shadows, eliciting a tiny shriek from Camellia.

"It's only a mouse." Mr. Matthews stood in the doorway once more, a half grin on his face.

Lily supposed he was trying to frighten them. "Once we get this place cleaned up, no vermin"—she tossed a meaningful glance at him—"will dare make their home here."

His grin widened. "I'm sure you're right. No mouse would dare remain near a shrew."

Lily turned from the irritating man. "Hang up your cloaks on those pegs, girls."

Tamar appeared, her arms full of linens. "I've brought the aprons."

"Good." Lily looked around for a clean surface, gave up, and pointed to a counter under the window. "If you'll help the girls get started, Mr. Matthews and I have a few things to discuss."

❧

Blake watched in fascination as Miss Anderson took over. How had it come to this? They had been invaded by a marauding army. An army of females. The enemy forces had taken over the *Hattie Belle* without firing a single shot.

He'd never met such a managing female. She had more backbone than many of the men he'd met in his travels. She reminded him of the women in his family—as innocent as Ada, as determined as his mother.

Not that Ma had ever been pushy. She always let Pa take the lead. He couldn't imagine Ma owning property, but if she had, she would have insisted on keeping it clean enough to serve dinner on the floor. And she never would countenance serving alcohol or gambling.

But that didn't mean he should let Miss Anderson get her way without a challenge. She headed toward the paddle wheel, chin high, skirts swaying back and forth.

He caught her elbow with one hand. "Where are you going?"

"I want to explore every inch of my boat. I need to start a list of repairs we'll have to make." She tried to shake him off, but her foot slipped.

To stop her from falling overboard, Blake grabbed the girl around the waist and pulled her close against his side. She clung to him for a brief moment. Her curves felt so comfortable against him—so right—like she was made to fit against him.

The thought shook him, challenging everything he held dear. To mask his confusion, Blake adopted a cynical tone. "Careful there, honey. If you're going to move onto *our* boat, you've got to learn to keep your feet under you."

"I am not your honey."

That was better. She was as stiff as a piece of plywood in his arms. He let go of her but remained ready to grab her again if she was still unsteady. "I didn't mean anything by it."

She sniffed. "Does the paddle wheel need any repairs?"

"Right to business. I like that in a partner." At her dark look, he assumed a more serious expression. "The Champneys had it repaired after the *Hattie Belle*'s last run from St. Louis."

"Good." She turned back and eased her way past him. "The deck looks like it's in good shape. How many staterooms?"

"Six. Jensen and I are using two of them, but that leaves plenty of room for your family."

She shook her head. "That will never do. We'll have to take on passengers as well as cargo. You and Mr. Moreau will have to share a stateroom. We'll share another one, which will leave room for four paying passengers."

"If you want to make money fast, you need to give up your plan to carry cargo or passengers. I can make you more money in a week without leaving the bank. I've been making tables for the ballroom upstairs. All I need is a little time—"

"Mr. Matthews, I want to get one thing straight—I am a respectable woman from a God-fearing home. I will not countenance games of chance on this boat. We can make a comfortable living moving cargo and passengers on the river."

"What if I don't want just a comfortable living? If we follow my plan, we'll both be rich beyond our wildest dreams. Then you can buy all the reputation you want. You can afford a big house in town where you can have tea and introduce your sisters to the best society."

"If you want to spend your time taking money from unsuspecting clients, pack up your things immediately and go back to where you came from." She lifted her nose in the air.

He wasn't about to leave. This was his dream as much as it was hers.

He studied her features objectively as she began enumerating all the reasons he would bow to her wishes. Miss Anderson would never be considered a beauty, but something in her face, something in her whole attitude, filled him with longing. What was it about her? She had some indefinable quality that he admired. She was very cute, too, standing up to him even though he was at least a foot taller and could toss her over the side of the boat without much effort.

"So you must see my point." She looked at him, her chocolate-brown eyes shining.

He gathered his wandering thoughts. "Just because you own a measly two percent more of this boat than I do doesn't mean I'm going to allow you to turn the *Hattie Belle* into a charitable concern."

"I don't expect you to." Her voice was earnest. She put her hand on his arm, making his muscles tense in response. "I'm sure we're going to work well together as soon as we establish a few basic rules."

He pulled his arm free and held up a different finger for each point he made. "So we can't have any gaming; I have to move in with my hired help; we won't have any workmen to help with the repairs; and we have to hire a captain."

"That's right, except for hiring a captain. I've taken care of that." She smiled broadly. "I'm glad we've got that all straightened out. After yesterday, I was worried we would have a problem. I had no idea you would be so reasonable."

"What do you mean you've hired a captain?"

"Yesterday on the ride home, Jean Luc Champney offered, on my behalf, to approach the man they used to employ."

A feeling of foreboding settled on his shoulders. "Not Lars Steenberg. . ."

She shrugged. "If he was the captain before you took over. Please don't tell me you disapprove of him, too."

Blake leaned against the wall. "I was not overly impressed with his abilities, but at least he has some experience on the river and with our boat."

"Good, that's settled, then." She dusted her hands and turned to go back to the kitchen.

Blake decided it would be better to bide his time than wrestle with Miss Anderson right now. Life on the river was difficult. She and her sisters would be ready to go back home after the first week of snags and tree islands. He would gamble his part of the *Hattie Belle* on it.

He climbed the stairs slowly as he thought about it. Yes, that was exactly what would happen. As soon as she saw how hard it was to move cargo, the determined Miss Lily Anderson would change her mind. Then he and Jensen could go back to their original plans.

Chapter Seventeen

"We've been cleaning for days." Jasmine's lip protruded. With her hair wrapped in a white cloth, she looked more like a servant than a young lady.

Lily withdrew her list from one of her apron pockets. "Sometimes we have to work hard to accomplish our dreams."

"But this is not my dream." Camellia perched on the edge of the bed they shared and wrapped a second cloth around her head. They had learned the importance of covering their hair after rubbing the brass fittings in the engine room. Their activities had raised a storm of dust that had settled on them like a quilt.

"I need to go into town this morning for some supplies Mr. Matthews needs."

"We're supposed to call him Blake, remember?" Camellia sighed.

"Would the two of you like to go with me?" Lily pinned a bright smile on her face. She was not happy about the way Camellia mooned over the gambler, but she had to admit he always treated the girl like a younger sister. In the past week, all of them had spent a great deal of time in close quarters as they polished, dusted, and scrubbed their way from aft to stern. And Blake had a knack for getting more work out of Camellia than anyone else. Lily wrestled with a touch of jealousy at the easy camaraderie he shared with her sisters. Why couldn't he be as charming to her?

"I do!" Jasmine executed a twirl in the center of the room, managing to bang her hand against the table holding their bowl and pitcher.

Lily grabbed the table before it could overturn, so relieved to have a new focus for her unruly thoughts that she didn't chastise Jasmine.

Camellia walked over to the mirror and leaned against one wall of their bedroom. "I don't want anyone to see me looking like this."

"Suit yourself, Camellia. You can stay in the carriage and wait for us." Lily ignored the exaggerated sigh and left the room to get Tamar.

Walking the length of the second floor, she had to admit to a feeling of accomplishment. The tables Blake had made for his gambling salon had become dining tables, lined up with military precision along one side of the former ballroom. Sparkling crystal chandeliers would illuminate the room during meals. A wood-burning stove in the far corner would offer warmth during cool, damp evenings. If she closed her eyes, she could almost see well-dressed passengers sitting around the stove as they discussed their comfortable travel. Maybe they could find a piano. That would please Camellia. It was the thing she bemoaned most often.

Blake's deep voice interrupted her daydreaming. "Jensen is waiting outside."

Lily could feel her cheeks heating. The man had a talent for making her feel inadequate. She tried to quiet her heart as she turned to face him. "Did he have any trouble finding a carriage?"

As usual, Blake wore only dark trousers and a flowing white shirt with sleeves rolled up above his elbows. His dress should have made him look like a greengrocer or laborer, but he carried himself with the assurance of a planter. From the set of his shoulders to his wide stance, Blake was a man one could not ignore. "I doubt it. Jensen has a way of acquiring whatever we need."

Had he stolen the equipage? She hesitated to voice the question. What if he confirmed her fear?

"I sent him to the livery stable." The lift of his right eyebrow and the half smile on Blake's lips indicated he'd read her thoughts.

More hot blood rushed to her face. She glanced down at the floor. "Have you seen Tamar?"

"She's already outside." He stepped closer and lifted her chin with a finger. "Unless I am mistaken, there is romance in the air."

Her brain sizzled. What did he mean? Had he formed an attachment for her? Impossible. They barely spoke.

"I only hope Tamar will not break his heart."

Her heartbeat slowed its frantic pace, and Lily pulled away from his hand. "Tamar would not be so foolish. She is here because of her love for us, not because she wants to find a husband."

He just raised that eyebrow again.

Camellia and Jasmine exited the bedroom and stood beside Lily. "We will be back before too long."

"Are you sure you don't need me to accompany you?"

She shook her head.

"You have the list I made out?" His question chased her down the stairs.

Lily shooed her sisters ahead of her. The sooner they left him behind, the better. She breathed deeply as they hopped off the deck and picked their way to the road.

She cast a furtive glance back toward the boat as she settled on the seat of the rented carriage, but Blake was not standing on the deck. The feeling that pierced her chest could not be disappointment. It had to be relief. Didn't it?

❧

"What do you think of this material?" Tamar held a length of navy-blue broadcloth. "Would it look good on the dining tables?"

Lily's eyes widened. "It's perfect. All it needs is lace edging." She looked around for a bolt of the lace she envisioned.

A bell tinkled at the front of the mercantile, and she looked up to see if it was one of her sisters. They had begged her to let them go to the park. Camellia wanted to stroll; Jasmine wanted to explore. Lily agreed to let them go after making them promise not to talk to strangers.

But instead of seeing one of her sisters, her gaze met the dark eyes of the intriguing Jean Luc Champney. "What a happy coincidence." She moved forward with her hand outstretched.

Jean Luc took it in his and placed a warm kiss on her skin.

The gesture should have made her heart race, so why didn't it? Why didn't blood rush to her cheeks the way it did every time Blake Matthews talked to her? Maybe because Jean Luc was not abrasive and challenging like Blake always was. Yes, that had to be the answer.

"I thought I saw you and your slave entering." He squeezed her hand before releasing it. "How are things going on the boat? Has

Captain Steenberg moved aboard? I trust he meets with your approval."

"Yes, thank you for sending him." She paused, choosing her words with care. Truth to tell she had not been overly impressed with the man. He was loud and did not practice the best hygiene. "He is quite a colorful character."

"Yes, well, he is an excellent captain. You will come to no harm while he guides the boat. He can probably supply you with an engineer and several crewmen."

"Thank you, but that won't be necessary." Lily could not imagine more of the same type of men on her boat. They would not impress the passengers she hoped to draw. "We've already hired a new crewman, and Mr. Moreau is going to act as our engineer for now."

He shrugged. "Whatever you—"

"Lily! Lily!" Jasmine barreled into the mercantile like a cannonball. She ran past Jean Luc, grabbed Lily's hand, and tugged her toward the door.

"Wait a minute, Jasmine. What's wrong?"

"Come quick. They're going to kill him."

Thinking someone must have attacked Jensen, Lily tossed a glance at Jean Luc. "Pardon me."

"Hurry, Lily! Please hurry." Jasmine pulled harder. As soon as they were outside, her little sister picked up her skirts and dashed across the street, disappearing into an alley between two buildings.

Lily plunged into the alley, following her sister and praying for their safety as sounds of a scuffle reached her ears.

"Leave him alone!" Her sister's voice carried to her from a shadowy corner.

Dazzled by the change from light to dark, Lily willed her vision to clear. Several boys stood in a semicircle looking down while one of them kicked whatever lay on the ground. It looked like a pile of rags, but from the solid impact made by each kick, someone was under the rags. "Stop what you're doing." Lily put all the authority she could muster into her voice.

The largest boy, who was doing the kicking, laughed. "We already took care of your friend. Do you want us to do the same to you?"

Lily's first concern was for her sisters. She pointed toward the street without taking her eyes off the bullies. "Jasmine, you and Camellia go find Jensen."

"But—"

"Go. Now." She listened for the sound of their retreat before raising her parasol in a threatening manner. "If you leave now, I won't have you arrested."

One of the other boys grabbed the leader's arm. "He's learned his lesson. He won't be filching our fish no more."

The other accomplice added his voice. "Let's get out of here."

After one more vicious kick, the third boy looked at her, a snarl twisting his face. "I oughta teach you a lesson, too."

Lily had never been so frightened, but she couldn't let him see her fear. She raised her chin and narrowed her eyes. "It won't take long for my sisters to find our coachman. He'd probably like to teach you a thing or two himself."

They took to their heels, leaving her alone with their groaning victim. Lily was about to go to him when Jensen, followed by her sisters, dashed into the alley.

"What's going on here?" His growl reassured her, slowing the rapid thump of her heart. He looked around for the miscreants. "I don't see no one here."

"They ran off." Was that weak sound her voice?

"Are you all right, Miss Lily?"

"Yes, Jensen."

Jasmine dashed past them and sat down in the alley, ignoring everything else as she lifted a young boy's head into her lap. "We have to take him back to the *Hattie Belle*."

Lily understood her sister's impulse to help the stranger, but they already had enough challenges to face. "I don't know if that's a very good idea."

Camellia pushed her out of the way and sat next to Jasmine, her hands gently prodding the boy's arms and legs. "We can't leave him here."

Lily sighed and looked from her sisters to Jensen.

"Don't you remember the story of the Good Samaritan?" Jasmine's voice held a hint of desperation.

Closing her eyes, Lily remembered the prayer she'd whispered as they'd entered the alley. The Lord had kept them safe. How then could she refuse to do her Christian duty? "I think it would be better to find his parents. They must be worried about him."

Camellia leaned back on her heels. "What if he's a foundling?"

"Then we'll leave him at the foundling home." Lily realized this was a losing battle. She knelt next to Jasmine and Camellia, bending to get a closer look at their victim. He flinched as she reached a hand toward his bruised face, an awful mat of gashes and bruises. It was the boy who had stolen her reticule. Her heart melted, and she looked over her shoulder toward Jensen. "Go get the carriage."

Chapter Eighteen

Jean Luc hung around the mercantile for another half hour, waiting for Lily Anderson. He pulled out his pocket watch and flipped it open.

"Are you sure I can't help you, Mr. Champney?" The storekeeper had already asked him the question twice before.

He shook his head and walked to the plate-glass window, staring at tall white clouds that were starting to pile up in the southern sky. How much longer could she be?

"Are you waiting for someone?" The man was at his elbow, as annoying as a mosquito.

Jean Luc sighed. "If you must know, I'm waiting to speak to Miss Anderson."

"She's not coming back." The man smiled as though conferring a gift. "Her man loaded her supplies in the carriage and left a quarter hour ago."

Anger burned in the pit of his stomach. How dared she ignore him? First she rushed off to see about some child instead of talking to him, and then she didn't bother to come back. His jaw tightened. Lily Anderson would rue the day she ignored him. He stormed out of the mercantile and headed toward his father's office.

"Good day, Mr. Champney."

Jean Luc almost bypassed the man. But then he realized he could begin to settle the score right away. He smiled at the man who owned one of the largest shipping companies in town. "Hello, Sweeney. I trust business is going well."

Sweeney nodded. "I heard your father sold the *Hattie Belle*."

"Yes." Jean Luc tapped his cane against his chin. "I was as surprised as anyone. Especially when I learned who the new owners are." He shook his head and put an arm around the other man. "Just between you and me, he must have gotten a really good price."

"Is that so?"

"Why else would he sell to a woman?" Jean Luc shook his head. "I hate to say it, but he may be slipping. Selling the *Hattie Belle* to someone who will likely run it aground on her first run? What sense is there in that?"

The older man looked pensive. Then he chuckled. "Maybe your father is wilier than you think. He's probably expecting this woman to come running back to him. Then he'll offer to take the boat off her hands, and he'll make a tidy profit in the deal."

Jean Luc raised his eyebrows. "You may be right." He stood as though considering the other man's suggestion then shook his head slowly. "Still, I worry about any shipper who lets her take his cargo out. He'll lose the whole load, and she certainly doesn't have deep enough pockets to repay the cost."

"But I thought she was Isaiah Blackstone's granddaughter. Surely they wouldn't hang her out to dry."

"Do you really think they approve of her going into business? They've probably washed their hands of her."

Sweeney looked thoughtful. "You may be right."

"No, no. Don't rely on what I've said." Jean Luc shook his head. "It's only speculation on my part."

"Of course not, my boy. Of course not. But I couldn't forgive myself if I didn't spread the word to my colleagues."

Jean Luc shrugged. "I can't speak to that, Mr. Sweeney. You must do as you think best."

The older man was shaking his head as they parted.

A sudden wind pushed Jean Luc along the street. Thunder rumbled, and lightning split the sky, matching his mood perfectly.

If Miss Anderson wanted to be his enemy, she would find herself in deep water. His smile widened. In very deep water indeed.

It was far too quiet. Blake held a peg as he brought his hammer down. He was an idiot. He actually missed the chatter and giggles of the Anderson girls.

In the distance a cannon boomed, announcing the arrival of a steamboat. It was such a common occurrence these days he was surprised the city of Natchez didn't run out of ammunition. Another reason Lily's daft idea was doomed to failure. With so much river traffic, who would want to take a chance on a boat full of females to ship their goods?

He missed the peg, and pain exploded in his left thumb. Harsh curses rose to his lips, but a week of choking them back had become a habit. "Owww!"

Blake checked his thumb. No blood. He would live. With a shake of his head, he went back to work. Lily wanted benches, so she would have benches. He was almost finished attaching them on the starboard side of the main room—the room she had turned into a dining hall, even though he would rather see it a gambling parlor. But she wouldn't budge.

He'd tried to wheedle her into allowing one corner of the room for friendly games of poker, but she would have none of it. It was a shame, really. All this work that he would have to tear apart when Lily quit. At least he could reuse this wood—it would make a good buffet table when he finally opened his casino.

Somehow his dream had gotten tarnished since the Anderson girls had moved aboard. They brought sunshine to every corner of the *Hattie Belle*, even the engine room.

Footsteps brought his head around. Were they back already?

The uneven rhythm of his heart settled when Captain Steenberg appeared, chewing on the stubby end of a cigar. Blake had never seen him light it, not that Lily would allow smoking on *her* boat. Steenberg removed the cigar, holding it between his thumb and finger. "It's kinda quiet around here."

"The ladies went to Natchez to do a little shopping."

The captain nodded. He planted his feet wide apart and stared at Blake.

Blake drilled a hole for the next peg, blowing it free of sawdust when he withdrew the bit.

The captain remained.

"Did you need me for something?"

"I was thinking about going to town myself. I hear there's a new saloon in town. I thought I'd try my luck."

"I see." Blake felt a tug to join the man. He'd been working hard. No one could say he didn't deserve a night off. He looked at the unfinished bench. Maybe later. "Try not to lose money you haven't earned yet."

"I was wondering about that." The captain studied his cigar. "I know we ain't gone on a voyage yet, but my time is valuable." He put emphasis on the last word. "I was thinking mebbe I could get a little advance for my first trip."

"I doubt it." Blake pounded a new peg into the hole he'd just created. "Money's going to be tight until we make our first delivery." He sank the peg and reached for the drill, falling back into a rhythm as he worked.

After a while he realized he was alone. Again. His heart clenched. He'd always been a loner. Well, not always. But for a very long time. And, he reminded himself, he liked it that way.

The sound of hoofbeats brought his head up. They were back. He was up and halfway down the stairs before he realized his intention. He halted; then with a shrug he decided he might as well see what Lily had managed to purchase. He stepped outside as Jensen jumped to the ground and tied off the horses.

Lily opened the door and waved at him. "We could use your help."

He didn't like the frown on her face. "What's wrong? Is it your sisters?"

She shook her head and disappeared back inside the carriage.

He strode to the door and looked inside. Lily and Camellia occupied one seat while Jasmine cradled someone in her lap. "Who's that?"

"He was attacked." Jasmine looked up, tears giving her eyes the velvety look of dew-sprinkled violets. "We're going to tend to his wounds."

"Really?" His gaze met Lily's. What was she thinking?

She lifted her shoulders. "We could hardly leave him bleeding on the street."

Thunder rumbled in the distance. "Let's get him inside." Blake picked him up and carried him to the *Hattie Belle*. "I suppose you want him to bunk in my room."

They decided to use the ladies' parlor for the time being. It was on the floor above the staterooms, a pleasant room with the most comfortable furniture, including a fainting couch, which they turned into a makeshift bed.

Camellia took control, directing the others to boil water, make bandages, and bring fresh clothing to replace the boy's filthy rags.

An afternoon thunderstorm rocked the boat. Rain made rivulets on the windows, chilling Blake despite the fact it was summer. Gloom seemed to have invaded the *Hattie Belle*. He had been assigned the task of watching over Miss Jasmine. After she told him about finding the patient, they stared at each other.

"I have an idea." Blake went to his bedroom and retrieved his deck of cards and an old bowler hat. Jasmine was sitting on one of the new benches when he got back, her pert little nose glued to a window. "Let's play a game." He riffled the cards in one hand.

Jasmine's eyes grew as wide as saucers. "I don't think Lily wants me to gamble."

"I'll keep that in mind." Blake set the hat upside down about ten feet away and moved to the bench where Jasmine sat. "How good is your aim?"

She regarded him with curiosity. "I once knocked the bloom off one of Grandmother's roses with a rock."

"Pretty impressive." He held a card between the first two fingers of his hand and flipped it toward the hat, watching as it turned over and over before landing several inches short of the target. "Do you think you can get closer than that?"

She took a card and studied it. He showed her how to bend her wrist to get the most action from the card. Her first attempt didn't make it to the table. "Can I try another?"

"Of course." He gave her half the deck while he retained the other half. "One at a time, now."

Soon the gloom had disappeared, and they were laughing as the cards flew all over the room like crazed butterflies.

"What's going on in here?" The laughter stopped. Lily stood in the doorway, arms crossed. "Are you teaching my sister card games?"

"Of course not. We were just—"

"I think I can trust my eyes more than your words, Mr. Matthews. You don't have to add lying to your list of sins." She pointed a finger at

Jasmine. "It's time for you to eat some supper and get to bed."

"Yes, ma'am." Jasmine handed him the rest of her cards and exited the room, her head down.

Blake was speechless. How dare she condemn him without giving him a chance to explain. It was ridiculous. All this time spent acceding to her every wish, and still Lily didn't trust him to watch over her sisters. Then again, he hadn't thought to prepare food for Jasmine.

A fist wrapped around his heart. Maybe Lily was right. Maybe he didn't deserve her trust.

Chapter Nineteen

*H*ave you lost your mind?" Blake paced the main room, stopping when he drew even with Lily. "Keeping that boy on the boat is sure to lead to trouble. We're liable to wake up one morning to find him gone and all our valuables with him."

"I don't care what you say. My mind is made up." Her voice was calm, but bolts of lightning flew from her brown eyes.

Blake took a deep breath. He should have learned by now that anger was not the right approach with this young woman. "You're about as contrary as a mule."

"Look, I don't like the idea any better than you—"

"Then why are we having this discussion? Send that cutpurse on his way."

"And leave him to the tender mercies of the thugs who were beating him yesterday?" She crossed her arms and tapped one foot.

"Then Jensen and I will take him to the foundling home."

Lily shook her head. "I sent Jensen to make inquiries earlier. The foundling home is overcrowded. They cannot take him in."

"I understand you're tenderhearted, but we cannot be picking up every waif we come across or we'll find ourselves without room for paying passengers. I've yet to see a city that doesn't support at least a dozen just like the one upstairs."

The fire in her eyes faded. "I cannot abandon David Foster now."

"David Foster!" He blew out an exasperated breath. "I doubt that's his real name. He was probably born out of wedlock to a mother who tossed him on the street as soon as he could walk."

"All the more reason to let him stay with us."

"You're not making any sense, Lily. He may be an object of pity, but it doesn't follow that we should take him in."

"It may not make sense to you, but I have very sound reasons for keeping him aboard."

"Then explain them."

She cocked her head. "If I throw him off the boat, my sisters will hate me."

Surprise made him take a step back. She couldn't believe such a silly thing. But she was a female, and females often got odd ideas—just one of the reasons they should content themselves with being mothers and wives. "That's utterly ridiculous, girl."

"How many times do I have to tell you I am not a girl?"

He ignored her interruption. "Your sisters adore you. They watch your every move. If you don't care for mussels, they won't touch them, either. They walk the same way you do, imitate your laugh and even the tilt of your chin when you feel challenged. That's the way it is with younger siblings."

"I don't know about all that, but I do know I cannot disappoint them on this matter. Besides, they have both promised to keep a close eye on him. For now David is recuperating, but once we are under way and he is better, I'll make sure he stays too busy to get into any trouble." She paused and looked over Blake's right shoulder. "Did you need me for something, Jensen?"

Blake turned around, surprised to see the sheepish look on his friend's scarred face. "Is something wrong?"

"No, sir." Jensen twisted his hands. "I was just going to offer to help with the boy. He reminds me a bit of myself at that age. I know how different my life woulda been had someone taken me in and cared for me."

"Am I the only one on this boat with a lick of sense?" Blake expelled a harsh breath. "All right then, I suppose I'll have to bow to your insanity. You do have controlling interest. But don't come running to me when your jewelry disappears."

He strode out, brushing past Jensen. "Traitor." Knowing Lily couldn't see his face, he added a wink to soften the accusation. "You're going to be the death of me yet."

"Where are you going?" Lily's question brought him up short.

Blake turned on his heel and smiled slowly. "I didn't know you cared."

Her cheeks darkened, and her gaze shifted away from him.

He shook his head. From conquering Amazon to shy maiden in the blink of an eye. It drove him crazy. "I have an appointment in town."

Blake didn't wait to hear her answer. He stopped by his room to grab his coat then left the boat. What was it about Lily Anderson?

She had begun their discussion this morning with an apology for jumping to the wrong conclusion last night, explaining her misunderstanding of the situation and thanking him prettily for keeping Jasmine occupied. Then she had told him about the boy, and they had gone right back to sparring mode.

He really shouldn't tease her, but the temptation was sometimes impossible to resist. Especially since it ended whatever argument they were having. He loved seeing that startled look in her eyes, as well as the ready color that flushed her cheeks. Besides, it was about the only way he could get the last word.

Whistling as he walked, Blake smiled at the green canopy above his head. He wondered what her reaction would be if he kissed her. . . .

"I'm not taking you, Camellia, because I'm not going shopping." Lily ignored the pout on her sister's face. "You would have to stay in the wagon all day. You'd be redder than the sunset by the time we got back."

"But I could help you—"

She put a hand on her sister's arm. "You can help me most by staying here and keeping an eye on Jasmine and David. Blake and I will be back as soon as we arrange for a paying cargo. Just think of it. We could be leaving for New Orleans as early as tomorrow."

"I don't want to go to New Orleans. I want to go home." A solitary tear traced a path down Camellia's cheek.

Lily sighed. "This is our home now."

"This is not a home." Camellia stomped her foot for emphasis. "It's a boat. A nasty, ugly boat. I hate it. I hate the way it rocks and creaks. I want to go back to Grandmother's house and sleep in my own bed. I'm tired of sharing a bedroom with you and the others."

Pulling on her gloves, Lily wondered what Blake would think if he could hear her sister now. Contrary to his belief, Camellia didn't admire anything about her older sister. "I am sorry for that, but it doesn't change anything. You are to stay here with Jasmine and the boy you begged me to keep. If anything goes missing, I am holding you personally responsible."

Camellia sniffed. "I can't wait until I'm older. I'm going to find a husband who'll take me to his home. It'll be larger than Grandmother's house. We'll have parties and balls and eat grapes every day."

"I'm sure I wish you the best in your search, but until then you will do as I say. Now go find your sister. We'll be back before you know it."

She watched as Camellia flounced off, her nose high. Lily sincerely hoped she hadn't taught her younger sister that particular attitude.

With a shake of her head Lily joined Blake, who was waiting in the wagon. They had decided to rent it rather than a carriage in case they needed to bring cargo back with them.

Blake reached down a hand to help her climb up. "Where do you want to go first?"

"I've been thinking about that." Lily was proud to show she had a head for business. "I think the market would be a good place to start. Tamar says they have all sorts of stalls selling goods. Perhaps we can offer to move—"

Her words were cut off by laughter.

Miffed, she frowned up at Blake. "What's so funny?"

"You are. You couldn't find your way out of a feed sack without directions." He laughed again. "Those people only sell their goods locally."

Lily tilted her chin up, thought of Camellia's flounce, and lowered it again. "That may be true, but they can probably direct me."

He shook his head. "You should have stayed back at the boat with the others and let me do this alone."

"I suppose you're an expert at shipping?"

"No, but I know a great deal more about business than you do."

No one had the ability to make her feel like an imbecile more than the man sitting beside her. With a gesture he could reduce her to the level of a dim-witted schoolgirl. "Where would you go, then?" Anger made her voice sharp.

A horseman careened around the corner. Blake pulled back on the reins, the muscles in his arms straining to stop the wagon. As though time had slowed, Lily saw his jaw clench, saw the horseman's shocked expression. She scrunched her eyes together, certain they would crash into the horseman, but somehow Blake managed to avoid a collision.

After a moment she remembered to breathe.

He pulled the wagon to a standstill and grazed her cheek with a hand. "Are you all right?"

"I'm fine." As she gazed into his eyes, Lily forgot about their near miss. She forgot her irritation with him, forgot everything except his mesmerizing blue eyes. How had she ever thought they were cold? They were as warm as a summer day. Up close they looked like flower petals with black centers.

His lids lowered, and for some reason her heart increased its speed. She should pull away, but it was all she could do not to lean toward him. His breath fanned her face. His pupils dilated. He blinked and pulled back. Then turned away from her.

Lily's heart pounded. She was breathing like she'd run all the way to Natchez. What had just happened? Had he almost kissed her? She put a hand to her chest, certain her heart was about to jump free. "I. . . I'm not hurt."

"That's good." At least he sounded as winded as she did.

Lily watched as he jumped down and went to the horse's head. He spoke quietly to the animal and checked to make sure it was unharmed. "You were amazing."

He glanced back toward her, his gaze unreadable, and nodded. "I would suggest you start with either Sweeney's or LeGrand's. They are two of the largest shippers in Natchez."

So they would ignore what had just happened? She supposed that was as good an answer as any. It wasn't as if they could develop any romantic feelings about each other. Neither of them wanted the same things from life. He saw the *Hattie Belle* as a means to achieve riches. She considered their boat her home, a place to raise her sisters and to live free from the strictures of local society. They had absolutely nothing in common.

Besides, she knew his type. Like Father, he would desert her. He'd get bored, or earn enough money, or find some other excuse. Then he would disappear. And leave her to pick up the pieces.

"Did you fall asleep?" His voice brought her back to the present.

Lily gathered her skirts in one hand and climbed down. "I'll go to Sweeney's since it's the closest."

"Fine. I'll just wait here."

She walked away from him without a backward glance—not to assert her independence but rather because she knew the less she looked into his blue eyes, the better off she would be.

Chapter Twenty

Lily tapped her foot. A wall clock told her she'd been waiting half an hour. What could be keeping Mr. Sweeney? Why had he left her in his office?

The door opened. "I'm sorry to keep you waiting, Miss Anderson."

"I understand you are a busy man, Mr. Sweeney." She pasted a smile on her face. "I hope you have found a load for the *Hattie Belle*."

"Who is your captain?" He walked to the large window overlooking the street.

"Lars Steenberg. He recently worked for the Champney family."

"I see." He turned to her. "Miss Anderson, I'm afraid I do not have good news for you."

"You couldn't find anything for us to transport?"

He shook his head. "Not so much as a bale of cotton."

"Yet I have seen any number of wagons unloading their goods at your warehouse across the street."

"Yes, but those clients are particular about the boats I hire."

"Exactly what are you saying, Mr. Sweeney?"

The older man cleared his throat. "They don't feel comfortable with a boat that has a female on it."

"I see." Lily thought hard. Suddenly she wished she'd invited Blake to join her. He would know how to broker the deal. Inspiration dawned. "What if I offer to charge half of what others are getting?"

"Miss Anderson, may I be blunt?"

She answered with a nod.

"Then let me encourage you to go back home to your parents and leave the dangers of river travel to men."

"My parents are dead."

"I'm sorry for your loss." His sympathetic words left her cold. "Isn't there any family you can turn to?"

"Mr. Sweeney, my personal life is none of your concern." She stood up and pulled her gloves over shaking fingers. "If you don't have any cargo for me, I suppose I will have to take my leave. Perhaps those at LeGrand Shipping will be interested in making a profitable deal." She swept out of the room on a righteous tide.

One day Mr. Sweeney would be sorry he had not given her a chance. One day the *Hattie Belle* would be so much in demand the shipping companies would be fighting over her.

Lily deflated when she reached the wagon. Where was Blake? Had he given up on her? She looked around as people passed, hoping she wouldn't see anyone she knew. She didn't feel like making small talk.

"Did you have any success?" His voice came from directly behind her.

She jumped. "You scared me." His half grin made her blush. "Where did you come from?"

"I ran into some old acquaintances, and I have good news." His grin widened, making him look years younger.

With a little imagination she could see the boy he'd once been. Her heart turned over. "You found some cargo?"

The gleam in his eyes confirmed it.

Lily squealed. "What is it? Tell me all about it. Is the pay good? Tell me, tell me."

He tweaked her nose. "It's a full gross of whiskey barrels. Not a full load, mind you, but if we pick up a few other items, we should be able to make a profit."

Her joy evaporated. "Whiskey?"

"That's right." His smile wavered. "Please don't tell me. . . ."

"We can't transport alcohol."

He groaned. "I can't believe you. We cannot afford to be picky about our first load. We need to make money."

Lily wanted to agree, but she knew it was wrong. She shook her head. "It's impossible."

"I should have known. You're such a little puritan. Always have to hold yourself to a higher standard. What kind of sanctimonious, self-righteous, judgmental girl are you?"

His words were sharper than a razor blade. But Lily knew she had to stand up for her beliefs. Anything less would doom her to the future she'd been trying to escape. "You'll have to cancel the deal. I'll go to LeGrand Shipping and see if I can find a respectable load."

❧

Jean Luc retraced his path through the park and climbed back into his carriage, a smile of triumph on his face. He could not believe how well things were going. It looked like the time was growing ripe to offer Lily a deal for her portion of the *Hattie Belle*.

He'd thought at first that Blake was going to bring everything to ruin, but Lily had rejected the whiskey on moral grounds. Perfect. After a few more setbacks, she should be ready to grasp at whatever solution he offered.

Of course, returning to her old life would not be possible. The gossip at parties, behind fluttering fans, was that Lily Anderson had ruined her reputation by moving aboard the boat with a man. He doubted she would ever be received again in polite society unless she married someone who could face down the talebearers. Perhaps he would do that—take pity on her, offer to marry her in exchange for the deed. Or maybe he would just set her up in a little house along the bluff and visit her from time to time.

He reached in his pocket and pulled out a coin. Too bad he'd wasted money bribing Captain Steenberg. Stopping to look back over his shoulder, Jean Luc pursed his lips. He had an idea. If it worked out, he could tell the captain his services were no longer needed.

❧

At least the couple at LeGrand Shipping had not made her wait for their bad news. Lily kicked at a clod of dirt. She got back to the wagon ahead of Blake and climbed onto the bench to wait. Maybe she should give up. Had she been wrong to turn down Blake's client?

"What a beautiful afternoon this has turned out to be."

Lily blinked and looked down. "Jean Luc?"

"I stopped by your house a few days ago, but I was told you were away from home." His dark eyes devoured her face. "I haven't offended you, have I?"

"No, no, not at all." She summoned a smile. "I have moved onto the boat I bought from your father."

"You're living on the *Hattie Belle*?"

"Yes, that's right."

"What about the gambler? Did you send him off with a flea in his ear?"

Lily shook her head. "He's still on the boat, too."

"I see." His mouth turned down.

A blush heated her cheeks. "I assure you everything is proper. My sisters and I have a chaperone."

"I see." He paused as though considering her explanation. "I was disappointed when you didn't return to the mercantile the other day."

"I am sorry for that. My sister encountered some trouble, and we had to go back to the boat straightaway. I'm sorry if our departure worried you."

"I don't know how to answer that...Lily." He put his hand over hers where it rested on the side of the wagon. When she didn't say anything, he continued. "If I say I was not worried, you will think I don't care; if I say I was worried, you will claim I am being difficult."

A giggle slipped out. She pulled her hand from under his.

"Please say you'll have dinner with me this evening."

"I don't know—"

His pitiful look stopped her.

Why not? Perhaps he or even his father could put in a good word with the local shipping companies. "I am very flattered, Jean Luc."

"I will come out to the boat around sunset to collect you." He touched his cane to the brim of his hat and stepped back. "Until then."

As she watched him walk away, the wagon rocked. She turned to greet Blake, but the words stopped when she saw his frown. Lily folded her lips together and stared straight ahead. It was going to be a long ride back to the boat.

Chapter Twenty-one

Lily had never been inside this dining establishment. The main entrance opened into a room large enough for a ball. Candles burned from the chandeliers, casting a golden glow over the dozen or so tables scattered about. "This is lovely."

Jean Luc held a chair for her. "I'm glad you approve. The food is remarkable."

She nodded. If the pleasing aromas were any indication, the same would be true this evening.

A waiter spoke briefly with Jean Luc while Lily stared at the other diners. Although she recognized one or two from the balls Aunt Dahlia had made her attend, no one acknowledged her. Starting to feel a little uncomfortable, she touched the loose hairs at the nape of her neck. Had Tamar's arrangement come undone? No. Her gaze settled on the unrelieved black material of her gown. Was she being judged for dining with Mr. Champney while she was in mourning?

Jean Luc's words interrupted her fretful thoughts. "Tell me about your sister."

Lily let her hand drop to her lap. "Actually, I have two sisters. Camellia and Jasmine."

"What interesting names."

"All the women in my grandmother's family are named for flowers. Her given name is Violet. She and Grandfather named their daughters

Dahlia and Rose. Rose, my mother, continued the tradition."

Jean Luc placed a linen napkin on his lap. "A lovely tradition."

"Yes, Grandfather even named the plantation he built Les Fleurs, which as you know means 'the flowers,' to honor his new bride's family."

"Obviously he really loved your grandmother." He leaned forward. "Now which sister came running into the mercantile, and what calamity overtook her?"

Where to begin? Jean Luc was a pleasant companion, but she doubted he would understand why she allowed David to remain aboard the *Hattie Belle*. "You will appreciate this story. It goes back to the party you and your family hosted on the *Hattie Belle* several weeks ago."

"The first time I met you." His voice was husky, intimate.

It brought a flush to her cheeks. "Yes, that's right. . .but before we arrived at the party there was a boy. . . . He took my reticule."

"I'm so sorry. Were you hurt?"

Lily shook her head. "Only my pride. I couldn't believe I'd been so unaware. Anyway, he snatched my reticule and ran away." She decided the chase and David's subsequent dunking in the river were irrelevant. Besides, she didn't care to describe her first meeting with Blake to Jean Luc. The two men didn't have a very good relationship. She sipped from her glass of water as she considered what to say.

"What does this have to do with the mercantile?"

"My sister Jasmine is a curious little girl. She heard a noise coming from one of the alleys and went to investigate. She found a group of bullies beating a young boy. That's when she came to get me. The older boys ran away, and we managed to get their victim to the carriage. I recognized him and thought we would take him to the doctor's office, but Camellia insisted she wanted to nurse him." She glanced up and waited for Jean Luc to get the point of her story.

He frowned for a moment before understanding dawned. "The pickpocket."

Lily nodded, and Jean Luc laughed out loud. It was a nice moment, but her heart plodded steadily on as if she were making biscuits or dusting furniture. Why didn't this debonair man make her heart trip? She took another sip of water.

"Where is he now?" Jean Luc chuckled again.

"Still aboard the *Hattie Belle*."

His face grew serious. "You have taken him in? He may take

advantage of your kindness while making plans to murder you in your sleep."

Irritation filled her. "Why does every man in my life think he has the right to dictate my actions?"

Jean Luc leaned toward her. "Surely you can understand how dangerous it is to open your home to a criminal?"

Lily studied his face. He was debonair. Earnest, kind, and thoughtful. And he seemed truly interested in her welfare. So why did her heart remain so stubbornly calm? Why didn't her cheeks flush with awareness and excitement? "I understand your concern, Jean Luc, but you must allow me to decide how to conduct my life."

He reached for her hand. "Please forgive me if I've offended. I can't help worrying about you."

Her heart fluttered as he squeezed her hand. "Thank you, Jean Luc. It makes me happy to count you as a friend. If I'm going to support myself and my sisters, I will need all the friends I can muster."

He raised her hand to his lips and pressed a warm kiss on it.

Lily should have enjoyed the sensation and the admiring glance in his eyes, but she felt uncomfortable. She pulled her hand away. "Please, Jean Luc. That may be acceptable behavior in Paris, but here in Mississippi, too much familiarity is frowned upon."

His cheeks turned red, and a look of exasperation crossed his face.

Before he could respond, a familiar lady's voice interrupted their conversation. "Hello, Miss Anderson."

Lily turned. An older, attractively dressed couple stood beside her. It took her a moment to recognize the owners of LeGrand Shipping, whom she had met that afternoon. "Good evening, Mr. and Mrs. Hughes."

"I am so excited to find you here this evening." Susannah Hughes turned to the man at her elbow. "I believe God's hand is in this, Judah."

He put a hand on her shoulder. "You make an excellent point, my dear." He turned to Lily. "After you left this afternoon, we received an unexpected shipment that must be in New Orleans before week's end. Our normal ships have already departed Natchez or have no room for additional cargo."

Mrs. Hughes took up the conversation. "I know you said you are doing some work on your boat, so you may not be able to do this, but we wanted to give you the opportunity if you think you can be ready to sail tomorrow."

Lily looked from one to the other, her excitement building with each word. She wanted to dance a jig or turn a somersault. Since those reactions were forbidden, she smiled widely. "Oh yes, we can be ready as soon as we get your cargo loaded." She paused as her earlier conversation with Blake came to mind. "What type of goods would we be transporting?"

"A hundred hogshead of milled corn," Mr. Hughes answered. "Our daughter and her husband run our New Orleans office. They moved there to take over after Monsieur LeGrand, the original owner, fell ill. I don't have fond memories of that area—it's where I lost my leg—but they love it. We'll give you directions to their office when you're getting your load stored away."

"You will love our daughter, Charlotte. She is a bit older than you, but I have a feeling you will become close friends." Mrs. Hughes had a twinkle in her eye.

Unable to remain in her chair a moment longer, Lily jumped up and hugged the older lady. "If she is half as charming as her mother, I'm sure we will. Thank you both so very much. I can hardly wait until tomorrow."

"Is this your co-owner?" Mr. Hughes gestured to Jean Luc, whom Lily had almost forgotten in her excitement.

"No, please excuse my lack of manners. This is Jean Luc Champney, a dear friend who has gone out of his way to help me." She could feel her cheeks burning. Grandmother and Aunt Dahlia would be horrified. "I thought you were acquainted since Mr. Champney's family is also involved in the shipping business."

Jean Luc stood and greeted the Hugheses with more reserve than she expected. Was he upset because their dinner had been interrupted? His behavior seemed out of character.

"We'll leave you to your dinner, then." Mr. Hughes bowed and took his wife's arm.

Lily smiled at them. "You have made me so happy. Thank you."

The handsome couple smiled before making their way to a table on the other side of the room.

After Jean Luc and Lily returned to their seats, he said, "I can hardly believe it's true."

Was there an edge to his voice? Lily could read nothing other than support in his dark gaze. She must be imaging things. "I can hardly believe it, either. Mrs. Hughes was right about God's involvement. When I spoke to them this afternoon, they had nothing, and now they have a shipment and no ship to deliver it. What else could explain such a happy string of coincidences?"

"What indeed?"

Perhaps Jean Luc was put out because he felt ignored. Lily reached across the table for his hand. "And you must be His instrument, too, in bringing me to this place where we would run into each other."

She thought his smile faltered, but before she could ask him what was wrong, he squeezed her fingers. "I am very excited for you."

His smile was back in place. Perhaps she had imagined his irritation. He pulled his hand away and began eating again.

Lily picked up her fork but put it down without eating another bite. She was too excited to concentrate on anything as dull as food. She sipped at her lime soda and began to dream of the coming day. Her life on the river was about to begin.

Chapter Twenty-two

Lily was partly terrified, partly elated as she watched the bank sliding past. The trip from their quiet cove to the bustling port of Natchez had gone without a hitch so far.

Jasmine darted from side to side of the pilothouse, looking like a ruffled dragonfly. "When will we see Natchez Under-the-Hill?"

Captain Lars rolled his eyes. "The pilothouse is no place for young girls."

Lily frowned at him. "Just because Monsieur Champney recommended you does not give you the right to dictate how *my* boat will be run."

Jasmine turned away from the scenery, her violet eyes wide as she looked from Lily to the captain. "I'm sorry."

"You have nothing to apologize for, dearest. We are all excited about our first voyage." Lily pulled Jasmine close for a reassuring hug. Jasmine's arms went around her waist. Lily basked in the moment. Was there anything sweeter than the love expressed by a child?

Captain Lars grunted and reached for a leather cord to his right. A low moan filled the air.

Tears stung Lily's eyes as she listened to the first long blast, followed by two short toots and another long whistle. "Mother would be so happy if she could see us."

Jasmine pulled away from her embrace and clapped her hands in excitement. "I want to learn how to do that."

Blake appeared at the doorway, his blue eyes reflecting the bright sunlit morning. "Don't you think we should head down to the main level? We'll want to make sure we get the right cargo."

Lily and Jasmine followed him, passing through the spotless parlor and on to the first floor where Tamar and Camellia were already positioned at the rail. They waved at the people watching their arrival. Their very first landing. Lily wanted to hug the whole world.

The boat churned the brown water slowly as they approached the wharf. Blake uncoiled a rope nearly as thick as her arm and fashioned a loop at its end that reminded her of a hangman's noose. As the *Hattie Belle* nudged against the wet, gray wood of the dock, he tossed the rope over one of the posts and pulled it tight, his muscles rippling with the effort. As soon as it caught, he strode past them to the back of the boat, grabbed a second rope, and repeated the process.

Lily could not help but be impressed. She had so much to learn. As soon as they were under way again, she would ask him to show her how to make that loop so she could help the next time they landed.

Jensen appeared from the engine room, wiping his hands on a handkerchief. "The engine seems in good shape." He took a position next to Tamar, his elbow almost touching her arm.

Tamar moved away and frowned before turning her attention to Lily's sisters. "Jasmine, you and Camellia come with me. It's time to check on your patient. We'll leave the cargo to your sister and the men."

A chorus of moans answered, but the girls obediently followed her to the aft cabin.

Lily spotted Mr. Hughes waiting beside a mountain of barrels. He doffed his hat in greeting.

Their crewman, Jack Brown, swung the landing platform over the dark water, and it contacted the wharf with a loud clap. As soon as it was down, Mr. Hughes crossed over and handed her two pieces of paper, one signed, one not. "This is the bill of lading. It specifies exactly how many barrels are being loaded on your boat and the value of each."

Lily glanced at the paper, frowned, and looked toward Mr. Hughes. This could not be right. "I don't understand. I cannot afford to pay you this amount of money."

He shook his head. "That amount will be paid to our New Orleans office once the goods are delivered. In turn they will pay you a percentage of their profit for bringing the shipment to them safely."

A burden seemed to slide off her shoulders. "I see."

"You should carefully count the items delivered, however." He patted her arm and chuckled. "Not all businessmen can be relied upon to be honest."

Another question occurred to Lily. "What happens if I don't deliver all the barrels listed here?"

"Unless you can afford to purchase insurance, you would have to pay the difference."

A lump formed in her throat. Lily swallowed hard. "Then I'll have to make certain every barrel arrives safely."

"I'll be praying for you the whole time."

A snort behind her made Lily turn. Blake leaned against one of the posts, a sour look on his face.

"You don't believe in the power of prayer?" Mr. Hughes voiced the question in her mind.

"I wouldn't go so far as to say that, sir." Blake sauntered toward them. He held out a hand toward Mr. Hughes and introduced himself before continuing. "Asking God for favor cannot harm us, but I'm not certain it will do us good, either. I'd rather purchase insurance and remove all worry."

Lily drew herself up. "I will not throw away money on insurance for such a short trip in good weather. By this time tomorrow, we'll be in New Orleans safe and sound."

"Insurance is quite expensive," Mr. Hughes added. "It would eat up a large portion of your profit."

Blake's half smile curled up one side of his mouth. "I'll bow to your superior knowledge."

His reply was obviously directed toward Mr. Hughes. She had less actual experience than anyone else on the boat except for Tamar and her sisters.

Lily folded her lips into a tight smile as Mr. Hughes glanced at both of them. He probably wondered what position Blake held on her boat, but she had no desire to explain.

Mr. Hughes cleared his throat. "I have signed this copy of the bill for you to keep. It also has directions on how to reach our New Orleans office. You need to sign the second copy and return it to me."

While Mr. Hughes directed loading operations, Lily retreated to the small office just ahead of the engine room. It took her a little while to locate pen and ink before she signed her name with a flourish.

By the time she returned to the loading area, Blake had disappeared, and all the barrels were stowed in neat rows. Oilcloth lashed across them would protect them from rain and spray. She smiled at the sight before turning to the wharf, where Mr. Hughes waited. She leaned against the rail to hand him his copy, noticing that the loading dock seemed higher.

A memory returned from the worst day of her life. She and her father were standing on Grandmother's front porch, watching an overladen steamboat struggle to make its way against the river currents.

"Filling your boat so full that the river washes across the deck is a sign of a foolish captain." Her father's gravelly voice spoke to her. "Always remember to balance your profit against your risks, Water Lily. All the money in the world cannot return loved ones to us once they're gone."

That was the last advice her father had given her before he'd walked out of her life. Before he'd abandoned them without a backward glance.

Mr. Hughes's kind voice brought her back to the present. "I wish you a safe journey." He tucked his copy of their agreement into a coat pocket and bowed.

Lily waved good-bye as the dockworkers released their ropes and tossed them onto the deck. The giant paddle wheel began moving, and a single, long, steady blast from the captain indicated they were on the move.

Their first voyage had begun.

Chapter Twenty-three

Tamar searched the dining parlor but found no sign of her youngest charges. It seemed she'd spent all her waking hours chasing after Jasmine and David since he'd been allowed to leave his sickbed the day before. She had a feeling the friendship between those two was going to give her a head of gray hair.

Where could they be? She hurried down to the first floor, but she saw no sign of Jasmine's dark curls or David's wheat-colored thatch of hair—just cargo and empty deck. A sense of foreboding filled her. She could almost see Jasmine leaning over the rail and falling into the brown water. Tamar put a hand over her chest and turned away from the rail.

"And the steam makes the pistons go back and forth—"

"What's a piston?"

At the youthful voice, Tamar sighed with relief. She pushed open the door to the engine room to find both young people standing next to Jensen Moreau, the one man she'd rather avoid. Whenever they were in the same room, she could feel his dark gaze on her. And he liked to sidle up close to her, like he was interested in courting her. It made her uncomfortable.

She had no time for romance, and even if she did, she wouldn't encourage someone like him. Jensen Moreau was younger than she and a man of the world. Beyond that, he was a freeman, and she was a slave. Any relationship between them was doomed to failure.

She tried to ignore him, concentrating on Jasmine and David instead. "I've been looking all over this boat for you, Miss Jasmine, and you, too, Master David. Not being able to find you has nearly scared me out of ten years of my life."

Jasmine jumped and twisted around. "Tamar! What are you doing here?"

"I was halfway convinced you'd fallen overboard and drowned."

Jasmine flipped her hair over one shoulder. "I wouldn't drown. I know how to swim."

"I wouldn't let her come to any harm." David's soulful green gaze was centered on Jasmine.

"They wasn't doing no harm, Miss Tamar." Mr. Moreau wiped his hands on a rag. "Just wanting to see how this old engine works."

Tamar put her hands on her hips. She should have known Jasmine would charm the gruff man like she did everyone else. The girl was going to be a handful when she became a woman, leading her older sister on a merry chase until some man took her off Lily's hands. "She can learn about her home after she studies history and arithmetic."

Mr. Moreau's eyes widened. "You teach the children?"

A reluctant smile turned her lips upward. "I don't hardly know how to spell out my name. I wouldn't be any good trying to teach them."

"Tamar is very good at other things." Jasmine moved to her side and put an arm around her waist. "She's an excellent seamstress, and she knows all the stories from the Bible."

Warmth filled Tamar at the way Jasmine rushed to her defense. She had once dreamed of having little girls of her own, but as the years passed, she had come to realize she would never marry. Her heart had never been touched by any man, and now she was too old to be thinking about such things. But the good Lord knew best. And He'd seen fit to give her the joy of raising the motherless Anderson girls. It was enough to satisfy her most times.

Jensen's unscarred eyebrow lifted. "I have the feeling Miss Tamar can do most anything she puts her mind to."

The engine room suddenly felt uncomfortably warm. The boiler hissed and popped. No wonder Jensen. . .Mr. Moreau. . .only wore a white shirt and loose-fitting trousers. He looked like a bloodthirsty pirate with his swarthy skin and scarred face. All he needed was a neckerchief and a broadsword to complete the picture. "Th–thank you."

What was the matter with her? She was acting like a love-struck girl.

"We need to leave Mr. Moreau to his important work." Tamar shooed the children out of the room. She ignored the urge to look back. She was a grown woman, an old woman. And she was a godly woman, not one given to carrying on with men—no matter whether one set her heart to fluttering. She would keep her mind where it belonged, regardless of how hard that might be.

Midafternoon heat made it impossible for Lily to nap with her sisters. She tossed for half an hour before getting up and returning to the kitchen to see if she could help Tamar. The older woman was sitting at the table, her hands folded together, her eyes closed.

Tamar was praying. It made Lily think of how little time she'd spent lately talking to God. She needed to do better. Unearth her Bible and get back to reading to her sisters and Tamar. Perhaps she could invite the men to a nightly devotional time. Happy with the idea, she carefully picked up a chair and carried it out onto the deck.

The bank slid silently past, and Lily considered how uneventful their voyage had been. No storms, no pirates.

They had caught up with a smaller steamer, the *Daniel Boone*, right after resuming their journey at dawn. Captain Lars had wanted to race the steamer, but Lily vetoed the idea. She had no desire to collide with a snag or stray out of the channel in such a frivolous pursuit. She wanted to get safely to New Orleans, collect their payment, and pick up their next load. They still managed to leave the smaller boat in their wake, not surprising since their paddle wheel was nearly twice as large.

Tamar's voice interrupted her musings. "I thought you were taking a nap."

"I'm sorry. I didn't mean to disturb you."

"You didn't disturb me, honey. I was just thanking the good Lord for protecting us."

"You're such a good example for us, Tamar."

The older woman looked down at her hands. "I don't know about that."

Lily stood and hugged Tamar. "I do." She pushed Tamar down into her chair. "Why don't you sit here and relax a bit? I'm feeling too restless to sit still."

Lily wandered toward the main staircase. Maybe she could talk to Blake about taking on passengers for their return trip to Natchez. Although they would have to hire more crew to help take care of the passengers' needs, they could still realize a profit.

She entered the shadowy room and ran a hand across the edge of the main dining room. They'd eaten in here last night, all nine of them. Blake had sat at the head of the table while she'd taken the spot at the foot, like they were a real family.

A smile teased her lips. An odd family indeed. From David, their rescued foundling, to Jensen, the reformed pirate, they made a motley crew. And she enjoyed all of them—Captain Steenberg and the tongue-tied crewman, Jack. They had become the heart and soul of the *Hattie Belle*.

A staccato sound made Lily catch her breath. Her warm feelings melted away. Blake Matthews had better not be playing cards. She would not allow gambling on this boat.

Anger carried her through the empty dining hall and into the gentlemen's parlor. Blake and their new crewman, Jack, were sitting on opposite sides of a small table. Her arrival apparently went unheard as neither looked up. Lily took a moment to size up the situation. Blake had his back to her, but a pile of coins at his elbow told the story. She had caught the man red-handed. "What are you doing?"

Jack gasped and stood, his movements almost oversetting the stack of coins.

After a brief hesitation, Blake continued to deal the cards. "We're enjoying a friendly game of cards."

"I thought you understood my feelings about gambling on the *Hattie Belle*." Lily walked to where he sat, acting as though her desires were of no interest or validity. "I won't have it."

"Don't get so upset. Haven't we earned a little relaxation?"

Just as she reached the table, the floor bucked upward. She screamed and grabbed the table with both hands. The boat lurched again, and a horrendous scraping sound filled the air. Blake stood and grabbed her around the waist, holding her close as the world shook and shuddered.

"What's happening?" she asked.

"I'd guess we've run aground." His deep voice tickled her ear.

How had she ended up in his arms again? Confusing emotions clamored for attention—fear, anger, pleasure. . . . Why was she clinging to him like some weak debutante? Lily made fists of her hands and pushed against his chest. "Let go of me."

When he complied, she staggered back but compensated by windmilling her arms. He was almost out of the parlor by the time she recovered, never having looked back to see whether she had fallen.

Lily swallowed her exasperation and followed him to the pilothouse. Coming out onto the hurricane deck made her realize how bad the situation was. From the sounds of it, the *Hattie Belle* was tearing apart at the seams. Lily could see the bank some distance away on both sides of them. What had happened?

She stepped into the pilothouse right behind Blake and groaned. Ahead of the boat was a wide expanse of sand. The captain had run them onto a sandbar. "Where is he?"

"Hey, there." The captain appeared at the door to the pilothouse. "We had an acci...ac...acshident."

"You're drunk." The disgust in Blake's voice was as deep as the main river channel. The channel their drunken captain had taken them out of.

"No, I'm not." The captain hiccuped and grinned. "Only had a nip." He held up a thumb and finger as a measurement.

Lily closed her eyes. She wanted to toss the man onto the sandbar and leave him.

"Take our gallant captain downstairs and get some coffee into him." Blake bit out the words as though he was angry with her. As if the whole fiasco was her fault.

She wanted to take exception to his tone, but this was not the time. They needed to get their boat back into the river. Besides, her sisters, Tamar, and David would be terrified. She needed to reassure them.

Guilt speared her at the thought of the trouble they were facing. She should have listened to Blake. He was right about the captain, and he was also right about purchasing insurance. A tiny sob escaped her as she realized her dreams might collapse. Why hadn't she let Blake convince her? Why was she always so determined to ignore his advice?

She was going to have to apologize to him, admit that he had been right. And she would...if she got out of this mess.

Chapter Twenty-four

He had to fix this mess, get them out of the disaster *her* choice of captain had caused while she gave him grief over an innocent card game. Blake pushed away the memory of Lily's stricken expression. He didn't have time to worry about her tender feelings.

A pang of guilt shot through him. If he'd been in the pilothouse instead of gambling downstairs, the accident might not have happened. But didn't he deserve a little relaxation? Was he supposed to shoulder all the responsibility for this venture? It hadn't been his idea, after all. He'd gone along with Lily Anderson because he had no choice.

Jensen appeared at the door to the pilothouse. "I've turned off the boiler."

Blake nodded. "Good. Can you tell how bad it is?"

"Bad enough," Jensen admitted, shaking his head. "I'm not sure if we'll be able to get free before the current turns us broadside."

Blake shuddered. They'd lose the boat for sure if that happened. The *Hattie Belle* couldn't compete against the force of the mighty Mississippi. "Can we dig our way out?"

Jensen shrugged. "We can give it a try."

"Good. I'll be downstairs as quick as I can to help. You go ahead and get started with Jack."

❧

Lily headed back toward the parlor, her ears stretched in hopes she would hear the churn of the paddle wheel. She had left the captain in the kitchen with a pot of black coffee. She needed to check on David and her sisters, warn Tamar to be ready to get them out safely, and then get outside to see how bad the damage was and what she could do to help.

"Lily." Blake's voice stopped her. "How is the captain?"

She turned to answer his question. The expression on his face deepened her foreboding. "He's nursing a mug of coffee, but I'm not sure how long it's going to take him to sober up. How bad is it?"

"I've checked on the cargo, and it's fine. . .for the time being." The corners of Blake's mouth turned down. "But half the boat is up on the sand. If we can't dig around it enough to get it floating again, the *Hattie Belle* may break apart."

Lily closed her eyes. *Please, God.* All her yearning went into the plea.

"We're doing everything we can, but you need to make sure the children are ready to abandon ship if necessary."

She swallowed hard, opened her eyes, and nodded.

The floor lurched. "I've got to get back out there." He turned sharply and ran down the passageway.

Lily wanted to follow him, but she knew she had to check on her sisters. David was the first one she saw in the parlor, his back to her as he peered through the window. She glanced around and found Tamar sitting on the sofa, hugging both Jasmine and Camellia close. Her sisters' faces were pale, their eyes large. They jumped up and ran to her.

"What's wrong, Sissy?" Jasmine barreled into her.

Camellia wasn't far behind her. "Did we hit another boat?"

Lily held both of them. "No, we scraped up on a sandbar. It's going to take us a while to dig out."

David moved toward them. "Can I help the men?"

Lily shook her head. "I need you to stay here and keep my sisters calm." She gave both of them a little shove. "Why don't you get out the checkerboard and enjoy a few games while we wait?"

As they got out the checkers, she pulled Tamar aside. "I don't want to alarm the children, but we are in trouble."

"What can I do?" Tamar asked.

"Stay here with the children. Be ready to get them out quickly if something happens."

"What are you going to do?"

Lily patted her arm. "I'm going to change clothes and help."

"Won't you be in the way?" Tamar's voice was pitched low, but it conveyed her concern.

"Not as soon as I get a shovel in my hand." Lily slipped out of the parlor and ran to her room. Putting on her oldest skirt, she prayed for deliverance. They needed God's intervention to survive this disaster.

⁊❦

The sun beat against Blake's shoulders through his shirt. It seemed he'd been digging forever.

"I need a shovel."

Lily's voice brought his head up. "What are you doing here?"

"I can't sit inside and wait for our dreams to be lost." She crossed her arms. "I may not be able to dig as fast as you, but every grain of sand I move is one you won't have to."

Part of him wanted to send her inside to safety, but Blake understood her frustration. He inclined his head. "If we have any more, they'll be in that bucket."

She nodded and marched away, her shoulders as straight as a sergeant's.

As he redoubled his efforts, Blake thought about Lily's temerity. He had to admire her spunk. He didn't know a single other woman who would volunteer to shovel sand. He only hoped it wasn't too little, too late.

"You look like you could use a helping hand."

Blake straightened and looked out at the river. A boat had pulled even with them, a boat he recognized. It was the *Daniel Boone*, the boat they'd passed earlier. He climbed out of his trench. "We sure could." For the first time since they'd landed on the sandbar, Blake felt his shoulders relax.

The captain shouted an order, and one of his crew tossed a towline out across the water. Blake and Jack secured it to the bow while Jensen and Lily picked up the shovels. As soon as they had all climbed back onto the *Hattie Belle*, the smaller boat's paddle wheel started churning. At first Blake thought it would not be able to pull them free of the grasping sand, but with a lurch, their boat began to move.

Jensen fired up the boiler while Blake loosened the grappling hook and tossed it back to the captain of the *Daniel Boone*.

138

Lily was standing next to him, her skirt covered in sand and muddy water but a wide smile on her face. "I can't thank you enough. I was beginning to think our first voyage was going to be our last."

The broad-chested captain tugged on his cap. "It's a harsh river we're riding. We have to help each other or we all lose."

Blake was humbled by the man's attitude. If nothing else positive came from this disaster, he would always remember the captain's actions and never forget to extend a helping hand to those in need.

They limped into New Orleans before the last ray of sun had slipped from the sky. By the time the *Hattie Belle* was secured, the shadows were running together into dusk. He was filthy, exhausted, and sore. And quite certain he didn't want to earn a living running cargo.

He was more suited to the life of a gambler. Tonight he couldn't remember why he hadn't walked away from the *Hattie Belle* when Lily first showed up and claimed majority ownership. As soon as he got paid for this trip, he would disappear. New Orleans was as good a place to start over as any other.

He felt rather than saw Lily join him at the rail. "We made it."

She put a hand over his. "Thank you. I know we wouldn't have made it without your hard work."

Blake liked the feeling of her cool skin on his. He wanted to turn his palm over and run the tips of his fingers across her soft skin, but he didn't want her to pull away. So he remained still and basked in her appreciation. Their differences sank beneath the surface of his tumbling thoughts, taking his frustration and weariness with them.

They stood close together like kindred spirits and looked toward the other boats in the harbor. Many of them were lashed together, and he made out the figures of men leaping from one deck to another with the nimbleness of experience.

The slap of water against wooden hulls was punctuated by greetings, shouts, and laughter, all melting together to create the unique sound of a floating city. The warm yellow flames of cooking fires glowed, and the air was heavy with the exotic fragrances of unfamiliar spices. He could have remained standing there for the rest of the evening.

Lily squeezed his hand and pulled away. "I suppose we need to get moving if we're going to find LeGrand's this evening."

Blake turned toward her, his gaze following the outline of her graceful neck up to the determined chin and pert nose he could barely make out in the growing darkness. "I doubt it'll be open."

"It will be. It has to be." Her chin rose a notch.

He sighed. He should have known she would insist on finding the business tonight. "Do you have the directions?"

It was for the best. Hadn't he just been thinking about cutting his losses and walking away? He needed the reminder that Lily was always going to want to call the shots.

She would never be a conformable female. If he ever decided to marry, it would not be to a woman so bossy and self-righteous. He would choose someone quiet, someone who adored him and would be a good role model for their children. Not a woman who strode about on the deck of a steamship and expected everyone to fall in with her plans.

A stab of regret pierced his heart, but Blake ignored it. After a nice long soak in a warm bath and a good night's sleep, the pains he had earned today would fade away. Including the ache beginning to lay claim to part of his heart.

Chapter Twenty-five

As they approached, Blake saw a lamp gleaming in the front window of LeGrand Shipping. Even though Lily had to be as exhausted as he was, she practically leaped from the wagon he had hired.

"If you'll wait a moment, I'll help you get down." He tossed the reins to a child who came running forward, then jumped down, holding back a groan with some effort. The sooner they concluded their business, the sooner he could rest.

He walked to the far side of the wagon and held out a hand. As soon as Lily's feet touched the ground, she let go of him and straightened her skirts. He moved up the two steps and opened the door to the shipping company, setting off a tinkling bell and causing the man at the counter to look up.

As a gambler, Blake had learned to size up people quickly. Thinning hair on the man's head was compensated for by a neatly trimmed beard and mustache. Probably about two decades older than he, the man smiled readily, a sign of an honest merchant. As the man removed his spectacles, Blake recognized the intelligence in his hazel gaze. "May I help you?" he asked as Lily and Blake entered the orderly office space.

Lily consulted the paper in her hand. "I'm looking for Lloyd Thornton."

The man's smile widened, and he put down his pen. "You've found me. What can I do for you?"

Before Lily could answer, the curtain covering a doorway behind Mr. Thornton moved, and a woman stepped into the room. She was short, even shorter than Lily, and her blond hair looked almost colorless in the lamplight. Her light-brown eyes contained the same combination of friendliness and canniness as the man she stood beside. "Well, I see we have some late business, or is this handsome couple seeking directions to the French Quarter?"

"I was about to find out their errand when you entered, dearest. They seem to be seeking us, however, since this lovely young lady has my name."

"*Quel charme.* It's charming to meet you." The woman's gaze was as bright and interested as a bird's. "I'm Mrs. Thornton."

Although both Thorntons looked to Blake, he glanced at Lily. She held out her paper to Mr. Thornton. "We have brought cargo from Natchez."

Mr. Thornton took the paper and returned his spectacles to his face. After a moment he looked at his wife. "This is the cornmeal we were hoping to send to Barbados. I wasn't sure your parents would be able to get it to us in time."

Mrs. Thornton nodded and turned to them with her attractive smile. "Did you and your husband have a pleasant voyage to New Orleans?"

"He's not my husband." The words flew out of Lily's mouth.

At the same time, Blake spoke forcefully. "We're not married."

"Oh." Mrs. Thornton looked toward her husband who answered with a shrug.

"I suppose their situation must be entirely proper or your parents wouldn't have trusted them with the cargo."

"My sisters and I own a majority share of the *Hattie Belle*. Mr. Matthews owns a smaller portion." Color had darkened Lily's cheeks. "A chaperone travels with us."

"I assure you our relationship is purely business." Blake picked up the explanation. "Miss Anderson convinced me we should try our hand at shipping, and here we are with our first delivery."

"I see." Mr. and Mrs. Thornton exchanged a glance before Mrs. Thornton continued. "Then I trust you and your business partner had a pleasant first voyage."

Blake nodded but saw Lily shaking her head. "We had the ill fortune of running our boat on a sandbar. Although we were blessed to be towed back into the channel by a passing steamship, I'm afraid we sustained some damage."

"Praise the Lord you made it to New Orleans." Mrs. Thornton put a hand to her chest. She stepped around the end of the counter. "But what do you plan to do until your beautiful boat is repaired?"

Blake cleared his throat. "We haven't gotten that far. We arrived only a little while ago."

Mrs. Thornton looked at her husband, an unspoken question in her gaze. Mr. Thornton removed his spectacles and nodded.

These two seemed able to read each other's thoughts. Past sermons from Blake's childhood came to mind. Could two people really become one? Or did one simply find a pretty, compatible female and marry her?

"All of you will come to our house and stay until your boat is fixed." Mrs. Thornton's words made Blake's jaw drop.

"We couldn't do that. It would be too much of an imposition." Lily's words had a wistful tone. "There are seven of us not counting the crew."

"Our town house seems so empty now that Eli and Sarah are gone. Tell them, Lloyd."

"Charlotte is right." Mr. Thornton cleaned his spectacles with his handkerchief as he spoke. "You would be doing us a favor. You can tell us about her parents and what's happening in Natchez."

"We do need somewhere to stay." Blake added his support to the Thorntons' suggestion.

Lily looked at him as though he had betrayed her. "I thought we'd stay in the *Hattie Belle*. Make sure the repairs are carried out properly."

He raised an eyebrow. "I doubt workers will appreciate having women and children running underfoot. Jensen and I can stay on board and supervise the work."

"That makes no sense." Lily frowned at him. "You're more exhausted than I. You deserve a chance to recoup your strength."

That was true enough. Blake would pay a large sum for a bed as long as his frame. "But—"

"I won't hear of it." Mrs. Thornton overrode both of them. "We may have to ask the gentlemen to share a bedroom, but we can manage things. Now go on back to your berth, gather your belongings, and come back here. Lloyd will wait for you while I make sure everything is ready."

Lily opened her mouth, but Mrs. Thornton raised a finger. "You're coming to stay with us. That's the end of it."

Mr. Thornton joined his wife, putting an arm around her waist. "I learned long ago when to let Charlotte win an argument. Besides, she will enjoy having you to fuss over. So you may as well give in gracefully and let us coddle you a bit."

Blake could tell the moment Lily decided to stay with the Thorntons. He breathed a sigh of relief. The Thorntons' generosity was like being dealt a royal flush—a stroke of good luck no gambler would ignore.

"Thank you so much." Lily smiled at the couple. "We would be happy to pay—"

Mrs. Thornton laughed. "Don't be silly, child. I won't hear of such folly. We can afford twice as many guests. Besides, you will be doing me a favor. Since my daughter, Sarah, got married, I have had no girls to discuss fashion and shopping with. We'll have such fun together."

"I can also arrange for a reputable company to do your repairs." Mr. Thornton moved back to the counter and began searching through some papers. "I'll have all the information together by the time you return."

Blake led Lily back to the wagon by the light of a gas lantern. On the ride to the boat, she was uncharacteristically silent. Did she regret agreeing to stay with the Thorntons? "I think you made a good decision. Who knows how long it will take to complete the repairs on our boat?"

She turned her face up to him. "Please promise you will come with us."

Warmth filled him, traveling outward from his chest in a flood of emotion. Was she worried about him? Or maybe she wanted his company. He really liked that idea. She was growing fond of him in spite of their differences. He patted her hand. "I won't desert you."

As soon as the words escaped, Blake wanted to call them back. Wasn't he ready to wash his hands of Miss Anderson and her troublesome troupe? Then why had he given his word to stay at her side? The question had no answer, or at least no answer he wanted to consider.

&

Early the next morning, Blake rolled his shoulders as he waited for the repair crew Mr. Thornton was sending over. He hadn't seen Captain Steenberg yet. Maybe the man had decided to disappear. Good riddance. It would save Blake the trouble of telling him his services were no longer required. The sound of footsteps on the back stairway drew his attention.

"I feel like a herd of buffalo's running through my head." The captain winced as a shaft of sunlight landed on his face.

Stale waves of alcohol washed over Blake. Was Steenberg still drunk? Or drunk again? "You should be glad we didn't leave your sorry carcass on that sandbar."

"For making a mistake?" the man said, his face showing surprise. "Don't I deserve a little relaxation?"

Guilt speared Blake as the man used the same excuse he'd given Lily when she'd discovered him playing cards. Had he been negligent in expecting the captain to shoulder all the responsibility of piloting? He shook his head. "You ran us aground. We could still be stuck out there on the river or trying to walk our way through the swamp to New Orleans."

The captain shrugged. "But we're not."

How could the man be so dense? So careless? And how could Blake have been so wrongheaded as to ignore his intuition about Steenberg? It was time to take action. Time to stop letting Lily Anderson call the shots.

"No thanks to you. Clear off this boat."

The man's jaw went slack. "What do you mean?"

Blake remained silent.

The captain's face hardened. "You didn't hire me. You don't have the right to tell me to leave."

"I most certainly do have the right. I can assure you Miss Anderson and I are of one mind on this matter." Blake winced inside as he made the statement. Surely Lily would agree once he explained the situation. "Get your things."

Fear and regret replaced the captain's rebellion. "Please give me another chance. I promise I'll do a better job. Besides, you need a licensed captain."

Blake shook his head. "Don't worry. We'll find someone."

"Lots of luck." The captain spat and took a step forward. He shook a finger under Blake's nose. "Where do you think you'll find someone to replace me? Do you think anyone else is going to take a chance on this doomed boat?"

He knew he ought to remain stoic, but curiosity overcame Blake. "What do you mean?"

"Everybody knows having a woman run a boat is bad luck. And I'm sure word has gotten out about her running aground. No one's going to want a berth, much less a job, on the *Hattie Belle*. You might as well change her name to the *Flying Dutchman*."

Blake laughed. Superstition? Ludicrous. He'd seen a lot of men blame luck and superstition for their own shortcomings. It seemed the captain was ready to take it one step further. "You're trying to blame your mistake on Miss Anderson?" Laughter bubbled up again. "Go ahead. Any man with sense will be able to see the truth."

A sound turned Blake's attention to the wharf. The repair crew. He wondered how much they had heard of the argument. At least no one was running away. "I'll be right with you." He turned back to the captain. "You have five minutes to gather your gear and get off this boat."

"You'll be sorry." Steenberg's bravado faded as he hissed the threat. "Everyone's going to hear about the way you've treated me. I'll make sure you and all those Anderson girls pay for this."

Blake shouldn't have been surprised at the threat. They were the weapons of a coward. "That's enough." He advanced two steps and pointed a finger of warning at the man. "Believe me, if anything *ever* happens to this ship or to any of the Andersons, I will find you, and you'll wish you'd never been born."

The captain backed away, stumbled over the bottom step, and then practically ran to his quarters.

Blake hoped he'd convinced the troublemaker to leave them alone. He turned back to the repair crew. "I'm glad to see you."

The burly man who boarded first nodded. "We'll just take a look at your paddle wheel and let you know how long it'll be."

The minutes dragged by, and Blake paced the deck, torn between his desire to oversee the repair crew and his need to make sure Steenberg wasn't packing any more than he'd brought. Loud footsteps took the decision out of his hands. The irate captain reappeared, a black leather bag slung over his back. Shouldering his way past Blake, the man stepped onto the wharf. "You'll be sorry for this."

"Are you threatening me?" Blake clenched his fists.

Captain Lars held his gaze then looked down. "No. I'm just saying captains aren't standing on every corner, waiting to find a boat."

"That's my problem, not yours." Blake strode to the rear of the boat to check with the workers.

He found the burly foreman taking measurements and recording them in a small book. "It's going to take at least two weeks to get your boat ready."

Blake took a deep breath. "Are you sure?"

A nod answered his question. "You're lucky to have made it to New Orleans. I'm not sure how you did without breaking up. You must have had an angel riding with you."

His lips turned up in a grin. He wouldn't exactly describe her as an angel. Lily was a little too forceful to spend her time strumming a harp. He dreaded telling her how bad the damage was. She was probably planning to get back on the river this afternoon or tomorrow at the latest. If she did have a halo hidden away somewhere, it was going to get a little bent.

Blake gave the order to proceed and left to check with Mr. Thornton on available captains. At least he had plenty of time to conduct interviews and find a suitable candidate. That should please Lily if nothing else did.

Chapter Twenty-six

Lily left Tamar helping her sisters get dressed and hurried downstairs, wondering how long it would take her to get back to the boat. She exited their bedroom on the third floor, surprised to realize she was eye level with a beautiful crystal chandelier that held dozens of candles. She reached out one hand for the wooden railing as she began descending the U-shaped stairwell.

Last night she had not noticed the intricate woodwork on the posts or the number of doorways in the Thorntons' town house. The craftsmanship signaled the luxury in which their new acquaintances resided.

Reaching the end of the stairs, she had a choice of direction. The door through which they had entered the home stood in front of her. She remembered the parlor was to her left, so perhaps she would find the dining room to her right.

Lily bypassed the first door since it was closed. She doubted their hosts would close the entryway into their dining room. Light spilled from the second doorway, and when she reached it, she found a spacious room with a large table at its center. The dining room.

Lily entered, surprised to find the only other occupant was Mrs. Thornton. "What a beautiful home you and Mr. Thornton have."

"Thank you, dear. I am glad to see you are looking less bedraggled this morning." She smiled. "Did you sleep well?"

"Yes, ma'am." Lily slid into the seat her hostess indicated.

Mrs. Thornton rang a bell. "Someone will be here with your food in a moment. We normally eat croissants with marmalade or fresh fruit for breakfast, but I can instruct our cook to fix something else if you prefer."

Lily picked up a snowy-white napkin and placed it on her lap. "Oh no, thank you. Your breakfast sounds wonderful."

A round-faced girl in a plain dress appeared and served Lily a plate with two rolls that had been twisted in a spiral and bent into a half-moon shape.

Lily thanked her and picked one up, breaking it open to see steam rising from the flaky interior. She placed a dab of butter on her croissant and bit into it, her eyes closing as the bread melted in her mouth.

Mrs. Thornton smiled. "Our cook is an artist with food."

Lily nodded. "I'm rather surprised Blake and your husband are not here. Have they already left for the office? I was hoping to talk to Blake before they departed."

"I'm sorry, dear." Mrs. Thornton picked up her fork and speared a fresh strawberry. "Mr. Matthews must have decided to stay on the boat last night. He never made it to the town house. But don't worry. I'm sure he simply decided to guard your cargo since it could not be unloaded last night. Lloyd was going to check on him this morning, make certain he has all the help he needs to get your riverboat repaired."

"I see." Lily's appetite fled. While she had been sleeping in luxury, Blake had been guarding the boat. They had worked hard to get the boat free from the sandbar yesterday. They all deserved to sleep well.

"If you're worried about Mr. Matthews, I can send one of the servants to check on him."

"Thank you, but that's not necessary. I'm sure he's fine." Lily pinched the end of one of her croissants. She still wasn't hungry, but her hands needed something to do. Besides, she did not want to offend her hostess by not eating the sumptuous meal.

As she continued to pick at her food, her mind was consumed with plans. She had thought they might have time to tour the fabled city of New Orleans, but that would have to wait for a future trip. As soon as her sisters ate breakfast, they would all have to go to the boat to help out with the repairs. Even if they couldn't do the heavy work, they could at least prepare meals and keep the rest of the boat clean. Maybe they could make up nice flyers to advertise for passengers.

Camellia and Jasmine made an appearance then. Lily was thankful for their nonstop chatter as it allowed her to concentrate on the proper wording of the advertisements, as well as the apology she owed Blake.

When her sisters had finished breakfast, Lily rose from her place at the table and turned to tell Camellia and Jasmine to come upstairs with her. All of them needed to change into their working clothes. The outfits they were wearing were more suited to a day of sightseeing.

Before she could issue her instructions, however, a commotion in the foyer diverted her attention.

Mrs. Thornton checked the watch suspended on her fleur-de-lis chatelaine pin. "I cannot believe we have visitors this early."

A familiar voice made Lily's heart race. "I believe it may be my business partner. He's probably come to tell me how much our repairs are going to cost and how long they will take." She ignored the wide smile on Mrs. Thornton's face and walked out into the hall.

Blake was striding toward the dining room but checked himself when she appeared.

Lily thought he looked a bit haggard and wondered if he'd spent the whole night standing watch at their boat. A wave of shame swamped her. She remembered how ugly she'd been to him right before the accident. Again. Was she turning into a shrew? Pushing the thought aside, she composed herself and produced a welcoming smile. "I'm so glad to see you. We have many things we need to discuss."

No answering smile turned up the corners of his lips. "I suppose we can make use of the Thorntons' parlor."

Lily's heart stuttered. Blake must have bad news. Her smile slipped away. What could be wrong now?

❦

Blake followed Lily down a black-and-white-tiled hallway and entered a well-appointed parlor. She sat on the upholstered sofa and fluffed her black skirts around her, fussing with the material as though it was imperative to have it just right. "Mr. Matthews, this is difficult for me—"

Blake held up a hand to stop her. "I want to apologize, Lily. You were right. I should not have been playing cards. If I had been in the pilothouse, I could have stopped the captain from overimbibing." He didn't realize that he'd been staring at his feet as he delivered his apology until Lily's skirts appeared before his gaze. He looked up, his gaze meeting her wide eyes, eyes that seemed filled with remorse. What was this?

"You're not at fault as much as I am, Blake. I seem to remember your trying to warn me Steenberg might not be a good captain. Because I refused to listen to you, I share a large portion of the responsibility. Please forgive me for placing the blame on you yesterday."

Surprise rippled through him. He who prided himself on being able to understand others was always caught off guard by Lily's behavior. Where was the puritanical firebrand who had condemned him? "You had every right, Lily. But please believe me when I say I'll make it up to you."

"I know you will, Blake. I've learned that you're a man I can depend on."

Was she manipulating him? No. A glance in those deep brown eyes told him she was being honest. He wanted to enfold her in his arms, dance about the room. She had faith in him. In that moment he knew he would do whatever it took to get their boat running again. He would make sure her dreams came true, even if he had to swim the Mississippi from end to end to find cargo for the *Hattie Belle*.

"How long will it take to complete the repairs?" Her question brought him back to reality.

Blake paced in front of the fireplace. He wished he could give her better news, but he couldn't lie to her. "At least two weeks."

"Two weeks!" She croaked out the words. "I thought you said it would be one week. We can't afford to be off the river for two whole weeks."

"Jensen and I will do what we can, but some of the supplies are in high demand because of a break in the levee system at the Bell plantation. The people on the other side of the levee are trying to shore things up, and they keep buying up everything available." He paused before continuing. "Since there's such high demand, the lumber is more expensive."

"Isn't there something my sisters and I can do to speed things up?"

"No. In fact, I don't want any of you out there as long as the repairs are ongoing. It's dangerous with all the strangers around, and there's nothing for you to do until we're ready to leave for Natchez."

Blake was ready to comfort Lily when she broke down and began to cry. He hoped she had a handkerchief, because the one in his pocket was not as pristine as he might have liked. He lowered himself onto the sofa next to her and reached for one of her hands, pressing it between his palms and rubbing as he waited. "Everything is going to work out."

No tears flowed. Instead she straightened her spine and lifted her chin. "Of course you realize the good Lord knew we'd be facing this problem. Since the day you and I were born, He knew we'd end up sitting on this very sofa in this town house discussing this problem."

Not seeing why she wanted to bring God into the discussion, he waited.

Lily turned to him. "He already had things worked out, Blake. Don't you see? He'll help us through this trouble. I'm sure of it."

"If you say so, Lily." She might want to rely on God, but he was more a man of action than of prayer. That was why he'd considered their predicament from every angle. He had a solution, but would she accept it? Could she let go of her strict moral code long enough to allow him to put his plan into action? He doubted it but felt he needed to try anyway. "There's another way around this."

The look she gave him was full of hope. It brightened her eyes and her smile. "What is that?"

"I can host a quiet evening or two of cards on *Hattie Belle* during the evenings once the repairmen leave. It shouldn't take me long to earn enough to pay for the repairs and whatever additional expenses we run up."

"I can't believe you'd suggest such a thing. You know my stance on gambling and drinking. They're immoral and wicked, and they lead to absolute debauchery. I will not countenance them on my boat."

He should have known she wouldn't listen to reason. "Don't you think it's about time you got off your high horse, Lily? I've gone along with your self-righteous rules and pretentions. Where has that gotten us? We're stranded in New Orleans with little cash and no prospects. Dependent on the kindness of strangers for a safe place for you and your sisters to stay. Isn't it about time you let go of your highfalutin morals and embraced a little common sense?"

"Banning your dissolute habits is common sense, and as long as I own controlling interest in the *Hattie Belle*, you'll have to live with my highfalutin morals." She pointed a finger at him. "So get used to it, or get yourself another boat."

He raked a hand through his hair. Why couldn't she see reason? "I'd like to do that very thing, but I've sunk all my assets and not a little bit of my time into *our* boat. I'm not about to walk away."

"Fine." Lily walked to the door, opening it a few inches. "I'll go meet with Captain Steenberg and see if he can find someone more capable than the repairmen you hired."

"You won't find him aboard *Hattie Belle*."

His words stopped her. Her knuckles whitened around the doorknob she still clenched. "Why won't I?"

"I fired him."

She slammed the door shut. "You what?"

"You heard me." He crossed his arms and leaned back. "I told him to clear his gear out and be gone before I got back. I don't expect you'll find him anytime soon. He's probably gone to a saloon to drown his sorrows."

"You had no right to do that."

"Why not? The man's a drunkard. He nearly got us killed."

Lily shook her head. "I could have controlled that by removing his alcohol from the boat and keeping him under tight scrutiny."

"You're lying to yourself. No one can stop a drunkard who is intent on his drink. Steenberg would have hidden a bottle in his boot, in his shirt pocket, even in his breeches if he needed to. And the minute your back was turned, he would have taken a little nip. And another and another. Until he was as drunk as he was yesterday."

"You should have kept him until we found someone to take his place. What if we have to hire someone without experience? How will we be any better off?" She paced the floor.

"At least there'll be a better chance to arrive in Natchez with an undamaged boat."

"But we know Steenberg's weakness. We won't know anything about the man who replaces him. He could murder us while we sleep."

"I don't understand you, Lily." He sat forward. "You'd have thrown me overboard if I did what Steenberg did. And he's not your business partner. Why is it you want to forgive him for something much more heinous than anything I've ever done? You say you know I'm trustworthy, but when it comes time to put your words to the test, to put your faith in me, you can't do it."

Lily stopped pacing and looked at him. A frown of confusion marred her face. "I. . .you don't have the right to fire someone I hired."

"You mean someone Jean Luc Champney hired. Is that it? Are you concerned about upsetting your friend?"

"Don't try to bring him into this argument. Jean Luc is a fine gentleman. A kind man who considers my wishes. He's been very considerate toward me and my family."

Blake couldn't stop his grimace. "That's because he's trying to romance you."

"It's not like that." Her words rushed out with force, but her cheeks reddened. "Besides, my relationship with Monsieur Champney is none of your concern."

"I see." He raised an eyebrow. "We'll get away from such an uncomfortable subject since my point has already been proven. You're very quick to defend everyone except me."

She took a turn about the room, her skirts swishing and swaying. When she stopped in front of him, her eyes were as frosty as a January morning.

Something inside him hurt like he'd been punched in the stomach. How had they gotten here? Why did they always seem to end up on opposite sides? He opened his mouth to apologize for firing Lars without consulting her, but she held up a hand.

"We'll have to hire another captain. You fired Captain Steenberg, so it's your responsibility to find his replacement. Fix it."

Anger swept through him. His desire to apologize was swept away by her demand. How dare she order him around like a hired hand? He started to challenge her but decided it might be better to take a different tack. "If that's the way you want it, that's the way it will be."

"Good."

He pointed a finger at her. "And you can't second-guess my choice, either. The man I hire will captain our boat."

"That's fine by me. But if I don't like him, don't expect me to keep him aboard after we reach Natchez."

Blake watched as she jerked open the door and swept through it. With a weary sigh, he pushed himself up from the sofa and trod to the door.

Arguing with Lily was as exhausting as anything he'd done in the past week. Part of him wanted to please her, wanted her to be as forgiving toward him as she was toward everyone else. But that seemed impossible. He supposed they would continue bickering until they dissolved their partnership and went their separate ways.

Chapter Twenty-seven

Lily trudged up to her bedroom on the third floor, her heart heavy. Would she and Blake ever see eye to eye? It didn't seem so.

Why had he gotten so upset when she suggested keeping Lars Steenberg? She understood what the man had done. But they could have controlled him while getting back to Natchez, back to a part of the world she was more familiar with. Back to an area where she knew people who could help them locate the right candidate.

If only Blake had consulted her, she would not have been so taken aback. Why couldn't he seem to remember they were joint owners of the *Hattie Belle* or that she owned more of their venture than he? Maybe she should have a flyer printed up for him—one he could hang in his room and read every night before he fell asleep: LILY CATHERINE ANDERSON OWNS 51 PERCENT INTEREST OF THE *HATTIE BELLE*.

Feeling a tiny bit better, she entered her bedroom. "Camellia? Jasmine?"

No one answered. Where were her sisters? Lily sighed. At least they would appreciate not having to work so hard over the next few days. When she'd first brought them on board the *Hattie Belle*, she'd promised exciting adventures in cities like New Orleans. Perhaps she could begin making good on her words today. If Mrs. Thornton agreed, they would take a tour of the city and maybe do a little shopping—as long as they didn't spend too much money, of course.

She opened the bedroom door and leaned out into the hall. Her sisters were not hiding on the landing. Where could they be? Faint music made her tilt her head. The tune sounded familiar. Was it a hymn?

She followed the sound down the stairs and found herself outside the conservatory, on the first floor opposite the staircase from the parlor. She pushed the door open.

Camellia was sitting on a piano bench, her fingers moving across the keys with sure movements. Jasmine sat beside her sister, facing the room. She was singing "O for a Thousand Tongues to Sing." The notes issuing from her were clear, strong, and sure.

Lily caught her breath. When had Jasmine developed that wonderful voice? She sounded like an angel. She knew how much Camellia liked playing the piano, so she was not surprised at the way her middle sister's hands coaxed such wonderful harmonies from the Thorntons' instrument. But Lily had never heard her youngest sister sing except during church services. And her voice had sounded breathy and scratchy then. Nothing like the pure tones Jasmine was producing this morning.

Jasmine held the final note for an extra beat as Camellia ended the song with a flourish.

Mrs. Thornton, ensconced in a leather wingback chair, applauded. "That was lovely. Both of you have so much talent."

Lily clapped, too. "I am proud to call you my sisters, as I always am."

"You should be." Mrs. Thornton nodded her agreement. "They're as talented as they are beautiful."

"Yes, they are." Lily hugged them both.

"Did you finish your business with Mr. Matthews?" asked Mrs. Thornton.

Jasmine reached up to tug on her arm. "Can we go to town now, Lily?"

"I don't. . . I'm not sure."

Her sisters groaned.

"I knew it." Camellia pushed away from the piano bench. "We're in the biggest, most exciting city on the Mississippi River, and we're going to be stuck inside the whole time."

Mrs. Thornton laughed. "I doubt that. Not with so much to see and enjoy."

"But we don't have enough money to do much." Lily hated to throw a damper on them, but someone had to be practical.

"Could we at least walk to Canal Street?" Camellia's blue eyes implored her to say yes. "It won't cost a thing to look in the store windows."

"Don't be silly." Mrs. Thornton clucked her tongue. "You made a great deal on the cargo you brought to New Orleans. And even though your *Hattie Belle* was damaged, you did not lose a single barrel. I'm certain you will be able to repair your riverboat and still have enough to enjoy a few distractions."

"But you don't know the worst of it." Lily squared her shoulders. She would rather have kept their financial circumstances to herself, but the others would not be satisfied until she explained her reluctance to fritter away their earnings. "Blake says the repairs will take nearly two weeks and the material is going to be more expensive than normal. We'll be fortunate to avoid going into debt."

Mrs. Thornton rose from her chair and enveloped Lily in a fragrant hug. "Don't worry. It's not as bad as you imagine. My husband, Lloyd, can work miracles. You wait and see. We will talk to him. And poof! All your troubles will be gone."

A hint of hope returned to Lily. "But we cannot—"

The older lady stopped Lily's word with a shake of her head. "Not another word. You will stay with us for as long as it takes. Lloyd and I have many rooms and would enjoy having you and your charming sisters as our guests for as long as you stay. We will send a note to my daughter, Sarah. You will love my Sarah. She is quite the popular hostess. Together we will have a wonderful time."

Feeling a bit like a leaf caught in a thunderstorm, Lily let herself be carried along with their hostess's plans. Doing anything else would be like taking on an army she could never defeat.

Chapter Twenty-eight

If Lily compared Mrs. Thornton to a thunderstorm, the next few days taught her that Sarah, Mr. and Mrs. Thornton's only daughter, was more akin to a hurricane.

A short, stylish hurricane, to be sure. Sarah Cartier, *née* Thornton, was barely five feet tall. But what she lacked in height, she more than made up for in energy. Married to an eminent surgeon, she had a generous nature and a caring heart. It didn't take long for Lily to realize that her hostess's daughter was a strong Christian who was always looking for opportunities to spread the Gospel.

All of Sarah's conversations were liberally sprinkled with references to the Bible. But she not only knew the Word, she lived it—spending her mornings at the hospital where her husband worked, praying with those who were sick and in pain, healing their spirits as her husband healed their bodies. The vivacious young matron also devoted one afternoon each week to meet with some of the ladies in her church. *Les Femmes du Patre*—the Women of the Shepherd—studied together, supported each other, and aided families from all walks of life.

Sarah also found time to host balls, soirees, and all manner of social events. One such was coming up at the end of the week. She and her mother had been trying to convince Lily to attend and bring Camellia. Sarah had come to the town house with the latest copy of *Godey's Lady's Book*.

Soon they were oohing and aahing over the dresses modeled by and for stylish young ladies. If fashion dictated that skirts grow much wider, Lily wondered whether she would be able to negotiate the passageways on the *Hattie Belle.*

"Look at this receipt for royal crumpets." Mrs. Thornton pointed to the next page. "They sound so dainty and scrumptious. I wonder if you could make those to serve with tea for passengers on your boat."

Lily glanced at the list of ingredients. "I have no idea. We rely on Jensen to plan our meals. He has a wide knowledge of many dishes."

"I can copy it down for Jensen." Jasmine made the offer from her position on a footstool in front of the sofa.

Camellia frowned at her younger sister. "I don't see why you should bother. We never have formal meals on the boat."

Lily shook her head. "That may have to change since we'll be taking on passengers for our next voyage." Blake had informed her last night that several people had inquired about passage. At least one thing was progressing as planned. Not like the repairs, which seemed to be taking forever.

"Can we have parties on the boat, too?"

Camellia's question turned Lily's mind from her unpleasant thoughts. "I don't know." Lily smiled to soften her words. "We'll probably be very busy preparing food and helping Tamar keep everything clean."

Jasmine, who had looked up at Camellia's question, made a face and went back to copying the receipt.

"I declare. You are the most glum group of ladies I have ever been around." Sarah jumped up and struck a pose. "I have it!"

Camellia focused on the animated young woman. "What do you have?"

"The answer." She clapped her hands. "We'll go shopping. No matter the problem, a little shopping always puts one in a better frame of mind."

Lily sighed and shook her head. "I don't think that's a good idea."

"Nonsense." Mrs. Thornton smiled at her daughter. "I agree with Sarah. The reason we are so melancholy is because we are surrounded by a river of mourning attire."

"Mama, you are a genius!" Sarah returned to the sofa and flipped the pages to a style they had all found attractive. "We will have this dress made in dove gray for Lily."

Lily shook her head. "It's too soon."

"Grandfather has been dead forever." Camellia drew out the last word to emphasize it.

"Look at this one, Camellia." Sarah pointed out another fashion plate. "If we choose a muted blue, it would be perfect for you to wear to my ball."

"But—"

Lily's words were cut off as Jasmine interrupted. "Which dress can I have?"

Sarah put a finger on her chin and tilted her head. "Lavender is the perfect color for you, little one. But it must be a simpler design."

Lily was relieved when Sarah pointed out a dress appropriate for a young lady instead of another debutante dress. Jasmine didn't even pout when she saw it.

The idea of spending money on three dresses made Lily feel a bit faint, but she could not ignore the hopeful look on her sisters' faces. Still, she had to try one more time to make them see reason. "We have no need for new dresses."

"*Mais oui.*" Sarah frowned at her mother. "Did you not tell them of my party on Saturday?"

Mrs. Thornton shook her head. "I thought I would need your support to convince Lily that she and Camellia should attend."

"Impossible." Lily's gaze shifted from mother to daughter. "We cannot afford such an extravagance."

"Jesus said nothing is impossible for those who have faith." Sarah crossed her arms.

Sarah's reference to scripture reminded Lily how often she had ignored her Bible of late. Her glance met the beseeching looks from both Camellia and Jasmine. She had a duty to provide shelter and sustenance for them. She squirmed in her seat. Was she providing them the spiritual guidance they needed? *Lord, forgive me. Show me how to be a better model for Camellia and Jasmine. Help me teach them Your ways.*

"Lily, you and your sisters are as dear to me as. my own children." Mrs. Thornton reached for Lily's hand. "It would be a kindness if you would let me pay for these dresses."

"I couldn't—"

"Please, Lily." Camellia's blue eyes were bright with unshed tears. "I would love to have a new dress."

How could she resist? Lily squeezed Mrs. Thornton's hand. "I suppose I could accept a loan."

"Perfect!" Sarah clapped her hands. "Let's go right now before Lily changes her mind."

Although she still wasn't sure it was a good idea, Lily let herself be swept up by the combined efforts of her sisters, Sarah, and Mrs. Thornton. Soon all five of them were crowded into the carriage, headed for the fabled shops on Canal Street.

Jean Luc slapped at an insect buzzing around his head. They seemed to be everywhere these days. Some said they were the carriers of disease, but while he found them irritating, he could not believe they were the reason for sickness. He never got sick. Avoiding the night air made more sense to him. Evil deeds and evil-minded people used darkness as a cover. Why not illness as well?

Plucking a bloom from the flower arrangement in the foyer, he tucked it into the lapel of his coat. He'd told his mother he was going to town. Anything to get away from the oppressive, disappointed glances she still directed at him. Would he never live down his mistake?

Jean Luc mounted his horse and headed to town, passing cotton fields being worked by dozens of slaves. They were planting seed, a job he did not envy as it required hour after backbreaking hour laboring in the sweltering heat. Papa had mentioned something about purchasing a few extra slaves before harvest. Jean Luc shuddered. He didn't like going to the slave market. It was foul smelling and filthy. No place for a gentleman to spend time.

Not like his current destination—his tailor. He was in need of a new dress coat and several shirts. The streets were crowded. Farmers with loaded wagons of fresh-picked melons and peaches trundled past immigrants in rough-spun work clothes. Fashionable ladies in bright-colored finery hung on the arms of their dark-coated escorts, eager to purchase everything from hats to shoes. Street vendors hawked fruit, vegetables, and meat pies.

Jean Luc wove his horse back and forth down the street, his teeth clenching as his progress was repeatedly halted. When he finally reached the storefront of Preston and Sons, Jean Luc dismounted with a relieved sigh and tied his horse to the hitching rail. Before he could enter the establishment, however, he was stopped by someone calling his name.

"I'm so glad to find you, Mr. Champney."

Jean Luc turned to see Lars Steenberg. "Is *Hattie Belle* back from New Orleans?" He shaded his eyes and looked toward the river.

Steenberg shuffled his feet. "No, sir. We ran into a bit of trouble."

Dread filled Jean Luc. "Is she sunk?" Most steamships did not last long. They either ran up on a snag and tore a hole in the keel, or the boiler exploded and set the deck on fire. If nature was not dangerous enough, pirates often lurked along the shore and attacked vulnerable boats. A paddle wheeler with a gaggle of females would fit that description pretty well.

"No, she made it to New Orleans."

"Then why isn't she here? And why are you here without her?"

Steenberg shrugged. "We ran aground north of the city and had to be pulled free."

"You what!" Jean Luc was horrified. "Didn't those idiots know not to travel in the dark? Were they in such a hurry to reach port that they risked my boat?"

"Not exactly. It was daylight."

Jean Luc stared at the older man. "Who was captaining the boat when it happened?"

"I was." Steenberg glanced at him, his expression rebellious. "You said you didn't want Lily Anderson to succeed."

"I didn't mean for you to put the *Hattie Belle* at risk." Noticing his angry tones had attracted the attention of some passersby, Jean Luc lowered his voice. "I only wanted you to keep an eye on things and report back. I didn't want you to sink the boat. If the *Hattie Belle* is lost, I won't have any chance to prove myself to my father."

"She's holed up for repairs, but they'll probably be sailing her back to Natchez in a few days."

"How bad was the damage?"

"Not too bad." The other man shrugged. "A little problem with the paddle wheel and a bit of shattered glass. Probably be as good as new."

"You'd better hope that's true." Jean Luc leaned closer to the captain. "Because if she's not, I'm holding you responsible."

Steenberg cringed. "I can't help it if they don't get her repaired proper."

"She wouldn't have to be repaired if not for your idiocy." Jean Luc started to turn on his heel, but a thought occurred to him. "Do you want to make it up to me?"

"Yes, sir. They let me go, and there's not many boats needing captains." His eyes shifted to the left. "I'd be glad to work for you."

Jean Luc nodded. "Then you watch for my boat to get back in, and let me know the minute it appears around Dead Man's Bend. I want to be on the docks waiting to greet Miss Anderson before her dainty foot touches dry land." He jangled the coins in his pocket. Pulling out a handful, he selected one and tossed it in the air.

"Yes, sir. Thank you, sir." Steenberg caught the coin before it hit the ground. "I'll be on the lookout, Mr. Champney."

"Good, because if you fail me this time, it will be your last." Jean Luc walked away, certain the man had gotten the point.

Now he needed to concentrate on the business at hand. If he was going to convince Lily to allow him to take over the management of the *Hattie Belle*, he needed to look his best.

Chapter Twenty-nine

Conflicting desires pulled at Tamar. She could barely concentrate on getting the two older girls ready for the ball because of wondering whether Jensen would come to visit while the others were out dancing. He'd come to the Thorntons' home several times over the past week, but that didn't mean he would come tonight, not after she'd told him to leave her alone.

She regretted her words even if they were sensible. He was too nice a man to get tangled up with the likes of her. She would be happy if he didn't come, wouldn't she?

The answer was simple. She wouldn't be happy at all. There were so many reasons to push him away. A thousand obstacles stood between her and Jensen, not the least of which was that she had no right to marry. She was too old, too plain, too dark, and too sensible to listen to his suggestions.

"I think you've pulled my corset too tight." Lily reached back to tug on her hands.

Tamar released some of the pressure on the laces. "I'm sorry. I don't know where my mind is tonight."

"I wish I could go." Jasmine sat pouting in a corner of the girls' bedroom. "I'm going to be all alone."

"No, you won't." Camellia stood in front of the mirror, admiring her new blue gown. "David and Tamar will be here."

"I'm practically grown up." The whine in Jasmine's voice contradicted her words. "Besides, you and Lily can't dance. You're still in mourning."

Tamar knew her girls well enough to know that Camellia would probably be on the dance floor before the beginning of the second song. Here in New Orleans no one knew about her grandfather's death, so she would see no reason to deny herself. Lily would probably remain seated with the matrons and old maids, content to watch the younger girls dip and swirl in the arms of their suitors. If she didn't watch out, she would find herself alone as her sisters married and began families.

"I hope both of your sisters will dance, Miss Jasmine." She reached for the hooped crinoline that would make Lily's skirt stand out in a bell shape. "I'm sure your grandfather wouldn't disapprove. He'd like to see his girls having a wonderful evening."

Jasmine crossed her hands over her chest. "I'm not so sure about that. He'll probably be upset to see me staying here with you and David."

"Don't be so anxious to grow up, Jasmine." Lily stood still while Tamar lifted her new skirt over her head and settled it around her waist. "You need to learn the trick of finding enjoyment no matter your age, or you'll always be so busy looking ahead that you'll miss a lot of grand adventures."

"But you and Camellia are wearing your new clothes. Why did you get a dress for me if I can't wear it?"

Tamar frowned at Jasmine. "You'll wear it tomorrow when you go to church."

Jasmine turned her face to the window.

Tamar tweaked the gray material of Lily's skirt, making sure every fold was perfect. Not many women could wear this color without looking like they were ready for a grave marker, but the soft color reflected on Lily's face, muting the line of her stubborn chin and bringing a special glow into her sweet brown eyes. She looked as young and fresh as Camellia, who came to stand next to her. Seeing them made Tamar feel old and worn out, like a well-used rag.

Camellia's golden curls were fastened on top of her head with three white camellia blossoms. A matching blossom was pinned to the front of her bodice, its delicate bloom standing out against the dark moiré silk of her gown. Her milky-white skin also contrasted against the material, glowing in the candlelight. She was sure to be sought after by all the young men at the ball.

Smothering the desire to wear something flattering instead of her shapeless brown gown, Tamar concentrated on her charges—collecting fans, smoothing gloves, and settling cotton lace shawls around their shoulders. She had no reason for the tears that sprang to her eyes as the two young ladies left the bedroom. Wishing for the impossible only made a body miserable. She was going to have to spend extra time on her knees this evening, asking God to root out the envy in her heart. She needed to concentrate on the blessing of having kind owners and a chance to see something of the world beyond the boundaries of Natchez and Les Fleurs plantation.

As soon as the bedroom was straightened up, Tamar went down the back stairs toward the kitchen, which was separated from the main house by a courtyard. She tarried in the cooler air, her fingers trailing across the wide leaves of a palm tree. Her gaze went to the sky, wonder filling her as she gazed at thousands of stars and the bright round globe of the moon.

" 'Tis a lovely evening."

She jerked in surprise. Her gaze traveled around the courtyard, searching for the person who'd spoken. "Jensen." She recognized his voice, of course. It was the voice that entered her dreams, whispering of things she shouldn't consider. Tempting her to reach out for a future that didn't belong to her.

He stepped from the far corner of the courtyard, nearest the stable. "Stay a moment and talk to me."

"I told you yesterday we don't have a thing to talk about."

"Of course we do, only you don't want to listen." Jensen moved closer.

Tamar's heart beat so hard she thought he could probably hear it. She knew she should turn her back on him, but her legs wouldn't move. "I'm listening." Was that her trembling voice?

He reached out slowly, his hand traveling toward her face. Tamar's breath caught, and her heart stopped beating altogether. His fingers gently smoothed her hair against her temple where it had escaped her cap. They left a trail of fire in their wake. She felt like she might die right there, right then. Then his whole hand cupped her cheek, warm and a little rough. She couldn't speak, couldn't step back, couldn't do anything but look into his eyes. What she saw made her knees shake. Fierce emotion burned inside this man. But rather than frighten her, it kindled a flame inside of her.

His lids drooped and the corners of his mouth turned up. "I want to steal a kiss from you, Tamar. I want it more than I want to draw my next breath." He moved even closer, his shoulders blocking out the rest of the world. "Please say yes."

Tamar lifted her hands. She had to put a stop to this now or be lost forever. "No." Forming fists with her hands, she pushed at his chest.

Pain entered his face as though she had struck him, but Jensen moved back. She felt like she had thrust a knife into the man's heart. Or was it her own heart she had wounded? Tamar wasn't sure. She wasn't sure of anything except that she needed distance from the feelings Jensen stirred in her.

With a sound of equal parts pain, fear, and frustration, Tamar ran to the kitchen. She jerked open the heavy wooden door and slipped inside. Slamming the door behind her, she leaned against it and gasped for breath. The other slaves looked up in surprise but didn't ask any questions. That was a good thing. She had no answers.

The Cartiers lived in a huge mansion in Lafayette Square, several miles south of the Thorntons' town house. Lily enjoyed the carriage ride but wished Blake and Mr. Thornton could have joined them inside instead of riding alongside on horseback. But she and Camellia could barely fit their skirts on one bench of the carriage, so wide were their crinolines, and Mrs. Thornton had instructed the men to take horses rather than crowd them.

"Don't leave the ballroom with any strangers, Camellia." Lily had a list of instructions for her sister. "Don't eat too much at the midnight supper. Don't accept any invitations to dance; we are still in mourning. Keep your fan attached to your wrist or you will lose it."

Mrs. Thornton leaned forward and patted her wrist. "It will be all right, Lily. Don't be so worried. Your sister is a sensible young lady."

"I know, but—"

"You're giving me a headache." Camellia touched her gloved hand to her forehead.

Lily sat back with a sigh. "Then perhaps we should turn the carriage around and go home."

"No!" Both Camellia and Mrs. Thornton chorused their disagreement.

"This is my very first ball, Lily. Please don't take away my pleasure."

"I know the feelings you're experiencing, Lily, my dear." Mrs. Thornton's voice hinted at amusement. "I felt the same way the first time I took Sarah to a party. But don't worry. We will all look out for Camellia. As to dancing, I don't see the harm since this is a family party. No one here knows you. They will assume you are my family, and they'll be confused if I am not also in mourning."

Lily found it difficult to argue with Mrs. Thornton's pragmatic view. Besides, this was Camellia's first dance. It should be a memory to treasure. If Camellia had to sit on the wall next to her sister and the other old maids, she would not enjoy herself very much. Pinning a smile on her face to cover her misgivings, Lily turned to Camellia. "If you promise to be circumspect—"

Camellia reached past the material of their skirts and hugged Lily close. "I promise to do whatever you say. I won't lose my fan or my gloves. I won't leave the ballroom with anyone, male or female. And I promise not to eat too much at supper."

Lily returned her embrace and sent a prayer heavenward that she was making the right decision.

The carriage stopped, and they disembarked. Mr. Thornton offered his arm to his wife, while Blake escorted both Lily and Camellia up the shallow steps to the main entrance.

Dr. Cartier, a man some ten years older than Sarah, was fashionably dressed in white from chin to toe. He was much quieter than Sarah, but the love they felt for each other was obvious in the way their gazes locked and the little touches they managed to exchange while receiving their guests.

"Good evening, Mother, Father." Sarah was resplendent in a pale-yellow gown, her dark hair upswept and held in place with a diamond tiara. "I have a surprise for you."

She turned around and grabbed a young man who'd been lurking in the shadows. "Look who got into town this afternoon."

The first thing Lily noticed was the thatch of thick auburn hair on his head. Below that was a pair of eyes as green as grass. Something about him looked familiar, but she did not place him until Mrs. Thornton stepped forward with a glad cry.

"Jonah, why didn't you come to the house to tell your mother you had arrived safely?"

So this was the youngest Thornton child. She glanced at Mr. Thornton and realized why Jonah looked familiar. He was a younger version of his father.

"I'm sorry, Mother. Sarah wanted to surprise you." He hugged her close before turning to shake hands with his father. "I'm glad to see both of you looking so well. We have many things to talk about."

"Yes, yes." Sarah stepped between them. "But for tonight you are to forget all that and enjoy yourself."

He shrugged and turned back to the receiving line. He smiled at Lily as they were introduced, but he couldn't take his eyes off Camellia. She blushed and nodded when he asked for the first dance.

Lily's glance met Blake's, and they shared a moment. It was as if they didn't need words to communicate. Her little sister was going to be a big hit in New Orleans.

Lily and Camellia, followed by a grinning Blake, trailed the Thorntons into the crowded ballroom. Over the next half hour they were introduced to so many of New Orleans' elite that Lily soon lost count.

The musicians began playing, and couples started walking to the center of the room. Jonah came to claim Camellia for the promised dance. He was soon replaced by others, as many of the young men vied for her attention.

One or two of them turned to Lily as a second choice if Camellia was not available, but she refused them all, preferring her role as chaperone.

Between the crush of people and the candles all around the room, Lily grew rather warm and wished she could escape through some french doors that had been flung open in the hope of coaxing some of the cooler night air into the room. She was about to seek out a chair along the wall when a hand on her arm stopped her.

"Would you like to dance?" Blake's drawl in her ear made gooseflesh pop up along her arms.

Lily shook her head resolutely. "I'm here as a chaperone for Camellia. This is her evening to dance."

"It looks to me as though she's had no shortage of partners." Blake stepped in front of her. He looked every inch the gentleman. Her gaze wandered from the high points of his shirt collar to the intricate folds of his necktie. His broad shoulders were razor straight in his black frock coat, and his striped silk waistcoat, blood red in color, gleamed richly in the light of the Cartiers' ballroom.

Lily realized something in that instant. He was as much a gentleman as Jean Luc Champney. More handsome in some respects than the polished Mr. Champney, although perhaps not as well traveled.

That thought led to another. Where was Blake from? Had he grown up in the lap of luxury? He certainly looked comfortable in the trappings of the privileged. But he'd never spoken of his home or childhood. She'd never really thought about it. She knew absolutely nothing about her business partner beyond his current lifestyle.

Perhaps if she accepted his invitation she could ask him about his past. "I believe you are right, Mr. Matthews."

His smile rewarded her acquiescence. Blake held out a white-gloved hand, and she placed her own in it. As soon as they reached the edge of the dancers, he swept her into his arms and swung her into the rhythm of a waltz. "You look lovely this evening."

"I'm afraid I owe Mrs. Thornton a substantial portion of our money in payment for the new dresses we bought for Jasmine, Camellia, and me."

"The expenditure is well worth it."

Had he actually complimented her? What a novel feeling. Lily's hand tightened on his shoulder as she and Blake moved around the room. The other dancers disappeared from her consciousness until all that remained was the music and the look in his deep blue eyes. She felt as though she were floating away on a melody as seductive as the song of the river.

Forgotten were the questions about his background. Forgotten were the warnings she had given her sister. Lily allowed him to pull her a tiny bit closer until only inches separated them. Until his mouth was so close he could lean forward to brush his lips against hers.

Panic struck her. She pulled away to a more discreet distance, racking her brain for some subject to introduce. Anything to avoid falling under his hypnotic gaze again. "How is the work going on our boat?"

His smile widened, as though he knew the real reason for her question. "Don't fret, Lily. We should be able to leave no later than Tuesday or Wednesday."

"Have you found a captain yet?" She pursued the subject of business doggedly.

"I think I have."

Didn't he think she would want to know more about the man who would take them back to Natchez? "Tell me about him."

"I haven't quite decided which one to hire, but Mr. Thornton has sent me a couple of excellent candidates. As soon as I check out a few more things and make my final decision, you'll be able to meet him." He hesitated a moment. "But remember your promise. The man I choose will be the man we hire."

She stiffened. "I haven't forgotten."

"Good."

Blake executed two more intricate turns, each in the opposite direction, a move that had her head spinning. Lily had to focus on her feet to avoid tripping. She was so overbalanced that she hardly noticed when he swept her through one of the open french doors and out onto the veranda. The sound of the music faded, and his steps slowed, winding down until they were standing still.

Lily pulled away from him and turned to face the manicured lawn. She took two steps forward, standing next to the low wall that ran along the outside of the dimly lit area. He didn't follow her, and Lily was thankful he gave her time to catch her breath. She opened her fan and used it to cool her face. When she finally turned to face him, her breathing had returned to normal.

Blake was leaning against the wall next to the french doors, watching her like a panther stalking its prey.

Another sprinkle of gooseflesh erupted. Lily pulled her shawl over her arms to counteract the effect. "Where did you learn to dance like that?"

"Along the river."

She moved a step closer to him. "That's an evasive answer."

"Maybe I don't like it when curious women pry into my past."

"When have I ever pried?"

He pushed away from the wall. "I have to admit, you've managed to avoid it. . .up until tonight, that is."

Lily decided a softer approach was needed. "I don't know anything about you, Blake, except that you're a hard worker and a dependable partner. Oh, and that you like to play cards."

Blake looked over her shoulder at something in the distance. She began to think he wouldn't say anything at all, but then he cleared his throat. "I left home after a disagreement with my father, and I haven't been back since. It was tough making my way for the first couple of years. One of my earliest jobs was in Oakdale, a little town in Missouri. The owner of the Oakdale Inn hired me to muck out the stables, cut timber for firewood, and do whatever jobs he didn't want to do."

Blake stopped and sighed, his gaze refocusing on her face. "It was a friendly little town without much to do on long winter days once the river froze up. The innkeeper and his wife opened up their dining room a couple of times a week and invited the locals to come for a party. They'd charge everyone a nickel to attend, even the men who brought their instruments and played for the rest. We'd sing and dance and have a good time." He shrugged. "I may not know the right steps to every song, but I can move with the music."

Something about his attitude made Lily melt. Blake Matthews was vulnerable. Uncertain of his skills. She wanted to reassure him. In all their weeks of squabbling and bickering, he'd never seemed to be anything less than supremely sure of himself. Of course she'd had to mount her own defenses to keep him from riding roughshod over her principles. Had she missed other evidence of his real nature? She looked at him with new eyes. "You're an excellent dancer."

He smiled, a slow, dangerous smile that set her pulse jumping. What he might have said was lost as another couple walked out onto the veranda. It was probably a good thing.

Lily gathered her skirts and moved toward the french doors. "We should return to the ballroom. I really do need to keep an eye on Camellia." She rushed back into the ballroom without glancing back, even though she thought she heard him chuckling.

Blake didn't dance with anyone else that evening, nor did she. But Lily found herself wondering what might have happened if they had not been interrupted. And wondering if she was glad or sorry that it had not.

Chapter Thirty

$\mathcal{B}$lake awoke with a start and looked around at his unfamiliar surroundings. It took him a minute to remember he'd stayed in the Thorntons' *garçonièrre*, the apartment their sons used when in town, which boasted a separate entrance from the main town house. The opulence of this family made him wonder if Lily was right. Maybe they could make more money shipping goods than gambling.

He dressed in the change of clothes Jensen had insisted he bring. Smart man. He would have to tell him so when he returned to the *Hattie Belle*. He was eager to get some work done before the weather got too hot. A twinge of guilt reminded him his father would not approve of his working on the Sabbath. But he was no longer living under his father's roof. He could decide for himself what to do with his Sundays.

A knock on his door made Blake shake his head. So much for a quick exit.

"Are you awake, Mr. Matthews?" The voice belonged to Jonah Thornton, the young man he'd met at the ball.

He went to the door and wrenched it open. "Yes, I'm awake."

Jonah blinked at him. He wore more casual garb this morning, making him look younger than ever. "Good. Mother sent a note saying we are expected for breakfast."

Wishing he'd awakened half an hour earlier and made his escape, Blake nodded. "I'll be right down."

"We usually eat in the courtyard on Sundays." Jonah tossed this information over his shoulder as he clattered down the stairs. "Don't be late or you'll miss the croissants."

Blake grimaced as he combed his hair. How was he to avoid attending church with the Thorntons without raising a ruckus?

He was the last one to arrive for breakfast, and the only place left was between Jasmine and David. He greeted everyone as he slipped into the chair.

Lily was no longer dressed in the finery she had worn the evening before, but she looked lovely. Ethereal. She glanced his way and smiled. Her gesture warmed his belly. He could grow used to sharing breakfast in a family group like this one. If only his childhood home had been as warm, his life might have turned out very differently.

A basket of croissants occupied the center of the table. Next to it was a crock of butter and a large platter of scrambled eggs. He started to reach for the basket but halted when Lily shook her head at him.

Mr. Thornton had been reading a copy of the *Picayune*, but he folded it and set it next to his coffee cup. "Good morning. I trust you slept well, Mr. Matthews."

"Yes, sir."

"Excellent." Mr. Thornton bowed his head, and the others followed his lead. "Father God, we thank You for the bountiful food and many blessings You provide. Please keep us ever mindful of Your grace and help us to live more fruitful lives because of Your example. Amen."

David reached for the croissants, took one, and handed the basket to Blake, who followed suit and handed it off to Jasmine.

"It's wonderful to have you back with us, Jonah." Mrs. Thornton beamed at her son who sat next to Mr. Thornton. "I don't know when I've been more surprised than when you appeared at Sarah's party last night."

Jonah ducked his head. "Thank you."

Mr. Thornton stirred cream into his coffee. "Did you stop and visit with Eli on your way back down?"

"Yes."

Silence fell at the table as everyone waited to see if Jonah would add to his brief answer.

Lily's gaze clashed with Blake's. Did she want him to do something? What could he do short of kicking Jonah under the table?

She sighed and broke eye contact before turning to Mrs. Thornton. "Is Eli your oldest son?"

"Yes, he runs the Memphis branch of our business." Mrs. Thornton's eyelids fluttered as though she was holding back tears. "We don't get to see him and his wife, Renée, as much as we would like."

Their host cleared his throat. "I hope he's come to his senses and stopped spouting that abolitionist nonsense."

Blake could see Jonah's irritation in the reddening of his ears. He hoped they were not about to be treated to a family disagreement. Positions on abolition, slavery, and states' rights divided many families these days. The whole country, for that matter.

Mrs. Thornton stepped into the uneasy breach. "We correspond regularly, but I still miss them."

"They are fine, Mother. They send their love." Jonah's shoulders relaxed as he smiled at her.

Blake could feel the tension dissipating. Relieved, he glanced around the table, the hair on his arms rising when he caught the look of intense yearning on Camellia's face. Did she fancy herself smitten with young Thornton? Of course she did. He was not fawning over her as the other young men had done last night. A girl like Camellia would find his disinterest irresistible. Blake wanted to groan out loud. They didn't need any broken hearts on the *Hattie Belle*.

Galvanized by his thoughts, he pushed himself away from the table. The sooner they could get back on the river and put physical distance between Camellia and Jonah, the better for all of them. "Thank you for your hospitality, Mr. and Mrs. Thornton."

"Don't forget it's Sunday." Mrs. Thornton's voice stopped him from leaving. "We'll be meeting in the foyer as soon as everyone has a chance to put on their coats and hats."

"I'm afraid I won't be joining you." He looked away from Lily's shocked expression. "I need to get back to work on the *Hattie Belle*."

Lily got up and moved toward him, putting a hand on his arm. "Please come with us. You've been working too hard as it is. And you may find you have more energy after you spend your morning at church."

What was it about her eyes that made him want to agree with everything she suggested? Before he could summon the strength to turn her down, Camellia and Jasmine added their pleas. It was less trouble to give in.

He would go this one time. But as soon as the service was over, he would explain to Lily why he was so reluctant to darken the doorway of any church. She was a smart girl. She would understand once he explained it to her. And even if she didn't, he was determined to refuse the next time, no matter what tactic she used.

ॐ

"I hope you girls will like our preacher." Mrs. Thornton nodded to a lady in a puce dress and matching hat. "He is rather young, but what he lacks in age he makes up for in delivery."

"I'll say he does." Mr. Thornton winked at them. "Some of our female members have swooned when he gets caught up in his sermon."

"Father, don't tell them such things." Sarah walked over to them, resplendent in a gold-and-white-striped dress. A dainty matching fan dangled from her right hand. "If Pastor Nolan hears you, we'll be asked to leave the church."

Lily's smile widened at the look on Sarah's face. "It would be the church's loss."

"I concur." A well-dressed little man walked toward them. He had a gentle smile topped by a thin mustache, hazel eyes under thick brown eyebrows, and carefully combed hair that was several shades darker than Camellia's. "We couldn't bear to lose our most dedicated families, no matter their opinion of the preacher."

Sarah and her parents laughed easily.

The man bowed. "Silas Nolan, at your service."

"I'm sorry, Pastor Nolan." Mr. Thornton stepped forward, still chuckling. "Allow me to present our guests, Mr. Blake Matthews, Miss Lily Anderson, and her sisters, Camellia and Jasmine."

"It's a pleasure to meet you." His warm glance touched each of their faces. "And I promise to control my. . .energy. If the Holy Spirit allows, of course."

They all laughed at his self-deprecating humor. Lily liked him immediately. She turned to look at Blake and was surprised to see him looking so stiff. He was usually comfortable in any situation. Why should the friendly pastor disturb him so? Or was something else wrong? Was he hiding something from her about their boat? Had they run out of money? Had he not been able to find a captain?

The questions continued distracting her as the Thorntons and the

Cartiers introduced them to friends who had not been at the ball the previous evening. She tried to concentrate on remembering names and faces, but it was impossible with the nagging questions.

As they entered the church, Jasmine grabbed her hand. "Are you okay, Sissy?"

"Of course I am." Lily glanced around to see if anyone else was listening. "I'm sorry, Jasmine. I guess I'm a little distracted." She took a deep breath. Whatever might be wrong, she would find a way around it. For now she would concentrate on the present. She would enjoy the service and let God take care of the future.

The sanctuary was a large rectangle with two rows of pews that were mostly filled. Abraham, Noah and his ark, and Joseph in his coat of many colors were depicted in stained-glass windows on one side of the room. Jesus in various stages of His life from the cradle in Bethlehem to the Resurrection was the subject of the opposite windows.

Tints of blue, green, and red painted Blake's face as he walked stiff legged beside her. The feeling of unrest tried to grasp her once again until Lily directed her attention toward the large cross that hung on the paneled wall behind the pulpit. Peace settled on her shoulders as she slid onto a pew next to Camellia. A peace she'd almost forgotten, a peace she needed as much as she needed air to breathe.

The murmur of voices died away as the pastor strode down the aisle and bounded onto the dais in two quick steps. He led the congregation in several hymns, familiar songs that brought Lily a great deal of comfort, especially when she heard Jasmine's talented soprano and Camellia's softer contralto joining the others.

How blessed they were to have each other. She smiled toward her sisters and thanked God for keeping them together. No matter what the future held, Camellia and Jasmine would always know how much she loved them. As long as she was their sister, she would find a way to provide for them.

The pastor read to them from the sixty-eighth psalm, one of Lily's favorites. After the death of her mother and the desertion of her father, she had often turned to verse five. She traced the words in her Bible as he read them to the congregation: " 'A father of the fatherless, and a judge of the widows, is God in his holy habitation.' "

When the pastor spoke of singing praises to God and rejoicing in His presence, a desire welled up in her to set aside more time for the Lord than she had been doing lately. As Pastor Nolan began the closing prayer, she concentrated on praising God to the best of her ability. She would start as soon as they got back on the boat. She would organize a Bible study. It would be good for everyone on board—crew and passengers alike.

Feeling better about the future, she raised her head and gathered her things. It was so rewarding to attend church. She would make a point to be in port on Sundays as they continued traveling the river. It was the best way to fulfill her most sacred duty to her sisters and ensure they were rooted in the faith necessary to sustain them throughout their lives.

Chapter Thirty-one

Blake intended to make a quick exit as soon as they got back to the Thorntons' town house. He had endured enough for one day.

The sermon had been unnerving—especially the part about God being Father to the fatherless. He wasn't fatherless. But sometimes he thought that might be better than having a father who ignored the needs of his family. What about children who had to escape their fathers in order to thrive? If God condoned that type of fatherhood, he wanted no part of it.

Nor did he want any part of the discussion sure to come about how wonderful the pastor was and how inspiring his sermon had been. Eager to escape the cloying atmosphere, he tapped a foot as the others chatted together in the front yard of the church.

The sun was beginning to warm the air. Prickles of sweat trickled down his back, making him long for the deck of the *Hattie Belle*. Would their infernal talking never end? Blake's jaw was so tight it ached.

Finally Lily walked over to him. "Is something wrong?"

He rolled his eyes. "Nothing much."

A frown appeared on her brow. "Why am I not convinced?"

"I have no idea." He nodded toward the Thorntons. "How much longer do you think they'll be?"

She shrugged. "I don't know. Why? Do you have a pressing engagement?"

"Do you have to control every aspect of my life?" He kept his voice low to avoid drawing attention. "Can I not have some tiny corner of my life that is safe from your prying questions?"

Her face paled, and Blake wanted to kick himself. When had he become the kind of man who attacked women?

"I–I'm sorry, Blake. I didn't realize. . . ."

"No, I'm the one who's sorry." Reaching for her hand, he tucked it into the crook of his arm. "I'm hot and hungry, and I'm taking it out on you. It's not your fault."

Sorrowful brown eyes stared at him, looking into his very soul. "Apparently it is."

"No." He took a deep breath. "As soon as we get back to the house, I'll tell you about it. You and I have very different backgrounds. Perhaps it's time for us to sit down and talk. Maybe if I explain a little of my past, you'll understand better why we don't always see eye to eye."

"I'd like that very much." The color had returned to Lily's cheeks. She looked around for Camellia, Jasmine, and David. The Thorntons appeared to have finished their conversations. "Let's start back."

As they walked, Blake tried to organize his thoughts. He wanted Lily to understand enough to leave him alone about certain things. He didn't want to risk repeating this day. Nor did he want her nagging him about going to church. He was never going to be a churchgoing man. Once he explained why he was so reluctant to attend, he hoped she would acquiesce and leave him out of her religious nonsense. It wasn't too much to ask. He'd given way in so many things since they became business partners, surely she would yield once she knew the truth.

When they returned to the Thorntons' town house, Camellia, Jasmine, and David went to their rooms to change clothes before lunch, but Blake and Lily hung back, explaining that they had business to discuss.

"Business?" The lilt in Mrs. Thornton's voice made Blake want to groan. She was raising questions he'd rather avoid. He and Lily did not have any romantic feelings for each other, but if he protested, those in the foyer would begin to share her suspicions. The way Lily's cheeks reddened, they might anyway.

He raised one eyebrow. "Yes, the repairs are winding down, so we need to prepare for our voyage back to Natchez."

"I see." Mr. Thornton looked from his wife to Blake before shrugging and turning to the staircase. "We'll see you shortly."

Blake opened the parlor door and motioned for Lily to precede him.

She sat down on the sofa, removed her hat, and waited for him to begin.

Unable to sit, he swung his arms back and forth a few times. Where to start? "I told you I left home years ago, and I've never been back."

She nodded.

"What I didn't tell you is that my father is the reason I left." He hesitated. "My father, Reverend William Matthews."

Her eyes widened. "Your father is a minister?"

"Yes, that's right." He could hear the bitterness creeping into his voice. "And he's a cold, uncaring man who thinks the word *Christian* is a synonym for *tyrant*."

"I don't understand."

Blake considered what he should tell her. The back of his throat burned in reaction to the memories. How could he share such things with anyone, even Lily? "I don't want to drag you through all the sad occurrences from my childhood, but suffice it to say that my sister and I had to sacrifice every comfort for the sake of my father's religion."

"What did your mother say about your father's treatment?" Her voice was a blend of sympathy and caring.

Lily's question touched on another sore point. "Not much. She was a 'good Christian,' the perfect submissive wife as defined by Paul."

She said nothing, apparently digesting his statements. "Was there no one you could turn to? Grandparents? Cousins? People in the church?"

"None of our relatives lived close enough to know what was going on." He shoved his hands into his pants pockets. "As for the church, who wants to challenge a preacher? A man called by God to lead the flock? They must have felt it would be blasphemy. At any rate, no one crossed my father. No one but me, that is."

"Is that why you don't like going to church?"

Relieved at her quick understanding, he nodded. "I went this morning because it seemed so important to you, but I was not at all comfortable."

"I'm sorry for whatever pain your father caused you, but perhaps you should forgive him for his past deeds. To hold on to your bitterness only hurts you."

"You think I should forgive him?"

Her nod felt like a betrayal.

Would anyone stand up against his father other than himself? Could no one else understand what he and his sister had gone through? He turned from her, not wanting her to see how much her suggestion hurt him.

"You should not condemn all pastors or all churches because of your experiences." Her voice was gentle, but her words struck his heart with the explosive impact of a bullet.

Lily didn't understand what it had been like. Why was that? She was intelligent and caring. Why could she not understand the pain and anguish he'd been through?

Pushing back his pain and anger, Blake took a turn around the room. Perhaps logic would appeal to her. "I've been doing fine without going to church for all these years."

"You may think you're fine, but that's only because you believe you can rely on your own strength. It's not enough, you know."

He stopped pacing to look at her, his jaw slack. "What an odd opinion coming from one of the most self-reliant ladies I've ever met."

Her head dipped in acknowledgment. "I thank you for the compliment."

Blake wondered if it occurred to her that he might not have meant his statement as a compliment. Some men—most men—thought self-reliance was not necessary for a lady. Women were supposed to depend on the strength of their husbands, fathers, or brothers. Lily had none of those to rely on, but it didn't make much difference.

"You should know that God is the source for my strength."

"I see." He raised an eyebrow. "So that's why you spend every Sunday in church?"

A hint of color appeared in her cheeks. "Whenever possible. I know my sisters and I have not been as faithful in our Bible studies or prayer life as we should be, but we've been rather busy."

Heat began to rise in his chest. "So you should attend church and read your Bible only when it's convenient?"

"At least I don't spend my leisure time at gambling halls and cabarets."

How dare she judge him? "No, you spend your leisure time spending money on clothing and dragging your family and friends to parties. If you were truly moved by the Spirit, wouldn't you be spreading the Gospel instead?"

"I certainly am not perfect—"

"That's one thing we agree upon." He couldn't resist the chance to bait her. If he kept her on the defensive, she'd have no time to attack him.

Her chin wobbled. Was she going to cry?

Remorse overcame him. "I'm sorry, Lily. I was only teasing."

She turned her head. When she faced him again, her expression was composed. "At least I don't fidget and fuss the whole time I'm listening to a sermon."

"I agree that I'm not a good Christian, Lily. So why don't we leave it at that? All I'm asking is that you consider my feelings. Show me the courtesy of letting me decide how and where I spend my time."

"If the only reason for attending church was to sing hymns and listen to a sermon, I might be able to do that." She stood and crossed the room, stopping directly in front of him. "But the reason is to draw closer to the One who made you, the One who loves you, the One who wants you to turn your life over to Him."

She looked so lovely standing in the light from the parlor window, her gaze earnest. Something inside him wanted to agree with her. Then sanity returned. Lily didn't know what she was talking about. She'd been raised in the lap of luxury. Buying a boat was the action of a spoiled child who was determined to live her life in opposition to the wishes of her family.

Lily was typical of the type of women he usually steered clear of—the reformers who wanted to save the world. She would never understand how someone could twist religion to suit his own needs. She had never seen the harsh realities he had experienced. Not that he would wish that on anyone, but he wanted to get his point across to her. She needed to stop trying to reform him.

He steeled his heart. He had to put a barrier between them or she would never give him any peace. "You can dress it up any way you wish, Lily, but this is really just another attempt to direct my life."

She stepped back, a frown crossing her face.

Realizing he was finally getting through to her, Blake continued. "I've never met a woman who was so determined to control every action and thought of everyone around her. You may own fifty-one percent of our boat, but you don't own any part of my private life, and I'll thank you to stay out of it."

Blake left her standing there. He knew he had to get out of the room before he recanted every word he'd just said.

Chapter Thirty-two

Jasmine stuck out her tongue at Camellia, who promptly glared back.

"Please don't argue. We don't have time for it." Lily folded her nightclothes and placed them in the trunk. She had allowed the younger girls and David to sleep while Tamar helped her dress. After making sure Camellia was packed, they made short work of getting David and Jasmine ready for their departure, which was slated for noon.

Blake had sent a note the evening before, the only contact she'd had from him since their argument two days earlier. The message had been brief and businesslike.

> *We have four first-class passengers, eight deck passengers, two new crewmen, and a captain. Will leave dock at noon sharp.*

He hadn't signed the note, apparently in too much of a hurry to waste time with niceties.

"I don't want to go." Camellia's steps dragged as they descended the staircase. "Can't I stay with the Thorntons?"

"Of course not." Lily frowned at her. "We're sisters. We belong together until the day you fall in love and get married."

Camellia made a face and continued her slow progress toward the dining room. Jasmine seemed more eager to face the day's adventures.

She bounded down the stairs like a rubber ball. By the time Camellia and Lily made it to the breakfast table, Jasmine was already seated and had filled her plate with preserves and a flaky croissant.

"I cannot believe it's your final morning with me." Mrs. Thornton offered a sad little smile. "I'm going to miss all the energy and excitement you've brought to our home."

"Yes, we will." Mr. Thornton folded his newspaper and reached for his coffee.

"I could—"

"We'll miss you, too." Lily interrupted Camellia's statement, kicking her under the table in warning.

Camellia sent her an injured look but subsided.

The rest of their breakfast was uneventful. David joined them, as did Jonah. When they had eaten their fill, Mr. and Mrs. Thornton called for their carriage.

David rode up front next to the driver. Lily and her sisters settled on the comfortable seats inside the carriage and waved at their hosts until they could no longer see them.

"Where is Tamar?" Jasmine asked.

"She went ahead with our trunks and some food the Thorntons sent." Lily's explanation eased the concern on her youngest sister's face.

Camellia slumped back against the velvet carriage cushions. "I wish we didn't always have to leave."

"Would you rather stay here without me and Jasmine?"

Camellia shrugged. "You could stay, too. Mrs. Thornton said she wished we would."

"She is a dear friend, Camellia, but she is not our mother. We cannot impose on her."

Lily tried to keep the hurt out of her voice. She knew the desire to accept Mrs. Thornton's unconditional love, to revel in the warmth of their home. But it wasn't the *Hattie Belle*. It wasn't home.

Blake's accusation came to the forefront of her memory, and she lifted her chin. She wasn't determined to control everything and everyone. She just wanted her sisters to be happy.

When they arrived at the boat, pleasure filled Lily's heart at the sight of white decks, black smokestacks, and the red-edged paddle wheel. The mighty river rushed beneath their feet as they crossed the gangplank.

Lily wondered where Blake was. She dreaded seeing him, but there was no way around it. They were partners and likely to remain together for quite some time.

David, Jasmine, and Camellia went inside, but Lily lingered on the first-floor deck. She wanted to see the repairs, check for herself that everything was shipshape.

Smiling a little at the pun, she heard footsteps on the deck above her and looked up to see Tamar and Jensen strolling together. Deep in conversation, they didn't see her. Lily was about to greet them when Jensen leaned forward and brushed a finger across Tamar's cheek. Was a romance blooming between them? Was Tamar falling in love? How wonderful that would be. The two of them could be married on the *Hattie Belle*. They would have a pastor come aboard and perform the ceremony. She couldn't think of a more beautiful setting.

Smiling, Lily crept away to give them privacy. She was about to search for Blake when she heard his voice coming from the boiler room. Following the sound, she discovered him talking to someone, probably a new crewman. He wore a red shirt reminiscent of the clothing captains used to wear in the wild days when flatboats and canoes were the only vessels on the Mississippi. Her father had often talked of the red shirts, the larger-than-life characters who carved out livelihoods before steam-powered engines made them obsolete.

Pushing away the memory, she bent her lips into a welcoming smile. "Good morning, gentlemen."

Blake jerked as though he'd been shot and turned toward her. Circles darkened the skin under his blue eyes. "Hello, Lily." He looked tired, and she got an impression of vulnerability.

A gasp from the other man drew her attention. She looked toward the stranger and noticed his face had gone pale. Was he ill? She took a step forward, ready to catch him if he fell over. "Are you all right, sir?"

His mouth opened and closed twice before he managed to make a sound. "Water Lily? Is it really you?"

She gasped and grew faint. "Father?" The two syllables spun out from her mouth for what seemed forever. To stop herself from fainting, Lily took several deep breaths. Then she balled her hands into fists and turned back to Blake. "What have you done?"

Blake looked from Lily to the man he'd recently hired. "What's going on here?"

"I can't believe you did this," Lily hissed. Her brown eyes blazed.

"Calm down, Water Lily." The captain held up both hands. "You don't have to fly off the handle. We'll figure everything out."

"Don't you call me that." She pointed a finger at Captain Henrick. "You may be my father, but you don't have any right to call me that."

Realizing he needed to defuse the situation before something went terribly wrong, Blake stepped between Lily and the older man. "I don't understand. I thought your father was dead. Didn't you tell me you and your sisters were orphans?"

His words seemed to hit her like a bucket of cold water. The fiery sparks in her eyes dimmed. Her cheeks reddened. She seemed unable to look at him. Her gaze focused on the floor. "It doesn't matter what you thought. I won't allow him to remain on board for another minute."

"Oh no, you don't. We have an agreement. I spent a great deal of time and energy finding someone we can depend on. Captain Henrick is the best of the lot. No matter what you say, he's taking us to Natchez."

Lily shook her head. Her face hardened into a look of belligerence. Blake wondered if he'd ever met a more stubborn woman.

"I can leave." The quiet voice reminded Blake that he and Lily were not alone.

"You stay put." He didn't bother to look at the man. The real problem was the persnickety, demanding, unforgiving woman in front of him. "I don't care if he's the first cousin of President Buchanan, he's staying on this boat."

When she looked back up at him, fire had returned to her brown eyes. "This is the man who deserted me and my sisters. We couldn't depend on him then, and we can't depend on him now. If you think we had a bad captain before, I can't wait to see your reaction when he jumps ship because a better offer has come along. And then we won't see him for another decade."

"I don't want to cause trouble, Wa—Lily." The captain pushed his way past Blake's shoulder. "I didn't realize this was your boat when I agreed to take over. I can understand your reluctance to have me here."

Lily crossed her arms over her chest and raised her chin.

Before she could reiterate her position, Blake needed to point out a few things to his business partner. "If he leaves now, we won't have anyone to take us to Natchez. Our paying customers are going to demand a refund so they can purchase tickets on a boat that will leave the dock as advertised. Be reasonable, Lily. There's not much chance he's going to desert us between here and Natchez."

"Camellia and Jasmine think he's dead." She talked past her father as if he wasn't there.

It was the one argument he could understand—the desire to protect her siblings. But there might be a way around this problem. "We don't have to tell them the truth."

He could see the family resemblance in their identical stares of disbelief, even though Lily's features were much softer than those of her father.

"Don't you think someone will notice that we have the same last name?" The question came from Lily. "Or do you think no one will ask who the captain is?"

Blake snapped his fingers. The solution was easy. "We'll introduce him by the name he gave me, Captain Henrick. No one will ever connect the two of you."

A look of yearning filled the older man's eyes as he listened to their conversation.

Lily's chin lifted another notch as she considered Blake's suggestion. She turned to her father. "Do you promise you'll not tell Camellia and Jasmine who you really are?"

Captain Henrick nodded, his expression grave. "I promise."

Uncrossing her arms, Lily sighed. "I suppose you can stay then, but only until we find a suitable replacement."

"Thank you. Thank you so much." Captain Henrick brushed his eye with one hand. "I promise you won't regret it. I'll make sure you and your sisters get to Natchez safely."

Lily sniffed and turned on her heel. "If I find you've broken your promise, I'll throw you overboard myself."

Her threat seemed to linger in the small room. Blake started to apologize for Lily's acerbic words, but then he saw the wide smile on her father's face. Was the man actually proud of his daughter's reaction? He could not imagine how his own father would have reacted in a similar situation. Given a choice, he'd take Lily's father any day.

Chapter Thirty-three

Jensen surprised them all by bringing a milk cow to the boat right before they cast off. Their new captain and crew built a small corral, filling it with hay and a bucket of water for the placid animal. His idea was to offer fresh milk to their first-class passengers since one of the most common complaints about riverboat travel was the lack of fresh dairy.

Tamar thought the idea inspired, but someone had to milk the cow, and they had to use the milk and cream before it curdled. So before the sun was up the next day, she searched out two buckets, one of which she scrubbed thoroughly. Fog swirled around her feet as she headed toward the corral with a bucket in each hand—one to sit on, the clean one to hold milk.

Others were moving about the boat already, stoking the boilers and releasing the vessel from its overnight mooring. The girls would be up soon, too, and she wanted to be back in the galley making biscuits and frying sausage for the passengers in the dining room.

"Good morning."

The unexpected voice behind her startled Tamar. Squinting, she looked back over her shoulder. Lily stood at the foot of the staircase. "Good morning to you, too."

"You already look busy."

"No sense wasting time." Years of rising early and working hard in

Les Fleurs plantation had made it second nature to her. "I'm going to milk our new cow."

"Are you sure you don't want me to do that?"

A laugh escaped Tamar. "I doubt you know how."

"You're right." Lily sighed. "But I'm sure I could learn."

"Why don't you watch me? Then you can try after a bit." Tamar held back the wire fence for both of them to enter the corral. "The cow will have to be milked every day, or she'll stop giving milk."

Lily's nose wrinkled. "The smell out here is rather strong. I'm not sure it was a good idea to bring that animal on board."

"She'll be nice to have for milk."

"That's true. Especially now that we've taken on passengers. Not many of the steamboats offer fresh milk for drinking and cream to put on biscuits and desserts."

Tamar sat on the upturned bucket. She placed the clean bucket under the cow's udder. "You have to get a good hold up here and then you press and pull as you move your hand down." She demonstrated the proper movements, gratified at the sound of milk hitting the bottom of the bucket.

After a few minutes, she traded places with Lily, laughing at the face her charge was making. It took several tries, but finally Lily managed to get some milk into the bucket. She turned and grinned, her pride evident.

The cow continued munching on hay, unconcerned with the efforts of the two women.

Tamar pulled a cloth from the pocket of her skirt and reached for the bucket as the liquid nearly topped its edges. "That's enough for one day. You did very well."

Lily stood up and reached for the second bucket. "Thanks. You're a good teacher."

Tamar held out one arm to balance herself as they walked toward the galley. The riverbank sliding past was green and beautiful. Who would have thought she'd like living on a boat?

Lily's voice drew her away from her daydreaming. "Tamar, can I ask you a personal question?"

"Of course."

"Are you falling in love with Jensen?"

The question was like one of those hidden snags in the river—

appearing without warning and threatening the peace of every-one around. Her thoughts ran in circles. Why did the galley seem so far away? She picked up her pace. "Why do you ask?"

Lily kept pace with her. "I saw the two of you talking yesterday when we got to the boat. You seemed. . .taken."

"Don't go getting any silly ideas. Mr. Jensen is a good man."

"Yes, he is. I think the two of you would make a wonderful couple."

Tamar wished Lily would drop this subject. She didn't want to examine her feelings for Jensen. "You don't know what you're talking about, Lily."

Lily halted, her face showing her surprise at Tamar's harsh tone.

Tamar plunked the bucket of milk down and put her hands on her hips. "I'm sorry, Miss Lily."

"No, I'm the one who's sorry." Lily no longer looked like the self-confident owner of a successful business; instead she looked like the little girl she'd once been—a little girl who needed someone to hold her. "It's none of my business."

Tamar sighed. "I didn't mean to be so abrupt. There's just some things you can't understand." Some things that were better left alone.

The vulnerability in Lily's expression changed to confusion. "Why not?"

How could she explain? The answer was simple. She couldn't. "You may be a woman, but that doesn't mean you're mature enough to understand everything about how the world works."

Lily turned toward the bank.

Tamar started to put a comforting hand around her shoulders but decided they would both be better off if she ended this conversation now. So she picked up her bucket and continued toward the galley, her head shaking as she considered the difference in Lily's and her own life.

How could a girl born to luxury and freedom ever understand the problems of a slave? As much as she loved Lily and knew she was loved by her, Tamar could see the unbridgeable gulf between them. Almost as wide a gulf as the one between her and Jensen.

❧

Lily held her breath as Camellia served the tea for the guests who'd gathered in the ladies' parlor. It wasn't that her sister was unpracticed at pouring tea, but doing so on board a boat that was likely to rock to one side or the other without notice could challenge the most experienced lady.

"I don't know how you do it."

Turning to the tall, spare woman next to her, Lily summoned a smile. "What is that, Mrs. Carlyle?"

"How a young thing like you can manage a large boat like this."

She glanced around the cozy room, furnished with three sofas and a scattering of Queen Anne chairs Sarah had donated, insisting they were gathering dust in her attic. Then she turned to the lady who reminded her rather forcefully of Aunt Dahlia. She'd spent most of the evening before arguing with the crew and other passengers and complaining about the rustic accommodations. Lily wondered if she would ever make the woman happy. *God loves her, too.*

The words in Lily's heart shamed her. She breathed slowly and widened her smile with an effort. "It's quite similar to running a household. Most everyone knows what must be done, and they don't need much more than my encouragement and an occasional pat on the back to keep things on an even keel. And you must remember that Mr. Matthews is my partner. I rely on him greatly, of course."

The words hardly stuck in her throat. She did owe Blake a lot. He had been essential in repairing the boat and finding passengers such as Mrs. Carlyle while she and her sisters shopped and socialized with the Thornton family. If only he had not hired her father.

The conversation turned general, and Lily's gaze wandered toward the other occupants of the room. Mrs. Abernathy, a kindly woman with iron-gray hair and deep-set brown eyes, traveled with her daughter, Karen. Karen was a dark-haired, younger version of her mother.

Lily sipped her tea and nibbled at one of the royal crumpets Jensen, David, and Jasmine had baked earlier this morning. They were an elegant addition to their tea service. She needed to remember to tell all three of them what a success their creation was. It looked a little like a pancake topped with a sprinkling of blackberry preserves and sifted sugar. Even Mrs. Carlyle seemed to be enjoying them.

Camellia engaged Miss Abernathy in a discussion of the latest fashions while Mrs. Carlyle and Mrs. Abernathy talked about the exorbitant price of fabric and the rising cost of most goods.

Given a moment to herself, Lily's thoughts returned to her business partner. She had not sought Blake out after their argument, preferring to concentrate on the welfare of the passengers while he oversaw the crew. It was a workable solution that seemed beneficial for all. Except that every time their paths crossed, she prayed for him to acknowledge her, smile at her, even argue with her. But he didn't. He simply nodded and moved away, apparently unwilling to heal the breach between them. Perhaps if she sought him out and apologized. . . But she couldn't. Not while her father was on board the *Hattie Belle.*

"Please excuse me, ladies." Lily could no longer sit in the parlor. She had to be up and doing something. "I need to check on my youngest sister, but I'll leave you in Camellia's capable hands."

Mrs. Carlyle frowned even as Mrs. Abernathy gave her an encouraging wink. "It must be quite a job keeping up with that young lady."

Nodding her head, Lily made her escape. She walked out onto the second-floor deck and stood at the rail, her gaze taking in the dense forest lining the banks of the muddy river. She ought to be checking the galley to make sure Jensen and Tamar didn't need any help, but after the disturbing conversation with Tamar this morning, she hesitated to interrupt them.

What had Tamar meant? She was no longer a child. Tamar had to have been talking about her status as a slave. But didn't she know Lily considered her an equal? Didn't she have the same freedoms as everyone else aboard the *Hattie Belle?* She worked hard, it was true, but so did the rest of them. Even Jasmine and David had chores.

Lily felt battered by the emotional upheavals of the past few days. She wished she had someone she could talk to, someone who would be on her side no matter what. But that was impossible. Seeing her father again after all these years had reminded her of one thing: no one was dependable. No one could be relied on. She had only herself.

It was all too much. More than she could bear. Then something touched her, light as the breeze, quiet as a whisper. Almost a voice, a reassurance. And she knew there was another she could count on: God. He was her eternal Father. Even if everyone else walked out of her life or this great wide river dried up to a bare trickle—no matter what happened, God would never desert her.

Tears burned her eyes. How could she have forgotten Him even for an instant? God was the only constant. He was the beginning of everything. Yet He was concerned about her. The words of the New

Orleans pastor came back to her. She should rejoice in the Lord. He was her Father, her Lord. He had made her, and He was always ready to embrace her.

Lily didn't know how long she stood watching the bank slip by, but when she turned to go, she felt much better. She would be able to handle whatever lay ahead as long as she depended on God to lead her.

She still wished her earthly father wasn't so close to hand, but she didn't see any way around that until they made landfall in Natchez. Wondering how soon that might be, she headed up to the hurricane deck to ask Captain Henrick. At least she could make use of the man's experience.

"That snag up yonder is what we call a sawyer." The voice she remembered so clearly from childhood wafted across the upper deck as she made her way to the pilothouse.

"I see." Was that Jasmine's excited voice? "Because it looks like a saw going back and forth."

"That's right. You sure are a bright young lady. You remind me of my own little girls—"

"That's enough." Lily raised her voice enough to cut off his words. "Jasmine, you have some reading to do in your room."

The child groaned. "Please don't make me go inside, Lily. I'm learning all about the river from Captain Henrick."

"It's an awful pretty day for a young'un to be cooped up inside."

Lily frowned. "I suppose you're an expert on parenting."

A look of pain deepened the lines on her father's weathered face. Her anger dissipated, but Lily reminded herself that she had good reason to keep this man separated from her sisters. She didn't want them to be hurt as she'd been all those years ago. They didn't deserve that kind of pain. No one did.

Jasmine slid past her without another word.

Lily waited until her sister's dark head had disappeared before turning her gaze back to the captain. "I don't know what you think gives you the right to embroil my innocent little sister in your schemes."

"I am not scheming or embroiling anyone, Lily." He turned back to the wheel. "I just answered a few of her questions."

All Lily could see of him was the drooping line of his shoulders under the ridiculous red shirt he wore. Choosing to concentrate on the shirt instead of his posture, she wondered if her father thought they were still living in the days of the keelboats. She wanted to lash out at him. She wanted to tell him how ridiculous he looked. She wanted to remind him he was only needed to steer the boat, not to teach her sister anything. But she couldn't quite force the words past her lips. So she watched him while he watched the river.

Why did you stay on this boat? Lily wanted to ask, but she didn't dare open up that topic. It was too dangerous.

Shoring up her defenses, she lifted her chin. Perhaps if she kept him isolated from her sisters, up here in the pilothouse where the pilot belonged. . .

"I don't want you talking to Jasmine anymore." She turned on her heel and practically ran toward the staircase as though some monster was chasing her.

Chapter Thirty-four

"Why can't David go with us?" Jasmine's plaintive voice interrupted the instructions Lily was giving Jensen.

"Because he's going to stay here with the other men."

Jasmine's lower lip protruded. "He stayed with us in New Orleans."

"And you spent most of your time bickering," Camellia reminded her. She looked toward Lily. "When can we leave?"

"In just a moment." Lily focused on Jensen. "If you need anything, we'll be at my grandmother's home. Blake knows where it is."

"We'll be fine, ma'am." Jensen rested a hand on David's shoulder.

David looked longingly toward the carriage where Lily's sisters and Tamar waited. Should she let him come home with them? But no, Lily reminded herself, there would be enough controversy at Les Fleurs without bringing a foundling. "Trust me, David, you're better off here. Just stay close to Jensen or Blake, and you shouldn't have any trouble with those bullies in town."

He gave a slow nod. "Yes'm."

Lily gave him an encouraging smile before climbing into the carriage. She hadn't seen Blake since the cargo was off-loaded. Their passengers had disembarked as soon as they made landfall. Blake and Jensen had taken charge of the cargo while the women cleaned the staterooms and made a list of supplies they would need for their next trip. Some of the crew had dismantled the pen on the main deck and scrubbed it with lye soap. She and Tamar had decided to ask Jensen to sell the cow, who had turned out to be a bit too pungent for their passengers. Blake hadn't needed to point out the advantages of keeping the captain. His experience and concern were proof enough that he should remain. . .as long as he didn't reveal his identity.

Camellia adjusted her hat to better protect her complexion from the sunlight. "Are they expecting us at home?"

Lily nodded. "I sent a messenger to Grandmother asking if we could visit. He returned with a sweet note saying that she couldn't wait to see us."

"Everything looks different." Jasmine's head swiveled as they ascended the hill leading away from the docks.

"Don't be silly." Camellia maintained her pose while managing to frown at her sister. "We haven't been gone that long."

Lily agreed with Jasmine. The city did look different. Under-the-Hill had been the same with its ramshackle buildings and throngs of steamboats, but new buildings seemed to have sprung up overnight On-the-Hill. Business was booming, a sure sign they would succeed in their shipping business.

"I want the two of you to be on your best behavior while we're at Les Fleurs." Lily broke into the discussion before it could escalate into an all-out fight. "I don't want Aunt Dahlia or Uncle Phillip saying I have turned you into hoydens."

Camellia elevated her nose and looked away.

Jasmine reached out for Lily's hand. "Of course we will, Sissy."

Lily sent a quick prayer heavenward. Her gaze met Tamar's sympathetic one. Lily couldn't wait to get back on the river. Even dealing with Captain Henrick and the likes of Mrs. Carlyle would be pleasant in comparison to her relatives' homilies.

As they topped the hill, she spied a man on horseback, waving in their direction.

It was Jean Luc Champney. A smile teased the edges of her mouth. She reached forward and tapped on the shoulder of the hired driver to get him to stop.

"Hello," Jean Luc said as he pulled his horse up next to the carriage. He swept a bow. "How wonderful to see you."

"It's nice to see you, too." She could feel the weight of her sisters' gazes on her. Were they shocked that someone so handsome had sought her out?

Camellia peeped at him from under the brim of her hat, but Jasmine was more open in her perusal.

"I trust your first voyage was successful." His dark eyes never strayed toward Lily's more handsome sisters.

"Yes, it was." Lily's cheeks heated under his intense scrutiny.

"Excellent. Perhaps you will have dinner with me so I can hear all about it."

She nodded. "I would like that."

"I'll call on you this afternoon." With a second bow, he resettled his hat and cantered away.

"I think you have a beau." Camellia's voice sounded petulant.

Lily supposed she was not used to having anyone ignore her. It was a novel experience for Lily, too. "Monsieur Champney has been very kind to me. I bought our boat from his father, you know. I think he just wants to help us succeed."

Why did all three of them look at her with varying degrees of surprise or pity? Lily stared at the countryside as the carriage began moving forward. Once again she felt she was being told she didn't understand the world around her. Maybe they were the ones who didn't understand things. They had not been at the dinner she and Jean Luc had shared. Nor had they been with them when he took her out to the boat—well, at least Camellia and Jasmine had not.

"How long will we be staying at Grandmother's home?" Camellia asked.

"No matter how long our visit is, it will be too long for me." Jasmine crossed her arms.

"That's no way to talk about your relatives." Lily frowned, and Jasmine sat back against the seat cushion with a thump. Lily turned her attention to Camellia. "I doubt we'll spend more than a day or two."

"A day or two?" Dismay colored both sisters' words.

"Can't we stay a little longer?" asked Camellia.

Jasmine shook her head in disagreement. "I don't want to spend the night there. It's so much fun on the *Hattie Belle* where we're not cooped up inside all the time."

"We'll be off as soon as we get another shipment. I am hoping to head north this time, toward Memphis." Lily tucked several loose strands of hair behind her ear.

"Really?" Jasmine bounced to the edge of her seat.

Tamar put out a hand to stop her from tumbling to the floor. "Settle down, Miss Jasmine, before you hurt yourself."

"Yes, do settle down." Camellia aimed a disdainful look at her.

Lily sighed. Was she being fair to her middle sister? While Jasmine thrived with the easygoing lifestyle aboard their boat, Camellia was eager to abandon it. Every time they landed, she wanted to disembark immediately and delayed going back until Lily forced her to return. Yet what else could Lily do? She was determined not to let her sister grow too self-absorbed.

The carriage turned into the drive leading to Grandmother's house. Lily should feel excited, but she couldn't summon much enthusiasm. Like Jasmine, she wished she were back on the *Hattie Belle*, floating on beloved muddy waters.

❧

Blake glanced at the floating island of boats lashed together for the night. Men moved from deck to deck, cooking, laughing, playing cards. He wanted to join them, but that wasn't possible. Not tonight. He had more important duties.

Blake turned to the interior of the boat. It was far too quiet aboard the *Hattie Belle*, as though the departure of Lily and her sisters had removed all the joy and laughter.

He wondered how she was faring with her family. Were they welcoming or rebuking her? Of course she would be able to handle herself no matter how her relatives treated her.

He loved the way she was so optimistic, so eager to embrace life on the river. It no longer mattered to him that her vision of that life was so different from the gambling salon he had imagined. He was rather enjoying himself. He might even try a little fishing during their next cruise.

He opened the door of the cabin he shared with David. The boy was lying on his back in bed, his textbook spread across his chest. A warm feeling filled Blake's chest. It didn't seem too long ago that he was the one falling asleep at his lessons. Affection wrapped itself around his heart. Who would have thought he would so much enjoy the role of older brother? He was glad Lily had insisted on letting David stay on board. Another of her policies that had proven to be right. Blake shook the boy's shoulder. "David?"

A grumble answered him.

"Wake up. You need to get out of those clothes."

David rubbed his eyes and pushed himself up.

Blake rescued the textbook before it could slide off to the floor. "I suppose you were absorbing the information in here straight through your chest?"

"I didn't mean to fall asleep."

Blake loosed a smile. "That's all right, David. We'll work on your studies together tomorrow." His smile disappeared. His father had said the same thing to him once upon a time. And had helped him the next day as promised. Why hadn't he remembered that before? Had he only clung to the unhappy memories? Unable to deal with the emotion his thoughts stirred, Blake shut them out and concentrated on helping the younger boy find his nightshirt and climb under the covers.

The light in the room was fading quickly now that the sun had set. He bid David good night and stepped back into the passageway. He wished Jensen had not gone into town. He needed a distraction this evening, something to keep his memories at bay.

"Where are you going?"

Blake stopped in midstride and turned to face Captain Henrick. "I thought you went to Natchez with the rest of the crew."

"No." The older man shook his head, a smile wrinkling his weathered face. "I'm a bit old and staid to enjoy the kind of. . .ah. . . distractions that interest the others."

"With all the storytelling going on out there?" Blake pointed his head toward the deck. "I'm sure you could keep a group well entertained with stories of Mike Fink or some of your own adventures. A man who's seen as much of the river as you must have a host of stories in his knapsack."

"Maybe so, but it's not the same as spinning yarns for the little ones."

Blake raised an eyebrow. "You sound more like a father than a river captain."

"I am, son. Or at least I want to be. But it seems the good Lord hasn't removed all the obstacles in my path even though He had to be responsible for leading me back to my girls."

The man's statement raised several questions in Blake's mind. "Are you interested in explaining what you mean?"

Captain Henrick shrugged. "I suppose. Seems you have the time to listen."

Instead of returning to the deck, Blake nodded toward the dining room. He'd never heard Lily tell the story of why she and her sisters had been raised by their grandparents rather than their father. He assumed her mother was dead. Surely no woman would desert her beautiful daughters voluntarily. But how had this man made the decision to walk away from his children?

Blake had grown to care deeply about all three of the Anderson girls. He couldn't imagine abandoning them. . .and he was not their father.

They sat at one of the empty tables. Captain Henrick leaned forward, placing his forearms on the tabletop. "What do you want to know?"

"Everything."

"That's a tall order."

Blake sighed and leaned back against his chair. "Okay, why don't you start with what happened between you and Lily?"

"There's a tale." Captain Henrick's brown eyes darkened. "It's not an easy story to tell." He sighed, seeming to steel himself to face something unpleasant. "I fell in love with Rose Blackstone. She was such a lovely, delicate, cultured young lady, but somehow I still managed to secure her affection. We married even though her parents never approved of me. Rose joined me on my boat. What a wonderful life we had."

He stopped as if reliving the early days of his marriage. "Then we had our first daughter, my Water Lily. She was a little sailor from the time she could walk. Her mother and I always took her with us on our trips. Then came pretty-as-a-picture Camellia. If you wonder what the girls' mother looked like, gaze on my second-born child." He sighed. "I have no doubt she'll lead some poor man on a merry chase. She never took to living on the river like Water Lily. She was scared of everything—the noises, the smells, the strangers. Traveling as a family grew harder, and her grandparents offered to keep her for us. It seemed like the right thing to do back then, but I'm not as sure now."

Blake nodded. He knew how much perspective was gained when one looked back. He would change several of his choices if he could.

"It's better to concentrate on the present and plan for the future instead of spending too much time reliving the past."

"That's true. But it's also important to remember the past, or we run the risk of making the same mistakes over and over. I only wish I'd had more wisdom back then."

They sat in silence. Blake didn't want to push the man. He'd learned that patience often yielded better results. He crossed one leg over the other and waited.

The captain finally continued. "When my sweet Rose told me she was in the family way a second time, I knew we'd outgrown our boat. But we had managed to put some money aside, and we used that to purchase a bigger boat. One that would accommodate our children and hopefully bring us more income. After a few more years, our little Jasmine came. Violet eyes and a fluff of hair as dark as midnight. She looked just like a miniature I once saw of her grandmother, Miss Violet."

A faraway look and wistful smile softened his features. "I could hardly believe we had three girls who were so different in looks and temperament. You must have seen the differences—my headstrong Lily, my comfort-loving Camellia, and joyful, exuberant Jasmine. I'm truly blessed to have three such wonderful daughters."

"Then why did you leave them?" Blake's question blurted out as though shot from a cannon.

"I had no choice." Captain Henrick's eyes were moist. His face showed pain. "The summer after Jasmine was born, Rose and I decided to leave the children with her parents while we traveled upriver. We didn't know a flood was bearing down on us. It hit during the middle of the night, the river rose twenty feet in minutes. Our boat didn't stand a chance. It was ripped free of its mooring and thrown into the main current."

The man halted, untying the scarf from his neck and using it to dry his eyes. He cleared his throat. "We broke up on something—a rock or snag. I never saw it. We were dumped into the water and tossed around like bits of flotsam. At first Rose and I clung to each other, but the water ripped us apart. My sweet wife drowned—" His voice broke.

Captain Henrick shook his head. "When I found her body, I wanted to die. And when I got back to Natchez and told her parents what had happened, they wanted me dead, too." His gaze lifted.

The pain in his eyes made Blake's gut twist. "I'm so sorry."

"Me too, son. That was the darkest time of my life. I didn't understand why God would allow such a terrible thing to happen. Why would He take Rose from her husband and daughters? Why didn't He take me instead? Rose and the girls would have been much better off. Mr. and Mrs. Blackstone would've made sure they never had to worry about finances. Rose probably would have married again. Everything would have been better. If He thought it necessary to take one of us, He made a mistake in taking Rose and leaving me."

Blake nodded. He could understand questioning God. He'd done enough of that himself.

"Old Mr. Blackstone told me that he and his wife would raise my daughters, give them every luxury, every opportunity. At first I refused to consider his offer, but finally I agreed. Then he told me he thought the children would adapt better to their new lives if I stayed away. What was I supposed to do? I was a riverboat captain without a boat. I couldn't take three children with me. We'd starve. It seemed the final proof that God cared nothing about us."

Blake looked away from the captain, suddenly wishing he'd never asked the man about his past. He sensed he was not going to enjoy the rest of the story.

"Over the next few years I wandered from port to port. I did things that bring me shame now. I was lost and angry. I picked fights with men who'd done me no wrong, anything to exorcise my rage. Strangely enough, that's what may have saved my life. . .and my soul."

Exactly as Blake had feared. And from an unexpected source. He might have been prepared for a sermon from a preacher, but not from this old gentleman whom he'd considered kindly and harmless. Blake wanted to push back from the table, but something held him still. Some macabre impulse. Rather like not being able to resist looking toward a dead body caught in a river snag.

"One night more than a year ago, I met a man who stabbed me during a fight and left me for dead. A preacher got me to a doctor. Between them they kept me alive. The preacher shared his rooms with me. While I was recovering, he had a captive audience. I'll never forget the afternoon when he asked me why I wanted to die."

"I'm certain you had an answer." Blake shoved his chair back. "And I'm sure it was a good one. But I don't have time to listen tonight."

Captain Henrick sat back. The look that crossed his face was not condemning. It wasn't even sad. The expression was one of understanding. He nodded at Blake. "I see."

"I doubt that." He stood and stalked to the door. "You don't know a thing about me, so don't go acting like you do."

Blake stomped onto the deck. A group of men sat around a small fire on a nearby boat. Close enough so he could keep a watch on the boat and be ready if David needed something. He headed toward them, eager to drown out Captain Henrick's words.

Chapter Thirty-five

Ashamed of his response to the captain's story, Blake got up early the next morning and fixed breakfast. Soon the aromas of fresh coffee and bacon filled the air. As the sun made its first appearance over the horizon, Jensen, Captain Henrick, and David showed up. Blake scrambled a small mountain of eggs and sat at the table with the others.

Silence reigned as they dug into their food.

Blake washed down his food with a gulp of hot coffee and turned to face the captain. He was determined to clear the air. "Look, I'm sorry for interrupting you last night."

Captain Henrick waved away his apology. "When the time is right, you'll listen. There's no doubt God is whispering in your ear. He wants you to come to Him."

David's eyes widened. "Did you have a fight?"

Blake brushed a hand through the boy's blond curls. "Nothing to worry about. Captain Henrick and I get along fine, don't we?" He shot a glance at the captain.

"That's right." Captain Henrick smiled. "In fact, I'm hoping we're going to be very close."

Nodding, Blake forced a smile to his face. He bent a look at the captain that he hoped spoke to his desire to talk to the man alone. They still had a few things that needed to be straightened out. Things that had nothing to do with religion.

"Let's get this food put away, and then you and I need to spend some time checking how much of that textbook you managed to absorb last night."

Jensen began gathering the dirty dishes and moved to the galley. Captain Henrick headed upstairs to the hurricane deck. Blake and David went to the dining hall to study. Blake hoped he remembered enough about arithmetic to help the boy.

David seemed a bit lost, so Blake pulled out his deck of cards, hoping Lily would not catch him again and accuse him of teaching the children to gamble. He thought by now she should have a better idea of his moral code, but he'd just as soon not test that theory.

"A deck has fifty-two cards." He shuffled the cards and dealt them facedown on the table. "I've dealt four hands on this table. Without counting, can you tell me how many cards should be in each hand?"

David's brow gathered as he tried to reason out the answer.

"If I had dealt two hands, how many cards would be in each hand?"

"Thirty?"

Blake shook his head. "You're guessing. What is half of fifty-two?"

David scrunched up his face, his mouth moving as he divided the number. "Twenty-six?"

"Are you guessing or telling me?"

"I. . .I'm telling you."

Blake nodded. "You're right."

The smile on David's face was a joy to see.

"That's good." He tapped a finger on the table. "So how many cards are in each hand here?"

Another frown from his pupil. "Thirteen?"

"I think you're beginning to understand." He picked up one of the hands and fanned the cards before laying them down. "Now if there are four suits in this deck, how many cards will be in each suit?"

"Thirteen." David's answer was more confident.

"You may have found a new way of studying." He picked up the cards and shuffled them once more. "I'm removing twelve cards from the deck, so how many cards will be left?"

They continued drilling—adding, subtracting, multiplying, and dividing. When Blake felt his student had grasped the subject, he sent David for the slate he and Jasmine shared. "Write your name."

He watched as David meticulously copied out the five letters of his first name, hesitated, and looked up. "I don't know how to spell Foster."

Blake pressed his upper teeth against his lower lip and pushed air through them. "What letter makes that sound?"

And so they continued. He wondered if Lily would be proud of the progress David had made. She might not even notice. "You've seen the name of our boat, right?"

David nodded.

"Good. Then write *Hattie Belle* on your slate."

David wiped his name off the slate with his sleeve and began concentrating once more.

The bond Blake had felt the night before returned in full force. This boy was bright. He would make sure David had a chance to make something of himself. Perhaps one day they would find the boy's father and reunite them. Or maybe he'd be better off staying on the *Hattie Belle*. Between Lily and him, they could see to it that the boy recognized his worth and learned to rely on his talents.

He gave David a series of tasks and left him for a while. Blake wanted to set Captain Henrick straight.

The captain was studying a map in the pilothouse but looked up when Blake entered. "Are you through tutoring that towheaded scamp?"

"For the time being."

Captain Henrick put down his map. "I don't suppose you came all the way up here to enjoy the sunshine."

Blake looked around. The view from the highest deck of the *Hattie Belle* never failed to amaze. Perhaps he should find time to come up here more often. The morning sunshine gleamed on the surface of the water. Most of the boats that had formed the floating island last night were already gone, but there would be more tonight. It was a daily ritual. The old adage of "safety in numbers" was true on the Mississippi. Brigands and pirates could target a lone boat unless it was well hidden.

"No." Blake turned his attention to the captain. "Now that I know Lily can't overhear us, I wanted to talk about what happened when I first brought you aboard. I can't say I didn't get a little enjoyment from taking your side."

"I do appreciate it. Otherwise I wouldn't have gotten the chance to see her or my other daughters."

Blake smothered a smile. "Yes, well, be that as it may, I won't stand for seeing Lily or her sisters hurt by anyone. If you ever cause them pain, I'll put you off this boat. Whether we're in Natchez, New Orleans, or Timbuktu, I'll make sure you don't get a second chance."

"If I hurt them and you didn't run me away, I would lose respect for you, Blake. I have to live with what I did all those years ago, no matter what my reasons. But I would never, ever do that to them again. I am their father, even if Lily doesn't want me to acknowledge that. I'd never walk away from my family again." The fervor in Captain Henrick's words was obvious.

Blake gave him a curt nod and turned on his heel.

"If you want to talk again, Blake, you know where to find me."

Ignoring the man, he headed for the staircase. Why did it feel like he was retreating? He had nothing to feel guilty about. Then what was the sharp pain in his chest? He hadn't done the same thing to his family. What had happened between him and his father was altogether different. Wasn't it?

⁊⧼

"I have come to ask for your granddaughter's company for a sedate ride." Jean Luc smiled widely. He'd found that charming a young lady's chaperone was a fruitful effort.

His gaze followed Mrs. Blackstone's to the sofa where Lily sat, her hands folded demurely in her lap. Her brown eyes sparkled with anticipation. "I don't see why not, Monsieur Champney." Mrs. Blackstone returned his smile. "The weather outside is perfect for a carriage ride."

"Thank you, Grandmother." Lily rose from the sofa. "I'll just get my shawl and hat."

Jean Luc stood when she did and bowed. "I await your pleasure, Miss Anderson."

He appreciated the pink tint to her cheeks as she exited the room. At least she was still an innocent. He'd had his doubts after she'd spent so much time in New Orleans. He knew firsthand about the opportunities to stray in that city.

"Do you follow politics at all, Monsieur Champney?" Mrs. Blackstone's voice captured his attention.

"I'm afraid I keep busy with other pursuits. While I was in Europe, I was plunged into the political world of the king and found it to be sordid and dangerous. My father, however, is well versed in political matters." Jean Luc resumed his seat to the old lady's right. "I suppose he needs to since he's a businessman."

"I'm sure you're right." Mrs. Blackstone sipped from her teacup. "I don't get out much these days, so the newspaper is how I stay abreast of the world. I was reading this morning of a race for the Illinois senate."

Jean Luc adopted an interested expression. "I'm surprised such a race is covered in the local newspaper."

"Perhaps you haven't yet realized how interested we are here in national developments concerning slavery and abolition." Mrs. Blackstone put down her teacup. "I read all I can about national policies."

He could not imagine spending that much time perusing anything. He preferred more athletic pursuits and the excitement to be found in gambling salons, although he limited his time there to avoid more disasters.

"You must be quite the scholar." Jean Luc tried to infuse admiration into his voice while glancing at her hands to see if her fingertips had been blackened from all the newsprint she perused. He hoped her penchant for reading had not rubbed off on Lily. While he appreciated a sensible woman, he had no desire to woo a girl who knew more about every subject than he.

Before Mrs. Blackstone could answer, Lily returned. She was tying the ribbon on a pretty straw hat and had a lacy shawl draped over one arm.

Jean Luc stood and offered his arm. "I am so glad you can join me."

"It's sweet of you to invite me."

Mrs. Blackstone waved them out of the room. "Enjoy your outing, Lily, but don't be late for dinner."

A frisson of irritation passed through Jean Luc. Did the woman think he was untrustworthy? Stifling the feeling, he smiled and bowed toward her before leading Lily out to his carriage.

After getting her settled, Jean Luc took the reins and set their vehicle in motion. "Before we get onto another subject, please let me apologize for the antics of the man I recommended to you."

"You don't need to apologize." Lily put a hand on his arm.

Jean Luc tightened his muscles in response, hoping she would be impressed with his strength. "Yes, I do. You are very kind to forgive me, but I need to tell you how devastated I was when he reappeared here in Natchez."

She removed her hand. "I really wish you would not persist, Monsieur Champney."

He pulled the carriage to the side of the road under the spreading branches of a live oak so he could concentrate on his passenger rather than his driving. "But I must. I must make you believe I had no idea what kind of man Captain Steenberg is." He placed a hand over his chest. "I would never have put you or your family in harm's way. I was so relieved to see the *Hattie Belle* sailing into port yesterday."

"You have convinced me of your innocence." She tilted her head back. "Please don't waste any more time. I never blamed you for his actions. You have been a good friend to me since the first time we met."

"*Merci*." He took one of her hands, noticing that she was wearing gloves, a barrier to his intentions. Jean Luc used his thumb to slide the white cotton away from the back of her wrist and pressed a fervent kiss against her skin. "I would like to be more than your friend."

She gasped and tugged at her hand. Reluctantly, Jean Luc allowed her to pull away. Color rode high in her cheeks, and the tenderness he had seen in her expression had disappeared. Lily looked uncertain.

Should he take the opportunity to embrace her? He needed to secure her affection. He didn't want her to leave town again without making her aware of his intentions.

"*Monsieur* Champney—"

He could tell from the tone of her voice that she was not as entranced as she should be by his attentions. He groaned, the sound stopping her words. "Please don't tell me I have overstepped."

"No, you're not the problem. I find your sentiments flattering. How could I not? You're a fine gentleman." She sighed and looked down at her lap. "I have so many things to worry about these days, I really don't have time to accept a courtship."

At least she hadn't demurred because she had no feelings for him. Jean Luc would capitalize on this scant encouragement. "I can see the burdens you carry, Miss Anderson. I hate to watch you work so hard. I want to be someone you can lean upon." He could tell his words had hit the mark by the returning tenderness in her expression.

"Jean Luc, you are very kind. But I cannot impose upon you any more than I already have."

"At least let me find someone to replace Captain Steenberg."

"That's not necessary. We found someone in New Orleans. The

crew and even my sisters seem to be taken with him, so I suppose we will keep him in our employ unless something drastic happens."

"Then what can I do for you, Lily?" He reached for her hand, massaging it gently, trying to project unthreatening support. "There must be something you need."

She shook her head. "I think Blake and I have things under control. He hired our current crew and oversaw the repairs."

"I'm glad Matthews is treating you well, but I must admit to reservations about him." He pulled her hand to his chest. "Please promise me you will not lower your guard with him. He may be trying to lull you into a vulnerable position before taking advantage of your trusting nature."

She stiffened. "I know you mean well, Jean Luc, but you must allow me some credit. I am not as naive as you might think."

Jean Luc released her and let his shoulders droop. "Now I've offended you."

"You haven't offended me, Jean Luc. I appreciate your concern. It's just that no one seems to have any faith in me. I am not a helpless debutante." She sat up straight, turning slightly away. "Please take me home."

He had to be satisfied with that. Jean Luc turned the carriage around and started the trip back to her family's home.

Why did Lily have to be so prickly? He had never met a young lady so difficult to please. He only hoped she was worth the effort. And she was, he reminded himself. She was the way to regain everything—his father's approval, his boat, his self-esteem. Lily was the key to his future.

Chapter Thirty-six

Please, please let me stay, Lily." Camellia's expression was filled with hope, yearning, and optimism.

Lily sighed and touched her sister's pretty curls with a finger. Her heart was tearing in half. Camellia had not thrived on the river like she and Jasmine had. Where they had enjoyed searching for the next adventure around the bend, Camellia had been happiest when they were staying with the Thorntons in New Orleans. But to separate the three of them? And would Camellia be truly happy here, or would she find herself in a situation similar to the one that had made Lily purchase the *Hattie Belle* in the first place? "What about Aunt Dahlia?"

Camellia's face sparkled like sunshine hitting the surface of the river. "She's promised me an exciting season now that I'm old enough to be a debutante. I may even find a husband by Christmas."

Concern flashed through Lily. Camellia was not mature enough to be responsible for a household and children. "You're only fifteen. Don't be in such a hurry to grow up."

"I won't." Camellia walked to the tall window that graced one side of the fireplace, covered for the summer with a hand-painted screen.

Lily followed her to the window and put an arm around her younger sister's waist.

Camellia leaned against her and sighed. "I'm sorry, Lily. I know you want to live on a boat, but I'm more suited to ballrooms. Please say you'll let me stay. I can continue my piano lessons. Uncle Phillip knows an art teacher who can improve my drawing."

Words choked Lily's throat. Was everything changing? Again? Feeling like she'd been stabbed in the chest, she nodded. "I suppose you can stay."

A squeal of excitement was followed by a big hug from Camellia. "Thank you so much, Lily. I promise I'll be good. So good you'll be amazed the next time you come home."

She returned Camellia's hug, hoping she'd made the right decision. It didn't feel right, but how could she force her sister to return to a life that didn't suit her? Perhaps if there were no other option, she would insist that Camellia come back to the *Hattie Belle*.

A thought came to her, an odd echo. Had their father faced a similar decision? She pushed the thought away. Their father had not offered them a choice. He had simply walked away. Perhaps if he'd come to visit them over the years, if he'd made any attempt at communication, she might understand. But none of them had seen him until the day Blake hired him to captain their boat.

Camellia kissed her cheek then danced around the room as if waltzing with a partner. "I hope Grandmother will let me take dancing lessons."

A laugh gurgled up from Lily's throat. "You certainly will be busy with all these lessons. Perhaps instead of remaining here, you should go to a good finishing school."

Camellia stopped abruptly, her blue eyes opening wide. "You would let me go to school?"

"Of course I would." Lily wondered if she could bribe her sister. "We'll be taking our next load to Memphis, but I imagine we'll head back to New Orleans after that. I'm sure either the Thorntons or Sarah Cartier could recommend several good schools. Of course if you're not with us, what good would that do?"

Her sister considered Lily's words. "Will you let me stay here while you go to Memphis? You could pick me up before you return to New Orleans."

Lily nodded slowly. Camellia had never had the problems with Aunt Dahlia that Lily had. But she didn't want to see her sister pushed into a loveless marriage, and minimizing the contact between the two was the best way to make sure Camellia was safe from manipulation.

The door to the parlor opened, and the subject of her thoughts walked into the room. Aunt Dahlia's black skirts swished as she crossed the room and settled on the sofa. "Have you gotten everything settled?"

The pain stabbed Lily again, caused by a sense of betrayal. She looked toward Camellia, who would not return her gaze.

"I hope you'll one day come to your senses, Lily." Aunt Dahlia's voice drew her attention from her traitorous sibling. "But whether you do or not, there's no reason to destroy Camellia's and Jasmine's chances of making advantageous marriages."

"I don't believe seeing a little of the world is a bad thing for a young woman."

"What more could they learn than can be taught here in Natchez? You may turn up your nose at the local society, but I can promise you that the best and brightest young men are to be found right outside our door."

Lily realized she shouldn't give her aunt the satisfaction of an argument, but she couldn't keep silent. "Not every woman thinks marriage is the only future for her. I want to make sure my sisters have choices."

"I want to thank you for giving me a choice." Camellia moved to the sofa and sat next to Aunt Dahlia. "And for accepting that my decision is different from your own."

Lily's mouth opened to refute her sister, but she snapped it shut. Nothing was to be gained by continuing this discussion. As Camellia had pointed out, she did believe in choices. It was the very reason she'd first embarked on her quest to make a home for them on the river. She just wished it didn't hurt so badly to contemplate the schism that seemed to be forming between her and Camellia.

She nodded and left the parlor, feeling like she was leaving part of her heart behind.

Chapter Thirty-seven

Lily took a moment to sit in the shade on the upper deck before beginning her next chore. They missed Camellia, but with the increased number of passengers, no one had much time to dwell on such matters. She had no free time at all. She rose at daybreak, dressed, and headed to the kitchen to help prepare breakfast. Then she scrubbed dishes, washed floors, took care of the needs of the women passengers. No matter how badly she wanted to, it seemed she could never find enough time to read her Bible and pray.

Maybe she should take her Bible to the afternoon tea in the ladies' parlor. Or would that be too pretentious? Would the passengers appreciate a daily Bible study? She could read a few verses and then ask everyone's opinion. Uncertain of exactly where to start, Lily wondered who might advise her. She wished her friend Sarah was with them. She would have bushels of ideas, and the energetic matron would infect all the ladies.

With a sigh, Lily picked up the bowl of butter beans she'd shelled to help Jensen. He was peeling potatoes to go along with his planned lunch of ham and redeye gravy. Her mouth watered as she imagined the delicious—

"Oof." Lily barreled into someone, her momentum causing him to rock back. Her nose was firmly buried in his chest. His hands caught her shoulders and held on as they teetered. In the moment it took him to recover his balance, she knew who held her. Blake's cologne was unmistakable, a heady mix of spice and leather. Why did it have to be him? She pushed at Blake's hard chest and took a step back. "Let go of me."

When he immediately complied, Lily was overcome by a feeling of loss. What was the matter with her? She glanced up at his face.

His gaze met hers, his blue eyes twinkling. A smile softened his face and set her heart thumping. "You've got to start watching your step, or you're going to fall overboard."

"I'm sorry." She forced the words out, her gaze falling to the deck. "I wasn't paying attention."

His hand caught her chin, lifting it with a gentleness that made her breath catch. When their gazes met, she felt it all the way to her toes. Everything in her trembled. Her fingers clung to the bowl of shelled beans as to a life preserver.

"You're working much too hard. We have several new crew members aboard. Let some of them ease your burden." His hand still held her chin, his large fingers cupping her face with disconcerting warmth.

Lily willed herself to take another step back, but her legs refused to obey. She didn't know what to say. Where was the disdainful glint she expected from him? If she didn't know better, Lily would think he was truly concerned about her well-being.

Butterflies fluttered against the walls of her stomach, their wings shutting off her breath. His eyelids lowered, and his head dropped a couple of inches. She swayed toward him, pulled by the gentle tug of his hand.

"Excuse me." The sound of her father's voice was like a bucket of cold river water drenching her. "What's going on here?"

Lily pulled away from Blake's hand with a jerk. Her face flamed as she met Captain Henrick's thunderous scowl. Was her father passing judgment? The man who'd had nothing to do with her upbringing could not think he had any right to dictate her behavior.

"I need to get to the galley." She held her head high and pushed past Blake. All the way down the corridor she felt their eyes on her, but Lily refused to give them the satisfaction of looking back.

As she turned the corner, she thought she heard her father's voice again. Was he angry? And why did she care? With a huff, she thumped her bowl onto an empty counter. "What else can I do?"

Jensen looked at her. "Why don't you go to the ladies' parlor? I served some refreshments awhile back. You look a little. . .upset. A nice cup of tea would calm your nerves."

Lily glared at the man's back, but Jensen focused on his skillet and pots. After a moment she gave up and followed his advice.

As she walked to the parlor, her thoughts drifted back to Blake. What had come over them? He probably couldn't help himself. He was a handsome man, most likely used to women throwing themselves at him. Perhaps he thought she had been making overtures when they collided. Her face burned.

Lily spent the next half hour chatting with the ladies in the parlor. She sipped at her tea and found it did settle her nerves. But she couldn't remain for long. Too much work remained to be done. She placed her porcelain cup on the silver service and excused herself to check on the lunch preparations.

Entering the dining room, she was surprised to find the tables still bare of cloths and plates. Where were Jasmine and David? She was about to look for them in the storage closet they used for a classroom when Tamar entered the dining hall, her arms full of linens. "Where are the children?" Lily took several of the bleached cloths and set them on an empty table.

"They went to the pilothouse to visit the captain." Tamar unfolded a tablecloth with a snap and settled it on another table. "They're not bothering him. I overheard him telling Mr. Blake he loves spinning stories about the river."

"How dare he!" Lily was marching toward the staircase before Tamar could say another word. She moved up the two flights of the boat so quickly it was as though she'd grown a pair of wings and flown. She couldn't wait to give Captain Henrick a piece of her mind.

❧

"And he always claimed he'd been chewed up and swallowed by that ol' alligator."

Blake laughed out loud as much at the round eyes of Jasmine and David as at the outrageous ending of Captain Henrick's tall tale.

"What do you think you're doing?"

Lily's wrathful question wiped Blake's smile off his face. He turned to face her. "What's wrong now?"

"It's nothing to concern you. This is between Captain Henrick and me."

Blake put himself between her and the pilothouse. "What concerns our employees concerns me."

"Let me pass." She tried to push him out of the way.

He put his hands on her shoulders. "Not until you calm down."

Lily redirected her ire at him, but Blake simply returned her stare. She might be able to cow old men and children, but she would find herself at a loss if she tried to intimidate him.

The staring contest continued a moment or two before the fire died out of her eyes.

He felt someone standing next to him and looked down to see Jasmine peeking at her oldest sister, a look of contrition on her face. "I'm sorry, Lily. Is it already time for lunch? David and I'll go downstairs right away."

"I'm not angry at you, Jasmine." Lily's voice had calmed. "But you do need to help Tamar."

"Yes, ma'am." Jasmine and David scurried past, their footsteps clanging as they rushed down the stairs.

Blake waited to make sure they were out of earshot before speaking again. "Now what's this all about, Lily?"

She glared past Blake's shoulder at the captain. "He broke his word."

"I have not."

Blake let her pass and turned toward the pilothouse. "Why don't you explain what's wrong instead of making accusations?"

Lily pointed a finger at Captain Henrick. "He promised he would not try to win the affections of my sisters, but he wants to make them love him. I'm not going to stand for that. I don't want to see their hearts broken like mine was when he deserted us."

Captain Henrick looked like he'd been slapped. Although Blake could understand why Lily was so protective of her sisters, he thought she had gone overboard. "I was here with Jasmine and David. All the captain was doing was telling them a story about Mike Fink."

Her expression didn't change. "I don't care what he was doing. I don't want him to influence my sisters in any way."

"So you want him to be unkind to them?" Blake shook his head. "That sounds like an odd request."

He glanced toward Captain Henrick in time to see the man hiding a grin.

"Of course I don't want him to be unkind. But he can maintain some distance."

Captain Henrick's face smoothed out. "Lily, I hate to contradict you, but I never promised I wouldn't talk to my daughters. I haven't seen Jasmine since she was a baby—"

"And whose fault is that?" Lily's accusation cut off his words.

Blake put a calming hand on her arm. He didn't want her to say something she would regret later.

The captain nodded. "I take full responsibility for that, but Lily, you don't know all the circumstances. You don't know how much I've changed since those dark days."

Blake could feel the tension in Lily's body. Like a taut bowstring, she was ready to unleash a hailstorm of arrows to pierce her father's heart. He could remember feeling the same way toward his father. And he knew from experience that the path she and her father were on would lead to loneliness, remorse, and grief.

"Although I think you and Lily should sit down together and talk about those days, this is not the right time." Blake squeezed Lily's arm to make sure he had her attention. "You need to do it when neither of you is this upset."

"I am more than willing to talk to my daughter about the past." Captain Henrick looked at him first before turning his gaze toward Lily. "I pray that one day she will find a way to forgive me. And I promise to continue loving her no matter how she feels about me."

Lily rolled her eyes. "And in the meantime you'll try to steal my sisters from me."

Understanding flashed through Blake. "Is that why you let Camellia stay with an aunt and uncle you cannot abide? Are you afraid you'll lose her love?"

"Of course not. I let Camellia remain with *my grandmother* because she begged me to let her stay and take part in the Natchez social whirl. It had absolutely nothing to do with him. I acceded to her wishes because I want her to be happy. It's what I want for both of my sisters. And I happen to know they won't be if they discover that our father is alive and then have to mourn him once again when he deserts us—them."

"I'm not sure you're being completely honest with yourself." Blake hoped his words would penetrate the wall of distrust she'd built. "You need to spend some time thinking about your actions and decisions."

"Lily is being very sensible given my history." Captain Henrick shoved his hands into his pants pockets. "I won't tell them who I am unless you say I can, Lily. That's what I promised in New Orleans, and you can count on me to keep that promise. But you can't expect me to be this close to Jasmine and not try to spend time with her."

Blake nodded his agreement. "The captain's not doing anything more than Jensen in keeping them entertained while you and Tamar are busy. You don't have a problem with that, do you?"

"Of course not, but Jensen—"

"Is no different in Jasmine's eyes than Captain Henrick." Blake let his gaze rest on a lock of Lily's hair that had come loose. It gleamed in the bright sunlight, and he found himself wanting to touch it to see if it felt as silky as it looked.

Lily's gaze met his, and her brown eyes widened as if she could read his thoughts. He needed to focus on the conversation, not her hair. Blake cleared his throat. "If you continue to object to her spending time up here, Jasmine is going to wonder why there's a difference. First she'll ask questions that you don't want to answer. Then she'll turn to the captain. She's an intelligent little girl. She will see through your pretense. And you'll have no one to blame but yourself when both of your sisters turn their backs on you."

He could see the pain in her eyes and the sudden paleness of her cheeks. Blake wanted to cut out his tongue. He hadn't meant to hurt her. He'd only wanted to get through to her. "I'm sorry."

"No." Her voice cracked a little. She cleared her throat. "I'm the one who should apologize. You're right, Blake. Both of you are right. I shouldn't have gotten so upset. It's just that I'm so worried they'll be hurt."

"You can stop worrying about that, Water Lily." Captain Henrick smiled at her, a wealth of sorrow in his eyes. "No matter what happens, I'll make sure I never hurt any of you again."

She nodded, the color returning to her face. "I'm trying to believe you."

Blake squeezed her arm to show his appreciation for her words. When she turned her gaze to him, his breath stopped. He'd never before seen so much depth or heart in a woman. A fierce desire rose in him to wrap his arms around her and protect her from whatever or whoever might try to harm her.

His hand moved up and tucked the loose lock of hair behind her ear. Her mouth parted, and her gaze dropped to his lips. If Captain Henrick had not cleared his throat, Blake had no idea what might have happened. But she pulled away and ducked her head.

"I have to get downstairs." She murmured the words and slipped out of the pilothouse, not glancing at either of them.

Chapter Thirty-eight

Tamar shook her head. She was worried about Lily. The poor thing was working herself to death. If she didn't slow down, she was likely to collapse. Then what would they do?

She covered the remaining tables and dusted her hands off. The plates and silverware were needed next. Heading to the galley, she breathed a sigh of relief to find it empty. With David and Jasmine otherwise occupied, she didn't have time for Jensen's tomfoolery. She grabbed a couple of the baskets they used for transporting dinnerware and begin filling them.

"What are you doing in my galley, woman?"

Jensen's voice made her gasp and spin around. "I thought you were busy doing something else."

"I see." He tapped a wooden spoon against one hand. "I guess you forgot I'm the one in charge of the cooking."

"Of course not." His presence made the galley shrink and grow much, much warmer. She tried to slow her pounding heart. What was it about this man?

"Why won't you be kind to a poor, heartsore man?" His gravelly voice held a plaintive note. "I'm only trying to win a smile from the woman I love."

Tamar pointed a finger at him. "If you don't quit talking such nonsense and leave me alone to do my chores, I'm going to take that spoon and use it on your head."

He chuckled. "It might improve my looks."

Tamar tried to keep from smiling, but it was a losing struggle. She turned to the baskets in an attempt to ignore him. Another impossibility. When the room behind her grew quiet, she sighed. He must've decided to take her at her word. Had she finally convinced him she wasn't interested in him? "Silly man."

"And here I thought you were the one being silly."

She jumped a foot and managed to overturn the laden baskets. Everything would have to be washed again. Tamar rounded on him. "Now look at what you've done."

Jensen stood next to the stove, his arms crossed over his chest. "Me? All I'm doing is trying to catch the attention of the purtiest girl on this boat." He lifted one of the lids and sniffed the contents. "You see, she's taken my heart, and I want hers in a sort of bartering deal."

Charmed in spite of herself, Tamar picked up the tableware that had fallen and moved to the large sink on the far side of Jensen. "I've told you before it won't work. You shouldn't be so stubborn."

He shook his head, one hand going to his scar. "Why won't it work, *cher*? Is it because I'm so ugly?"

"Of course not." She put the dishes in the sink and reached for a dishcloth. "I'm too old for you."

"Age don't matter to me." He sidled up next to her and put a hand on her arm, stilling her movements. "You'll have to do better than that."

Tamar looked down at the soapy water, tears burning her eyes. She would've thought he was smart enough to figure out the real reason she had to deny him. But apparently she was going to have to be brutally honest. Once he understood, Jensen would have to stop pursuing her. One hot tear leaked out and landed on his hand.

"What is it, Tamar?" His voice no longer teased. "Do you think I want anything less than marriage with you? Is that the reason you're crying?"

"No, Jensen." She pulled away and wiped her tears. "I know you're an honorable man. That's not the problem."

"What is it? Please tell me."

She closed her eyes. "I—it won't work because you're a freeman." There, she'd said the words. Tamar wished expressing them made her feel better. She felt like she'd aged at least a hundred years.

"Is that what's been worrying you so, woman?" He stepped back a pace, his laughter filling the air.

Shocked at his response, Tamar turned to face him. She had to make him understand. Jensen was a warm, caring man who deserved better than a worn-out old slave for a wife. "You cannot tie yourself to me. Don't you see, Jensen? I work for Lily and her sisters. I don't have time or the right to be a wife and mother."

A noise at the door warned her they were no longer alone. Tamar looked past Jensen's shoulder and saw Lily, a look of dismay on her face. Tamar dropped her rag and moved to the girl. "I don't know what you heard. We were just talking. You have so much to deal with, please don't make this your concern."

"But it is. How can it not be when I'm the one coming between you and Jensen?"

Tamar recognized the determined look on Lily's face. It was the same look she'd worn when she'd decided to rebel against her relatives and set up housekeeping on a riverboat. But this problem could not be solved by determination.

She opened her mouth, but Lily shook her head. "You needn't try convincing me otherwise, Tamar. I'm going to set you free so you can live your life in a way you choose."

"You don't know what you're saying, Miss Lily." She pointed a finger at the younger woman. "You don't own me. Your grandmother does. And when she dies, I'll become the property of whoever she wills me to. I was born a slave, and that's what I'll be until they lay my body in its grave."

Tamar had been so focused on convincing Lily of the folly of her words that she'd forgotten Jensen was still there. He cleared his throat. "I think I have the answer for both of you."

Lily lowered her chin a smidgen, but a frown still marred her face. "What's that?"

"I'll pay the purchase price to your relatives and set Tamar free."

"You can afford that?"

A confident smile accompanied Jensen's nod. "I've managed to put some money aside over the years."

"I can help, too. We made a small profit from our first voyage, and we're going to make even more once we dock in Memphis this evening." Lily's chin moved to its normal level. "We can make this work."

"Wait a minute." Tamar couldn't believe they were talking about her and her future as if she wasn't in the room. "What if I don't—" She stopped. What could she say? That she didn't want to be free? Tamar sent a pleading look toward Jensen. "I can't let you spend that kind of money."

Jensen snorted. "You can't stop me. I'm free, remember?"

Tamar looked from one to the other. A whole new world seemed to be opening for her. It was an exhilarating, absolutely terrifying idea. She'd always known what was expected of her. She'd even had the added benefit of loving all three of her charges as if they were her daughters.

If she let Jensen and Lily do this, everything would change. Lily and her sisters would replace her with another slave. Then what would she do? Tamar had never considered a different future, and she didn't know if she could do so now.

With a wordless cry, she tossed the rag down and ran from the room. Why did life have to be so difficult?

Lily recognized Eli Thornton the minute she saw him. He had his father's good looks and his mother's wise gaze. As soon as he found out who she was, he welcomed her with open arms, offering to let Jasmine, David, and her, along with Tamar, sleep in their home for the duration of their stay. David had asked to remain on board the *Hattie Belle* with the other men, and she had agreed.

They would be leaving in two days, and Eli assured her they would be fully loaded with cargo. One thing was certain—Uncle Phillip had been right about the money available in the shipping business. They were already making more money than she had imagined. Their profit margin was good enough that she would soon be able to buy out Blake's interest in the *Hattie Belle*. He could purchase another boat and fleece innocent victims.

Dinner that evening was a lively affair. Lily took an instant liking to Eli's wife, Renée, a perky beauty with dark hair and hazel eyes. With all three of Eli and Renée's boys joining them, there was scarcely a lull in the conversation. They peppered their guests with questions about current events in New Orleans and the rest of the Thornton clan.

As soon as the meal was over, Lily pled exhaustion and escorted her yawning sister to their bedroom. So tired were they that she didn't even notice the locations of the other bedrooms. She almost fell asleep while

Tamar brushed and plaited her hair, her head nodding like a snag in the river. Even Jasmine's animation was muted as they said their prayers and climbed into their shared bed.

Her youngest sister was asleep as soon as her head settled on the pillow, but Lily was so exhausted she was unable to rest. Scattered images spun in her head. Had Blake been about to kiss her? A shiver passed through her. He was not the right man for her, even if he was devastatingly handsome. Good looks had nothing to do with what was in a man's heart. No, she would be better off with someone like Jean Luc, someone she could count on to support her.

She wondered why no shiver erupted as she considered being kissed by him. Probably because he was such a fine gentleman. He would never take advantage of her. Not that Blake had taken advantage. But he had wanted to. She'd seen it in his expression. Or was that her imagination?

Lily sighed and redirected her thoughts to Camellia, wondering if she missed them. Probably not. Jasmine twisted in the bed and punched her with a bony knee. Lily smiled. Camellia certainly would not have enjoyed sharing the bed. If Jasmine kept moving, she was not likely to enjoy a restful slumber herself. . . .

"Wake up." A small hand shook Lily's shoulder. "Wake up, Sissy. Something's wrong."

Lily rolled over and blinked at the unfamiliar room. "Wha—" A hand covered her mouth, pulling her into wakefulness with a start. Her heartbeat slowed as she realized it belonged to Jasmine.

"I think someone is breaking into the house," Jasmine whispered close to her ear. "What should we do?"

Holding her breath, Lily stretched her hearing to its limit. At first she heard nothing but silence. Then a thump, bump, bump. She could feel her eyes widening.

"Did you hear that?" Jasmine's whisper was fearful.

In the dim light, she could barely make out her sister's face. She nodded and pushed back the sheet. "Stay here."

Lily tiptoed to the door and opened it an inch. Crash! Her heartbeat ratcheted up another few notches. She glanced around the room for a weapon and picked up her parasol. It was not much better than her bare hands, but the sharp point at the end of the spine might make an effective threat. Looking over her shoulder, she summoned a smile for Jasmine, who was sitting up, her knees drawn to her chin.

Should she knock on Eli and Renée Thornton's bedroom door? Lily took a moment to look at the other three doors that faced the second-floor landing. Which one belonged to the parents? She didn't want to wake the children, so Lily crept to the top of the stairs, her parasol held high.

Yellow light made a pool in the hallway leading toward the back of the house. A dark figure must be the burglar. He stumbled into a wall. Then another figure appeared. How many burglars were in the house? Praying for courage and protection, she crept down the stairs.

"Halt!" Her voice came out in a squeak. Both figures stopped. She couldn't see their features because of the light behind them, but she brandished her parasol, holding it like a sword in front of her.

"Miss Anderson? What are you doing down here?"

Lily lowered her parasol as she recognized Eli Thornton's voice. "What's going on?"

She could barely make out his features. And who was standing next to him? A servant? Was he being forced to help a burglar?

"Everything is fine, Miss Anderson. You need to go back to bed." Eli spoke as both he and the other man stepped into the light. The staid butler? Why were the two of them creeping about the house in the middle of the night?

"Not until you tell me what you're doing up at this hour."

Eli's sleeves were rolled up to his elbows, and he held a bowl in his hands. His expression was tense, much more drawn than earlier in the evening. Before he could answer her, a door opened farther down the corridor. "Where's that warm water?"

The butler took the bowl from Eli and moved toward the voice.

When Lily tried to follow him, Eli stepped into her path. She brandished her parasol even though the action felt a bit silly. "Whatever is going on must be serious. Perhaps I can help."

"It would be much easier if you returned to your bedroom, but if you'll promise not to tell anyone about what you see. . ."

Lily nodded, and they entered the Thorntons' library.

Several of the Thorntons' slaves were in the room, most of them focused on a figure propped against the edge of Eli's desk. The poor fellow looked a mess, his clothing in tatters, his feet bare. The coppery scent of blood filled the air. She glanced at Eli. "Is he a fugitive?"

Eli nodded. "He escaped from a plantation a few miles south of here because his master whipped him nearly to death for answering too loudly."

Lily's mouth dropped open. She'd heard whispers of mistreatment by slave owners, but at Les Fleurs, no slave ever suffered. "That's inexcusable."

Everyone had been watching her with fear, but apparently reassured by her reaction, they went back to their tasks, some offering food and water while others cleaned the poor man's back.

Eli removed a vial from his shirt pocket and shook it vigorously. "Would you pour some water into one of those glasses?"

Looking about, Lily spied a serving tray on Eli's desk. It held two glasses and a pitcher of water. "How much?"

"Half full."

Lily complied and held the glass while Eli poured his concoction into it. "What's that?"

"Laudanum. It will help him sleep." Eli grabbed a spoon from the tray and stirred. "Then perhaps he can continue on his way tomorrow night."

"The Underground Railroad?" Lily whispered the words. She'd heard of the escape route but never dreamed she would be privy to one of the way stations.

Eli nodded. "Now you know what a dangerous secret we're keeping."

"I's sorry." The fugitive groaned out the words. "I didn't mean to. . ."

A rounded woman who might be the housekeeper patted his hand. "Don't worry. We're doing nothing more than our Christian duty."

The man subsided and let Lily hold the glass of water to his lips.

"Lily?" Jasmine's whisper drifted down the hall. "Where are you?"

"You need to go back upstairs." Eli's gaze met hers. "We can't have the whole household waking up and catching us."

Conflicting desires warred within her, but Lily could not ignore the needs of the frightened, desperate man. "I'll reassure Jasmine, but then I'll be back to help."

Before anyone could argue, she retraced her steps. Jasmine was leaning over the balustrade. "It's okay, Jasmine. It's only a late-night guest." She helped Jasmine return to bed. "Go to sleep."

"Where are you going?"

"Back to help."

"Can't I help?" Jasmine's voice was plaintive.

Lily kissed her cheek. "You need your sleep."

Jasmine's lower lip protruded as Lily left her, but she must have fallen back asleep quickly, as the only sounds emanating from her were the deep breaths of restful slumber. Lily was relieved. Although Jasmine's tender heart would have been touched, she was still a child. Helping an escaped slave was a hanging offense. She might risk her own neck, but she would not risk Jasmine's.

The next hour passed quickly as Lily helped bandage the man's wounds. While she worked alongside the others, the fugitive described his ordeal. He spoke of the girl he'd married by jumping the broom, as slaves couldn't legally marry, and how he'd probably never see her again because she'd been sold to another plantation. He talked about the daily quota of cotton expected of every able-bodied slave. He even spoke about other punishments he'd endured. His back, crisscrossed by a web of gashes, bore mute testimony to the truth of his story.

Thinking of his pain made Lily sick. No human should be so cruel to another. The events of this night had been seared into her memory with the force of a brand. She would never forget.

The sun was turning the sky a pale pink as she trudged upstairs and fell into bed. Sleep overtook her as soon as her head hit the pillow, but Lily's dreams were filled with fractured images of being chased through swamps, her parasol in one hand as the muddy water dragged at her skirts.

Chapter Thirty-nine

Walking past the storeroom filled with crates and barrels, Lily realized the nightmares had begun to fade. Over the past weeks, they had repeated the run between Natchez and Memphis, making regular stops in Port Gibson, Vicksburg, and Greenville. Business was thriving.

If only Camellia had not been adamant about staying with Grandmother and Aunt Dahlia until they took the promised trip to New Orleans. But every load seemed slated for delivery to Memphis. Feeling torn between business and family obligations, Lily had reluctantly yielded to her younger sister's wishes. She wanted to avoid the type of coercion that had sent her fleeing after Grandfather's death. It wasn't the easiest option, but she prayed it was the best one.

Lily sighed as she turned toward the ladies' parlor. At least the Lord had blessed her idea of using afternoon tea as an opportunity for Bible study. No matter how diverse the women passengers were, they seemed to enjoy discussing how to apply the Bible to their daily problems. Today she would suggest reading John 7 about the rivers of living water, the Holy Spirit, which flowed inside all believers.

The afternoon was far advanced when Blake called her out of the ladies' parlor. "Captain Henrick says we'll need to stop and purchase more firewood."

Stopping at wood yards was a normal occurrence, so Lily wondered why Blake thought it necessary to let her know. Did he have another reason to seek her out? Her heart turned over, rushing blood to her cheeks. "That doesn't sound like much of a problem."

His brow furrowed. "It will stop us from reaching Natchez this evening unless you want to risk the boat by continuing after dark."

Comprehension brought a sense of irritation. "Why didn't we stop at an earlier yard? The captain must have known this would happen. We've been up and down this stretch of river several times."

"Lily, can't you let go of your distrust a little?"

His question speared her conscience. Was she being too hard on her father? No. He was supposed to be a seasoned captain. "I would expect the same thing from any captain. By making a mistake like this, he's put the *Hattie Belle* at risk. Why can't you see that?"

The furrow deepened. "What I see is that you are as quick to condemn Captain Henrick as you have been me. I don't understand, Lily. No one on this boat wants to fail, least of all your father. Can't you see how he's trying to win your approval? Last month when we were in New Orleans, you were full of advice about how I should reestablish a link with my family. Maybe it's time for you to listen to your own counsel."

Not wanting Blake to see how his words had affected her, she turned away. A tear trickled down her cheek. Lily refused to be the type of woman who used tears to blackmail a man into doing what she wanted. She was stronger than that. Brushing the tear away with an impatient finger, she took a deep breath and tried to understand why Blake was championing Captain Henrick. What possible reason could the man have for failing to have enough wood on board? If he was as good a captain as he'd claimed, he would not put them in peril. She slammed the door on her emotions and took a deep, cleansing breath.

Blake's hands came down on her shoulders and pressed gently to turn her around.

Lily didn't want to look up. "He's supposed to be captaining this ship. That's the only thing I need from him."

"Lily, both of us know what it's like to make mistakes. You can be so warm and accepting toward others. You are a gracious hostess and a capable manager. Why can't you yield just a little to the captain?"

She glanced up. His eyes drew her in. Their blue depths promised understanding and comfort. Then his lids drooped a bit, and the blue fire in his gaze singed her. Whatever she'd been about to say slipped from her mind. No wonder all their lady passengers—all ladies in general—found him so attractive.

"No matter how hard you try to ignore it, he is your father." Blake's voice was as tempting as a soft pillow.

Lily could feel herself yielding. She pulled away, and as soon as he let go, her mind began working again. She needed to focus on their current problem. "Can we spend the night at the wood yard?"

"I suppose so. According to Captain Henrick, Sanderson Wood Yard is only a few miles away. But stopping now means we'll lose several hours of travel."

She chewed at her lower lip. "Whether we stay here or stop somewhere else, we won't make it home in time to attend church in Natchez."

He shrugged. "Maybe you could have a service on the boat."

Was Blake actually suggesting a church service? She considered the idea then shook her head. "We don't have a preacher on board."

"Captain Henrick could lead a service."

Her jaw clenched to hold back the flood of emotions that once again threatened. "He's not a preacher."

His shoulders lowered a notch. Was he disappointed? "He may not be a preacher, but he has a great deal of insight on matters of faith. If you spent a little more time with him, you might change your mind."

Lily wanted to shout a denial. She had to protect herself. Otherwise— She reined in her thoughts once more. For now she would concentrate on the original problem. She needed to answer the question of what to do after purchasing wood. "There aren't any other ports between here and Vicksburg, so if we continue, we'd be alone when we docked." Lily shuddered. "We'd be vulnerable to pirates."

"That's true, but there've been no reports of pirates operating on this part of the river for years."

Lily spread her hands, palms upward. "We have several children on board—passengers as well as David and Jasmine. I can't take a chance that someone might be hurt. At the most we'll lose a day."

"Do we have enough food?"

She gave an emphatic nod. "I think we have enough for an extra week."

"That's fine then. I'll notify Captain Henrick and the crew."

Lily reached for the doorknob to the ladies' parlor. "I'll tell our passengers." But before entering the room, she watched Blake's retreating back, her mind replaying his words. She didn't like admitting it, but he had a point. She didn't want to be the type of hypocrite who dispensed advice but refused to follow it. Yet she couldn't reach out to her father—not unless she asked for God's help.

Which led to a concern at the heart of the matter. How would she respond if God did smooth out a path toward reconciliation?

Blake slid into the empty seat next to Lily, nodding to David and Jasmine on her far side. The dining hall looked very different this morning. The tables had been pushed to one side, and all the chairs had been placed in rows for the Sunday service.

Tamar and Jensen stood with the passengers' slaves at the back of the room. Jensen's face was clean shaven, and he wore a recently pressed suit. Tamar was in a uniform but looked different—younger and more relaxed. Blake thought perhaps her hair had a new style, or maybe it was the half smile on her lips. Whatever the change, he approved.

His gaze came back to Lily, so prim and proper. He wondered what she thought of his presence.

When Henrick told him Lily had invited him to preach, Blake had been shocked. The captain had seemed pleased about the opportunity although aware his daughter was not ready to seek reconciliation. Blake had reminded him that Lily's actions were a good sign and might be the beginning of a real relationship between father and daughter.

Blake wondered if his conversation with Lily had gotten through her stubbornness. It was a sobering thought. For her to listen to his advice meant she valued his opinion. Was that why he found himself attending this morning? A response to her willingness to change? Or was he just curious?

He would rather believe he was here because of his admiration for Captain Henrick. At least the man was trying to make amends for his past misdeeds. The captain had told Blake how he'd plunged into despair after his wife died. But the man had managed to pull himself out of the hole he'd dug. He'd created a new life for himself. He was even trying to reconcile his past.

Captain Henrick gave all the credit for his transformation to God, but Blake thought he should accept a measure of recognition himself. It took a lot of determination to turn one's life around. The river towns were full of men like the captain had once been—men who eked out a miserable existence, slogging through life with a minimum of effort, looking for handouts or opportunities to prey on others.

After the passengers stopped entering the dining hall, Captain Henrick stood to get their attention. Dressed in his trademark red shirt and dark pants, the man still managed to look very natural standing before a group of people. His smile was wide and infectious. "Good morning. What a beautiful Lord's Day we are enjoying. This morning I thought I would talk to you about a passage from Isaiah."

He stopped and looked at the floor. Blake wondered if he'd been stricken by fear. He could certainly understand an attack of nerves. He wished he could reassure the captain. Shuffling his feet, he wondered if he should do something to ease the building tension in the quiet room.

Captain Henrick looked up, a serious expression on his weathered face. "Before I get started, I think you should know how proud I am to stand up here. When my. . .employer asked me to talk to you this morning, I thought she was joking." Several chuckles came from the audience. "I'm not a preacher, but the Good Book says you don't have to be to talk to others about God. You only have to be willing. I thought about that and how I want to serve God. Then I thought you might like to hear about how an angry old sinner like me came to be a believer. So I went back to the passage that the Lord used to get my attention."

He opened his Bible and began reading. " 'To appoint unto them that mourn in Zion, to give unto them beauty for ashes, the oil of joy for mourning, the garment of praise for the spirit of heaviness; that they might be called trees of righteousness, the planting of the Lord, that he might be glorified.'"

He bowed his head. "Dearest Lord, we come to You today with hearts full of thankfulness, hearts full of love and devotion. And for those among us who are struggling or grieving or lost, I ask that You fulfill Your promise to give them 'beauty for ashes.' Thank You, Lord, for listening. Please pour out Your Spirit on us today. Amen."

A rustling swept the room as the listeners settled in for the sermon, but to Blake's ears it sounded different. The hair at the back of his neck stood up. He had heard of the Holy Spirit, of course, but he'd never put much stock in such things. He wanted to look around, see if some ghostly mist floated in the air behind him, but he resisted the impulse.

"I remember the first time I read this scripture." Captain Henrick's face was relaxed. "I was in a deep, dark hole. I had done a terrible thing, for which I could not seek forgiveness." He looked over the crowd. "Some of you may be feeling the same way this morning. Some of you may think you can never seek the Lord."

Captain Henrick's gaze settled on Blake. What did the man think he'd done that was so awful? Blake thought back over the years since he'd left home. He hadn't been so bad. He'd never killed anyone or stolen anything. He squared his shoulders and stared back at Lily's father, his sympathy gone. What did Captain Henrick know about anything?

"I was lying in the ashes of despair. I mourned for things from my past. The heaviness described by the prophet Isaiah weighed heavily on my spirit. But God reached out to me. And I stand here today as a testament to His power. I am a different man. I have the peace promised by Jesus. My life is filled with beauty, with the oil of joy, and the garment of praise." Captain Henrick stopped speaking. He closed his Bible.

"Now you may be tempted to seek His blessings just as I was. And I encourage you to do so. But be warned. It doesn't stop there. Your life will become something beautiful and glorious, but that's not the end of it." He opened the Bible again and flipped a couple of pages before continuing. "Listen to the second part of this verse. 'That they might be called trees of righteousness, the planting of the Lord, that he might be glorified.'"

The captain lifted his face up toward the ceiling. "We're not on earth to make a decent living, or to marry and start a happy family. Those aren't bad things, but they are things of this world. They are things we should never see as our goals. We're here to glorify our Maker. He has planted us here for His purpose."

Captain Henrick's lips turned up in a smile of the purest joy Blake had ever witnessed. "Think of it. The Master of all, the glorious Creator, the mysterious I Am. He created you and me to glorify Him through our righteousness. What more wonderful task can we have?"

Blake felt himself caught up in the joy of the captain's sermon. He almost felt the touch of God. He glanced at Lily. Her face was also lit as though from within. She had it, too. Intense yearning swept him. He wanted to feel what they felt. He wanted the joy of knowing God, of living for a higher purpose. The need was so deep and consuming that it nearly brought him to his knees.

But reality seeped in. He couldn't do that. He didn't deserve such a future. It was probably a sham anyway. His own father had been a preacher. Blake knew better than to fall for the empty promises of religion. He would be better off if he'd never given in to the impulse to listen to Lily's father this morning. It would have been a better use of his time to have stayed in bed.

The voice in Blake's head drowned out the rest of Captain Henrick's testimony. He had no need of the emotional flood the man's words could cause. He needed to keep his feet on the ground. Keep working hard.

He and Lily were making a lot of money. Soon one of them would be able to buy out the other. Then they could go their separate ways. He wouldn't have to worry about her prickly morals, and she wouldn't have to fret about his talent with games of chance. All he had to do was keep his focus on the real world, the one he knew so well.

He bowed his head when the others did, his gaze trained on the floor. The yawning jaws of a trap seemed to open at his feet, a snare to deceive those who felt unable to rely on themselves. He refused to fall for it.

Ignoring the dull ache in his chest, Blake followed the others out of the dining hall after the closing prayer. He promised himself he would never submit to another church service.

He ignored Lily's glance and headed toward the engine room. He could not afford to be swept away by pretty words and fake sentiments. Someone on board this boat needed to keep a cool head.

Chapter Forty

Lily stood at the rail as Captain Henrick skillfully navigated them into the dock at Natchez, her mind full of all they needed to do. If the temperature continued to drop, she'd have to ask Tamar to pack warmer clothes for their next trip. Maybe she should learn to pack for herself. Maybe it was time to stop relying on a slave.

After the cargo and passengers had been off-loaded, she went to find Blake. A fruitless search around the lower floors led her to the hurricane deck. She heard his voice before she saw him. He and the captain were talking.

Not wanting to be accused of eavesdropping, she raised her hand. "Hello there."

Both men turned toward her.

"Do you need something?" Blake asked. "I thought you would have gone to your family's home by now."

"I had an idea I wanted to discuss." She hugged herself. It was even colder on the hurricane deck due to the wind. "It's about David."

Blake excused himself from her father and stepped toward her. "Is he causing a problem?"

They walked down the stairs side by side. What would it feel like to walk hand in hand? Suppressing the image, Lily cleared her throat. "No, of course not. David couldn't cause a ruckus if he tried. But he seems more withdrawn lately. Do you have any idea what's bothering him?"

Blake shook his head. "Have you talked to him?"

"I thought I'd ask you to. He seems to look up to you."

"That's just because I'm a foot taller than he is."

A laugh gurgled up Lily's throat. "Stop teasing. You're like a big brother to him. Jasmine told me his father left to search for gold in California. She said he's certain his father is going to return for him someday."

They reached the third floor, empty except for the crewman cleaning the guest rooms. Although the port was as busy as ever, a hush seemed to envelop them.

Blake's expression had grown serious. "I'll talk to him."

Lily put a hand on his arm. "Thank you. I appreciate this, especially since you never wanted to take him aboard in the first place."

"He's been a good companion for Jasmine." He stopped and cleared his throat. "And I have to admit I've grown fond of him, too."

Was it her imagination, or had Blake's cheeks darkened? She squeezed his arm. "Thanks."

⁂

Whenever they returned to Les Fleurs, it seemed to have grown smaller. Perhaps it was because Lily had rediscovered how huge the world really was. She smiled at Tamar, who seemed a bit distracted. "I think your mind must still be back on the *Hattie Belle*."

Tamar grimaced. "The longer I'm away from that man, the better."

"What man?" Jasmine's gaze moved from Lily to Tamar and back.

Lily shook her head. "I'll not tell any tales. If you want to find out, you'll have to ask Tamar."

Jasmine's eyes widened. "Who is it, Tamar? Is someone courting you?"

Tamar groaned. "Now why would you say such a thing to Jasmine? You know she'll badger me day and night."

"Jasmine, you are not to bother Tamar with her private business." Lily hoped her command would control her youngest sister's curiosity. Attempting to distract her, she broached a different subject. "Do you think Camellia has a suitor?"

Jasmine moved next to her sister. "She may have a whole line of them."

"I hope not." Lily chuckled at the picture Jasmine's words conjured. Wouldn't the butler be amazed if he answered the door to find not one or two, but a dozen suitors? She would brook no argument from Camellia this time. All three of them would go on the next trip.

Grandmother was sitting on the front porch when the carriage pulled up. As soon as she recognized them, she gave a glad cry, stood, and hurried toward them with widespread arms. "I'm so happy to see you. We were worried something might have happened when you didn't return yesterday as planned."

Lily emerged from the embrace and smiled at the older woman. "You shouldn't worry so. You know we cannot always adhere to a schedule."

"I know, but I will always be concerned for your safety."

Jasmine dashed inside and ran upstairs as Lily and Grandmother followed more sedately. Their happy reunion turned bittersweet as Lily realized Grandmother was probably thinking of the daughter she'd lost to the river.

As soon as she settled her grandmother in her usual chair, Lily sat on the sofa and arranged her skirts. "Is Camellia home this afternoon?"

Grandmother shook her head. "She's out riding with a few young people. That girl has turned into a social butterfly."

The door opened, and Aunt Dahlia entered the room, her head high, a sour look on her face. "I see the wanderers have come home."

Lily decided to ignore her aunt's bad mood. "It's nice to see you looking so well this afternoon." She supposed a lukewarm welcome was all she would ever receive from this woman. And why? Because she had not been interested in the one suitor they had presented? Or was it because she was afraid they would drag the family into scandal? Whatever, it didn't excuse her catty behavior.

Grandmother intervened. "Lily was just telling me about her wonderful crew, giving me a most marvelous idea."

Lily's stomach twisted in a knot.

"How long are you planning to stay with us, dear?"

"Several days, maybe as long as a week." Lily didn't go into all the details. Besides work on the boiler and pistons the captain wanted to see to, Blake wanted to help David find information about his parents, and she wanted to give David every chance to reconnect with his father.

"Oh good, then we'll have time to plan a casual evening."

"Whatever are you talking about?" asked Aunt Dahlia.

Grandmother looked more animated than Lily had seen her since

Grandfather's death. "Not a party, mind you. We don't need music or dancing, but we would all enjoy a nice dinner." She paused, beaming a smile toward Lily. "We'll invite Mr. Matthews and your new captain and any other of your business associates. It will be a chance for your family to meet the people who have helped make your venture successful."

Lily blinked several times as her mind spun.

"Well, what do you think?" Grandmother's question was directed at her. "Would you rather schedule it for Thursday or Friday evening?"

"I'm not sure it's a good idea." Lily shuddered as she imagined her family's reaction if Captain Henrick Anderson showed up at their front door. Grandmother would probably faint dead away, Uncle Phillip would throw him out on his ear, and Aunt Dahlia would use him as an excuse to keep Camellia and Jasmine from returning to the *Hattie Belle*.

"I agree with Lily." Aunt Dahlia frowned. "We don't need to advertise the fact that your granddaughters and my nieces are living on a riverboat instead of attending finishing schools."

Although she was much too old for finishing school, Lily did not argue with her unexpected ally. Part of her wanted to defend their lifestyle, the experience they gained by visiting other ports and being exposed to the world of business. Lily hoped she was giving her sisters knowledge they would need to make their own way in the world, but she stopped short of expressing her thoughts. Stopping her grandmother's plans was more important.

"You're being absurd, Dahlia. Everyone knows what Lily and her sisters are doing. We live in much too close a society for something as big as their life on the river to be kept secret." She turned back to Lily. "I think it would be a delightful evening."

"I appreciate the offer, Grandmother, but I doubt whether Captain—" She bit off the word as she realized using even his first name could raise questions she didn't want to answer. "Whether the captain or Mr. Matthews would enjoy themselves."

"I don't see why not."

Breathing a sigh of relief that no one seemed to catch her gaffe, Lily twisted her hands together. She had never foreseen the problems she would face in hiding the captain's identity. The desire to be done with the subterfuge warred with her wish to avoid further confrontations with her family. She had never been—and did not want to become— good at lying.

Grandmother continued to make suggestions. "Why don't you ask them, Lily? If they say no, I'll drop my idea. But they would probably love to meet your family and spend time with us."

Knowing how impossible it would be to convince her grandmother that her plan was an invitation to disaster, Lily decided to avoid further discussion by simply putting her off. "I'll ask them the next time I'm down at the dock."

Her grandmother's eyes lost their luster, and for a moment Lily almost relented. But she needed to keep her heart from misleading her. Delaying a confrontation was the only course to take. Eventually Grandmother would forget her impulse to meet the men.

"I can send them a message if you're not going tomorrow." Grandmother glanced toward her writing desk. "It wouldn't take but a moment. And you can stand over my shoulder to make sure I don't say something that would offend them."

Another crack formed in Lily's heart. "Don't go to any trouble. I'm sure I'll see both of them in a day or two."

"I want the whole world to know how proud I am of you, Lily. You've done something remarkable. You've made your own way in the world. That's an accomplishment we can all appreciate, can't we?" She glanced past Lily to Aunt Dahlia.

"Of course." Aunt Dahlia's confirmation lacked the ring of truth.

Lily wasn't surprised by her aunt's lackluster response. She raised her chin a bit. "Thank you, Grandmother. I'll let you know what they say."

If the captain was any other man, this moment would be filled with unalloyed joy. The acceptance of her family—her grandmother at least—meant a great deal to Lily. But the truth about her father threatened to leech all the pleasure from her grandmother's accolades. She could never let her relatives meet him. Not if she wanted to avoid a disaster that could completely shatter her relationship with her family.

Chapter Forty-one

Jean Luc regarded himself in the mirror, noting with satisfaction the way his hair had been combed toward his face. Combined with the close fit of his coat and the expert twists of his cravat, his appearance epitomized a fashionable gentleman of means. He practiced a wide smile. What female could resist such a handsome fellow?

Lily Anderson. His dimples disappeared. Why did the single woman he needed to woo seem impervious to his charm? At least when he'd called on her at Les Fleurs, she had agreed to dine with him this evening.

He pulled on a pair of gloves and left his bedroom, his mind still chewing on the problem of how to win Lily's affections. Nothing he'd done so far had been very successful. Steenberg had been an absolute disaster, and she and that Matthews fellow had hired a full crew complement before he could suggest someone who would report to him.

Jean Luc considered his plans for their evening. He would take her to the same dining establishment they'd visited before. But this time he had secured a quiet table in a secluded corner. Candles and a fresh flower arrangement would decorate the table, a romantic touch that should impress Lily.

It was a pity she eschewed alcohol, as a glass or two of bubbly champagne would probably put her in a more convivial mood. But perhaps the bottle of effervescent springwater he'd secured would be equally salutary.

He climbed into the family carriage, the conveyance he'd chosen so he wouldn't be distracted by the traffic, and planned what he would say to Miss Anderson on the way to town. He would need to compliment her looks, of course, tell her she was the most charming, witty companion, that he felt honored by her agreement to spend an evening with him. All the things ladies yearned to hear.

His arrival at Les Fleurs was enthusiastic. He sat and chatted with Lily's grandmother, aunt, and uncle while he waited for her appearance. She entered the room, and he stood, allowing his smile to widen as he caressed her with his eyes. He moved toward her, bowed, and kissed her hand. "You look especially beautiful this evening."

As he straightened, Jean Luc saw that Lily's cheeks had reddened. It was a pity she was not a beauty. There was nothing really wrong with her looks, but her face was a little too plain. Her hair was a nondescript brown, and her eyes were about as lovely as a mud puddle.

Perhaps if she wore a color other than black. He recalled the first time they'd met, when she'd been dressed in something white and frilly. Perhaps when she emerged from mourning, she would look better.

"You are very debonair this evening, Monsieur Champney."

He bowed again. "I am honored to please you."

The aunt simpered as though he'd directed his compliments at her.

Jean Luc tucked Lily's hand into the crook of his arm and faced the rest of her family. "Thank you for trusting your treasure to my care."

The grandmother waved a hand at them. "Save your suave compliments for my granddaughter. Now go on, you two, and enjoy your evening."

They climbed into the carriage with a minimum of fuss. As soon as they were settled on opposite benches, Jean Luc rapped on the roof of the carriage with his cane.

"Where are we going this evening?"

"I hope you don't mind, but I wanted to return to the place where we first enjoyed a meal together."

"That will be delightful. I'm sure you remember that I secured my very first cargo that evening."

Jean Luc's jaw clamped. If not for that coincidence, Lily would probably have returned ownership of the *Hattie Belle* to him months ago. "Yes, that's right."

She chattered about her trips to Memphis and yet another branch of the shipping family who had befriended her. He sat back and nodded, biding his time.

They arrived at the hotel, and he escorted her to the dining room. The host caught sight of them and hurried over. "Welcome, welcome. We have your table ready, Monsieur Champney." Bowing repeatedly, he escorted them to the linen-covered table.

Jean Luc hoped Lily noticed how eager the man was to please him. She needed to understand how influential his family was.

After he helped Lily into her seat, Jean Luc slipped an extra coin into the man's palm, which earned him yet another bow. Sliding into his seat on the opposite side of the table, Jean Luc frowned. Although the flower arrangement was lovely, it hid his dining partner from his view. Reaching out, he moved a silver candelabrum closer to the edge of the table and scooted the crystal vase over so he could see Lily's face. "That's better."

If the smile on her face was any indication, he had managed to impress her. She opened her napkin and placed it on her lap. "You must have gone to a great deal of trouble."

"Once you accepted my invitation to dinner, I wanted to make sure this would be a memorable night."

"How could it be otherwise? I always enjoy our time together."

"Then you have forgiven me for offending you the last time we met?"

A fleeting frown crossed her expression. "I could never be truly offended by you, Jean Luc. I value your friendship too much."

That was a start. Jean Luc led their conversation in a different direction as their meal was delivered. Lily ate hers with a bit more gusto than he found attractive, being more used to ladies who picked at their food and abandoned whole plates after only managing to swallow a bite or two. But for now that habit could be overlooked. Once he secured her affection, she would want to please him enough to adopt more genteel habits.

He signaled for their dessert, a chocolate custard accompanied by steaming cups of dark, rich coffee. "I trust you approve of my choices for our dinner."

"Yes." She picked up a spoon and dredged out a mouthful of chocolate. "I'm flattered by your thoughtfulness. You make me feel like a princess."

Jean Luc summoned a burning stare to convince her of his desire.

"I would like to do more."

The words fell between them, stilling her spoon halfway between plate and mouth. Her eyes widened. She put down the bite of dessert. "But you've already done so much. I owe you a debt of gratitude."

Leaning forward, he took her hand in his. "Let there be no discussion of debts between us. It is not appropriate when I have such feelings about you. My heart is troubled when you are away. I worry about your safety and think of you almost without ceasing. I wish we were not so often separated by distance."

"But it is delightful to see you whenever I am in Natchez." Her hand fluttered in his hold like a frightened bird.

Jean Luc hid his irritation. "I pine for your smiles when you are not close."

"Your sentiments are very flattering, Jean Luc. I put so much stock in our friendship. You must know how much I rely on your advice and expertise." Her hand stopped fluttering.

"And I will be most happy to advise you, but please tell me that our friendship could evolve into a warmer relationship." He summoned his most devastating smile, one that had won him many favors in the past.

"I don't know. . . ."

He tightened his grasp on her hand. "Has someone stolen your heart from me?"

"Of course not." She tugged her hand free. "I've been much too busy to think of romance. Running a business commands my full attention."

"You must feel overwhelmed by the responsibility." Jean Luc drummed his fingers on the tablecloth. He hoped this was the right time to broach the subject that had been on his mind for several days. "In fact, I have an idea that may help."

"Really?"

He watched her face for a hint of how to proceed. Her features smoothed out so quickly it was like looking at a mask. Was her mind open or closed?

She glanced at the table, and he realized he was still drumming his fingers. He clenched his hand and brought it to his lap. "How would you feel about letting someone else, someone you trust, someone who has your best interests in mind. . ." Jean Luc paused and took a slow breath. "What if such a person offered to take over the day-to-day decisions of your shipping operations?"

"What are you suggesting?"

"I am offering to run the *Hattie Belle.*" There. He'd said it. Now he must convince her that his idea was the perfect solution.

"Why would I want to burden you with such a task?"

"Lily, you have seen the river up close. You must know that you are the only woman trying to run her own boat. By your own admission, it is a terrible burden." He reached for his coffee cup. "I think it is admirable that you've given so much to your endeavors. You have proven what you can accomplish, but now it is time for you to come back home. . .settle down. . .perhaps even marry."

"I am quite happy on the *Hattie Belle.*"

Jean Luc sipped some of the dark liquid from his cup and set it back on the table. "But you are working much too hard. Don't you see? You should be treated like a princess. If you were here more often, I could court you properly."

She pushed her chair back from the table. "I am not a princess, nor do I aspire to become one."

Jean Luc rose when she did. Was she going to storm out of the hotel? "I meant to compliment you, Lily. I only want you to lead the life to which you were bred."

Her brown eyes filled with flashes of hot emotion. "The life to which I was bred? My father and mother spent many years together on the river. They thought it was a good place to raise a family. I'd say that remaining in Natchez and allowing you or some other man to fawn over me would be contrary to the life my parents imagined for me, wouldn't you?"

He raised his shoulders in a gesture of agreement, but inside he was seething. How dare she spurn his offer? How dare this little nobody—a girl who'd never even seen Europe—look down her nose at him?

Like a volcanic eruption, he felt the anger gathering force. She may have been raised at Les Fleurs plantation, but she was proving a great deal of common blood ran in her veins. "I'm sorry, I must have been mistaken. I suppose you're right. I should have realized that your head has been filled with nonsense from the likes of Blake Matthews and the other wharf rats you've been rubbing shoulders with."

Her mouth open and closed several times, but no words came.

Good. Maybe she was beginning to regret her earlier disdain. But he would be slow to accept her apology. He gestured for their cloaks. "I should take you home."

The ride back was quiet and uncomfortable. Jean Luc got out first and offered her a hand.

She ignored his gesture, climbing out with one hand on the carriage frame and the other lifting her skirts. "Thank you for the meal." Her voice was as cold as winter rain.

Jean Luc bowed and watched as she ascended the stairs and disappeared through the front doors. The minute she was out of sight, he wanted to kick himself. Why had he let himself get so angry? Why hadn't he apologized instead of waiting for her to come to him? He knew how stubborn she was. He would have to demean himself tomorrow and send her a note of apology, maybe a bouquet of flowers. He had to get back in her good graces.

He climbed back into the carriage, his mind on possible solutions. As the coachman headed back to his parents' home, an idea occurred to him. He rapped on the roof of the carriage and shouted new instructions before settling back to contemplate his situation. Maybe he wouldn't need to grovel in front of Lily Anderson after all.

Chapter Fourty-two

The housekeeper, Alice, bustled into the crowded kitchen and snapped her fingers at Tamar. "Go see Mrs. Blackstone. She's in the front parlor."

Tamar put down the ear of corn she'd been shelling. "What's wrong?"

Alice settled her hands on her hips. "Can't be Miss Lily or Missy Jasmine. They gone to town to see about that boat y'all been living on."

"Mebbe she's got something special for you to do," suggested the cook.

Mrs. Blackstone's personal maid pursed her lips. "Seems like she'd a-called me for that."

Tamar shrugged as she moved to the pump. "It's probably some rumpus Miss Camellia's caused." She worked the handle and washed her hands in the stream of cool water. After drying her hands on her apron, she removed it and smoothed the skirt of her dress.

"Don't forget your cap." Alice nodded toward the white cloth hanging from a hook on the wall.

"You sure you're not in trouble?" Mary shook her head. "You ain't done nothing wrong, have you?"

"No." Tamar retrieved the cap, shook it out, and settled it on her head. But as she stepped out of the warm kitchen and crossed to the back of the big house, she wondered. Could Mrs. Blackstone have found out about Jensen wanting to court her?

Her heart clenched as she moved from the narrow hallway in the back of the house to the wider corridors the family used. By the time she reached the front parlor, however, her good sense righted itself. No one at Les Fleurs knew Jensen, so she had nothing to fear. She knocked on the door and waited for Mrs. Blackstone's command.

Lily's grandmother was sitting in her chair next to the fireplace. She didn't look angry. "There you are, Tamar." Mrs. Blackstone waved at her to enter. "I need your help with a little project."

"Yes, ma'am." Tamar curtsied and waited.

"I'm sure you know I'm planning a dinner party for tonight as my granddaughters are about to depart once again."

Tamar nodded. It was the reason she'd been helping in the kitchen.

"I can't get Lily to give me a straight answer about her business partner and boat captain. She was supposed to deliver an invitation, but neither of the gentlemen has responded. I would think they would be flattered and even eager to meet Lily's family and friends."

Wondering why Mrs. Blackstone was telling her this, Tamar shifted her weight from one foot to the other.

"I hate to suspect my granddaughter, but I have decided something must have happened to the invitations and she is loath to confess the problem." She sighed and held up two white envelopes. "So I have written out new invitations. Now I need someone to hand deliver these and wait for a response. Of course I could send one of the footmen, but since you know both of the men and they will know you, I thought I would send you instead."

Tamar's heart tripped. She would see Jensen. He had not attempted to contact her since she came back to Les Fleurs more than a week ago. She ought to be glad that he'd stayed away. She'd told him to do just that many times. But now that he'd taken her at her word, she found herself missing his teasing compliments, his easy smile, and the gleam in his coffee-brown eyes.

The door to the parlor opened and Miss Dahlia breezed in with Camellia following a couple of steps behind. "Mama, it's the worst disaster ever."

Mrs. Blackstone turned to her daughter. "What's wrong, Dahlia?"

Her daughter sighed as she sank into a chair. "It's Camellia's dress, the one she is supposed to wear to the dinner party tonight."

"I'm so sorry, Grandmother, but it was an accident." Camellia's eyes were red rimmed. "I was upstairs painting a still life of bananas and apples, and I upset the paints with disastrous results."

"There is a bright spatter down the front of Camellia's new dress." Miss Dahlia took up the tale. "We must take it to the dressmaker to see what may be done to repair it."

Tamar put a hand over her mouth. A disaster indeed. If it had been Miss Lily's dress, she would have shrugged and chosen an older one, but Miss Camellia put much more emphasis on her appearance.

"That's a shame, Camellia." Mrs. Blackstone's calm tone quieted the other two women. "Of course you must take the carriage. I was about to send Tamar to town, so she can ride with you."

Miss Dahlia looked surprised that someone else was in the room. "Of course we can take Tamar."

"That's settled, then." Mrs. Blackstone handed the envelopes to Tamar. "The top one is for the captain."

"Where are you sending her, Mama?"

"To the *Hattie Belle*. I have not heard from either Mr. Matthews or the captain, and it would be a shame if they did not attend because their invitations were not properly delivered."

A spark of interest entered her daughter's eyes. "I was a guest on the boat before Lily purchased it. I've been wondering what changes she's made."

"But I don't want to go back to the river until I have to." Camellia's forehead crinkled.

Tamar edged out of the room as Miss Dahlia warned Camellia to stop frowning or risk premature wrinkles. The joy she'd felt earlier faded as she realized the addition of the two ladies meant she would have no chance of seeing Jensen alone. She might not even be able to leave the carriage if Miss Dahlia decided she wanted to deliver the invitations herself. What had looked to be a delightful outing had become nothing more than another chore.

What else should she expect? She was a slave, not a free woman who could go wherever she chose. For one of the first times in her life, Tamar found herself resenting her lack of freedom.

❧

Lily was more than ready to leave for New Orleans. It seemed so long since she'd seen her friends there. They would have so much catching up to do.

"We should be ready to leave as soon as you get here Monday morning." Captain Henrick glanced toward Blake for confirmation.

"Good. I'll have the girls in the carriage by first light." She was relieved she wouldn't have to continue trying to sidestep Grandmother's plan to have the two men at her dinner party.

Jasmine, followed closely by a laughing David, brushed past Lily's skirts.

"Don't knock any of the crates over," Lily admonished.

David skidded to a halt and looked back at her. "We'll be careful." She would have to be satisfied with his promise, although Lily doubted he could control her youngest sister's exuberance.

"We've come to see where you girls have been living for all these weeks."

Recognizing the voice, Lily whirled toward the gangplank, her mouth falling open as she came face-to-face with Aunt Dahlia and Camellia.

"What on earth are you doing here?" Aunt Dahlia's gaze was fixed on someone standing behind Lily. Then she turned back to Lily. "Why is your father on board your boat?"

"Father?" Camellia gasped out the two syllables. Her shocked face turned toward Lily. "That can't be right. Our father is dead."

"I'm sorry." Lily reached toward her. "I didn't wa—"

"What?" Camellia's shriek rivaled the clamor of a steamship whistle. "You didn't want us to know our father was right here with us?"

"Camellia." Their father stepped toward her. "Don't blame your sister. This is not her fault."

"Of course it is. She knew." Camellia looked past him to Lily. "How long have you known? Why didn't you tell us?"

Lily didn't know what to say. Her sister was right. She should have told them. Even though she'd been only a child when her grandparents decided to tell everyone, including Camellia and Jasmine, that their father was dead, she could have let her sisters know the truth when each grew old enough to understand. She put a hand to her forehead.

"How could you deceive us so?" Camellia's voice broke. She picked up her skirts and ran back to the dock.

"Isn't anyone going to answer me?" Aunt Dahlia's querulous voice drew Lily's attention.

"No." Lily faced down her relative. She wanted to get to Camellia but had the feeling her sister would not listen to her at the moment.

"Not right now. Not while my sister is sitting in that carriage crying her eyes out. She trusts you. Please go comfort her and get her back home. I'll be there soon to sort everything out."

The shock on Aunt Dahlia's face should have been amusing, but Lily couldn't find any humor in this situation. "Please go, Aunt Dahlia. Go take care of my sister."

Her father added his voice to Lily's. "You cannot wish the whole town to know our family business, Dahlia. Your father would be mortified."

"Papa is past worrying about such earthly matters." Aunt Dahlia gathered her skirts. "But I suppose you're right." She glared at Lily. "See that you are home soon."

"What is all the shouting about?" Jasmine and David appeared as Aunt Dahlia marched off the boat. "Where's Aunt Dahlia going?"

Lily looked toward Blake. His sympathetic gaze nearly wrecked her control. Tears burned at the corners of her eyes. She tried to hold the tears at bay.

Apparently their aunt heard her name. She turned back to the boat and pointed at Jasmine. "You need to come with me now."

Jasmine glanced toward Lily for confirmation. Although Lily didn't want her youngest sister to hear about their father from Aunt Dahlia, it couldn't be helped. She needed to figure out how to handle this situation, and she couldn't do that until she talked to her father. Why had she ever let him remain on the *Hattie Belle*?

"Why don't you come up to the hurricane deck with me?" Their father put a gentle hand on David's shoulder. "I've been wanting to show you how to whittle a turtle, and I think now would be a good time." His shoulders drooped as he led the boy away.

Wondering what to do, Lily jumped when someone touched her arm. "Tamar."

"I'm so sorry. I didn't mean to startle you." She held out two envelopes. "Your grandmother wanted me to deliver these to Mr. Blake and Captain Henrick."

"Captain Anderson." She took the envelopes and sighed. "We need to start calling him by his full name. I suppose that's as good a place to start unraveling this knot as any."

"Yes, ma'am."

Blake stepped closer. "I know a certain fellow who's been ornery as a bear since a certain hardhearted female told him to stay away from her."

Tamar's head dropped toward her chest. Were her cheeks darkening? Lily almost smiled at her friend's response to Blake's teasing. But then her problems came crashing down on her once again. What was she going to do? Where could she turn?

She fought a strong desire to loose the *Hattie Belle* from her moorings and float away. But where could she escape her bad decisions? By the time she realized no place would be far enough away, Tamar had disappeared.

"What's going through that head of yours?" Blake's voice was warm, containing none of the condemnation she deserved.

Lily shook her head. She wouldn't—couldn't—cry in front of him.

His hands cupped her elbows, pulled her closer. "It's not that bad, honey."

His reassurance crashed through Lily's defenses. She needed to rest, to lean on his strength. Melting into him, Lily sobbed against his shoulder. After a moment he reached an arm under her knees and picked her up, cradling her against his chest as the hot tears continued unabated. On some level she knew he had moved her out of the way of prying eyes and ears. But mostly she simply released all the worry and dread that had been building inside for so long.

How had everything gone so wrong? Where had the first misstep happened? Was it when she bought the *Hattie Belle*? Or even earlier, when she'd refused to bow to her aunt and uncle's bidding? Perhaps she should have married Mr. Marvin in spite of her misgivings. Or maybe everything would have been different if she'd sent her father away the moment she discovered that Blake had hired him.

Finally the tears ran out. Drained by the storm of emotion, Lily lay against Blake's chest and breathed unsteadily. Little by little she noticed several things. She was sitting in his lap at one of the dining-room tables. His hand was rubbing gentle circles on her back. His shirt was wet under her cheek. She wanted to push away from him but didn't know if she would ever gather the nerve to look him in the eye.

"Feeling better?" His low voice eased some of her embarrassment.

Lily sniffed and lifted her head, her gaze not quite reaching his face. "I'm sorry."

"You don't have to apologize."

She pushed back and reached for the floor with her feet.

"Be careful." He released his hold on her.

"I don't know what's wrong with me." Her voice still sounded shaky, but Lily stood up anyway. "I'm not usually so overcome."

He thrust something under her nose. A handkerchief.

Lily used it to wipe her face.

When she tried to hand it back to him, Blake caught her hand. "Keep it for now."

She shrugged and tucked the damp square into the waist of her skirt. "I don't know what I'll do."

"I'd suggest a cool, wet cloth to wash your face."

A giggle bubbled into her throat. Finally she looked at him. "That's not what I meant."

"Are you asking for my advice?" His eyes, as clear and blue as a summer sky, considered her. For a moment they stood, watching each other. How did he manage to look so handsome, so capable?

"Yes." Lily felt an almost overwhelming urge to place all her burdens on his shoulders, but for now she would only ask for his advice.

"You're going to have to be truthful with your family—every one of them, your sisters, even the aunt and uncle you don't agree with."

She thought she had emptied the reservoir of tears on his shirtfront, but suddenly she could feel the burning of a fresh supply. "I'm afraid they won't forgive me, especially Camellia. She was so hurt and angry when she left."

"Of course she will, Lily. She's your sister. She may be angry with you for a day or two, but she'll come around. She loves you. Both of your sisters adore you. They will forgive you."

The tears receded a bit as his words gave her hope. But another thought intruded. "How can they when I cannot forgive my father for what he did all those years ago?"

A light entered his eyes. "You once told me to make peace with the past and with my father. I'm telling you the same thing today. You have to forgive your father."

She gulped, remembering how easily she had dispensed that advice. Odd how her words had come back to haunt her. Could she let go of the fact that her father had abandoned them when they needed him the most?

Backing away from Blake, she moved toward the bedroom she shared with Camellia and Jasmine. "I'll think about it." She turned and fled before he could extract a promise from her. She needed to do some praying before she decided what to do next.

Chapter Forty-three

The room was as tidy as they'd left it. Lily moved toward her trunk and opened it. She dug through the clothes inside until her fingers closed over the solid edges of the item she sought. Her Bible. Pulling it free, she perched on the edge of her bed.

Clasping the leather volume to her chest, she knelt next to her bed, closed her eyes, and began to pray. The words came slowly at first, but then they began sliding across her mind as she felt His presence beside her.

Lord, You know what's wrong. Please help me figure out how to fix it. I've gotten so far from Your Word, and I'm sorry. Please don't hold that against me. I come to You with my head hung low. I know better than to let my faith grow weak and forgotten in the press of days. I ask for Your forgiveness and patience. Help me to do better. Show me how to lead my sisters so that they will continue to embrace You no matter what our futures may hold. Thank You, Lord, for being so faithful. Amen.

Getting up to sit on the bed, Lily opened her Bible to the New Testament. She flipped a few pages of Matthew's Gospel, her eyes sliding across the familiar verses and stopping when she reached the Lord's Prayer. The words soothed her, bringing peace. Then her breath caught. The warning contained in verse 15 jumped out at her: " 'If ye forgive not men their trespasses, neither will your Father forgive your trespasses.' "

This was the answer she'd been searching for. If she wanted God to forgive her for ignoring Him and trying to do things her own way, she would have to forgive her father. She glimpsed the seriousness of her sin—how she had turned from her Creator, how she had considered herself better than others, how she had relied on her own understanding.

The look of betrayal on Camellia's face haunted her. Yet hadn't she nurtured her own feeling of betrayal? Why had she never told her sisters that their earthly father was alive? Why had she gone along with the lies her relatives had fabricated? Her arrogance had stopped her from telling them, even making him promise to hide the truth. She had thought it would be best for Camellia and Jasmine. Best for everyone. But when had Jesus ever taught that lies were better?

She had to forgive her father for walking away from them. No matter the reasons, no matter the circumstances. Lily looked up at the ceiling. "I want to forgive him, God. I don't want to hold on to the anger and blame any longer. Please help me see him through Your eyes." Warmth spread throughout her body. The pain of betrayal slipped away. Freedom filled with love took its place.

Lily closed her Bible and stood. She couldn't let any more time pass without telling him. She left the room and hurried down the passageway toward the stairs. He would most likely be in the pilothouse. Her feet took wing. She felt like a prisoner seeing the sunshine for the first time in years. She hadn't realized how dark her life had been, overshadowed by anger and distrust.

He stood on the upper deck, looking out at the sea of boats surrounding the *Hattie Belle*, but turned as she walked toward him. "Lily, are you all right?"

Shaking her head, Lily stopped in front of him. "You're not to blame. I'm the one who insisted we hide the truth from my sisters. I want you to come back to Les Fleurs with me. I don't want any more lies between us."

"You don't know what you're saying. You don't know why I left."

"It doesn't matter." She took a deep breath. "What matters is that you want to be near us now. I should have seen that earlier. Please say you'll forgive me. I want things to be different from now on."

His eyes filled with tears. "Lily, you don't have to ask for my forgiveness."

"Yes, I do. . .Papa."

He gasped, and his face crumpled. He opened his arms wide.

Without any hesitation, Lily stepped into his embrace. "I love you, Papa, and I'm glad God brought us back together."

"I'm just so happy to have my Water Lily back." His voice choked with emotion. "You've given me a gift beyond belief, second only to that moment when He entered my heart and changed it forever. I love you so much, my little Water Lily."

Lily hugged him hard, closing her eyes and thanking God for setting them both free. It had taken her far too long to get to this point, but thankfully she was no longer holding on to her bitterness. She only hoped Camellia would forgive her more easily.

❧

The sun was setting as the rented carriage pulled to a stop in front of her grandmother's door. Lily's gaze met her father's as he helped her down from the carriage. He was dressed in borrowed finery loaned to him from Blake's wardrobe. The fit of the blue coat was not perfect, since it would not quite button over her father's midsection, but it looked much better than his usual attire. For this occasion his hat, also borrowed from Blake, had the taller crown and narrow brim befitting a gentleman.

"I still don't think this is a good idea." His face mirrored his uncertainty.

Lily smiled at him. "It's going to be fine. It's about time Mama's family acknowledged you." She swept up the steps and pushed open the door.

Before she took more than three steps, Uncle Phillip emerged from his study. His expression changed from curiosity to outrage. "What is he doing here?"

"He's here at Grandmother's express invitation." Lily lifted her chin and faced her uncle, daring him to continue.

"I don't believe it. Your grandmother would never go against your grandfather's wishes."

Now it was Lily's turn for confusion. Her grandfather, the man who had treated her sisters and her like princesses, had forbidden their father's presence? She turned to Papa. He was studying the marbled floor. "Is it true? Is that why you never contacted us?"

His nod was all the confirmation she needed. If Lily had held any doubts about forgiving this man, they vanished completely. What had that forced separation cost him? "Why would Grandfather do such a thing?"

Her father looked up and met her gaze. "He loved your mother so much. I think it drove him a little crazy when she died. He blamed me, and I agreed with him that I bore the responsibility for her death. He was determined to protect you girls from a similar fate."

"And as his heir, I feel obligated to continue his wishes." Uncle Phillip cleared his throat. "Besides, he's the reason your aunt nearly collapsed from shock. Both of your sisters are in their rooms. I understand Camellia is inconsolable."

Her uncle moved as though to step past Lily, but she stopped him with an angry glare. "All of that is my fault, not his. I'm the one who demanded he keep his identity hidden. When Aunt Dahlia came to the boat, she recognized Papa." Lily shrugged. "I don't see why she should be so overcome, but she is a practical woman. This is a matter between me, my siblings, and our father."

Her uncle sputtered. "I still—"

Lily cut off his words. It was time to remind him that he was far from blameless. "In reality, you have only yourself to blame for Papa's appearance here tonight. If you hadn't tried to force me into marriage with a man I did not love, I would never have gathered the courage to buy a riverboat, and I would not have met my father in New Orleans."

Uncle Phillip's response was drowned out by Grandmother's voice as she opened the parlor door. "Whatever is going on out here?"

Aunt Dahlia was close on her heels. "I can't believe your effrontery."

It seemed her aunt had recovered. It wasn't clear if Aunt Dahlia was addressing her or Papa, but Lily didn't care. She lifted her chin and squared her shoulders. "What effrontery? All I've done is bring my new captain to dinner as Grandmother requested."

"You should know he's not welcome in this house." Aunt Dahlia's voice was heavy with spite. "But trust you to flout the wishes of your family. You have always thought you knew better than anyone else."

Her words struck at Lily's heart. Hadn't she promised God she would not be so rebellious? Did He mean for her to meekly follow her relative's directives, even when they were wrong?

Grandmother clapped her hands and waited until everyone had turned to her. "That's enough melodrama for one evening." She nodded toward Lily's father. "You are looking well, Henrick."

Aunt Dahlia's mouth dropped open. "But—"

"Calm down, Dahlia, and close your mouth before you swallow a fly."

Uncle Phillip put an arm around Aunt Dahlia. "I don't see—"

"Although I dearly loved my husband and would never have countermanded his dictates, I don't believe Isaiah was right to keep my granddaughters separated from their only living parent." She turned to Lily's father and offered him her hand. "I hated seeing them so lost, but I didn't want to oppose my husband. Perhaps now we can bury the past along with poor Rose."

Lily's father bowed over her hand before straightening. "If I could have traded my life for hers, I would have."

Grandmother tucked her hand in the crook of his arm. "I know that feeling well. It is difficult to bury one's spouse."

Grandmother turned to Lily. "Why don't you go talk to your sisters? It's about time for them to celebrate instead of experiencing all these histrionics that Dahlia has encouraged."

"Camellia is overwrought, Mother." Aunt Dahlia pulled away from her husband. "I don't think it's a good idea for Lily to bother her."

"While I am the first to admit that I've made a lot of mistakes, Aunt Dahlia, I am not going to allow you to come between me and Camellia."

"Why do you always imagine I am your enemy, Lily?" Aunt Dahlia put a hand to her forehead. "The good Lord knows I only want what's best for you and your sisters."

Lily could feel her eyes widening. "What's best for—"

"Lily." Her grandmother's voice interrupted her scathing response. She turned to her daughter. "Dahlia, you will not interfere with Camellia further. I believe we can allow Lily to handle the situation in the way she thinks best. And you will smile and converse politely with your brother-in-law tonight and in the future."

Lily escaped to the upstairs bedrooms before anyone else could stop her. Leaning her head against Camellia's door, she took a deep breath and said a prayer for wisdom. Then she knocked and entered.

"What do you want?" Camellia was sitting on the window seat in her dressing gown.

Lily closed the door behind her. "I need to explain why I didn't tell you about Father. I realize now how bad a mistake that was. I'm so sorry. Please say you'll forgive me."

"Do you think it's that easy?" Camellia hunched her shoulders. "Do you think you can waltz in here and tell me you're sorry and I'll say it's okay?"

"No, but I want to explain why I did it."

"Maybe I don't want to listen."

Lily sat beside Camellia and touched one of her sister's ringlets. "I've made a lot of mistakes in my life."

Camellia's eyes opened wide in a perfect imitation of Aunt Dahlia. "Do tell."

Disliking the influence she saw in her sister's behavior, Lily sighed. She had to get her sister away from this world. But for now she needed to concentrate on the current problem. "I know. But please believe me when I say my intention was only to protect you and Jasmine."

"By hiding the truth from us?"

"You're right. It was a terrible idea. But honey, I was afraid our father would burrow his way into our hearts and then disappear like he did when you were barely more than a baby. It was only after I started listening to him that I realized how much he's changed. He asked Jesus into his heart, and it's made him a new man. I no longer think he'll desert us." She hesitated, but now was not the time to hide anything. "And if he does, God will see us through it."

Camellia stood up and walked to her dressing table. She fingered the pearl-handled brush and moved a couple of hairpins around. "I wish you'd let us make the decision to accept Papa or not." Camellia looked toward her, her pale-blue eyes wet with unshed tears. Her bow-shaped mouth was pursed as she considered Lily. "You shouldn't try to keep such things from us, especially me. You're not my mother, you know. And I'm no longer a child."

"I am reminded of that every time I look at you."

"Then why do you treat me like a baby?" Camellia tugged at the sash on her dressing gown. "Why won't you let me take real responsibility? I could help you, Lily. I could do more things on the boat. I am fifteen years old, after all. You can trust me."

Understanding dawned on Lily. Although their father was the ostensible reason for Camellia's anger, the real problem went far deeper. "I'm so sorry. I didn't realize what I was doing."

A tear fell on Camellia's cheek, but it didn't diminish her beauty. Her nose didn't redden like Lily's did when she cried. "That's one reason

I like to stay here with Aunt Dahlia. She treats me like I'm grown up."

The comparison was hard to accept, but Lily would have to change if she wanted to remain close to Camellia. "I promise to do better."

A sniff came from Camellia. She managed a wobbly smile. "Thanks."

Lily stood and opened her arms wide. "I love you, Camellia. I can't stand to think I've made you so unhappy."

"I love you, too." Camellia ran into her embrace. "And I haven't been that unhappy. I just want to go to parties and enjoy life."

They hugged each other, and Lily closed her eyes, thanking God for giving her another chance with Camellia. *Please help me do better, Lord.* "Let's get you dressed so we can go downstairs and introduce you properly to our father."

This time Camellia's smile was much steadier. "What about Jasmine?"

Lily nodded. "While you're getting ready, I'll explain things to her. Then we'll go downstairs together and spend some time with Papa."

❧

Jasmine entered the parlor and ran toward their father. She hugged him with enthusiasm. "I'm so glad you're here."

"Me, too." His voice choked with emotion. "Me, too."

At least her youngest sister wasn't going to have trouble adjusting to Papa's reappearance. Lily envied her. How liberating to be young, without all the responsibility of adulthood. She wanted to warn Camellia to stay young as long as she could. But Lily knew that would be a waste of breath. She could well remember when she'd been as eager as Camellia to embrace adulthood.

"Hello, Camellia. . .Lily." Papa nodded in their direction. With one arm still around his youngest daughter, he stepped forward.

Camellia curtsied, her skirts wide, her face downcast. "Good evening. . .sir. I am happy to welcome you to Les Fleurs."

So that was how her younger sister was going to react? She was hiding behind etiquette. Lily couldn't blame her. Who knew better than she how hard it was to trust a man who had deserted them. Perhaps if she showed that she had forgiven their father, Camellia would follow her example.

She moved toward her father and gave him a quick kiss on the cheek. "Would you prefer we call you Father or Papa?"

While he considered his answer, Lily sat and motioned for Camellia to join her. Jasmine left her father's embrace to perch on the tufted footstool in front of Grandmother's chair.

After they were seated, Papa sat in a wooden chair near the fireplace. "Whichever you prefer."

Lily cocked her head. "I think Papa suits you best."

He nodded, a thankful smile lighting up his features. "Papa it is, then."

Jasmine sprang from the stool. "Papa, I'm so glad you found us."

His smile widened. "I am, too, little one. God is very good to me."

"Will you be continuing to captain Lily's boat. . .sir?" Camellia's hands were clenched in her lap. She let out a brittle laugh. "Or will you be chaperoning us here in Natchez?"

Like an anxious parent, Lily watched the emotions flitting across her sister's face. Anyone else might have thought Camellia poised and self-confident. They might not have caught the slight hesitation before she decided not to call him Papa. But Lily was her sister. She knew Camellia well. She recognized the uncertainty in her blue eyes. And she had the advantage of knowing firsthand the distrust her sister was experiencing. Until she had turned back to God, Lily had felt the same way.

Camellia needed to return to the *Hattie Belle*. Once she was around Papa more, she would accept him. He might not be perfect, but the love he had for them was plain to see. He had respected Lily's wish that he remain anonymous, showing a patience and understanding that she realized now could be likened to Jesus' love for mankind.

Now that she and Camellia had a better understanding, maybe Camellia wouldn't resist coming back to the boat. Lily hoped she wasn't trying to manage her sister. But regardless of what Camellia might think, she would be much better off aboard the *Hattie Belle*.

Lily put her arm around Camellia's waist. "Shall we join Grandmother for dinner? I'm sure they are wondering where we are."

"May I come, too?" Jasmine asked with a hopeful expression.

Lily shook her head. "I thought you already ate your supper before I got back to the house."

Jasmine's face fell. "I don't get to do anything fun. I wish I was back on the *Hattie Belle*."

"Don't worry." Their father stood and placed a comforting arm around her shoulders. "We'll be leaving in a few days, and you and I will have plenty of time to become close friends."

After Jasmine climbed the staircase, the others entered the library. Lily wished Blake were here to offer support, but he had declined, saying that her family needed time to themselves. At least they didn't have to contend with other guests. She could not imagine trying to make polite conversation with some vapid planter's wife after the emotional upheaval they had been through.

Why was Camellia so eager to join the gossip-filled, narrow-minded world of the Natchez debutante? Lily would much rather spend the evening with Jasmine in the nursery or on the deck of the *Hattie Belle*. She had promised to treat her sister as an adult who could make her own judicious choices, but it was going to be a difficult task.

Perhaps by the time Camellia was eighteen, she would understand how empty and unfulfilling the trappings of wealth could be. Lily could only pray she would come to her senses before she found herself bound by her eagerness to embrace luxury and privilege.

Chapter Forty-four

Women don't belong on the river.

Jean Luc studied the note he'd written to make sure his handwriting was disguised. Satisfied, he folded it and handed it to the man standing in front of him. "Make sure you leave this where they can find it."

Lars Steenberg licked his lips. "I got it. When do you want me to do it?"

Did he have to explain everything? "Wait until everyone's off the boat. They don't take many precautions, so I'm sure you'll be able to get on board without much trouble."

A snarl twisted his features. "I'll need some money to pay for helpers if you want this job done right."

Of course the man wanted money. Didn't he always? Jean Luc removed his pocketbook and withdrew a few bills. Irritated to see how little cash was left, he realized it was time to ask his mother for another loan. "Make sure no one's hurt. Remember, I only want to frighten the women, not do any lasting damage. My goal is to recover my boat. And when I do, you'll be able to captain her again."

"I got it." Steenberg pocketed the money and the note.

Jean Luc wished he was not forced to work with someone so shady. But sometimes it was necessary to make compromises to reach a goal. Especially since Lily Anderson was not going to be reasonable. Dealing with Steenberg was better than pleading with her to come to her senses.

No matter what it took, Jean Luc had to regain control of the *Hattie Belle*. He would use whatever tools were available, spend whatever money he could lay his hands on, do whatever he needed to. One day the boat would belong to him again.

"Keep close watch on the *Hattie Belle*. If you mess up again, you won't see any more money from me."

Steenberg's laugh gnawed at Jean Luc's patience. "It's not like you're making me wealthy."

"I've told you I won't have much until the *Hattie Belle* is mine again. When that happens, I'll see you're rewarded." Jean Luc tamped down his anger. He needed Steenberg for now. Once he got his boat back, he'd decide if he wanted to keep Steenberg on. Trusting him wouldn't be easy. "Just remember my instructions."

"Don't worry. That woman will be ready to sign the *Hattie Belle* over to you when she sees what can happen to an unguarded boat." He slinked down Silver Street, disappearing into the mist rolling up from the river, quickly blending in with the other shadowy figures in Natchez Under-the-Hill.

&

Lily couldn't remember enjoying an evening as much in a very long time. She shared a glance with Blake, wondering if he knew how much she appreciated his advice to forgive her father.

"I'm so excited about finding a school in New Orleans." Camellia's pleasure shone through her expression.

While Lily wasn't looking forward to the eventual separation, it was better than letting Camellia remain in Natchez or forcing her to accompany them to New Orleans against her will.

"What do you think they'll be able to teach you that you can't learn on the river?" Papa propped his elbows on the table and leaned forward.

Camellia frowned. "To sit with my hands in my lap, for one thing."

The volume of Papa's laugh drew the attention of several other restaurant patrons.

"Camellia." Lily shook her head. Another thing they should teach her sister was to show respect for her elders.

Camellia's cheeks grew pink as she focused on the food on her plate.

Lily turned to Blake. "Did you have any success with your search for David's parents?"

Blake shook his head. "His mother lives in a shack next to one of the saloons. No one has seen his father in more than a year. He hasn't returned from California or sent word for his family to join him. I suspect he may be dead."

A pall fell over the group as they absorbed his words. Lily's heart sank. She had been so hopeful Blake would be able to uncover better news. "What about the orphanage?"

"I spoke with the manager. She says they can take him in."

"Why can't we let the boy stay with us?" Papa's question turned everyone's attention back to her.

Lily tucked her napkin under the edge of her plate as she considered how to voice her concerns. "David is a sweet boy, and I appreciate the affection he lavishes on Jasmine." She glanced toward Blake, buoyed by his encouraging smile. "But adoption is not a responsibility I'm ready to shoulder. I don't know the first thing about raising a boy. I hope his father will return, and David needs to be where he can be found, not traipsing up and down the river."

Blake continued the explanation. "David doesn't want to be adopted, either. He loves his father and believes he will come back one day to rescue him. He wants to stay in Natchez so he'll be here when his father returns."

"Blake and I didn't want him living on the streets, so we told David he could stay here if he would agree to remain at the orphanage and apply himself to his studies." Lily finished the story. It was odd how well their minds worked together. As though they were an old, married couple. She supposed it came from their business partnership.

"Does Jasmine know?" Camellia had recovered her equilibrium enough to reenter the conversation. "She'll miss him terribly."

"I haven't told her yet." Lily dreaded that moment. Jasmine was with Tamar at Les Fleurs this evening. While she had spent almost all her waking hours with David since they'd rescued him, Jasmine would have her family to support her. Lily sent a thankful prayer to the Lord for that blessing.

A servant removed their dinner plates before serving small bowls of chilled quince pudding, one of Lily's favorites. "I wonder if we could serve this during our next trip."

"I imagine so." Blake spooned a bite of the fluffy pink dessert, his face registering pleasure. "I don't think I've ever tasted it before. What is it?"

"Quince pudding." Papa answered. He turned to Lily. "I saw an island covered in quince trees a few months back. Unless someone else has harvested the fruit, we can plan on stopping there on our way to New Orleans next week."

She smiled. "Perfect."

Blake settled their account while Papa escorted them to the waiting carriage. "We'll walk back to the boat."

Lily shook her head. She wanted to extend the pleasant evening. "We'll take you. I wanted to ask Jensen about our linens. He mentioned something about new ones the other day, and I haven't had the chance to get back with him."

Blake walked up as she spoke. "What time will we see you on Monday?"

"She wants to go to the boat right now."

The two men exchanged glances. Blake turned to her. "I don't like the idea of you and Camellia riding through that area at night."

"We'll be perfectly safe inside the carriage." She indicated the empty seat opposite her. "Now get in and stop being contrary."

Blake shrugged. "I suppose we'd better do as she says."

The men climbed in, and the carriage began the steep descent. The streets were dark, as was the waterfront. Only the saloons showed activity. The saloons and one of the steamboats.

Lily's heart plunged. She hoped it was not a fire. As they drew closer, she realized the light was coming from lamps, not a fire. Her heart resumed its normal position until she looked more closely and realized the boat was hers. "Something is wrong."

The carriage came to a halt, and Blake pushed the door open. "Stay here while I see what's going on."

Lily ignored his command, climbing down before anyone could stop her. Whatever was going on, she did not want to remain in the dark. Her livelihood was at risk.

She crossed the gangplank on Blake's heels and saw the destruction firsthand. Barrels had been overturned. The door to the staterooms hung at an angle. Her heart thudded. She dreaded seeing her room, but that would have to wait.

Blake was bent over someone propped against the outside rail. A group of strangers, many of whom carried lanterns, stood in a loose circle around him. Jensen! She hurried forward until she could see

Jensen's face. "Are you all right?"

Jensen held a handkerchief to his head. A stain—looking like blood—covered part of his shirt. "Yes, ma'am. The varmints surprised me. Gave me a bit of a headache. I'll be fine, but the rooms are pretty bad."

Blake frowned at her. "I thought I told you to wait."

"You are neither my father nor my husband." She turned to go toward their quarters, but a strong grip on her arm held her still.

"Lily, listen to reason. I don't want you going anywhere on this boat until we're sure the thieves are no longer on board."

Papa and Camellia appeared at her elbow before Lily could respond. Blake's words had given her pause. Especially since Camellia was here.

"I think they've gone." Jensen lowered his hand and pointed to one of the strangers. "He's the one saw what was going on and called for help. Them cowards went running when they realized they might get caught."

Papa dragged out a chair for Jensen from the dining room. "Did you recognize any of them?"

"I never got a chance." Jensen took the offered chair. "They come up behind me and tapped my head with a cudgel. I didn't see nothing until this fellow here helped me sit up."

"Don't worry." Blake's mouth tightened. "We'll catch them."

Camellia leaned toward Jensen. "Do you feel woozy?"

He grinned. "Nah. It'll take a lot worse to break this head of mine. But I am a bit worried about my handsome face."

Comforted by his quip, Lily turned her attention to the boat. Papa was questioning the other men about what they'd seen, but Blake had disappeared. Anger carried her into the passageway. How dare he sneak off while she was distracted?

She headed for the room she shared with her sisters. The paintings they had hung to enliven the passageways had been torn down or sliced to ribbons. So much hard work undone in a matter of minutes. She supposed she should be thankful. It could have been much worse.

The light faded as she got farther from the main deck. Why hadn't she asked to borrow a lantern? A movement ahead made Lily's breath catch. Had Jensen been wrong?

A door opened—her stateroom—and flickering light outlined a familiar shape. She breathed a sigh of relief when she recognized Blake. "I thought I told you to remain with the others." He folded a piece of paper and tucked it into his shirt pocket.

"How bad is it?"

He shrugged. "They didn't do as much damage here as on the main deck."

She considered his face. Did the lamplight make him look so distressed? "What are you hiding from me?"

Blake shook his head. "Nothing. Let's go check on Jensen." He put an arm around her shoulders. "I'll get all of this cleaned up, Lily. Don't worry. It's not as bad as it looks."

She wanted to believe him, but it was difficult. Lily remembered her earlier assurance that she and Camellia would be safe driving through Under-the-Hill. How could she have been so naive?

Chapter Forty-five

New Orleans seemed even busier than during their first visit. It took nearly two hours to secure a decent berth for unloading their cargo, and they would have to move to another location for the duration of their stay. Blake wondered how long it would be. Lily had mentioned finding a finishing school for Camellia. She'd probably want to interview several before making her decision.

"There you are." Lily's voice pulled Blake from his reverie.

As she walked toward him, her footsteps sure and fast, he could not but admire this woman. Ever since the day she'd broken down in front of him, something had changed in the way he viewed her. Although she appeared self-confident, he knew firsthand the fears she hid from the rest of the world. She might be autocratic and jump to the wrong conclusion from time to time, but no one was perfect. And she had shown him a flawless picture of forgiveness.

During the voyage to New Orleans, Lily had been unfailingly warm and loving toward Captain Henrick, introducing him as her father to their guests and spending her afternoons visiting him in the pilothouse. They had delayed their voyage one day when they stopped at the island that held quince trees. Jensen cooked the fruit, and they enjoyed a quince pudding that put to shame the one they'd enjoyed at the restaurant.

Lily seemed happier, as if letting go of her resentment had healed her in some way. He wondered if the resentment he felt toward his father was weighing him down. But how could a person let go of resentment when he'd been wronged?

"I've arranged for a carriage to take you and Tamar and your sisters to the Thorntons' home." His fingers itched to touch the strand of hair that blew across her face. "I will also hire some guards to remain on the ship."

She looked troubled. "Do you think we will be targeted again?"

"Not really, but I don't want to take any chances." He still hadn't mentioned the note he'd found in her room because he didn't want to add to her concerns. But he was determined to find the culprit who had engineered the attack. When he found him, the man would wish he had left them alone.

"You look so solemn. I'm beginning to be worried. Are you hiding something from me?"

"I don't want to have any trouble." She was too perceptive. To distract her attention, he changed the subject. "How is Camellia doing?"

Her brows drew together in a frown. "I'm not sure. She is still so stiff with Papa. I wish she could let go of her anger. I worry that she is still upset with me, too."

"I don't think so, Lily. I imagine she's preoccupied with that finishing school you promised her."

"It worked as a bribe, but I'm beginning to have second thoughts. Camellia sometimes seems to be hiding behind a mask." Lily pushed the strand behind her ear, but it escaped and blew back across her face. "What if the school we choose reinforces that tendency? She is at the very cusp of adulthood. What if I make the wrong choice, and she is ruined for life?"

Blake smiled. "I'm sure Mrs. Thornton and her daughter can help you avoid making a mistake."

"Thank you for knowing exactly the right thing to say." She tucked the errant strand back once more. Once more it blew free.

"Turn around."

She looked up at him, a question in her gaze.

"Trust me, Lily."

"I do." She turned to face the dock. Blake stepped behind her and pulled one of her hair clips out. He used his hand to smooth back her hair, especially the strands that had broken free. Then he refastened the hair clip and stepped back to the rail.

She shot him a glance. "I don't want to know how you learned to do that."

Laughter rumbled through him. "I have a younger sister."

"Really?" She looked up at him. "I didn't realize that."

Silence fell between them, a companionable silence. His thoughts wandered back to the burglary. "I wonder where Captain Steenberg is working."

"Do you think he attacked the boat?"

Why had he spoken out loud? "I don't know, but he did threaten me when I told him to leave."

She turned at his admission. "I didn't know that."

"I didn't want to tell you because I knew he was recommended by your friend Monsieur Champney."

Her sheepish look brought a smile to his face. "I'm so sorry. But believe me. Jean Luc Champney is not exactly my friend. I have discovered we do not see eye to eye."

His smile deepened. He looked away from her. Was the sun brighter than it had been moments ago?

She leaned against the rail, her arm very close to his. "How long before the carriage will be here?"

Contentment bathed Blake in warmth. He wanted to linger next to Lily. "It will wait until you and the others are ready, but I have a question."

"As long as it has nothing to do with finishing schools." Her gaze teased him.

"Okay, I'll ask the other question." He took a deep breath. "I was thinking you and your sisters might enjoy an evening at the theater."

Another sideways glance. "Are you offering to escort us?"

"If I was, would you accept?" He held his breath, his heart pounding so hard he thought she might be able to hear it.

"Why certainly, sir. How could I resist such a sweet offer?" Her smile made his heart triple its speed.

"Why, Miss Anderson"—he fought to keep his voice light—"I do believe you have a bit of the debutante in you. Are you sure you haven't spent time in a finishing school yourself?"

Her giggle was music to his ears. She had been too serious of late.

As though she had read his mind, Lily sobered. "I need to ask you for something, too."

Now what? He braced himself for bad news. "Go ahead."

"I want you to consider contacting your family."

He should have known. "You don't know what you're asking."

She turned to face him. Her chocolate-brown eyes pleaded for him to listen. "Yes, I do. When you told me I should tell my family the truth, you were right. But before I could face them, I had to go to God and ask for His help in forgiving my father."

He felt her hand on his arm. He wanted to shake it off. He wanted to tell her to get in the carriage and leave him alone. To preserve their friendship, he folded his mouth into a straight line and said nothing.

"You were there when I needed you, Blake. I'll never be able to repay you for supporting me during a very difficult time. I want to offer you similar support." She squeezed his arm once before releasing it. "I'm sorry if I've upset you."

He shook his head. Maybe one day he would be able to talk about this subject. But that day was not now. He watched as she walked away from him. Then he turned back to the dock. He didn't know if that day would ever arrive.

❦

Lily looked in the mirror atop her dressing table and caught sight of Tamar's pursed lips. "Do I look that bad?"

Tamar shook her head. "I like your gray dress better. This is a special evening. You know you should dress up."

A knock on the door stopped Lily's protest. "Come in."

Mrs. Thornton opened the door, a broad smile wreathing her face.

It had been so good to see her friend again. Lily enjoyed the pampering she received at the Thorntons' home, but she valued even more the relationship she and Mrs. Thornton shared. Why couldn't Aunt Dahlia be a little more like her?

"Oh no, dear, you must wear the dress you bought on Canal Street. It will complement the little gift I brought for you to wear." She opened her hand to reveal a pair of exquisite pearl-gray hair combs.

Lily could feel her mouth drop open. "They're beautiful, but I cannot accept such an expensive gift."

Mrs. Thornton frowned. "I bought these last year on a whim. But I've never found anything to wear them with. You must accept them. It would make me very happy."

Tamar took the combs and set them on the dressing table. "They will be perfect with your dress, Miss Lily. You can at least wear them tonight."

"I suppose so." Lily didn't want to hurt Mrs. Thornton's feelings.

The casement clock on the mantel began to chime the hour. "I will leave you to change your dress." She whisked her skirt back through the doorway and disappeared.

Tamar picked up Camellia's hairbrush and used it to part Lily's hair.

"You and Mrs. Thornton are making too much of this outing. It's nothing more than the kindness of my business partner in wanting to entertain my sisters and me."

"And why not?" Tamar brushed her hair until it shone and then began twisting it up. "You have a handsome escort for a fancy night out. Who knows what magic could happen?" A shadowy emotion darkened Tamar's eyes. Was she envious?

A thrill of anticipation zipped through Lily at the thought of the surprise in store for her maid later this evening. She didn't know exactly what Jensen planned, but when he had asked for her permission to take Tamar out for the evening, she had given it gladly. Tamar deserved a better life, one that offered all the freedoms Lily and her sisters enjoyed.

In order to keep Jensen's plans secret, she adopted a casual attitude. "It's nothing special. I've half a mind to tell you to remove the combs and put away the gray dress."

Tamar's expression was so serene Lily wondered if she'd imagined the emotion she'd seen earlier. "You can tell yourself that falsehood if you want to, but I've seen Mr. Blake make you blush. And his gaze turns to you when he thinks no one else is looking. He's your beau, all right, or he would be if you'd give him a little encouragement."

A telltale blush rose toward Lily's cheeks. Why did she have to be so transparent? She grabbed her fan from the dressing table and swept it back and forth to cool her face.

Tamar sent a knowing look then helped Lily with the gray dress and nodded. "You look very nice."

Lily turned to the mirror and was surprised by her image. Her hair was pinned by the gray combs above her ears and cascaded in soft waves around her head, giving her a much softer look. Her dress, with its wide skirt and fancy stitched design, accentuated her small waist and looked most fashionable. Lily felt like a fraud. She was no beauty.

Confused by her thoughts, she decided to focus on Tamar. Now that her maid had an opportunity to escape the yoke of slavery, she wanted to make certain nothing stood in her way. She pointed her fan at the maid. "This situation cannot continue."

"What do you mean? Have I done something wrong?"

"Of course not. You've done nothing but care for Camellia, Jasmine, and me as if we were your own children."

A smile chased away the worried look on Tamar's face. "I couldn't love you any more than my own children."

"I know, Tamar. That's why I'm going to make certain you gain your freedom. The last time I suggested this, I thought you may have reacted so badly because Mr. Moreau was there."

Tamar stepped back, her head shaking. "That's not it at all, Miss Lily. I don't want him or anyone else to spend good money for me. Besides, if I was freed, I wouldn't be able to care for you or your sisters."

Deciding to dispense with the easier issue, she smiled. "Maybe not, but you'd be able to marry Jensen and have children of your own."

Tears shone in Tamar's dark-brown eyes. "I don't need to marry that man."

"So, it's fine for Blake to court me, but you don't deserve to be with the man you love?"

Silence filled the room as they looked at each other. Finally Tamar's gaze fell to the floor. "Sometimes I just want everything to go back to the way it used to be. Back to the way I felt before I ever met Jensen. But then, when I'm near him—" She twisted her hands in her apron. "He makes me want to have a different future."

"That's wonderful." Lily hugged Tamar, her heart practically bursting with happiness.

At first the older woman resisted, but then she returned Lily's embrace.

"Don't you see? You're in love with Jensen. I knew it! And the two of you are going to have a chance for happiness. You're going to have children of your own you can love as wonderfully as you've loved us for all these years."

Tamar shooed Lily out of the room. "Get on downstairs before Mr. Blake comes looking for you."

"I will, but only if you promise to give Jensen a chance." Lily waited for Tamar's nod before she skipped down the staircase. She found her sisters and their escorts in the front parlor. Jasmine was talking nonstop to Mr. and Mrs. Thornton about the evening ahead. Camellia sat on the sofa, her arms crossed and a pout on her face. One look at the disinterested expression on Jonah Thornton's face told Lily why. Camellia was not used to being ignored. Lily struggled to keep a straight face.

Blake leaned against the fireplace mantel, his tall black hat dangling from one hand. She had never seen him looking so elegant. The brass buttons of his striped waistcoat gleamed in the candlelight. His black boots had been polished to a mirror finish. Suddenly Lily was glad she'd worn her gray dress, especially when she saw the light of appreciation in Blake's eyes.

"The carriage is ready." Blake bowed and walked toward her.

Lily wanted to say something witty, but nothing came to mind. "You look very nice this evening."

His lips curled in a tender smile. "Thank you. So do you. You've done something different to your hair, haven't you?"

He had noticed. Lily touched a hand to one of the combs. "Mrs. Thornton loaned these to me for the evening."

Blake nodded. "Are you ready to depart?"

She smiled and placed her hand on his proffered arm. Not sure whether she was walking or floating, she passed through the doorway and into the foyer.

Tamar had been right. This was going to be a very special evening.

Chapter Forty-six

Freedom. The word had been an idea without substance to Tamar. At best it was a scary word, yet she found herself increasingly drawn to it.

She picked up Jasmine's pinafore and smoothed it with a gentle touch. Wouldn't it be wonderful to have a family of her own? But what would the Anderson sisters do without someone to watch over them?

Shaking her head, Tamar folded the pinafore and put it in Jasmine's trunk. She checked the room one last time to make sure everything had been put away before going down the narrow staircase used by the slaves.

The housekeeper met her at the back door. "You have a visitor."

Her heart leaped. "Is it Mr. Moreau?"

The older woman winked and nodded. "He's dressed up awful pretty, too. I'd say he's got courting on his mind."

Tamar ducked her head. If Jensen was dressed up, she didn't want to be wearing her apron. She grabbed at the strings holding it to her waist and wrestled with them.

"Let me help you." The housekeeper turned her around and untied the strings. "I'll put this in your room. You go on out to the kitchen and meet your young man."

Putting a hand on her hammering heart, Tamar walked through the garden and stepped into the bright, warm kitchen where most of the servants gathered in the evenings. Tonight was no exception. Two maids, the butler, and the cook were sitting around a large table. But the only person Tamar saw was standing next to the hearth.

He stepped forward, his brown eyes shining with love. "I've got plans for the evening."

She cocked her head to one side. "You do?"

"Yes."

Tamar raised her hand toward his hair. "I think your head may still be broken."

Jensen captured her hand and placed it on his arm like she was a real lady. "I'm good as new. You didn't have nothing else planned, did you?"

She couldn't stop the giggle that slipped out. "What kind of plans could I have?"

"Good." Pulling her out of the kitchen, away from the prying eyes and ears of the Thorntons' staff, he escorted her to the outer entrance.

Her eyes stretched wide when she realized a hired cab awaited them. "Wait. I can't leave. I don't have permission."

"Yes, you do. I talked with Miss Lily earlier. She said you could."

She was free. For the evening at least.

Tamar let Jensen hand her into the cab. He climbed in and sat beside her, his closeness threatening her breath. "I can't believe you did this. Lily didn't say a word about it."

"I asked her not to so's I could surprise you." He put his hat on his lap. "Are you surprised?"

Another giggle filled the air. "Of course. But are you sure?"

"I never been surer, Tamar." His gaze caressed her. "I love you."

"Don't say those things." She turned away and watched the passing scenery.

"I have to. Else my heart would explode. There's lots I want to say to you, Tamar. But the most important is that I love you enough to buy your freedom."

That brought her head back around. "You don't have to do that. Lily promised to make sure I'm given my freedom."

He rubbed his knuckle against her jaw. "I love you with all my heart. As soon as you're free, I want to marry you."

"Don't say that. There are so many reasons we can't get married." Tamar tried to pull back, but he trapped her chin with long fingers.

"We belong together."

"I'm too old and too dark."

"I'll leave off my hat. The sun should help me look both older and darker." His grin was infectious.

Tamar found herself smiling at him. "I can't marry a man who's not a Christian."

"I have given my heart to Him." He waggled his brows at her. "I don't always do what I should. I just need a good woman to help keep me in line."

Infected by his jolly attitude, she summoned a fierce frown. "Well, if you want to be married to me, you'll have to change some. I'll not have anyone say I married a heathen."

He laughed out loud. Raising his other hand, he cupped her face. "I love you." He pressed a soft kiss on her lips.

Tamar felt like she was floating on a cloud. *So this is what the Bible meant about a man and a woman becoming one.* She could almost feel the joining of their souls.

The cab stopped, and Jensen let her go. "Are you ready?" He helped her out of the carriage and paid the driver.

They walked hand in hand down Gravier Street until they came to the St. Charles Theater. Her mouth dropped open at the size of the building. It could probably hold most of the citizens of New Orleans. Jensen led her past the line of carriages at the front entrance, walking toward the east side of the building. Part of her wished they could go inside, but Tamar knew that was impossible for a slave.

Refusing to let her thoughts spoil the evening, she looked toward the open doorway. The performance must have already started. She could hear someone singing. Dozens of people crowded around the door, jostling against each other to get a better position. They must have a view of the stage.

Jensen pointed to an empty bench a few feet away. "Why don't we sit over there?"

Tamar nodded. If they were very quiet, they would be able to hear almost every word. She couldn't think of any better way to spend the evening than sitting next to the man she loved.

Thankfulness filled her as she realized the truth. She loved Jensen Moreau. His arm encircled her waist and drew her close. If freedom offered other such delights, she would embrace it with a joyful heart.

Blake was a fool. All the gilded arches and velvet curtains of the theater were lost on him. He barely noticed the sparkling chandeliers or the crowds of tiara-crowned, bejeweled women. The only thing on his mind was that he was falling in love with a girl who was all wrong for him.

He glanced at her. Lily was leaning slightly forward, so caught up in the action on the stage that she had forgotten he was sitting next to her. Yes, he was an idiot.

Nothing about Lily should appeal to him. She was stubborn, idealistic, and a prude to boot. Never mind that she came with a ready-made family who would always be a big part of her life. Lily had a caring heart and a mind that worked at the speed of lightning, but those things shouldn't appeal to a man. He glanced at her again, his gaze caressing the fullness of her mouth and the jut of her determined chin. Funny how over the past months his idea of feminine beauty had changed.

A whisper from Jasmine at the front of the box drew his attention. She was seated next to Camellia and the Thorntons' son Jonah, while he and Lily were directly behind them. It was the perfect arrangement for chaperones.

When had he grown so old? And why was he spending his days surrounded by this motley crew of a family when he should be wining and dining lovely women from one end of the Mississippi River to the other?

Yet he found himself reluctant to sell his portion of the *Hattie Belle* to Lily. Although opportunities to open a gambling boat abounded, the thrill of gambling had faded to a distant fantasy. Blake had discovered he enjoyed the variety of alarms and challenges that chased Lily and her family.

Part of him even enjoyed listening to her father talk about his beliefs. Not that he would attend any more sermons in the dining room. But he did like asking Captain Henrick questions about faith in the modern world.

The curtain came down, and he joined the general applause even though he had no clue what had happened during the final act of *Richard Coeur-de-lion*. But when Lily turned to him, her brown eyes gleaming in the light of the sconces, he took pleasure from the knowledge that she had enjoyed the performance.

Her hand gripped his arm. "That was splendid. Thank you so much for taking us."

Blake covered her hand with his own. "I'm glad you liked it."

Jonah stood and stretched his arms over his head. "Their performance was a little unpolished. You should have seen the performance of *Don Giovanni* last month. The music was much better."

"I thought it was wonderful." Jasmine's eyes were even brighter than Lily's. She clasped the playbill. "I would like more than anything to become an actress like Miss Tabitha Barlow."

Camellia sniffed her disdain for the idea.

Blake felt the shudder that passed through Lily right before she pulled away from him. "That's ridiculous. I can't think of a more scandalous occupation for a young lady."

"It looks glamorous to me." Jasmine's chin lifted in the same manner Lily employed when she was determined to get her way.

"You'll feel differently when you grow up." Camellia tossed a smile toward Jonah, which the young man ignored.

Blake decided to step in before the discussion disintegrated into a quarrel. "I don't think we need to worry about such things tonight." He bent a cautionary gaze on Lily. "Let me help you with your cloak."

Jonah waved at someone on the opposite side of the theater. "Excuse me." He vaulted over the low wall that separated them from the pit before Blake could stop him.

With a sigh, Blake settled Lily's cloak around her shoulders. "I suppose he'll join us before too long." He helped the girls gather their wraps and gloves.

They exited the box, and he spotted Jonah with a group of youths about his age. Warning the others to wait for the carriage, he went to fetch the young man.

As he approached the group, they stopped talking, looking at him with suspicion. Did they think he was too old to join them? They couldn't be more than five years younger than he. Had the weight of experience aged him so much? For the second time that evening, he felt old. "Jonah, I need your help with the ladies."

Jonah rolled his eyes, garnering sympathetic looks from his friends, but he followed Blake back to the *porte cochére*. "I thought I would walk home to leave more room in the carriage."

"I appreciate your concern." Blake didn't try to hide his sarcasm.

"But we have sufficient room."

They found the others without incident, and Blake guided them to the carriage, feeling like a sheepherder. On the way to the theater, the girls had sat on one bench while he and Jonah shared the opposite one. But somehow this time the girls managed to split up as they entered the carriage. Camellia sat on the forward-facing bench, Jasmine between her and Jonah. Lily sat by herself, leaving only one place for Blake, a development that made his heart beat a couple of extra times before returning to its normal rhythm. He settled in, his knee brushing hers through the material of her skirt.

Each time the carriage turned a corner, Lily's shoulder leaned against him. She smelled of almonds and honey, a light scent that teased his nostrils. He wouldn't care if the ride home lasted half the night.

Of course it didn't. But when Blake helped Lily alight from the carriage, their gazes met. She offered a secret smile that promised she had enjoyed the ride home as much as he.

He was an idiot, an idiot in love with Lily Anderson. It was time for him to make his intentions known.

ஃ

"It was so exciting, Papa." Jasmine's violet gaze was fastened on him, seated across from her at the Thorntons' dinner table later that evening. "Blondel gets free, and Lady Marguerite has a party, and then her soldiers rescue poor King Richard."

Lily exchanged a glance with Blake. They communicated without words—sharing their amusement at Jasmine's enthusiasm. Jonah Thornton may have found the evening beneath his standards, but the rest of them rated the music and acting delightful. It had also changed something between her and Blake. He had become a member of their family.

"Only because they tricked Florestan. He loved Laurette, and they used that against him." Camellia did not hesitate to set her younger sister straight.

Jasmine considered Camellia's words. "He got what he deserved for putting a king in jail."

Everyone laughed at her logic.

Jasmine looked a little put out, but she managed to smile. "It was magical. I'm going to sing in the opera when I grow up."

"I'm so glad you enjoyed it." Mrs. Thornton smiled at her youngest guest. "It is good to be so passionate. Perhaps one day you will become a great patron of the arts."

Lily appreciated the woman's kind words. They soothed Jasmine's sensibilities as well as her own concern that her youngest sister was too fervent in her response to the opera. All evening Jasmine had been humming the melody. Imagining her sister performing on stage was enough to cause nightmares. Although Lily's choice of occupation was not traditional, other ladies traveled on the river. If Jasmine decided to pursue a career on stage, she would be disappointed at how tawdry it was.

Mrs. Thornton placed her napkin beside her plate and rose, signaling that the ladies should retire. The gentlemen rose, too.

Lily glanced at Blake once more. How had she ever thought Jean Luc Champney interesting? He might have lived in Europe, but he seemed shallow compared with the man standing across from her.

Blake was a man of honor, and she prayed he would let go of his prejudice against God. Her father had told her about the conversations he'd had with Blake, conversations that let her know God was trying to reach him. It was enough for now. But would it be enough for a more permanent relationship?

So lost was she in her contemplation, Lily almost missed the slight motion Blake made with his head. She frowned at him. Again Blake tilted his head, his gaze intense. He must have some information to impart, probably about the *Hattie Belle*. Had they been robbed again? She nodded to him, praying his news was nothing serious.

Mrs. Thornton, Camellia, and Jasmine went to the front parlor. Lily hung back until Blake joined her. "What's wrong?"

He shook his head and steered her toward the back of the house.

The air had cooled as night settled around them. Although the full moon had risen, its silver light did not impart warmth. Lily's arms were covered by long sleeves, but she wished she had a shawl. Maybe the problem wouldn't take long to solve.

They strolled along a dim path, saying nothing until they reached a stone bench. "Would you like to sit?" His voice sounded odd. Strained.

She sat and watched as he paced back and forth. "Whatever the problem is, Blake, you had best just tell me."

He stopped and looked at her, opened his mouth, shut it, and took another turn around their quiet corner of the garden.

"If you continue walking around in circles, one of us is going to become dizzy."

Moonlight touched his black hair as he sat beside her, taking her hands in his grasp. "I want to talk to you about the future."

Lily's heart missed a beat. "What?"

"We've made a lot of money on the *Hattie Belle*. I never thought shipping would be so lucrative, but you have pulled it off, Lily."

Did he want to end their partnership? She tugged on her hands, but he wouldn't release his hold. "I couldn't have done it alone."

He smiled. "I appreciate your kindness, but both of us know I had a completely different view of how to use the *Hattie Belle*."

Lily hoped she had mistaken Blake's intention. She hated the idea of living on the *Hattie Belle* without his reassuring presence. Who could she trust as much as she did this man? "It took both of us using the talents God gave us."

He leaned toward her, and Lily thought he was going to give her a brotherly hug. Anticipation warmed her. His hands released their grip, and his arms came around her shoulders. "Lily, you're a special woman." His head dropped lower. His eyelids drifted downward. And his lips covered hers.

She melted for a fraction of a second. But then reason returned. What was she doing? She pushed at his chest with enough force to stop his kiss. "S–stop, Blake." Was that breathy sound her voice? Lily cleared her throat. "I value your friendship deeply, but I cannot allow this."

Shock was evident in every line of his body. "I thought we understood each other."

Lily's mouth still tingled from his touch. She had never dreamed a kiss could feel so right—and so devastating. But she would have to consider the implications of her very confused emotions when she was alone. For now she needed to explain to this man why they were not right for each other. "Blake, you gave me the most excellent advice anyone could have offered at a time when I desperately needed it. You're the reason I've grown closer to God. You're the person who helped me see how far I'd strayed from Him. I'll always be grateful to you."

"I don't want your gratitude." He stood and faced the house. All she could see were his clenched hands behind his back, the same hands that had held her so gently moments ago.

"You're my best friend, Blake. You're the one who counseled me to tell my family the truth. I wish I had listened, as things would have been much easier."

He kicked at a stone, making her think of an angry child.

She hated being the cause of his anger. Hated hurting him. Praying for the right words, she drew another breath. "Letting this thing between us continue would be a lie."

He swung around. "A lie? What I feel for you is as real as that house. How can that be a lie?"

"I'm a Christian." She let her words sink in before continuing. "That means I can't link myself to someone who does not love God with his whole heart. I cannot put my eternal soul at risk for a transitory feeling. I beg you to understand."

"Understand?" He swallowed hard. Then his face smoothed out, becoming an emotionless mask. But the moonlight was bright enough to reveal the pain in his eyes.

Tears threatened to overwhelm Lily. With a wordless cry, she stood up and rushed past him to the house. Running up the stairs to her bedroom, she slammed the door and threw herself across the bed.

Hot tears streaked her cheeks and soaked the pillow. She didn't cry for herself but for the man she had deserted. The man who might never understand why she had rejected his love.

Chapter Forty-seven

Wondering why her father had summoned her, Lily pulled her cloak tighter as she plodded up to the pilothouse. The wind scraped at her cheeks and tugged at her skirt. The weather was a perfect reflection of her emotions.

She had seen Blake only once in the past week, the day of their departure. He'd moved out of the Thorntons' garçonnière the day after he kissed her. She'd wanted to talk to him, explain why she had spurned his advances, but when she got to the boat, a single glance at his cold features destroyed that impulse.

Papa pulled a cord, and the long, low note of the steam whistle filled the cold air.

Lily stepped into the pilothouse and looked out over the water. Another stern-wheeler was churning south, riding low in the water. Bales of cotton were piled high on every available surface of the other boat. "How do passengers move about on that deck?"

He waved her forward, giving her a hug before answering. "I doubt they're carrying passengers. Their cargo alone will make the trip profitable."

The cotton must be getting wet from the water washing onto the deck. "If the boat doesn't sink before it makes port."

Her father withdrew his prized telescope from the inside pocket of his coat and held it up to his right eye. "She is riding low, but the pilot is taking his time. I doubt he'll sink her."

A feeling of peace stole over Lily as she and her father watched the boat until it passed them. She couldn't thank God enough for reuniting her with her father. "Did you need something from me, Papa?"

He studied her, his brown eyes filled with compassion. "I'm worried about you."

"Worried?" She lifted her chin and wished she had done a better job of hiding her sorrow. "Everything is going well. We found the perfect school for Camellia, we're making money faster than I dreamed possible, and you're with us. My family is reunited. What more could I want?"

Her ruse didn't work. "Water Lily, I know I haven't been around like I should have been for you and your sisters, but I'm not blind. Maybe God intended for me to be here now so I can help."

"I don't need your help, Pa—Papa." Trying to pass her stutter off as a reaction to the cold air, she shivered. "It's cold out here today, isn't it?"

He shook his head. "You can't fool me, honey. You and Blake spent a lot of time together in New Orleans. I tried to talk to him when he showed up here early one morning last week, but talking to that boy is like trying to swim upstream. When I saw how the two of you avoided each other yesterday and again this morning, I started to understand the problem." He cleared his throat. "He didn't try to take advantage of you, did he?"

Lily's cheeks felt as if they were glowing like twin flames. "No—"

"Good." The word cut off her explanation. "I would hate to have to toss that boy overboard."

Lily would have laughed, but his gaze told her he was not making a joke. "I care about him very much, Papa. But we have no future together other than as co-owners of the *Hattie Belle*."

"Is this because of his past?"

A sigh filled her chest. "Not exactly."

"Then what's the problem?"

"He's turned away from God."

A frown wrinkled her father's weathered brow. "Has he told you this? That he doesn't believe in God?"

She nodded, her heart breaking again as she remembered Blake's refusal to release the pain of his past and turn to God.

"That surprises me." Papa adjusted the ship's wheel to avoid a snag ahead. "He and I have spent some time together, you know. He's been as full of questions about God and Christ as anyone I've ever met. When someone is determined to avoid contact with God, he usually doesn't want to stay around Christians or give in to his curiosity."

His words buoyed her, offered her hope. But what if he was wrong? "He probably wants ammunition to use against Christians."

"I don't know, Water Lily. I only know that God doesn't want to bring either of you pain."

With great effort, she summoned a smile. "I know, Papa."

"Good." He focused on the horizon then returned his attention to her. "We need to ask God to reveal the truth to Blake, and not just for your sake. This is more important than whether the two of you love each other—it's about where he'll spend eternity."

Papa's words were stark, frightening. A shudder shook her. Lily looked at her father. "Can we pray right now?"

He held out his arms to her. "Of course we can. I can't think of a better time to do so."

☙

Blake watched Lily cross the gangplank and enter her grandmother's carriage. A piece of his heart traveled with her. He had to win her esteem. But was he ready to surrender control of his life? And if so, who was he surrendering to? The cold, uncaring God of his childhood or the warm, loving Savior that Captain Henrick and Lily worshipped?

He'd spent years chiseling out a life for himself, learning how to rely on his own strengths. Was he supposed to give all that up?

A hand clapped him on the back. Blake turned and met Captain Henrick's gaze. "You look like someone is tearing out your heart."

"I don't know what you're talking about." The accuracy of Captain Henrick's analogy stunned him. When had he grown so transparent? And what did his inability to hide his thoughts say about being able to return to the gambling tables? His future didn't look very hopeful. What was a washed-up gambler supposed to do? He couldn't stay here. Being around Lily without being able to claim her was harder than he'd thought it would be.

Captain Henrick shrugged. "If you say so." His glance went to the carriage that was pulling away.

Time to change the subject. "Why aren't you going to Les Fleurs with them?"

"I've spent a great deal of time on my knees since I turned to God, and I've learned a lot from that position."

"What are you talking about?"

"I'm talking about the way God uses weakness to His benefit."

He had Blake's full attention. "What kind of God wants weak followers?"

The smile on Captain Henrick's face widened. "The kind of God I serve." He closed his eyes as though thinking hard about his answer. " 'And he said unto me, My grace is sufficient for thee: for my strength is made perfect in weakness.' "

Frustration boiled in Blake's chest. "That makes absolutely no sense."

The captain opened his eyes. "Think about it like this, son. God is eternal. He doesn't think like we do. If you took the strongest person in the world and multiplied his strength a hundredfold, it would be as nothing to the God I serve. When Paul asked for the strength to overcome his weakness, God gave him the answer I just quoted to you."

"Then what's the point of striving for anything? Why not rely on God for everything we need?"

"Exactly right." Captain Henrick clapped his shoulder. "I knew you were close to understanding."

Blake had not expected the man to agree with him. He didn't understand why Lily's father was grinning, but then the truth hit him. He didn't have to control anything. All he had to do was turn to God. The God who was stronger than his doubts, his questions, his weaknesses, and even his strengths. Hope sprang up inside him, choking out the doubt and anger that had controlled his life for so many years. "You've given me a lot to think about."

"That's all I need to hear."

Blake wished Captain Henrick's eldest daughter felt the same way. But perhaps if he continued searching for the truth, perhaps God would show him the way to Lily's heart, too.

✥

Jean Luc's father pulled his pocket watch from his waistcoat. "You're late. . .again." He snapped the silver cover closed and replaced the timepiece.

One of the other clerks snickered.

Jean Luc wanted to turn on his heel and walk out. Why did he have to be so humiliated? Most fathers would appreciate his exemplary behavior. Jean Luc had taken such pains to please the man since the disastrous night when he'd lost his interest in the *Hattie Belle*. Yet all his father did was embarrass him in front of his employees. Tamping down his irritation, Jean Luc removed his gloves and hat. "I'm here now."

His father blew out a harsh breath. "None of my other employees arrive as late as you."

"Any time you want me to stop working, I will be most happy to oblige." Jean Luc sauntered to the small desk tucked into a corner of the office. He sat and pulled forward a sheet of paper, pretending to study it while his father continued to fume. A list of goods was handwritten in the margin of the bill of lading he held, but he had no idea whether someone had delivered the goods to Natchez or if they were being ordered from some other port. Nor did he care.

"I don't know why I put up with your impudence." His father stormed out, slamming the door.

Jean Luc sat back in his chair and crossed his ankles. A large window on the front of the office building showed passing carriages, carts, and horses. How he wished he were outside instead of stuck in this office. But as long as he needed funds, he would have to pretend to work for his father.

He hoped his pretense wouldn't be necessary much longer. His mother had told him they'd been invited to a party at Lily Anderson's home tomorrow evening. He needed to meet with Steenberg and arrange for another unfortunate incident. Perhaps something a little more damaging. He would offer to comfort Lily and see if he could convince her to give up her dangerous lifestyle. If he could present himself in the proper way, he should be able to convince her to turn over the management of her boat to him. It would only take a matter of weeks for him to cement his control. Then he could take his proper place in local society.

"Aren't you going to begin listing those goods in your ledger?" Another clerk, Randolph something-or-other, pointed to the pile of papers someone had stacked on his desk.

Jean Luc shook his head and leaned his chair back until only the back two legs touched the floor. "My eyes are crossed from trying to make sense of that top one. Why don't you be a good friend and take care of these for me?"

Randolph swallowed hard, his Adam's apple moving up and down.

"I have a stack of my own."

Letting his chair fall forward, Jean Luc picked up the neat stack and held them out to the fellow. "I'm sure you'll do a much better job than I."

A slight lift to Randolph's shoulder indicated acceptance.

Jean Luc dusted his hands and reached for his gloves. "I believe I'll go check on the ships that are supposed to be arriving today."

He left the office and whiled away the morning being fitted for a new pair of boots. After a leisurely lunch, he purchased a newspaper and took it to the park for perusal. After he finished his reading, Jean Luc strolled across the park, renewing acquaintance with several of the ladies he'd met over the past months. He managed to escape without too much trouble and decided he should visit his tailor to see if the new suit he had ordered would be ready for tomorrow evening's party.

When he finally made his way back to Champney Shipping, the office was closed. A pity. But what was he supposed to do? A gentleman had to keep his priorities straight.

As the sun was setting, Jean Luc made his way down to the docks, pleased to note that the *Hattie Belle*'s berth was at the far end of the waterfront. It shouldn't be difficult for his men to board her without being spotted.

He found Steenberg standing in an alley next to a waterfront warehouse, the brim of his hat pulled low over his face. "Do you have the money?"

Jean Luc ignored the ill-mannered question. "The party is set for tomorrow night. The whole family will be in attendance. Blake Matthews, too. Are you ready to get back on board?"

"All I need is the cash."

"I want you to make sure they cannot leave the next day." Jean Luc wished he could hire someone else. But at least the man in front of him knew how to keep his mouth shut. No one suspected that either of them was involved in the earlier robbery. "And make sure no one gets hurt."

"That guy sprung up out of nowhere." Steenberg put out his hand for the money. "But I managed to knock him out before he could see who I was."

"This time wear masks." Jean Luc counted out three bills.

"That's not enough money."

"Be glad I'm giving you anything, given your incompetence. You've failed me twice. Next time, I won't be as forgiving."

"But you need me." Steenberg stepped closer. "You don't want to get your hands dirty."

Jean Luc refused to be intimidated. "You'll get the rest when I am satisfied with the results."

Steenberg looked like he was going to argue but then shrugged and accepted the cash, tucking it into the pocket of his trousers. "Tell me exactly what you want done. I can wreck the boat so she won't move for a month or more."

Jean Luc considered the options. "Stay away from the paddle wheel. Those things take too long to repair. I'll leave it up to you. Just make sure the damage is not irreparable. I need Lily Anderson to turn to me for help. Then I'll be able to convince her to relinquish her interest in my boat."

"I'll make sure she comes crying to you." Steenberg's laugh was as irritating as his greed. "Did you write another love note for me to leave for her?"

"No." Jean Luc turned to go home. Then he stopped and looked at Steenberg. "Remember, if you do your job right, you won't need to be looking for any more handouts. I'll reinstate you as captain of the *Hattie Belle* as soon as the ownership reverts to me. But if you fail me one more time, you won't work on the river again."

Steenberg's face twisted, and for a moment Jean Luc feared for his life. His heart pounded as he wondered if he had been a fool to come here alone. What would stop this man from killing him and taking the rest of his money?

Jean Luc straightened his shoulders. If he allowed his fear to show, nothing would stop Steenberg. He wished he'd been smart enough to bring his pistol, but he hadn't thought of it as he was getting ready to go to his father's office.

Someone stepped out of the warehouse, breaking the hold the other man had on him. Jean Luc began walking away, his shoulders twitching as he wondered if he was about to be attacked.

He was halfway down Silver Street before he looked back over his shoulder. Steenberg was still looking at him, wearing a grin made up of equal parts greed and malice.

Wondering if he had made a terrible mistake, Jean Luc headed back up the hill. He would be glad when this was over.

Chapter Forty-eight

Blake loved holding Lily close. He wished he had the right to do so all the time.

She was wearing the same outfit she'd worn the night they kissed—well, the night he kissed her. But he had thought for a moment she had responded to the touch of his lips. Maybe that was why it hurt so much when she pushed him away.

"I hope you're enjoying yourself this evening." Lily's brown eyes searched his face. "I know you don't know many of the townspeople."

He wanted to laugh out loud at her naïveté. "You might be surprised how often I've sat opposite some of these men."

Her pink cheeks made him want to cut out his tongue.

He hadn't meant to make her feel bad. "I'm sorry."

She shook her head. "I should have realized."

They danced in silence for several minutes. Blake searched for something to talk about. What was wrong with him? He never had trouble making conversation. But Lily was a different matter. "Your sister seems to be having an exciting time."

Lily nodded and favored him with a crooked smile. "The young men are lined up to ask for her hand in a dance. I knew she would be popular. She is so beautiful."

"If you have a liking for porcelain dolls." Blake bent his head closer to hers, his mouth almost touching her ear. "I prefer a woman with determination, courage, and intelligence. A woman who can take on the world with a smile on her face."

She caught her breath, and her cheeks darkened, but this time he didn't regret being the cause for her discomfort. It was proof she did care for him. "You are quite the flatterer, Mr. Matthews."

"I am simply expressing my taste, Miss Anderson." He turned his head slightly, his lips ever so close to her cheek. She was adorably awkward and would have stumbled if he had not held her so close. Taking pity on her, he straightened, allowing a few inches between them. He didn't want to make her a target for the gossips.

When the music ended, he wanted to whisk her out to the veranda, but someone else was waiting to partner her. Jean Luc Champney. Smothering a snarl, he let her go and turned to find another partner. Maybe he could keep Lily's attention better if she realized other women found him attractive.

One dance led to another. Too bad Blake could not recall a single name of his dance partners. His brain had been numbed by all their banalities, flirtatious glances, and suggestive movements. None of them stood out in his memory, none except Lily.

Mrs. Blackstone, Lily's grandmother, had managed to introduce him to half the young ladies in attendance at what she was calling her "little dinner party." Where he came from, this evening would be described as a formal ball. From the full orchestra providing the music to the chaperones sitting in chairs along one wall of the ballroom, this evening had little in common with a simple dinner party.

A familiar voice hailing him made Blake's jaw tighten. He didn't want to have to exchange pleasantries with Jean Luc Champney, not after he'd had to watch the man fawn over Lily.

"I wanted to congratulate you on your success."

Blake bowed. "That's kind of you since it was born on your ill luck."

A polite smile camouflaged the scowl Blake's words had caused. "I hope all of that is behind us now. I have taken a position in my father's office to learn the shipping business from the inside. By the time I take to the water, I should know enough to make my own fortune."

"Good. Then perhaps we'll see you on the river soon."

"I hope so."

When Blake would have turned away, Mr. Champney put a hand on his arm. "I heard about the incident when you were docked here a few weeks back. I trust no lasting harm was done to the boat."

The hair on Blake's arm rose. How had this man heard of the burglary? Lily, Jensen, and he had decided to tell no one. Suspicion filled him. "Yes, but we have decided it was a random act of bored young aristocrats. The only thing they managed to do was destroy a couple of barrels of wheat. Since then, I have hired several guards to keep watch."

Jean Luc shook his head. "It's a shame you have to take such precautions. Perhaps one day the waterfront will be safe for everyone. Lily is so adventurous, but I worry about her remaining in that environment. I have tried to convince her that the river is no place for a lady."

Thinking of the note he had discovered in Lily's room, the one he had crumpled and later tossed overboard to keep Lily from seeing it, Blake gritted his teeth. "You need not worry about her or her sisters. Their safety is my primary concern." He glared at the other man, wondering what role he had played in the burglary.

"Forgive me, I didn't mean to insult you." Surprise raised Jean Luc's eyebrows, but the emotion seemed false to Blake.

He tried to temper his dislike of the man, but it was difficult. When he'd first met him, Jean Luc had been nothing more than a young man with more money than sense. Then Lily had put so much stock in Jean Luc's advice while she managed to ignore his at every turn.

He looked across the crowded room for her brown hair and gray dress, a fierce pain in his chest. Even though she had spurned him, his love burned as intensely as ever. "I'd better not catch you anywhere near the *Hattie Belle*. If I do, you'll find yourself treading water."

The polite mask disappeared as Jean Luc's face filled with bitterness and hatred. "If you were a gentleman, I would call you out for that threat."

"Lucky then that I am not."

"One of these days your luck will run out." Jean Luc's voice was little more than a growl. "I only hope I am there to see it." He turned and pushed his way through the crowd.

Blake watched him then decided it was time to make his excuses to Lily and return to the *Hattie Belle*. He had a sudden urge to make sure their boat was safe. He moved toward Mrs. Blackstone.

"Is there someone else I can introduce you to, Mr. Matthews?" Her widow's dress seemed dull in this room of pastel-skirted debutantes.

"Not at all." He bowed and reached for her hand. "I'm afraid I must take my leave. I need to check on the men I left aboard my boat."

"What is this about *our* boat?" Lily put extra emphasis on the word as she joined them.

Mrs. Blackstone put an arm around her granddaughter. "I won't have the two of you arguing in my home."

All of them laughed, and Blake winked at the two women. "I stand corrected."

"I've enjoyed meeting you, Mr. Matthews." Mrs. Blackstone's smile included both of them. "I hope you will not be a stranger. Anytime you and my granddaughter are in Natchez, I will expect to see you." She turned and left the two alone.

"I wish you would not go by yourself, Blake. I will be glad to join you."

Blake shook his head. "I don't think I need a protector."

"At least promise you will be careful."

He tweaked her nose. "Don't worry. Jensen is there, as well as the two men we hired. I'll be safer there than I have been amongst these matchmaking matrons."

Her frown lingered as he headed for the door, but Lily would probably forget about him when the other guests claimed her attention. He only hoped she avoided Jean Luc Champney. The thought of her dancing with him again made Blake's jaw harden. The self-absorbed Monsieur Champney was not a man to be trusted.

During the quiet ride to the dock, Blake began to think his overreaction could be attributed to a lack of sleep. Water lapped at the bank, its surface reflecting the light of the moon above. Natchez Under-the-Hill was rarely quiet, but sometimes in the hours before dawn, the community slumbered, exhausted by its wickedness. Even the stray dogs that normally wandered the streets had found safe places to rest.

Blake had to wake the liveryman to return his hired horse. After settling his account with the sleepy man, he walked the dark street to where the *Hattie Belle* was berthed, relieved to see her as quiet as the town.

"Jensen, where are you?" He crossed the gangplank and headed for the galley. He needed a cup of strong coffee if he was going to stay awake until the sun rose. The boat rocked under his feet, setting off a warning in Blake's mind. He brushed the feeling aside. Probably just a guard making his rounds.

Opening the door to the galley, Blake was blinded by bright lantern light. He raised his arm to shield his eyes and tried to look into the room. "How many lanterns do you—"

"What are you doing here?"

The voice sounded familiar, but Blake couldn't match it to any of the men he'd hired for the evening. He squinted, trying to see who was in the galley. He was so focused on who was in front of him that a blow to the back of his head caught him by surprise.

Fighting off the blackness that threatened to overtake him, Blake realized he'd been ambushed. The floor rushed up to smack him in the face, and the light became a dark chasm into which he fell. . .and fell. . . and fell.

Chapter Forty-nine

Jean Luc worried when he noticed Blake leaving. He glanced at a clock above the fireplace mantel. Steenberg should be through by now. At least he hoped so. He should have been done an hour ago. Blake would find nothing more than anonymous destruction.

Taking a deep, steadying breath, he moved toward Lily. Perhaps she would be more cordial now that her business partner was gone. He had noticed how her gaze followed every step the gambler took. He had never dreamed the two of them might have more than a business partnership.

Were they lovers? He rejected the idea. They had half a dozen chaperones on the boat. And he was experienced enough to know that Lily was still a wide-eyed innocent. He walked to where she stood talking to her grandmother. "May I have the pleasure of a dance with you, Miss Anderson?"

She glanced around before nodding. Was she looking for an excuse to turn him down? The polite smile on her face held little warmth as they moved to the center of the ballroom. They stood facing each other, waiting for the orchestra to begin.

"Your family must be pleased with the number of guests in attendance this evening."

Her smile warmed a fraction. "Yes, especially Camellia."

He looked to the pretty blond who was laughing and flirting with a group of young bucks. "You do not mind her popularity?"

"Of course not." Lily's brown gaze returned to him. "She's my sister. I love seeing her so happy."

Jean Luc realized he had offended her...again. A sigh filled his chest, but before he could begin an apology, a disturbance at the entrance to the ballroom claimed his attention.

A man had pushed his way past the servants. He stood swaying in the doorway, his clothing ragged.

"What's going on?" Lily began moving toward the man, her concern showing on her face.

Jean Luc followed her, as did most of the other people in the room. As he drew closer, he heard two words that struck fear into his heart. "Blaze...steamship." He gasped as realization flooded his mind. Steenberg had set the *Hattie Belle* on fire! He knew it! On the heels of his thought came remorse. What had he done?

Several of the women fainted, falling gracefully into the arms of the nearest men.

Jean Luc fought his way through them to a white-faced Lily. "Don't worry. I'll take care of this."

He didn't stay to see her reaction. What she or anyone else thought was secondary to his need to stop this disaster. He'd never meant for the boat to be destroyed or for anyone to die. All he'd ever wanted was to get his boat back and regain his father's approval.

As he tried to mount his horse, the enormity of Steenberg's actions pressed against Jean Luc's shoulders, threatening to pin him to the ground. He finally managed to struggle into the saddle, desperation strangling him as he pushed the horse to a gallop. The *Hattie Belle* could not be destroyed. If the stern-wheeler was lost, he would never be able to earn redemption.

❧

Blake tried to raise his hands to rub his aching head, but they were trapped at his side. What had happened? Why wouldn't his arms work? He struggled before realizing he was bound. Panic filled him before he managed to push it back. He needed to assess the situation.

Thinking back, he remembered the party at Lily's home, then boarding the *Hattie Belle*...and a bright light in the galley. He must have surprised another gang of thieves. They had attacked him and tied him up.

The floor swayed, telling him he was still on the boat. But where were the guards? And Jensen? Had they been overcome, too? Were they tied up in another part of the boat?

He pushed himself up, feeling much like an inchworm as he used the wall behind him for leverage. The stench of lamp oil burned his nose and throat, making him cough.

The noise must have brought one of his attackers closer. "I see you're awake."

He opened his eyes at the sound of the familiar voice. Standing over him was a recognizable figure, although he looked worn and bedraggled. "Steenberg."

The former captain laughed. "I told you I'd get even with you. I've been busy while you were taking your little nap." He set down his lantern.

Blake looked around to see if any of the other men were in the room with him. They weren't. Only he and Steenberg occupied the storage room. He poured all his energy into getting free of the ropes holding him. "I am guessing that. . .you take your orders from Jean Luc."

Steenberg's laugh died. "Jean Luc Champney doesn't control me. I just use his pocketbook to finance my future. He's got no idea what I'm planning to do to you and your boat."

Blake could feel one of the ropes loosening. He redoubled his efforts. If he could keep Steenberg talking until he could get free, he could overcome the man without much trouble. "Where are my men?"

"They're tied up and taking little naps of their own, but my plans have changed since we overpowered them." Steenberg pushed against a cargo barrel, toppling it with a loud crash. His smile returned. "One of my men gagged them and took them to the train station so they couldn't raise a ruckus. They'll be found in a few hours, but by then everything will be over."

"You'll never get away with this. And I'll make sure you never work on the river again."

"Those are some mighty fine words for a fellow who's not going to be alive much longer. Don't worry about me." The former captain stuck his thumbs in the waist of his pants and pulled in his stomach. "I've been bleeding Jean Luc for months now, doing jobs he's too soft to do himself. Even if someone suspects me, I can make a run for it. I've got enough money to leave this stinking town and never come back."

"Enjoy your freedom while you can." Blake gritted his teeth against the pain caused by his efforts to free himself. "I'll have the sheriff after you like I should have done in New Orleans."

The other man's grin didn't fade. He strutted around the tight space. "I knew that the minute I saw you. That's why I had to make new plans. You see, Jean Luc gave us orders not to destroy his precious boat. I went along because I didn't really care if we broke a few windows or blew the whole boat up, but everything changed when you walked in on us. Now I've stoked up the boiler and jammed her shut. She's already hissing like a bunch of alley cats."

His words struck fear in Blake's heart. Boiler explosions were the most deadly cause of accidents on the river. Worse than sandbars, snags, or even floods. When a boiler blew, the force was enough to throw fiery chunks of the boat hundreds of feet into the air. Then like lava from a volcano, the burning debris rained down on everything around. It was every river boatman's worst nightmare. For a moment he forgot his plan to escape. His cough returned.

"Yes, the smell is rather strong in here." Steenberg pushed over another barrel, and it crashed to the floor, spewing out its load of flour. "That's because we're going to set your boat on fire."

His threats brought Blake's mind back to earth. He couldn't afford to panic. "That sounds a bit redundant."

"I can't take the chance someone will arrive in time to stop the explosion." He pushed at Blake's leg with the toe of his boot. "You see, I don't like jails. And I'm not planning to spend any time in one."

The ropes around him refused to give. Could he talk Steenberg into loosening them? He coughed again. "Could I have some water?" Was that pitiful voice his?

Steenberg considered his request before shaking his head. "Don't you worry, though, it won't be long before your thirst is gone. I'd guess it's about time to put you out of your misery." He kicked over the lantern and walked out, leaving the door to the outside open.

His position in the room gave Blake a limited view of the sky, which was still as black and featureless as his winter cloak. He coughed again as the flames took hold and smoke began to rise around him. As the futility of the situation became apparent, his will to live bled away. He was going to die.

Anguish overtook him with the acknowledgment. Why now? So

many things remained that he wished he had done, so many things he had yet to do. Was this all there was to life? Was he to end his life as the victim of a bloodthirsty crook? Did a man struggle and fight against the odds only to find himself facing death with no hope of redemption?

Sorrow and fear filled the empty spaces in his heart as Blake came face-to-face with his mortality. What was about to happen to him? Would he live on in some other form? A vision of hell rose up through the flames surrounding him. Why had he not repented when there was time? Why had he resisted the One who wanted to save him from eternal destruction? Why hadn't he realized the importance of faith until it was too late?

The flames licked higher, greedily consuming the space around him. Smoke wrapped its tendrils around him, choking out the air he needed to breathe, choking out all other considerations.

Blake slumped over as the heat intensified, regrets spinning away as death claimed him.

Chapter Fifty

*L*ily ran to her father. "We have to get to the river."

"I'll go. You stay here."

She refused to be left like some addled debutante. "I might be able to do something to help. You're going to need every able-bodied person you can muster, or every boat docked is liable to be lost, including ours."

He hesitated before nodding. "I'll get the buggy while you change out of that dress. But if you're not ready by the time I am, I'll leave you here."

Knowing his words were no idle threat, Lily pushed her way past their guests. Many of the men had already departed or were awaiting their carriages outside—not surprising since most of them depended on river traffic for their livelihoods.

Careless of the spectacle she might make, Lily took the steps at a dead run. When she reached her room, she jerked her skirt around so she could see the buttons and worked her way through them. Then she had to untie the ribbon holding her hoops to her waist. When she was finally free, she quickly donned one of her work skirts. The gray bodice would have to stay as Tamar was not here to help her and she could not reach the buttons.

She scurried back down the staircase, ignoring the raised eyebrows of the other women. Camellia was one of them, bless her heart. But her sister had always been much more concerned with her appearance than

Lily. Perhaps that came with being a beauty. If so, Lily was glad she was plain.

She ran to the stable, relieved to meet her father at the door. "I'm ready."

He held out a hand, and she pulled herself into the buggy. She was hardly seated before he whipped up the horse and they raced down the drive toward the river. It never took more than a few minutes to get to town, but tonight the ride seemed to last forever.

As they headed down the steep hill to the waterfront, her heart climbed into her throat. She could tell the *Hattie Belle* was on fire. Where was Blake? Was he one of the men tossing buckets of water into the flames?

Her father urged the horse faster, ignoring safety in his haste to reach the boat. He didn't pull up until they were almost on the men. Her gaze frantically searched their faces and figures, but she could find no sign of Blake. He must still be on the boat.

She leaped to the ground and raced to the gangplank, her father only a few steps behind her. At least the whole boat was not on fire yet, but it would burn to the waterline if God didn't provide a miraculous downpour.

Lily squinted, trying to see anyone through the billows of smoke. Then she caught a glimpse of someone in a dark coat. He was dragging something out of a room. Was it Blake? She knew almost instantly it was not. She could make out his dark hair, but his head was a different shape and his shoulders were not wide enough. He turned his head to cough, and she recognized him. "Jean Luc, what are you doing?"

"Get out of here." He coughed and turned again to pull at whatever he was dragging.

She and her father moved forward. Her eyes were streaming from the smoke, but she recognized Blake when they reached Jean Luc's side. He was bound in ropes and unconscious. Blood stained his face close to his hairline. He looked so pale she feared he might be dead.

Horror slammed through her at the thought of what Jean Luc had done to Blake. "Let go of him!" She tried to push Jean Luc away.

"Stop it, Lily. Do you think I'm the one who hurt him?" Jean Luc's dark gaze showed pain. "I'm trying to get him to safety."

"The two of you will have to work together." Her father stepped between them, his voice calm. "I've got to see about getting this boat out into the channel before it sets fire to everything docked here."

Lily's fear diminished a little because of his unruffled demeanor, but then the implications of his strategy hit her. Her father wouldn't survive if he stayed on the boat. "You can't do that, Papa."

"It's going to take all three of us to get Blake to safety." Jean Luc's voice was scratchy from exposure to the smoke.

Papa looked from Blake to the water. He nodded. "I'll come back as soon as we get him to the gangplank."

They tugged as a team, and Lily wondered if they were hurting Blake. But it didn't matter at this point. Ending up with broken bones was better than being burned alive. The smoke thickened as they moved toward the front of the boat. One step. . .pull. Another step. . .drag. She fell into a rhythm, ignoring the chaos around them. When they reached the end of the boat, the eager hands of several men lifted Blake's weight from between her and Papa and carried him to dry land.

That's when Lily felt the thrum of the paddle wheel. She looked around. "Where's Jean Luc?"

Her father's gaze followed hers, searching the deck around them. "He must be running the engine."

The wood crackled as flames licked greedily at the double doors leading to the staircase. The heat seemed to draw air from her lungs. She felt the tug of the boat as it began to inch away from the dock.

"Run!" Her father held out his hand, and she put hers in it. Together they dashed across the gangplank, barely making it before the whole thing fell into the river.

Slowly at first, then with increasing speed, the *Hattie Belle* began her final voyage. Lily's heart ached for Jean Luc. He was giving his life for the sake of others, showing he was a better man than she had ever dreamed. Tears streamed down her face as she caught sight of his figure in the pilothouse. "Jean Luc is a very brave man." Her voice broke, and her father cradled her in his arms.

After a few minutes, he leaned over and whispered in her ear. "There's a fellow standing here who seems mighty anxious to say something to you."

Lily raised her head, and her heart took wings. "Blake? Are you all right?"

He nodded, but the paleness of his face and the way he cradled one arm belied the gesture. "I'm sorry about the boat."

The meaning behind his words flashed across her mind. The boat was the only reason she and Blake were together. Without it, they had no reason to see each other. She would have no chance to convince him of God's love. He would have no reason to stay at her side. It wasn't like they were a married couple. He would be free to return to his former way of life and leave her to pick up the pieces.

An explosion rocked the water, and a blast of heat scorched Lily's face. "Jean Luc. . ." Horror and sadness filled her as her father put his arms back around her. They watched as flaming wood and metal splashed on the surface of the water and struck the surface of other boats.

She held her breath, fearing another boat might catch fire. Shadowy figures scurried around on their decks and doused the flames before they could take hold. Lily breathed a prayer of thankfulness to God for sparing them.

"I know where Jensen is."

"Is he. . . ?" Lily couldn't bring herself to complete the question.

"Not if Steenberg was telling the truth. He and the guards should be at the train depot."

Lily's head spun. "Steenberg?"

"He was getting even with me as he threatened when I dismissed him."

Knowing she would need time to absorb all the details about the night, she moved from the circle of her father's protection. "We need to get you back to Les Fleurs where someone can look at that arm."

He widened his stance as though he needed extra support. "First we need to find Jen—"

"You get some help for him. I'll take care of Jensen and the others." Papa walked away, calling out to one of the other men who huddled close to the empty berth where the *Hattie Belle* had been docked.

She turned her attention back to Blake and realized he was leaning to one side, much like a derelict boat. Lily stepped closer and grabbed the arm he was not favoring. At first he resisted leaning on her, but by the time they crossed the street to the buggy, she felt like she was supporting a mountain.

"I'm. . .s—sorry." Blake's voice was slurred.

Lily let out an impatient sound. "Don't be silly. You were nearly burned to a crisp. Just a few more steps and I'll help you get aboard.

Then you can rest until we get home."

He didn't answer, which frightened her more than his apology. Blake was never at a loss for words. He must be more injured than he'd let on. Once they were both in the buggy, she slapped the reins and backed the buggy away from the somber crowd.

Blake sagged against her as they drove away, and Lily prayed with all her heart that he would recover. She couldn't imagine a life without his teasing smile and intriguing gaze. Or accept the idea that he might die before he became a Christian.

Chapter Fifty-one

$\mathcal{B}$lake was still in bed when someone knocked on the bedroom door. "Come in."

He expected one of the maids to enter with a cup of coffee and tell him breakfast was waiting for him downstairs. So when Lily entered, a breakfast tray carefully balanced between her hands, his mouth fell open. He grabbed at the bedcover, making sure his limbs were not exposed. He had never felt so vulnerable.

"I trust you are beginning to recover from your ordeal." She set the tray on a table at the foot of his bed and moved to where he lay.

Blake pushed himself up to a sitting position, keeping the cover tightly around him. He bit back a groan when his head bumped against the headboard. "You shouldn't have gone to so much trouble."

Lily walked to the window on one side of his bed and opened the curtains covering it. Weak light drifted into the room while she moved to the window on the other side of his bed and repeated her actions. "They caught Steenberg and his gang."

"What about Jean Luc?"

Her eyebrows crinkled in a frown. "He saved yours and Papa's lives."

Now it was Blake's turn to frown. Had Steenberg not told them about Jean Luc's role in the destruction of their boat?

"Such a heroic act. If he had not taken the boat out into the channel, the whole port would have gone up in flames when the boiler blew. A

308

lot of people would have died if Jean Luc had not been so brave."

Every word she spoke was like a blow. How could he tell her the truth? And why should he? Blake didn't want to destroy her faith in the man. It was true that Jean Luc's actions had benefited the others. And since Jean Luc was dead, no one could bring him to justice for his attempts to harm the *Hattie Belle*. "I still haven't pieced together how you managed to get to the river."

She fluffed a pillow that had fallen on the floor. "Papa brought me in the same buggy that I used to get us back here."

Blake would have nodded, but he didn't want to aggravate the pounding in his head. "What I don't understand is how you went from dancing to rescuing me."

"One of the Champneys' slaves came in and said there was a boat on fire." She shrugged. "Nothing would have kept me in the ballroom."

He should have known that.

"Enough about me." She dropped the pillow on the bed and picked up the tray, settling it on his lap. "Are you recovered enough to feed yourself, or do you need some help?"

Blake's eyebrows rose. "Are you offering to be my nursemaid?"

Her blush was one of the things he loved most about Lily. That and her dogged determination. Like him, she had lost everything last night. Some women would have moaned and cried about the fire, but not Lily.

"How is your head?"

"It aches, but not too badly." He picked up his fork to prove that he was fine. The first taste of the fluffy scrambled eggs was delicious and seemed to light a ferocious hunger. Blake wolfed down the rest of his food and sat back with a sigh of contentment.

Lily reached for the tray. "I believe you are going to be fine."

Blake wrapped his hand around her wrist. "I don't know how you do it."

"What are you talking about?" She wouldn't meet his gaze, but she didn't try to pull away, either.

He didn't want to let her go, not until he understood her better. In all the months they had been together, he had never realized how strong she actually was. But now? "I don't have the energy to look on the bright side. All I can think about is that everything is gone. All my clothes, my cards, everything I owned was on the *Hattie Belle*."

She looked at him. Really looked at him. Her lips twitched, her smile appearing and disappearing like a shy child. "God can turn every tragedy into good."

Blake practically threw her hand away. His head pounded once more. "Is that all you have to say?"

She picked up the tray and moved away. "You asked the question."

Suddenly Blake knew what he had to do. "I'm leaving."

The tray dropped to the floor, making him wince and put a hand to his forehead. She looked at him, her face full of pain. "You can't leave. You're not well."

"It may take a day or two, but Camellia fixed me up pretty well last night. Besides, there's no reason for me to stay here any longer." He closed his eyes to keep from looking at her. He couldn't weaken. Couldn't let Lily's sweetness change his mind. Blake knew what he had to do.

The soft sound of his door closing made Blake open his eyes. She was gone. Now he realized that the pain in his chest was worse than the pain in his head. Blake sank into the soft, clean bed and groaned. He had to get away before he did something stupid. . .like kiss her again.

⚘

Hopelessness claimed Lily. She knew she should not have expected anything else.

Two days after the destruction of the *Hattie Belle*, when it became obvious Jean Luc had died in the explosion, Monsieur and Madame Champney held a memorial service for their son. Her heart had gone out to the grieving couple. They seemed to have aged a decade. The only thing she could think of that might alleviate some of their pain was to tell them how brave Jean Luc had been, how he had sacrificed himself so no one else would die. They seemed to appreciate her words.

As sad as the service had been, Lily would have recovered from her sorrow. Then Blake announced that he was not going to stay in Natchez, and she fell into despondency, a yawning pit of blackness she couldn't seem to climb from.

She had said nothing as he recovered his strength, nothing when he bid them good-bye. What could she say? He would never change. He would not turn to God and become the man she could spend the rest of her life with.

The only reason he had stayed in the first place was because he was invested. . .in the *Hattie Belle*. Nothing else. If she had ever doubted that, Blake had proven it when he walked out of her life.

She sighed and looked out the parlor window. Clouds skittered across the sky. It was a gloomy day, one that matched her mood. Tears filled her eyes. Lily sniffed and tried to keep them at bay. She didn't want to waste any tears over Blake Matthews. Not when she was sure he'd already forgotten her. The door opened behind her, and she wiped at her eyes, wishing she'd brought a handkerchief.

" 'In every thing give thanks: for this is the will of God in Christ Jesus concerning you.' " Her father quoted the scripture quietly as he walked across the room.

His words brought back her answer to Blake when he bemoaned the loss of all his worldly goods. How self-righteous she had been when she told him that God turned tragedy into good. Lily had not realized that God would call on her to live her beliefs.

She twisted her lips into a smile and looked toward her father. "Thanks, Papa, for reminding me of His promise. I know it's true, but I'm finding it so hard to live that way when it feels like my heart has been torn out of my chest."

A frown appeared on his face. "I know it's not easy." He sat beside her on the sofa and patted her hand. "Especially when someone you care about is no longer at your side."

Determined not to cry, Lily folded her lips into a straight line and nodded. "I didn't realize how much I cared about Blake until he disappeared."

"God must have someone really special in mind for you, Water Lily. Someone who will love God with all his heart and love you as Christ loves the Church. It may be hard to believe right now, but you will be so happy with that man."

"I suppose so." Lily wished she could believe him. The hole Blake left in her life was an awfully big one to fill. He had challenged her to do her best, dared her to cling to her morals, and supported her when she least expected it.

Papa stood and walked to the window she'd been looking through. Silence gathered around them, deepening her feeling of dread. What was he thinking? Was he about to leave her, too? Lily wasn't sure she could handle two desertions in one week. "I need to check on Camellia and Jasmine."

He turned around as she was rising from the sofa. "Have you thought about your future?"

Here it was. Papa was not going to allow her to escape before he told her his plans. Lily shook her head. "Not much."

"I understand. You've suffered a huge blow. It takes time to get over loss and grief. But one of these days you're going to wake up and realize life is going on whether you like it or not. One of these days your faith is going to rise again to the surface."

She wondered if he planned to come back and visit his daughters once he returned to life on the river.

"I want you to know I am here for you, Lily." He walked back to her and put an arm around her waist. "If you want to buy another boat, I'll gladly captain it for you."

Touched by his offer, she returned his hug. "Thanks, Papa. I appreciate that. You're a great captain. It's a special talent God gifted you with. No matter which boat you guide, the passengers and crew will be in good hands."

He lifted her chin with a bent finger. "You've loved the river almost since you drew your first breath, but if this disaster has taken away your desire, I'll stay right here in Natchez with you and your sisters. I'm never going to desert you again."

"You would do that for us?" Her last doubts disappeared in a landslide of emotion. "I love you, Papa."

They hugged for several healing minutes. When they separated, Lily had to wipe her eyes again. Was she turning into one of those weak women she so despised? The ones who relied on tears to manipulate others?

Her grandmother opened the parlor door and started to enter. "Oh, I'm sorry. I didn't mean to interrupt."

Lily shook her head and smiled. "You're not interrupting us at all. Papa and I were talking about what we're going to do."

Grandmother looked from one of them to the other. "I hope you don't plan on leaving right away."

"Don't worry about that." Lily stepped forward and took her grandmother's hands into her own. "It's going to be a while before I'm ready to purchase another boat."

"Well, I can't say that I'm entirely unhappy to hear that. Although it saddens me to see you moping about, I still like having you around.

You've proven you are capable of taking care of yourself and your sisters. Your aunt and uncle may have suggestions for your future, but you will decide which path to follow."

Grandmother looked past her to where her father stood. "I hope you will stay with us, too, Henrick. My Rose loved you so much, and I hope you'll forgive us for keeping you separated from your children for all these years."

He cleared his throat. "Thank you. The past is behind us, and there's no reason to hold on to it. God has been so good to me, revealing Himself to me and giving me a reason to keep moving forward. He takes the worst circumstances and turns them into something beautiful. That's what I was telling Lily right before you came in."

"Amen." Grandmother released one of Lily's hands to reach out toward Henrick.

Lily's heart filled with love and thankfulness as she stood between her father and her grandmother. It was time to stop dwelling on her losses. She had a lot of things to be thankful for. The reconciliation of her relatives was proof that God could work out anything.

Peace settled on her shoulders with that realization, the peace that Christ had promised to all who believed in Him. She claimed that promise with all her heart, trusting that He would work out her future in a way more marvelous than she could imagine.

Chapter Fifty-two

Blake had never felt more alone in his life. He still remembered so clearly the day when Lily, along with her sisters, had appeared aboard the *Hattie Belle*, determined to get her clean and ready for travel. At that time he'd wondered if he would ever again enjoy peace and quiet. Now he wondered how he had ever enjoyed the solitude of his life before she. . .they entered it.

Even Jensen had deserted him, opting to stay near Tamar since she appeared more receptive to sharing her future with him. He hoped the two of them would marry and be happy.

He wanted to go back to Natchez. What was wrong with him? Lily had made her position clear before he left.

Blake left the room he had rented two weeks earlier when he'd decided to stop in Vicksburg. Walking toward the riverfront, he mused about the differences between Vicksburg and Natchez. Both were situated on high bluffs on the eastern side of the river, overlooking Louisiana lowlands on the west. But fewer plantation homes dotted the landscape of this town, and the dock was not as busy. Perhaps that was because Vicksburg had only been a settled area for a few decades.

At least he could play cards. Blake tipped his hat at a lady riding by in a carriage. For a moment his heart nearly stopped. Lily? She had the same light-brown hair brightened by golden strands that reflected the afternoon sun, but that was where the similarity ended.

Blake regained his composure and continued his trek to the waterfront. His footsteps dragged. He didn't feel like going to a gambling boat. The allure of gambling seemed to have faded now that he had enough money to live comfortably. Maybe he should consider buying a home and settling down. But that wouldn't solve his lack of companionship.

A flyer someone had tacked to an oak tree caught his attention. DISHEARTENED was the first word, followed by a question mark. He stopped to read further. The next line read, DISCOURAGED? and the third line was equally compelling: LONELY? The hair on the back of his neck rose. The sign might have been written for him.

Blake took a step forward and peered at the rest of the announcement. It was about a revival in Vicksburg beginning this very night and promised that all who came to listen to the Word as preached by Rev. Nathan Pierce would find the answers they'd been seeking. Blake almost passed it by, but what would he do with his evening? Perhaps this Pierce fellow had a message that would make him feel better.

He walked to the livery stable and rented a horse, getting instructions on how to reach the revival. As he rode past the outskirts of Vicksburg, he heard singing. It seemed to come from all around him, wonderful, uplifting chords. He couldn't make out the words, so he pushed his mount faster.

He reached the meeting place and felt like he'd been transported back in time. A brush arbor stood at the edge of a meadow, its roughhewn posts and leafy roof reminding him of his childhood. Early in his father's career as a preacher, the church had met in a similar arbor.

Blake almost turned back, but his arrival had been noticed by some of the congregation. He didn't want to seem like a coward, so he dismounted and tied his horse to a tree. He found a seat in the shady arbor as the preacher stepped up to the pulpit made out of a hickory post.

"Good evening." A tall, handsome man with a piercing gaze and blond hair stepped up to the podium as dusk settled on the meadow.

Some of the men in the congregation answered the preacher. "Good evening."

"I've come to Vicksburg to share a message of hope and redemption with all of you. A message that was first shared a long time before you and I came here. It's a message that all men need to hear. A promise that we can cling to even when it seems we've lost everything."

Blake leaned forward, his attention caught by the preacher's words. "I'm sure a lot of you here tonight know who Daniel is."

Blake searched his memory. There was something about dreams and visions in that book of the Old Testament. A lions' den?

"Well, tonight I'm going to tell you a story about a set of young men who were his friends—Hananiah, Mishael, and Azariah. They were slaves of King Nebuchadnezzar, but they were also devout followers of the Most Holy God. So when King Nebuchadnezzar told them he wanted them to worship at the feet of a huge golden statue he'd made, they refused. This made King Nebuchadnezzar so angry he had them tied up and thrown into a fiery furnace."

The preacher paused and looked out over his congregation. It seemed to Blake the man was looking directly at him. "That's when things got really interesting. King Nebuchadnezzar looked at the furnace and saw that Hananiah, Mishael, and Azariah were no longer tied up. And they weren't alone in that furnace. Let me read this part to you directly from the Bible so you can hear it for yourself. 'Lo, I see four men loose, walking in the midst of the fire, and they have no hurt; and the form of the fourth is like the Son of God.'"

Blake's heart tripled its speed. This story was so familiar to him. He'd been bound and left for dead. He thought back to that night, to the despair that had claimed him before he lost consciousness. Like the three men in the Bible, he'd been rescued. He should have died that night, but God in His goodness spared him—sent others to pull him from the fire. He'd received a second chance, and here he was about to waste it.

As the preacher brought his sermon to a close, he asked all to bow their heads during his prayer. Then he invited anyone who had felt the hand of God on them to come forward and declare their faith.

Blake hesitated as others stood and made their way to the pulpit. Then he could not wait any longer. He stood and took a tentative step. It felt good. So he took another step. Joy was stalking him, making it difficult to restrain himself from running forward. When he reached the pulpit, Blake kneeled and bowed his head. He had learned from a young age what one said when giving one's heart to God, but tonight the words, the thoughts, had real meaning. He asked Jesus to come into his heart and felt the assurance flood his body. He was a new man.

The preacher put a hand on his head and prayed, giving thanks to God for saving another lost lamb. Blake had no idea how long he knelt there in front of the pulpit, but by the time he rose it was fully dark. He found his horse and rode back to the livery stable, wonder and excitement filling him.

He needed to tell someone, but who would care? *Lily.* The answer was in his heart as soon as the question formed. He needed to get back to Lily.

Blake thought of an advertisement he'd seen in the *Vicksburg Whig*, and everything came together as though God had planned it. Chills ran up his spine. God was omnipotent. Plans for surprising Lily filled his head as thankfulness flooded his heart. Blake knew exactly what he needed to do.

Lily threw a kiss toward Jasmine as she mounted her dapple-gray mare and headed to town. The effort would be wasted. No boat her father had found so far was the right one. Too big, too small, or too decrepit, none fit the vision she had.

Now that she no longer had a partner, she didn't want a riverboat as large as the *Hattie Belle*. If she and her father could find something on a smaller scale, they could keep the crew to a minimum.

They would hire Tamar and Jensen, of course. They had gotten married right after Blake left. It was the one bright spot in Lily's life. She loved seeing Tamar blossom into a different person, walking taller with her shoulders back and head high. It was amazing what a combination of freedom and the love of a good man could do.

She wished Camellia would stay with them but had finally realized her sister would only be happy if she could attend the finishing school they had chosen in New Orleans. Perhaps they would at least curb some of her flirtatiousness. Lily was also concerned about losing her youngest sister. Jasmine seemed to be growing faster than the weeds in Grandmother's garden.

Lily reined in her thoughts as she descended the steep hill to the dock. Natchez Under-the-Hill was as busy as always, boats of all sizes vying for passengers and cargo before they once again braved the river currents. Why was it she always felt more alive when she was close to the river? Papa had nicknamed her well. She had to be on the water to thrive. Living with her relatives was not as difficult as it had once been, but this was where she belonged.

Papa's bright-red shirt and felt hat with its single feather made him easy to spot in the bustling area. He stood to one side of a new warehouse that partially blocked her view of the boats in the harbor. Lily walked her horse to where he stood and dismounted. "Where is this boat you've found?"

"It's not far." He gave her a kiss on the cheek, his eyes twinkling. "I think this one is going to be perfect."

Lily smiled at him. He was trying so hard. Even though she had climbed out of the despondency Blake's desertion had caused, it was difficult to regain her enthusiasm. "I hope you're right."

He tucked her hand into the crook of his arm, and they ambled toward the river. A bevy of steamboats bumped shoulders, their tall stacks puffing as muscular, sweating men filled them with cargo. Next to them were the smaller craft—the few flatboats, barges, and keelboats that struggled to survive alongside the larger boats. But where was the boat her father had brought her to see?

Then a boat caught her eye, a shiny white vessel with red lettering on the side. A pinprick of interest touched her. The boat was about half the size of the *Hattie Belle*, just what Lily had thought she might want to purchase. It only had three decks: the main deck, the boiler deck, and the hurricane deck. She would need to get closer, but from where she stood, the stern wheel looked as though it was in good condition. Maybe Papa had found the perfect boat this time.

Her eyes widened as she read the words stenciled on the side of the boat. She read the words out loud before looking at her father. "WATER LILY. What have you done?"

A wide grin crinkled the corners of his eyes. "I'm not the one." He spread his free arm out in an arc.

Lily's confused gaze followed the gesture. Her heart stopped as a familiar figure stepped out of the shadows and bowed in their direction. Blake. The man she thought she'd never see again.

She wanted to run across the gangplank, but her feet seemed to have forgotten how to move. She watched as he sauntered toward them, his stride as long and self-assured as ever. Her heart ached with love for him. The time they'd spent apart seemed to disappear as he reached her side.

"Hello, Lily." His voice sent a shiver through her.

Lily looked up at his face, her gaze tracing the lines of his cheeks, her fingers itching to feel the silkiness of his dark hair. With great difficulty she swallowed her emotions. "I love your new boat."

His eyebrows rose. "I was hoping it might be *our* boat."

She noted the emphasis on the pronoun, but a thousand questions arose. "I suppose I could buy into it, but who would own controlling interest? I'm not about to let you turn any investment of mine into a gambling casino."

He tilted his head, and his eyebrows climbed higher. He was not going to agree with her.

Lily braced herself for an argument.

Blake's eyes darkened in a way that made her heart leap. "Did you know that wives in Mississippi can own property?"

"What difference does that make?" Irritation colored her voice. "I'm not mar—" Her throat closed up as the implication of his question struck her.

Blake nodded. "It wouldn't have worked in New Orleans, Lily. I know that now. You were right to push me away. But I've found God. It's changed me so much. I'm not saying I'm perfect—"

"I'm sure of that." Lily recovered her equilibrium as joy exploded within her, a feeling so strong and so pure she knew it came from God. "But I've never wanted to love a perfect man."

"All I've been able to think about is sharing my life with you, living in His will." Blake moved closer and brushed a tendril of hair out of her face.

Lily turned to her father. "Papa?"

He shrugged. "Blake came to me yesterday and asked for permission to court you, but if you don't love him. . ."

"But I do. I do love him." She blushed as she spoke the words and looked up at Blake.

Slowly and with great care he took her hand from her father's arm and wrapped her in a hug. "I love you, too, my Water Lily."

Diane T. Ashley, a "town girl" born and raised in Mississippi, has worked more than twenty years for the House of Representatives. She rediscovered a thirst for writing, was led to a class taught by Aaron McCarver, and became a founding member of the Bards of Faith.

Aaron McCarver is a transplanted Mississippian who was raised in the mountains near Dunlap, Tennessee. He loves his jobs of teaching at Belhaven University and editing for Barbour Publishing and Summerside Press. A member of ACFW, he is coauthor with Gilbert Morris of the bestselling series, The Spirit of Appalachia. He now coauthors with Diane T. Ashley on several historical series.